NEXT MAN UP

L.A. WITT

HUMAN POWERED CREATOR

No generative artificial intelligence was used in the making of this book or any of my books. This includes writing, co-writing, cover artwork, translation, and audiobook narration.

I do not consent to any Artificial Intelligence (AI), generative AI, large language model, machine learning, chatbot, or other automated analysis, generative process, or replication program to reproduce, mimic, remix, summarize, train from, or otherwise replicate any part of this creative work, via any means: print, graphic, sculpture, multimedia, audio, or other medium. This applies to all existing AI technology and any that comes into existence in the future.

I support the right of humans to control their artistic works.

Copyright Information

Next Man Up

First edition

Copyright © 2026 L.A. Witt

Edited by Mackenzie Walton

Cover Art by Lori Witt

eBook ISBN: 978-1-64230-370-4

Paperback ISBN: 978-1-64230-371-1

Hardcover ISBN: 978-1-64230-372-8

ABOUT NEXT MAN UP

When tragedy strikes the Pittsburgh Whiskey Rebels, winger Avery Caldwell loses more than his longtime linemate. Without warning, his best friend in the world is just... gone.

There's no time for grief, though. The season is starting, and now Avery is captain of his devastated team. He's determined to be strong for them and lead them by example—putting aside his emotions and focusing on hockey.

But he can only pretend he's okay for so long.

Peyton Hall was looking forward to a new start on a new team. He'd expected to land a place on the second line and play among men he's been admiring for years... including a winger he's been crushing on since forever. Now he's suddenly centering the top line and trying to fill the skates of a beloved star who's gone too soon.

Avery is determined to ignore his heartache and carry his devastated team. Peyton is determined to find his place among grieving teammates.

But can the new guy stop Avery from self-destructing beneath his grief and the pressure of the captaincy?

And is there any room for the crackling chemistry they're both trying desperately to ignore?

Next Man Up is a standalone M/M hockey romance.

TW: Off-page death, grief, self-medicating, self-destructive behavior, addiction. Also mentions of pregnancy loss/infertility. If you have questions or would like clarification about any of the potential triggers in this book, please contact the author.

AUTHOR'S NOTE

Next Man Up was written before the tragic and senseless deaths of Johnny and Matthew Gaudreau. Out of respect for their memory and for the family, publication was delayed, and the book was revised to minimize some unfortunate and highly coincidental similarities to reality.

30% of the author's royalties will be donated to the John and Matthew Gaudreau Foundation, an organization started by the brothers' family to support causes that were near and dear to their hearts.

https://www.johnandmatty.org/

CHAPTER 1
AVERY

August.

"Are you even going to be able to skate with him around?" My best friend, Leif Erlandsson, glanced up from the ball he was about to putt. "Didn't you lose an edge last time we played against—"

"Shut up." I gestured toward the hole with my club. "Less chirping, more putting."

He cackled. Then he tapped the ball, which took its sweet time rolling right toward the hole... only to veer a few precious degrees to the side before coming to rest six inches from his target. Leif's humor vanished and he huffed. "For shit's sake."

"Ha! That's what you get."

He flipped me off, but his smirk quickly returned. "You know I'm right, though. You're going to have to spend all of training camp learning how to skate on the same ice as him."

My face burned, and it had nothing to do with the

August sun blazing overhead. "You're a dick, you know that?"

"But I'm right."

"You're a *dick*."

He just chuckled, and we continued with our game. I knew this wasn't over, though. One of our teammates had texted a few minutes ago to let us know our GM had worked some kind of wizardry with two other teams. When all was said and done, our team had offloaded a couple of forwards who weren't gelling with the team, three mediocre prospects from the minors, and a veteran defenseman who we all knew wanted to retire closer to his hometown. On top of that, the GM had managed to shed two pricy contracts we'd retained after some awful trades by his predecessor.

In return, we had two goalie prospects, a handful of third and fourth round draft picks... and Peyton Hall.

Peyton. Fucking. Hall.

Center. Seventeenth overall draft pick five years ago. Rookie of the Year. Runner up for a scoring title two seasons in a row. Two conference championship rings and a goddamned Cup.

And yeah, I may have had a *little* bit of a crush on the guy, because in addition to being a top-notch hockey player, he was *smoking* hot. A little taller than me—five eleven, I thought his stats said—with wicked blue eyes and sandy blond hair that had no right to look that hot when it was sweaty and mussed. The last couple of years, he'd often sported a dusting of scruff that made him unreasonably sexy.

When we'd played against Detroit last season, he'd scored a hat trick, and his celly on that third goal really had almost cost me an edge. That smile, those eyes—I'd been so screwed.

I wouldn't admit it out loud under torture, but Leif might've been on to something. I probably *would* have to spend training camp—which was coming up in about a month—remembering how to skate in Peyton's presence.

I was so stupid for him, and I knew I shouldn't have let that slip to Leif over a few beers one night.

"No, I'd never do a teammate," I'd slurred as we'd watched a game in his man cave. Had I been slightly closer to sober, I'd have stopped there, but no, I was drunk with my best friend, so I'd added, *"I mean... not unless Gary signs Peyton Hall."*

"Ha! I knew there had to be one!" Leif had gestured at me with his beer bottle. *"I should tell Gary to try to get him just so you have to—"*

"Leif!" His wife, Rachel, had whapped him with a pillow. *"Oh my God. You are the worst."*

Yeah, he kinda was.

And now Hall was going to be on our team.

"For the record?" I said to Leif as he drove the golf cart toward the next hole. "If you breathe a word about this to Hall, I won't just get revenge—I'll recruit Rachel to help me get revenge."

He shot me a wide-eyed look. "Don't you fucking dare."

"So we have an understanding?"

Leif made a pouty sound and shook his head. "That's so not fair. You can't just weaponize the fact that my wife is seventy percent feral."

"Why not?" I shrugged, grinning with triumph as I claimed the upper hand. "You knew what she was when you married her."

"Yeah, but I didn't think you'd try to use her against me!"

"I won't... as long as you keep your goddamned mouth shut about Hall."

He pushed out a harsh breath. "Christ, Calds. You take the fun out of *everything*."

"I know. I'm such a dick."

"You really are." He paused. "And a hundred bucks plus three steak dinners on the road says you screw him before the season's over."

I barked a laugh that seemed to echo through the rolling golf course. "What? I told you I don't do teammates!"

"Uh-huh." He flashed me a toothy grin. "But you also said this one was an exception. So, are you chickening out of the wager or not?"

I scoffed. "I'm not going to bang a teammate. Especially not if it costs me a hundred bucks and three steak dinners."

Leif made a quiet sound, and as it crescendoed, I recognized it as a chicken noise.

"Oh, fuck you."

More chicken noises.

"For fuck's sake—fine! You're on."

"Ha! I knew it." He extended his hand, carefully keeping the other on the golf cart's wheel. As we shook hands, he asked, "Does it still count if I—"

"*No.*"

"You don't even know what I was going to ask!"

"I know you. So no. Whatever it was... no."

He huffed and rolled his eyes. We exchanged glares, then laughed as he continued driving toward the next hole.

This wasn't over, and I knew it. I trusted Leif not to tip my hand far enough to make me or a teammate uncomfortable, but he was an expert level troll. His subtlety bordered on magic both on and off the ice. When he played hockey, those little moves he did to protect the puck or sneak it past a goalie were mind-blowing. Off the ice, he was a *master* at deadpanning the perfect line to make us all choke on our drinks. A tiny upward flick of his eyebrow could scream sarcasm, amusement, or "that's what she said."

And when there was a wager involved, well...

Oh God. What did I just sign up for?

Yeah, he'd be discreet enough to keep my cards face-down, but I knew without a doubt that next season would be peppered with more chirping than I'd ever experienced in my life. For as long as he and I were on the same roster as Peyton Hall, Leif was going to be merciless.

What could I say?

I was looking forward to it.

That evening, Luis Abadiano gestured with his beer at the empty stool at our high top table. "Is Early coming or not?"

"I don't know, Baddy." I smirked. "If you have to ask him, you're probably not doing a very good job of—"

"Oh, fuck you!" He kicked me under the table as our other teammates howled with laughter.

"You kind of walked into that one," Willie—Henri Ouellet to everyone else—snickered.

Baddy rolled his eyes, shook his head, and took a deep pull of his beer.

I sipped my own beer, then checked my phone. I'd texted Leif about fifteen minutes ago to see if he was still coming. He was the most punctual of all of us by far—his nickname, Early, didn't *just* fit him because his last name was Erlandsson—so it wasn't like him to be late, never mind forty-five minutes late.

He hadn't read the message, which probably meant he was on the road. He never so much as glanced at his phone while he was driving, and if he was on his motorcycle, he wouldn't hear it anyway.

Maybe he'd parked and was on his way in? Maybe he still hadn't heard his phone?

"Hey. Avery." Davis elbowed me. "You good?"

"Yeah. Yeah." I laughed softly and put my phone facedown on the table. "Just texting Early to find out where his sorry ass is."

"Didn't he say he and the missus are trying for a fourth?" Baddy shrugged. "Maybe he got, uh, waylaid?"

"Well," Willie deadpanned, "that would answer the question about whether or not he's coming."

Everyone at the table groaned, and Davis gave Willie a shove.

I chuckled, half-expecting Leif to suddenly appear and ask what he'd missed. We would, of course, fill him in just so he could come up with some even snarkier remark to put Willie and Baddy in their places.

But he didn't.

And my phone stayed quiet.

As I neared the bottom of my beer, something coiled in the pit of my stomach. This wasn't like him, and I didn't like it.

Especially when an hour had passed since he was supposed to be here, and my texts still hadn't been read.

I pushed my stool back and got up, gesturing with my phone. "I'm going to step out and give Early a call."

They all nodded, and I headed for the bar's front door.

I was halfway there when the phone in my hand

vibrated with an incoming call. I looked at the screen, and I halted so abruptly, a server almost crashed into me.

Rachel.

I couldn't explain the cold dread wrapping around my spine like frozen barbed wire.

God, please tell me he lost his phone again and he's calling from his wife's to let us know where he is.

But somehow, somewhere deep down…

I knew.

"Mrs. Erlandsson is in here." The nurse pushed open a door marked *Private Family Waiting Area*, and she gestured for us to go inside.

As soon as I stepped into the room, Rachel was on her feet, and she threw her arms around my neck. She was shaking all over and sobbing against my shoulder, and I just closed my eyes and let her hold on for a moment.

I sensed my teammates around us, and someone put a hand on her shoulder. Someone else murmured that we'd stay with her as long as she needed us.

A couple of the other wives were here, too, their faces pale and full of worry as they sat around the chair Rachel had been occupying.

As she collected herself a little—as much as any wife could be expected to—she drew back and wiped her eyes with shaking hands. "Thank you guys for coming. It means a lot."

"Of course." I kept a hand on her shoulder. "Do they, um… Do they have any updates?"

Fresh tears well up and she pressed her lips together as she shook her head. "He's still in surgery."

My stomach somersaulted for about the fiftieth time since her voice had come through my phone.

"Leif's in the hospital," she'd sobbed. *"I don't know what happ—It's bad, Avery. He's... They said it's really bad."*

Here in the waiting room, she swiped at her eyes again. "God, he's going to be devastated if he can't play anymore."

I nodded numbly, as did my teammates. I had a feeling everyone in the room was thinking the same thing—if we focused on whether Leif would ever play hockey again, then we could ignore the bigger, uglier question. The question that had bile burning in the back of my throat.

We all settled into chairs, everyone exchanging worried glances in a room that was silent except for the occasional sniffle.

My mind flicked back to when we'd said goodbye in the parking lot outside the country club this afternoon.

"You going out with us tonight?" I'd asked as I hoisted our golf bags into my trunk.

"Are you kidding?" He'd laughed as he'd adjusted the strap on his helmet. *"We have to get back to work soon. I'm going to take all the going out and relaxing I can get."*

"Is that why you weren't at the gym this yesterday?"

Despite his sunglasses, the roll of his eyes was unmistakable, and he flipped me off with a glove-covered hand. *"Fuck you."*

I chuckled. *"All right. We're meeting around eight."*

"Sounds good. I can take the kids off Rachel's hands for a few hours before I go."

I made a gesture like I was cracking a whip.

He just snorted, fired up the engine, and rode out of the parking lot.

Sitting here now in this waiting room... Had that conversation been our last?

No. No, of course it hadn't. It couldn't be.

From what I'd been able to piece together from Rachel, he'd been on his way to meet us when he'd started getting dizzy, so he'd pulled over. He'd sat for a few minutes, hoping it would pass. It didn't, so he'd called Rachel and said he didn't feel safe on his bike, and maybe he needed to go to the hospital. Then he'd texted that he suddenly had a massive headache, and he *definitely* needed to go to the hospital.

When she'd arrived minutes later, his bike stood abandoned beside an ambulance as EMTs frantically loaded Leif into the back. He'd collapsed, and a bystander had called 911.

He'd made it to the hospital and into surgery. Brain bleed, they said. An aneurysm. People survived those all the time, didn't they? There might be a long recovery ahead, but he'd pull through. He was too goddamned stubborn not to.

I couldn't say how much time went by before the waiting room doors opened again.

But then they did.

And just like I had in the moment I'd seen Rachel's name on my phone...

I knew.

CHAPTER 2
PEYTON

September.

The first day of Pittsburgh Whiskey Rebels training camp was easily the most surreal thing I'd ever experienced.

As with any training camp, there were prospects, players from the farm teams, pros on professional tryouts, new acquisitions from trades and free agency, and the veterans who'd been on the roster the previous season. At every camp I'd ever attended before, there was always an electric vibe. Everyone was ready for the new season—time to shake off last season's lows and try to replicate its highs. The younger guys were eager to learn from the veterans, and they all held out hope this would be the season they were selected for the roster. The PTOs and new acquisitions who'd played elsewhere in the League were ready to find their footing within their new team's systems.

It was an exciting, stressful, and exhausting time for everyone.

But this year, the usual optimistic vibe of camp was MIA. The younger guys and us new additions were quieter than we should've been. No one knew quite what to say. How exuberant we should be.

Because holy shit, the men who'd been on Pittsburgh's roster last year were... God, it was like they weren't even here.

Most of the new guys and prospects changed in the facility's other locker rooms, but since I was expected to be on the roster, I already had a stall in the team locker room. As we all put on our gear, the room was so absolutely silent, I could hear every rip of tape being pulled off a roll. Every zipper. Every creak of padding.

Cautiously, I stole a few glances at my teammates. I'd known most of these men for a long time, even if I hadn't played with them. Mike Mitchell, who everyone called Eminem, had been on my major junior team a year ahead of me. Willie had played in Detroit the first two years I was there before he'd signed with Pittsburgh. I knew every face on sight.

And as the silence hung over all of them, I was painfully aware of the empty locker stall four over from mine. No one had dared put anything there, and no one had needed to be told; the nameplate made it clear that was a sacred space for now.

Sooner or later, someone would fill that spot. There were only so many stalls in here, and it wouldn't stay empty forever. But right now, while his teammates were still grieving—while they wore their pain on their sleeves as plainly as they wore the patches with his number on their chests—no one used that locker.

Right now, there was nothing in that space except for

about a dozen sticks leaning against it beneath the name-plate that read *Leif Erlandsson.*

One by one, guys clomped away toward the sheet so training camp could get started. I didn't even have to look to know if someone leaving was a new guy or a returning member of the Whiskey Rebels. The new guys all had the same heavy, purposeful gait.

The returning members...

Jesus. It was like I could feel their grief in their slow, halfhearted steps.

I didn't envy them. Teams were extremely tight knit, and I didn't know how I'd come back to the ice after a team-mate's death. It had been crushing enough when, during my second season, a teammate in Detroit had spiraled, his drinking problem turning into a painkiller addiction that had ultimately ended his career. We'd all been devastated, especially when we'd lost contact with him. To this day, I had no idea where he was.

That had been a long, awful thing for everyone on the team, even those of us who hadn't been especially close to him. It had been hard to come back from. I couldn't begin to imagine having a teammate's death just come out of nowhere like Erlandsson's had.

As I got up to head for the ice myself, I let my gaze drift to one of the few remaining stragglers, and my chest tight-ened beneath my gear.

Everyone in the hockey world knew Avery Caldwell and Leif Erlandsson were as tight as brothers. They were legendary as linemates, and so joined at the hip that there'd been more than a few rumors they were a couple. Especially since Caldwell was out and proud just like I was; even after he was best man at Erlandsson's wedding, the theories persisted that the bride was just a beard, or they weren't monogamous, or... something.

Whatever they did or didn't do in private, no one could deny they had a special bond both on and off the ice.

Now Caldwell was sitting in front of his locker stall, geared up except for his jersey, and he just looked... lost. He had one sock taped and the roll of tape still in his hand, and he stared blankly at the logo in the center of the floor. Long strands of dark hair fell over his forehead and in front of his unfocused eyes. I didn't even think he noticed.

Goddamn. I couldn't imagine what he was going through, never mind trying to play hockey through it.

Before I could pull my gaze away and pretend I hadn't been watching him, he turned his head and caught me staring. Nothing really registered on his face. No recognition. No irritation or offense. Just... nothing.

I didn't know what to say or what to do. What *could* I say to someone I'd spoken to maybe three times in my entire career?

I cleared my throat and tilted my head toward the ice. "I'll, uh... I'll see you out on..."

God, was that the best I could do?

Yeah, it kind of was, because I had no clue about shit like this.

Caldwell pushed out a heavy breath and brushed his hair out of his face. "I'm right behind you." The words came out flat and hollow. Like a recited line. Something automatic.

I just gave a nod and headed out into the hall. Once I was out of his sight, I paused to take a deep breath.

I'd watched dozens of interviews with Avery Caldwell since he'd come onto the scene three seasons before I was drafted. He was one of the few openly gay players, so I'd followed him and his career closely.

And also, I mean, who was I kidding? He was gorgeous. Like me, he was white, and I thought he was an inch or so shorter than me. He had dark hair that tickled the collar of his sweater and the most stunning hazel eyes I'd ever seen. That smile? Oh, God. In a game against Pittsburgh last year, I'd blown a tire, which had been embarrassing enough, but fortunately, no one knew it had happened because I'd caught a glimpse of him laughing at something.

In all his interviews, he was so funny and charismatic, with the kind of smile that did ridiculous things to my pulse. Reporters sought him out just to get a few sound bites because he always had a joke or something. He was the kind of person I not only had a crush on, I wished I could just sit down and have a beer with him because it would be so goddamned entertaining.

And now... my God.

That lifeless look in his eyes had been heartbreaking.

The sound of his voice? Devoid of all the humor and playfulness that seemed to define him? Holy shit.

I shook myself and continued toward the ice. I'd seen grieving players before. Those who'd lost grandparents, parents, friends, and even a sibling. The teams would always rally around them and keep them upright through their grief. Hockey teams were families, and we always looked after our own when they lost someone.

So what did we do when that family lost one of its own? How did those of us who were new to the Whiskey Rebels hold up the men who'd just two weeks ago flown to Sweden to bury their teammate?

It had already been announced that Erlandsson's number would be retired at the home opener. The first time these men took to the ice after his death, it would be right after watching his jersey raised into the rafters. How the hell did someone play through that?

And how the hell did those of us who hadn't been close to Erlandsson support them?

CHAPTER 3
AVERY

The weeks since Leif's death had been a blur of horrible emotions and some of the worst moments of my life. I was still having nightmares the moment the doctor's grim words had registered with Rachel.

"I'm so very sorry, Mrs. Erlandsson," the man had told her.

What followed had been the most gut-wrenching, heart-breaking sound I'd ever heard, and every night since, I hoped I wouldn't hear it again. So far, no luck.

Like my teammates and their wives, I'd spent as much time as I could with Rachel. We'd helped with the kids. Kept up with the yard and the house. Sometimes I thought the only thing keeping any of us moving was helping to keep Leif's family moving. I'd take whatever I could get.

Every day since, I'd dreaded the start of camp. I'd kept up my workouts if only to have an outlet and a distraction, but for the first time in my life, I hadn't wanted to come back to the ice. More than once, in my absolute lowest moments, I'd seriously considered asking my agent to find some way to get me out of my contract.

All it had taken each time was one look at Rachel and the kids. They were already taking the loss so hard. They needed to see us strong. They needed to see the Whiskey Rebels—the team Leif had poured so much of himself into—rallying and moving forward so maybe they too could move forward.

I wasn't sure I could do that, but I was damn sure going to try.

Returning to this place where I'd spent so much time and made so many memories—most of them with Leif—had been harder than I'd expected. Putting on my gear. Existing in that room where nothing was left of him but his nameplate. Leaning my stick in his stall—God, that had nearly destroyed me.

A couple of seasons ago, Leif had been out with a broken wrist. That had been tough, but at least it had been finite. We'd all known he was coming back. And he was such a goddamned rink rat, he'd been there almost every day anyway just to hang out.

This absence wasn't going anywhere.

But I *had* to move forward. I had to do this. If nothing else, for Leif's memory and for his family. For our team.

So I'd pulled myself out of bed. Dragged myself to the rink. Forced myself into my gear. Made myself get out to the ice.

And...

And for the first time in weeks, I did feel better. Not good—good was a long way off—but better. More centered. More like me.

The comfortable burn of muscles getting back into the swing of skating. The familiar presence of my stick through my gloves. The vibration of the puck landing on my blade. The satisfaction of watching the my shot go deep into the back of the net, even when there was no goaltender to stop it.

I took some slow breaths as I warmed up for practice. For all I'd felt like my entire world was off-kilter, the ice beneath my feet was level and solid. It wasn't like everything was right again, but the taste of cold rink air on my tongue gave me that first inkling of hope that maybe things would get better.

I'd lost a friend in major juniors. We hadn't been as close as Leif and me, but his death had still hit me hard. The grief had seemed insurmountable. Normal had been gone forever. But over time... little by little...

I still thought about Alex a lot, and I still missed him, but life had gone on. There'd been happiness and joy again, and I could think about him now without choking up.

Was it too much to hope I'd get there with Leif, too?

"You know what Alex would say if he could see us now, right?" Leif had asked when we'd been sharing a behind-closed-doors and very manly cry after the funeral.

Wiping my eyes, I'd managed a halfhearted chuckle. My first laugh in days. *"That we're a couple of pussies?"*

"Exactly." Leif had sniffed. *"Judgy-ass bitch."*

At that, we'd both burst out laughing. We'd still been crying, but we'd laughed, and it had felt good.

I exhaled a cloud and skated a small, lazy circle as I scanned the faces of my teammates and the prospects.

Is there anybody here I can have that manly cry with this time?

Right then, my gaze snagged on one of the new players, and my breath hitched.

In all the chaos, I'd forgotten about Peyton Hall. That we'd acquired him during the off season.

Before I'd come out here, we'd made eye contact across

the locker room and held it for a few seconds, and suddenly I'd been back on the golf course with Leif. There'd been a wager on the table and good-natured threats and his promise to troll me for my crush until the end of time.

The sight of Peyton Hall wearing a Pittsburgh Whiskey Rebels logo in our familiar practice facility had only carved the emptiness deeper. Every time I so much as caught a glimpse of him, I heard echoes of the chirps Leif and I had exchanged. I saw the void where there should have been my friend's smirking face making me blush without saying a word, just flicking his eyes toward Hall and chuckling. Instead of snarky remarks about how much I wanted our new teammate, I heard painful silence.

And I felt how *little* I wanted the man.

There was nothing wrong with him. Distantly, I registered that he was as attractive as he'd been before. How his crystal blue eyes had always scrambled my concentration. The way just seeing his smile in a social media post or something could make my brain record-scratch. How I'd always caught myself watching him skate; I'd been mesmerized by the distinctive sway of his shoulders and how his legs moved and how he made it look so effortless.

Now we were on the same ice and in the same jersey. He was here. A teammate. Still hot as ever.

But all the places that should've been warm and fluttery with all my fantasies about him were empty. Even when he laughed at something one of the guys said to him, that thousand-watt smile didn't ignite anything in me.

Christ. My libido was so dead and gone, it was hard to imagine I'd ever had one. Impossible to believe I ever would again.

I tore my gaze away from my new teammate and found a puck. Practicing some stick handling was always a good way to warm up, and it gave me a reason not to look at my new teammate.

"You know," I heard Leif saying as he'd skated up to me during warmups in Detroit last season. *"I could totally tell him you have a crush on him."*

I'd glared at him. *"Don't you dare."*

"Why not?" His eyes had been full of mischief behind his visor. *"He's right over there."* He'd tipped his head ever so slightly in the direction of the other end of the ice where Peyton's team had been warming up. *"I could just skate up to the red line, get his attention, and—"*

"Do you want me to show Rachel that karaoke video?"

He'd shut his trap and eyed me. *"You said you deleted that."*

"Uh-huh." I nodded toward the other team. *"How sure are you that I actually did?"*

Leif had pursed his lips. Then he sighed heavily and rolled his eyes. *"Christ. You really do take the fun out of everything."*

I'd laughed and punched his arm. *"Not my fault you suck at karaoke."*

"Pfft. Whatever." He'd shot me a pointed look. *"Did you delete it or not?"*

It was my turn for a toothy, mischievous grin. *"Wouldn't you like to know?"*

Then I'd skated away as he called after me, *"You're a dick, Calds!"*

Had we been anywhere other than an arena full of fans and cameras, I'd have flipped him the bird. I'd done that later.

In the present, I shook myself and looked around the rink. I needed to get into the moment. Into hockey. I was here, and I had work to do, and we had a whole crowd of prospects who needed us veterans to have our A-game on so they could learn and develop. Skating around and feeling sorry for myself wasn't going to help anyone with anything.

Of course, all it took was another glance at Hall for me to slip right back into my own head. He was doing some relaxed passing with a couple of prospects who looked about ten—was I getting old? Shit—and he seemed oblivious to me.

In that moment, Leif should've skated by me and muttered, *"You're drooling, Calds,"* at which point I'd have smacked him with my stick and called him something the fans and reporters hopefully wouldn't hear.

I hated that he wasn't here to chirp me about my stupid crush. I hated that I couldn't get my goddamned head together. I hated that Leif was going to lose our wager. Not because Hall wouldn't be interested in me—maybe he would be, maybe he wouldn't—but because I wouldn't even try. I couldn't.

Some part of me wished I could flirt my way into Hall's bed just so Leif could win our bet and maybe so I could feel something good again.

Part of me was pretty sure that would be a disaster. I didn't imagine I had it in me to go through the motions of a hookup with anyone. Not even my longtime crush.

Oh my God, I'm a mess.

Right then, someone did skate up to me, but it wasn't Leif.

Coach Tabakov peered at me from beneath his black baseball cap. "How are you doing, Calds?"

I forced a smile. "Here and skating. That has to count for something."

"It does." He clapped my shoulder. "It counts for a lot."

The sadness in his eyes didn't help me pull my brain on to the rails.

"Listen, before we get started," he said, glancing at the rest of the guys as if to make sure we had some relative privacy. "We're going to be trying out some new lines today."

"Right." I nodded sharply. "Training camp. It's—I know the drill."

"I know you do. How do you feel about being paired with Hall?"

I think my heart actually stopped for a beat or two. "I... Hall?"

Coach nodded and gestured in Hall's direction with his clipboard. "I want to see how the two of you gel."

It took me a couple of seconds to process that. Somehow I'd still assumed Hall would be on the second line, since that was why we'd acquired him. I guess I just hadn't thought about it. When my mind finally caught up, all I managed to say was, "Oh." What could I do? Tell Coach he was pairing me up with the player I'd had a wicked crush on since forever? That Leif and I had even had a wager on whether or not I'd get into Hall's pants?

Coach offered a sympathetic grimace as he put a hand on my shoulder. "I know this is tough for you, kid. No one can fill the hole Early left on this team. No one. Ever. But I have to fill his position. Next man up. You know how it is."

I swallowed hard against the lump in my throat. "I know. I get it."

I did. I honestly did. Somewhere in my mind, I'd known it on the way in here. There was no offensive line without a center and two wingers.

I just hadn't realized my line's new center might be Peyton Hall.

CHAPTER 4
PEYTON

I was, fortunately, not the only new member of this team. After I'd warmed up my legs, I skated over to Brandon Laramie, who'd been acquired to back up the starting netminder.

As I approached, he pushed up his mask. "Hey, man." He gave my arm a little smack with his blocker. "How's Pittsburgh treating you?"

I tapped one of his pads with my stick. "Haven't really had time to explore, but so far, so good. You?"

He shrugged. "Same." He looked around the ice, brow pinching beneath the shadow of his mask. Voice low, he murmured, "Is it just me, or...?"

"The vibe in here?"

He nodded slowly.

"No, it's not you." I glanced around before meeting his gaze again. "Can you blame them?"

"Not at all. I don't think I'd have even made it to the ice."

I grunted in agreement. "Something tells me it's going

to be a rough ride for a while. Best thing we can probably do is encourage everyone else to step up."

"The new guys and prospects?"

I nodded. "Whoever makes the roster is going to have a hell of a lot on their shoulders this season, but I don't know what else to do."

He studied me for a moment, then cracked a small smile. "You sound like a captain."

"I don't think I'd go that far." I swept my gaze around the ice again. "Somebody's gotta keep everyone going while they pick up the pieces, you know?"

The smile faded and he nodded solemnly.

Shortly after that, Coach Tabakov blew the whistle, and everyone skated toward the whiteboard on the glass beside the bench. We'd all been divided into three groups—black, gray, and gold jerseys. I wore a black jersey, as did Laramie. The gold team went to the other rink for their first session, and the gray team would arrive in another hour to join one of us for some drills and a scrimmage.

As I took a knee with everyone else, I gave my group a glance. It wasn't hard to pick out the returning Whiskey Rebels; the somber faces gave them away. The coaching staff wore similar expressions. Some of the other new guys looked at each other uncertainly, as if they had no idea what to do with this uncomfortable vibe. Did anyone really know how to interact with people who were grieving? Add that to the demands of hockey, and... yeah, this was going to be tough as hell.

At the whiteboard, Coach took a deep breath. "Gentlemen, I know this is going to be a challenging season for everyone. No one is expecting it to be easy, especially for those of us who knew Early." He rolled his shoulders, and he seemed to struggle a little to hold on to his composure.

"There's a big piece of this team missing, and it's missing in a way none of us are used to. It's just... going to take time."

My gaze landed on Caldwell. There was a little more life in his eyes now. Some more determination. Maybe he'd just needed a moment to process things in the locker room before he came out here, and now that he was on the ice, he was pulling himself together.

You're a stronger man than I am, Caldwell.

Or maybe I'd do the same in his skates. Maybe I'd find that reserve of strength or stubbornness or whatever the hell it took to push through.

All I could do now was hope I never had to find out.

Coach finished his pep talk and shifted gears to discuss the drills he wanted us to run through. Last season's offensive lines had some obvious holes in them thanks to a trade, a couple of free agents, and... well. One very conspicuously missing center. Coach had deliberately put his top six candidates in the black group, and the bottom six candidates would be duking it out on the grey and gold teams. We'd no doubt get shuffled around and even moved to different teams until he had the four lines he wanted for the opening roster.

Gary, the general manager, had specifically come looking for me to take the center position on the second line. Given that, I suspected Coach would be trying me out with different wingers until we solidified that second line.

So I wouldn't lie—I was a little surprised when the right winger assigned to me from the start was none other than Avery Caldwell.

Oh, shit. He'd been on the top line since halfway through his first season; now he was getting bumped down to the second? I mean, I supposed that made sense. If I were him, I didn't think I'd be able to handle that kind of pressure right now.

But then Coach sent a left winger our way.

Cody Davis.

Who'd been on the top line with Erlandsson and Caldwell.

Wait... instead of bumping Caldwell down to the second...

Was Coach putting *me* on the *top* line?

Putting me into the position that had suddenly and tragically been left unfilled?

Oh. *Fuck.*

But Coach had spoken, so off we went.

Our first few drills were reasonably easy. Though Davis would be our left winger, Coach rotated a few other players through—mostly prospects. That was normal at training camp. Even an offensive line or defensive pair that would be together on the final roster were often assigned other players as part of their development and to see how they gelled with the team's systems.

When we were in the midst of a drill, the only thing I could focus on was hockey. Following the instructions of the drill, passing to my linemates, getting around the defense— there was no time to pay attention to anything else.

In between, though, while other lines took their turns and we caught our breath, I surreptitiously watched Caldwell. There was more life in his eyes now than there'd been in the locker room. Maybe it helped to be away from his friend's empty locker stall. Maybe he just needed something to concentrate on, and God knew hockey was good for that. He was playing well, too—the drills were fairly simple at this stage of camp, but they weren't exactly pee-wee level drills.

He had to protect the puck, navigate around the defense, know where his linemates were, and get the puck to the right person, all while skating at nearly full speed. He scored twice during one of the drills, and Ziggy—Dimitriy Sigayev—was *not* an easy goalie to score against. Not even during practice.

Every time there was a lull—usually while we were waiting our turn for a drill—I tried to talk myself into approaching Caldwell. Just making some small talk. Break the ice, so to speak. I wanted to connect with him as a team-mate, especially since it looked like we might also be *line-mates* for the foreseeable future.

But I also couldn't deny that there was a very not-hockey-related reason why I'd been so excited to come to Pittsburgh. I could name at least a dozen players in the League who'd I'd have dropped trou with in a heartbeat, but I'd have forgotten them all entirely if Avery Caldwell ever gave me so much as a suggestive grin.

I hadn't really known what I would do with that infor-mation once I got here. Yes, he was openly queer, but that didn't mean he got involved with teammates or that he was interested in me. So I'd hoped to just play on the same team, maybe make friends with him like I usually did with team-mates, and if chemistry happened—great!

Now that I was here, I was afraid to approach any of them, especially Caldwell, because they were all in an understandably awful headspace. We had to connect—that was the only way teams functioned together—but making those connections right now felt risky. Like I was skating on eggshells because I didn't know these men well enough to gauge them.

So naturally the one I most *needed* to connect with was the one whose grief was the most palpable. How did I do this? What if I approached him when he was in the middle of giving himself a moment to compose himself?

Right now, as we caught our breath after another run through the drill, he still seemed more or less focused on hockey. He was watching a line of prospects going through the drill, his brow furrowed and his focus sharp.

I hesitated because I was afraid I'd say something stupid, but nothing ventured...

Pretending I wasn't as nervous as a high school sophomore trying to ask a senior to prom, I skated up beside him.

Caldwell tensed a little, and when he glanced at me, something flickered across his face. Something like fear? What the hell?

I pretended not to notice. "So, um... do you think Coach is going to keep us on the same line?" *Smooth, Hall. Real smooth.*

Caldwell recovered from that weird, momentary shock, and he shifted his attention to the players currently running the drill. "He told me we're going to be the top line."

Oh. Shit. So this wasn't just a trial run.

I swallowed. "So... you, me, and Davis?"

Caldwell nodded. His eyes tracked the players, and then when the whistle blew and the next line started, he faced me again. "I'm not surprised. You're one of the best in the League on the faceoff dot."

The little rush of giddiness that went through me almost had me groaning with embarrassment.

Come on, Peyton. Can we not fanboy Avery Caldwell right to his face?

"Oh. Uh." I laughed self-consciously. "Does, um..." I nodded toward our coach. "Does Coach Tabakov have wingers practice faceoffs too? Like, regularly?"

Caldwell nodded. To my surprise, a faint blush darkened his already flushed cheeks. "I'm, um... I'm not very good at them. So, you know, try not to get kicked out of the circle?"

I chuckled. "We can practice them, if you want."

He met my gaze again, and oh God, those hazel eyes were gorgeous. I'd always known they were—not that I'd ogled him in magazines or social media posts or anything— but up close? Wow.

Fortunately, my brain stopped short-circuiting in time to catch him ask, "Really?"

"Why not?" I smirked. "I do get kicked out of them sometimes, so..."

The way he laughed did things to my head that I did not want to think about right then.

"I mean, I won't say no," he said. "Maybe after camp. When we settle into practice a bit more."

I nodded. "Deal."

A moment later, it was our turn to run through the drill again, so that was the end of the conversation. Still, it had gone better than I'd anticipated, so I couldn't complain.

I also couldn't quite work up the courage to strike up another one. Even when we were standing together in between drills, I wasn't sure what to say. He wasn't stand-offish or giving off any signals that I shouldn't talk to him, but he didn't try to initiate anything either.

Fine. It was the first day of training camp. Between practicing, traveling, eating, playing, and staying in hotels, we'd have plenty of opportunity to get to know each other over the next season.

At least he still seemed to be in a better mood now. The more we practiced, the more he seemed to come to life. He clearly still had that dark cloud hanging over him—who could blame him?—but he smiled a little more as the day went on. He talked a lot with the prospects, helping them and giving them pointers. He sometimes chatted with some of the guys he'd been playing with for the past few seasons.

A handful of times, though, I caught him staring at nothing, his expression as distant as it had been in the locker room. More than once, I saw him shake himself and clearly try to remember what was going on or what he was supposed to be doing, as if he'd truly zoned out for a minute or two.

I could guess where his mind was going.

This had to be so damn hard, trying to play through that kind of grief. I'd been a mess for the first half of the season after my grandma died. Early had been *here*. In Pittsburgh. On this ice. On this team. Avery was surrounded by constant, inescapable reminders of the reason he was grieving.

I wondered which would be worse for him—if the club left Erlandsson's nameplate up in the locker room, or when they ultimately took it down.

Avery had been by far the closest to Erlandsson, but the other guys had been hit hard too. Though they tried to be stoic, they all let the masks slip now and then. Baddy had spaced out a little during a drill earlier. I'd caught Willie gazing at something on the stick rack with a far-off look on his face. As I'd swung by the bench for a swig of water, Eriks and Ollie had been having what sounded like a somber conversation in their native language. I didn't know the intricacies of Swedish, but their expressions hadn't left much to the imagination.

Their teammate had only been gone for a handful of weeks now. It was a fresh loss, and grief was not a fast process. On top of that, I'd heard that several of them, including Caldwell, had been at the hospital when the doctors broke the grim news. That *had* to be traumatic.

Returning to hockey without him probably pulled at the healing wounds and set them back. It was probably also what kept everyone who knew Erlandsson going. Hockey players were notorious for not being able to sit still anyway, and the way these guys threw themselves into hockey during camp was conspicuous.

I didn't know if that was healthy. Honestly, what *was* healthy after something like that? Therapy was great and all, but for better or worse, the grief still had to happen.

I scanned the ice for some of the players who, like me, were new to the Whiskey Rebels. Laramie. Dave Kemper. Lance Trewin. Emil Lavoie. It was still a little early to make predictions, but if I had to guess, those four would most likely be on the roster. Trewin was a rookie fresh out of college, and he'd been practically joined at the hip with Matias Astala, one of the veteran defensemen. Kemper and Lavoie looked like a solid match with Nate Johnson for the third line. Aside from Trewin, I knew them from around the League and—in the cases of Lavoie and Laramie—major juniors. They were standup guys. Great assets to a locker room.

Between us, maybe we could carry the team while the rest of the guys found their bearings after Erlandsson.

CHAPTER 5
AVERY

Getting into the groove of training camp and now preseason practice helped me get my head together. I was still a mess, still reminded of Leif at every turn, but I had something to focus on. Little but little, that shook me out of my funk, at least when I had my skates on.

Hockey was a mixed blessing like that. It was a constant reminder of the man I was missing, but it was also a balm to my soul. It was a lightning rod for my concentration and all my messy emotions, and gelling with my old and new teammates felt like moving toward normal. Not back to normal by any means, but moving in that direction.

Whenever I was off the ice, I was a mess, so any time I wasn't helping Rachel with something, I was a full-on rink rat. Here as much as I could, lingering after practice for as long as they'd let me.

Today, practice had ended, and I'd been lazily skating and chasing pucks, looking for some reason to stay longer.

My excuse came from an unexpected place:

"So." Peyton—we were on a first name basis now—

bounced a puck on the blade of his outstretched stick. "You in a hurry to go? Or do you want to practice faceoffs?"

I was at the bench for a swig of water, and I paused to consider the question.

Practicing faceoffs with the man I was supposed to have a crush on—*Hello, libido? Anybody home?*—sounded more enjoyable than what I'd do as soon as I got home. A lot healthier too. And I was down for any excuse to keep my skates under me for as long as possible.

"Sure." I shrugged. "Couldn't hurt."

In my past life, the way he smiled would've made me miss an edge and land on my ass. Today, there was an unexpected zip of... something. Like the faintest ghost of a thrill. Not excitement, but the promise that I still had the capacity for excitement, I supposed?

Either way, I didn't argue with it. I returned the smile, ready to suggest we get Davis to join us, but... was I imagining that blush? The way his gaze darted away from mine?

Yes. Yes, I absolutely was. Because he was my teammate, and my sanity was a distant memory.

Clearing my throat, I tried again. "Should I get Davis? Might not be a bad idea to have a few of us."

Peyton looked around the rink at our remaining teammates. "Yeah, why not?" Then he frowned. "I think Coach LeBon is busy, though."

He was right—our offensive coach was busy doing some work with some of the guys from the bottom six. Fortunately, we had other options.

"Actually," I said, "Jayson coaches faceoffs too."

"Oh, does he?"

I nodded. "I'll grab him if you can get Davis and some of the other guys."

Jayson, our skills coach, was in the locker room, but he

hadn't taken off his skates yet and he wasn't in a hurry. Though faceoffs were usually the domain of the offensive coach, Jayson had been amazing at them during his playing career, and he was a really good coach.

When Jayson and I returned to the ice, Peyton had wrangled Davis, Baddy, and Willie, and we all gathered around one of the faceoff dots.

"Calds, Hall." Jayson gestured at the dot. "You're up first."

Great. So I had to go up against one of the best in the League at faceoffs? Eh, it would be good for me. Humbling, if nothing else.

And yet another very welcome distraction from the world that existed outside this rink.

As I positioned myself, I flicked my eyes up, and I forgot all about the puck, faceoffs, hockey.

Looking at those piercing blue eyes in an interview or across the ice was one thing. Up close like this? Holy hell.

Movement in my peripheral vision reminded me a second too late what we were doing, and by the time I went after the falling puck, Peyton had already won the faceoff.

"Goddammit," I laughed. "See? You're way faster than me!"

Jayson huffed. "Well, for starters, you need to watch the puck. Not your opponent."

My face was instantly on fire, and I refused to read anything into the way Peyton ducked his head and bit his lip as he skated a circle.

"Right," I said. "Watch the puck. Got it."

"You sure?" Jayson deadpanned.

"Fuck you."

He snorted.

Peyton and I both skated back to the dot. I focused on the puck Jayson was holding.

Despite my best efforts, though, I glanced at Peyton again, and we both immediately burst out laughing.

"I'm sorry," I said through my laughter. "I'm sorry. I don't know why that—I'm sorry."

Peyton just let his head fall forward and shook it.

Jayson rolled his eyes. "You know, I've never *heard* of anyone getting kicked out of a faceoff for giggling, but there's a first time for everything."

That didn't help at all.

Ironically, that got us both kicked out of the circle, and we got out of the way so Willie and Davis could set up. They started snickering, too, and the exasperated sigh from our skills coach had all of us laughing.

Maybe we were just slaphappy and tired. That happened sometimes during the preseason when we were all still getting back in the swing of regular practices. And at least some of us were a little extra tired lately because—

Because nothing about this preseason had been normal.

That thought sobered me, but I tried to shake it off.

No, it wasn't normal, but it could be. We could get there. Life went on, and that included hockey.

While Jayson gave Willie and Davis some pointers on their faceoff, I chanced a look at Peyton.

He was looking right at me, and his eyebrows rose. The corner of his mouth did too, pulling his lips into an uneasy smile.

I couldn't help the quiet laugh that escaped, and it seemed to relax him, too. Hell, maybe that was what I needed today. What we *all* needed.

By the time we all headed back to the locker room, I

hadn't improved my faceoff much, but my mood was a little lighter than it had been recently.

On the way to the showers, I wasn't sure how I felt about my interactions with Peyton during that impromptu practice session. We got along well—we'd been linemates since the start of training camp, and we worked great together. But working on faceoffs with him—being right in each other's faces like that—had sparked some feelings I'd thought were dead and gone.

Those eyes had teased the edges of that dormant crush. His smile—his *flirty* smile?—had made something in me try to crackle to life.

And no, getting overcome by a fit of giggles might not have been the most professional thing in the world or the best example to set for the rookies, but... fuck it. It felt good. Better than anything had in a while.

I was still a long way from anything normal. Still miles from the person who could say he was moving past his grief.

But after laughing and joking my way through faceoff practice...

I was less numb than I'd been in weeks.

I ran my fingertips over the C on the jersey hanging in my dressing room stall. Somehow it messed with my head more than the memorial patch with Leif's number on it. The blue and white 61 above the right breast carried the weight of the whole team's grief, but that gold C was even heavier.

Leif had always said that if he ever left Pittsburgh, he'd tell anyone who'd listen that I should be the captain after him. I'd laughed it off, figuring we had years before it would be an issue. He'd been signed to a seven-year deal with a no-move clause, and he'd expected to sign another one after that. Everyone—including Leif—had expected him to be captain of this team until he retired.

"Oh, you're so generous," I'd snarked after he'd said I'd wear the C eventually. *"I'll get, what? One season of being a captain before I have to retire because I'm old as shit?"*

Smirking, Leif had shrugged. *"Tell you what—I'll retire when I'm forty, and then you can have—yeah, I guess one year. If you can keep playing that long."*

I'd rolled my eyes and flipped him off, and he'd cackled.

I swallowed hard as I ran my thumb over the slick fabric of the letter again.

I hadn't given much thought to the pressure of the captaincy except to realize it was way more than I'd wanted to shoulder. I'd had on one of the As for the past two seasons, and that had been enough. Leif had the C and he could *keep* it. By the time he retired, I'd be in my mid-thirties, and maybe then I could handle that letter on my jersey.

But now, here I was. My teammates had unanimously spoken. Leif was gone, and his C was mine, and that thin piece of fabric was heavier than I'd ever imagined it would be.

I gazed around the room as everyone suited up for our home opener. All these men—all nineteen of them, plus the staff, plus anyone called up from the minors—expected me to live up to the captaincy. They expected a leader, and they'd chosen me.

Not for the first time, I debated asking the team to select a different captain.

I couldn't do that to them, though.

Most of the guys had played with Leif, and they were all grieving him. Everyone was leaning hard on everyone else, trying like hell to be stronger for each other than we were capable of being for ourselves.

I didn't think I was strong enough to shoulder the captaincy, but the men in this room needed me to do it. If I could wear the C and lead this team, if I could keep putting one skate in front of the other, then they could too.

I pulled on the C-laden jersey and finished getting my gear together for warmups. Tonight would be hard, but we could do this. *I* could do this.

Warmups weren't too bad. Fans cheered. We tossed them some pucks. We went through our usual routines. I mostly managed to ignore that I couldn't shoulder check Leif tonight and he wouldn't thread the puck between Eminem's skates while he was stretching. We'd always done those for good luck—not that hockey players were superstitious or anything—but I'd had similar rituals with teammates who'd left over the years. It came with the territory; if your superstition involved someone else, you'd find a different one after that person left.

I shoulder-checked Baddy, earning me a shout of "Hey!"

A few minutes later, Davis threaded a puck between Eminem's skates, and they exchanged smiles.

Yeah. We could do this. We could move forward as a team, superstitions at all.

Warmups came to an end. We returned to the locker room briefly, then came back out for the game.

Since this was the home opener, we came out in numerical order as the announcer introduced us by our number, name, and hometown. As one of the alternate captains, I'd gone second to last for the past two seasons. Baddy had always gone before me, and then Leif, being the captain, went out last.

Tonight, we had a new alternate captain.

"From Samara, Russia, number twelve, alternate captain Nikandr Mikhailov."

Mix took off, waving to the crowd as he headed for the circle.

"From Houston, Texas, number thirty-six, alternate captain Luis Abadiano!"

Baddy skated out.

No one left but me.

I swallowed. *Here we go.*

"And finally, from Abbottsford, British Columbia, captain of your Pittsburgh Whiskey Rebels—number seventy-two, Avery Caldwell!"

The roar of the crowd made me smile, and I waved at the fans as I hit the ice.

Then I joined my teammates in the circle, and the announcer repeated, "Please welcome this season's Pittsburgh Whiskey Rebels!", which prompted even more cheering. My heart pounded, and not in an entirely bad way for a change. The fans were pumped. Maybe I could feed off that and get into the game the way I needed to tonight.

The cheers started to die down. At this point, most of the team would normally retreat to the bench while the starting lineups for both teams stood at the blue lines for the national anthems. This time, every player remained in the circle around center ice, and the visitors joined us, slotting themselves between Whiskey Rebels

I gritted my teeth. Even though I knew what was coming and I'd been steeling myself for it all damn week, I wasn't ready.

The arena went dark, and I stole a second to close my eyes and swallow hard. This was going to be hell, but I was determined to make it through.

For my team. For our fans. For Leif's family. For Leif's memory.

For myself.

The lights stayed down, and the screen lit up, showing a photo of Leif in his jersey, no helmet on and his dark hair neatly arranged, with his stick in one gloved hand and that brilliant smile on his face.

The announcer's voice was unusually subdued as he said, "In August of this year, the Pittsburgh Whiskey Rebel family suffered a terrible loss when Leif Erlandsson unexpectedly passed away."

I pushed out a ragged breath, the thin cloud forming in front of me as I stared up at the screen. I didn't hear much of what the announcer said. I was too focused on the clips of Leif. There were some highlight reel shots of his most incredible goals, and that time he'd come out of the penalty box, taken a pass from Davis and scored before the other team had known what hit them. There were shots of him and Rachel with their kids at the family skate on Christmas Eve, on the ice during practice, and at home. There was the image the team had displayed of the smiling parents with their minutes-old daughter at the hospital one night when Leif had understandably had to miss a game. Pictures and clips showed him with his teammates over the years, both on and off the ice. I laughed even as some tears spilled down my cheeks when the video switched to some of us pranking one of the rookies last season, followed by some of our other hijinks.

The crowd applauded, laughed, and cheered, and it was hard not to fall apart as I listened to an arena full of people showing my best friend love.

The video shifted back to the still image of Leif.

"In honor of Early's memory," the announcer went on,

"his number is now officially retired." A spotlight appeared in the rafters, illuminating a black piece of fabric hanging beside the retired numbers of two legendary Pittsburgh players. "Welcome to your place of honor, number sixty-one."

As the crowd roared again, the black fabric was rolled up, revealing his number, his name, and the years spanning both his life and his hockey career. Both were too short. Much, much too short.

I struggled to choke back my tears. I'd told him a long time ago that his jersey would end up in the rafters someday.

"They're gonna put you up there with Wilcox and Reynolds," I'd said during one morning skate. *"I bet you a thousand dollars."*

He'd laughed and smacked my shoulder. *"You're on. Because I'll either get my jersey up there or some of your money. I can't even decide which I want more."*

I'd flipped him off, and we'd both laughed, and here in the present, I'd have given anything to be counting out that money for him a decade or two from now. I'd have sold my soul to listen to him chirping at me and rubbing it in that I'd lost. Or, even better, to be standing at a podium and telling him *"I told you so"* in front of a packed arena.

Oh, but this wasn't over yet.

Rachel and the kids were introduced, walking out from the bench onto a long black carpet. She held little Elsa on her hip, and the twins, Linnea and Kalle, walked close beside her. Linnea clutched Rachel's hand while Kalle gazed around with huge eyes.

The announcer spoke again, "We now ask that Houston captain Jon Zachary and Pittsburgh captain Avery Caldwell join Early's family for the ceremonial puck drop."

I swallowed hard as I skated away from my teammates to join the family.

When I made eye contact with Rachel, her chin quivered. She let go of Linnea's hand and hugged me fiercely with one arm. When she let me go, she tapped the C on my jersey and managed a smile through her tears. "The team is in good hands."

I almost cried, but instead pulled her into another hug as I tried to keep myself together.

There was a little tug at my sleeve, and I looked to see Elsa pulling on the fabric.

"Hey, kiddo." I gave her a gentle hug and kissed her forehead. She smiled. At not even two years old, she didn't understand what was happening tonight or what had been happening the last several weeks. She was blissfully unaware of why everyone around her was so sad, and tragically too young to have much if any memory of her father.

God, this whole night was going to destroy me.

Then I shifted my attention to Kalle and Linnea. They were older—they'd turned six in July—and from what Rachel had told me, while they were still learning what death truly meant, they did understand that their dad wasn't coming back. Linnea was crying, but her brother was trying hard to hold it together. Tears beaded on his eyelashes, and his chin quivered when he looked at me.

I crouched, took off my glove, and rested a hand on his shoulder. "It's okay to cry, buddy. Trust me—" I gestured around us, and my voice cracked as I said, "You're not the only one."

With that, he had his arms around my neck, and he was sniffling against my shoulder pad. I closed my eyes and hugged him. Linnea joined, and I closed my eyes and tried to keep myself together. The network was probably apoplectic about this ceremony taking forever, and the team might even get fined or some shit for delay of game. In that moment, I honestly didn't care. These poor kids were at center ice a month after they'd lost their dad. Everyone could fucking *wait*.

After a moment, they both let me go, and they wiped their eyes with shaky hands.

"I'll see you and your mom after the game, okay?" I said.

Without speaking, they nodded. Then they both stepped back and clung to Rachel's legs.

Zachary, who I'd known from around the League but wasn't close to, waited patiently. When Rachel and I were ready, he took his position opposite me. Rachel held out the puck. We all offered smiles for the camera. Then she dropped the puck.

I gave her and the kids another round of hugs. As they headed back to the locker room, Zachary turned to me and extended his hand.

"I'm sorry, man," he said. "Always hard to lose a team-mate, but I know you two were tight."

God, was everyone conspiring to make me lose it on live TV tonight?

But as I'd done every goddamned day of training camp, practice, media availability, and just... *existing*, I kept it under the surface.

Accepting the handshake, pretending my jersey wasn't damp with the tears of two kids who'd lost their dad, I nodded sharply. "Thanks. It's, um... It's been tough."

Mercifully, that was the end of the memorial for Leif. Thank God, because I didn't think I was going to last another minute.

And at the same time...

It was over? Now we were just supposed to... move on? Play hockey?

Apparently so, because everyone but the starters returned to their respective benches, and we took our places on the blue lines for the anthem.

Holy fuck, this was surreal. It was such a normal thing—standing here, listening to the anthem, getting my head in the game—but I didn't know how to breathe around normal right now. It had been less than ten minutes since they'd unveiled Leif's jersey in the rafters, even less since I'd been comforting his kids, and now I was supposed to step back into normal like it was nothing? I couldn't go back in the locker room and catch my goddamned breath for a minute?

No. No, I couldn't, because my team and our fans and my best friend's memory were counting on all of us—were counting on *me*—to stay upright and play hockey.

I wasn't sure how I was going to *do* that, only that I needed to. I had to.

"You all right, Calds?" Davis's voice pulled me out of my thoughts.

I shook myself, then nodded. "I'm good." I gestured with my stick toward Houston's goal. "How about we put a few in the back of their net for Early?"

My linemate grinned. "Can't imagine a better tribute. Let's do it."

We set up at center ice for the faceoff.

Peyton glanced at all of us as he skated up to the dot. Apparently satisfied we were all in position, he faced the other center.

The puck dropped. He easily won the faceoff, and just like that, we were off.

In an instant, the weight of the night tumbled off my shoulders. Now that the game was moving, I fell into the groove. Passing. Bodying my way past a pest of a defenseman. Calling for the puck. Catching it on my stick and shooting it. No goal, but the puck rebounded and Peyton notched a shot, too. This time the goalie froze it, and the whistle blew.

Fine. Offensive zone faceoff. I could work with that.

Peyton won that faceoff too, but we quickly lost possession. Houston tried to break away, and they were promptly stopped at the blue line by our D.

Our shift was over. The second line came out, and a moment later, our defense peeled away to let in a pair of fresh bodies.

The game went back and forth, and every time I was on the bench, I twitched with frustration. I needed to get out there. We needed to *score*. We needed to *win*.

A few times when I was on the bench, the impulse to look up at Leif's number was too much to resist. After glancing up three separate times and then having to pull myself together, I kept my gaze very firmly at ice level. I didn't even look up at the Jumbotron unless I was checking the time, and I pointedly didn't let my gaze drift toward the retired jerseys. Leif belonged up there. I belonged down here. That was the way it was now.

And Houston was playing like they wanted to win this one, but like hell were we losing after we'd raised Leif's number.

"Next shift," I told Davis and Peyton. "One of us"—I gestured at them and myself—"is getting one into the net."

"Sounds good to me," Davis said.

Peyton held up his gloved fist. "Let's do it."

We bumped fists with him, and when it was our turn to hit the ice, we flew over the boards.

Willie was holding the puck behind our net, waiting for

us to complete the shift change. When Ollie went to the bench, Willie passed me the puck and skated off the ice himself.

Houston was trying for a line change too, but they'd waited too long while Willie had been behind the net. By the time they went for it, we were already heading into their zone. Peyton had the puck and he danced between a couple of skaters who tried but failed to get in his way.

I was already almost to the crease, and when I realized he'd broken free of the defense, I smacked my stick on the ice.

Without hesitation, he fired the puck at me, and I whipped it right on goal.

The netminder never saw it coming.

I roared with triumph as the goal horn sounded and the fans went wild. It was only the first goal of the game—hell, the first goal of the season—but... fuck it. We needed this momentum.

All we had to do now was keep it going.

By the time I dropped onto the bench in the locker room after the final buzzer, I was exhausted. Some of that was just getting back into the swing of playing in the regular season; the first few games were always a little bit of a rude awakening no matter how conditioned I was.

Some of it, though, was definitely the emotional start to the night.

I would never be used to seeing Leif's number up there in the rafters. Not now. Not this soon. Not when he hadn't retired in all the glory he'd deserved.

The club had done right by him, though, and they'd

honored Leif. The fans had cheered for him, and I had no doubt there'd been a lot of tears up there in the stands.

And we'd won. On Leif's night, with his widow and children in the building, we'd crushed Houston 4-1, and it felt absolutely incredible.

Was this closure? Something *like* closure? I didn't know. In some ways, the ceremony had left me ragged, but in others, it had soothed me in ways I couldn't explain, but had desperately needed soothing. In the end, I'd composed myself enough to play hockey.

My teammates had, too.

After sixty minutes of hockey, I was as tired as if I'd just played a grueling seven-game series. I was trembling as I stripped off my gear. Physically and emotionally, I was completely wrung out. I'd held it together all goddamned night, making myself stay strong for everyone *including* myself. I'd succeeded. I'd stayed together. Maybe that meant I was finally done falling apart at the slightest provocation. Was this what it felt like when grief started to lift? Was it too much to hope that after just a few weeks, I might start feeling better instead of worse?

I thought so... right up until Coach's postgame speech. It was a lot of the usual, but then came his closing words:

"You boys did good out there," he said. "You did the fans proud. You did me proud." His voice cracked as he added, "You did Early's memory proud."

And fuck me, but the dam broke.

CHAPTER 6
PEYTON

I had to give the team staff credit—they made damn sure no cameras got anywhere *near* the locker room.

The one that was in here—the team's reporter and crew —had seemed intent to keep filming, but a low growl of, "Turn that *off*" made them think twice. Right now, Coach was having a very terse one-way conversation with them, and I suspected it had a vibe of "If I see this footage on any screen or device, there will be hell to pay."

Good. Get 'em, Coach.

The team's reporter, Falon, was nodding along and not arguing. She'd seemed like good people, and my teammates all liked her, so I had a feeling she wasn't pushing back.

The reporters who were still out in the hallway didn't sound pleased as Glen, our PR director, explained to them that media availability was going to be delayed. After all, they had to get these interviews on the air ASAP.

Laramie and I exchanged glances, nodded, and got up.

"Hey, Glen?" I gestured at Laramie. "We can talk to them out in the hallway. If that'll pacify them until..." I pointed over my shoulder at our teammates.

Glen glanced past me, then nodded sharply and shooed us out into the hall, mumbling, "I owe you boys," before shutting the door behind us.

I didn't relish facing the media under the best of circumstances. Surrounded by lenses, microphones, and annoyed reporters in a hallway crammed with equipment boxes? Not fun at all.

But it took the pressure off Glen and our teammates, and I couldn't lie—it got me away from the absolutely heartbreaking sight and sound of Avery collapsing under his grief.

That was seared into my mind anyway. The way he'd buried his face in his hands and leaned forward, trembling all over as the sobs wracked his whole body—helpless didn't even describe how I'd felt in that moment. Eminem and Baddy, sitting on either side of him, had been doing their best to comfort him. One of the assistant coaches had joined in. I had no idea what they'd been saying or if any of it was working—was there anything someone *could* do to stop that kind of emotional break?

There'd been nothing I could do because I didn't have that bond with him. There were a lot of shoulders better suited to holding him up than mine.

So, I did the one thing within my power—I gave the media something to do besides circle him like camera-wielding vultures.

"How has this team been in the wake of losing their captain?" a reporter asked me as casually as if she were asking if we liked our new jerseys.

Calling on every second of media-training I'd ever had, I kept my expression neutral and met her gaze. "It's been hard for them. Teammates—we get really close, you know? We're family. Just having someone get traded away or sign somewhere else in free agency can be hard. It's been tough for those of us who *didn't* know Early. What those guys are going through?" I gestured at the closed door behind me. "I can't even imagine."

Laramie picked up the thread. "It's always hard when you lose someone, especially a member of your core. When they retire or if they leave—it's an adjustment. You feel kinda..." He furrowed his brow.

"Untethered?" I offered.

"Yeah," he said with a nod. "So then on top of that, there's... Well, there's *why* Pittsburgh's captain is gone. Any team's going to have a hard time picking up and moving forward after that."

"What are your thoughts on your new captain?" came the follow-up question. "Do you think Avery Caldwell is the leader this team needs through this difficult time?"

Laramie and I exchanged glances. I hoped the reporters and anyone watching the videos interpreted it as *"you want to answer first or should I?"* instead of *"are these clowns for real?"*

Laramie said, "He's been great. I haven't played with him long enough to be able to say one way or the other, but I watched him with the kids at training camp, and I've watched him play for years." He half-shrugged. "He was an alternate captain already—doesn't seem like much of a leap for him to wear the C."

Though I'd been surprised we'd made him captain when he was obviously grieving harder than any of our teammates, and I still worried we were putting too much pressure on him, I nodded. "Yeah, exactly. I don't know the whole roster that well yet, either, so I can't say this or that player would be better suited for the captaincy than Calds.

We'll see how the season goes, you know? But I've got total faith in him. I can't imagine why I wouldn't."

I wondered if any of them caught the unspoken dare— *why do* you *think he* shouldn't *be our captain?*

Because if they answered that, then I could remind them who'd scored two of our goals tonight, including the game winner, and pulled us through even after he'd obviously struggled to get through the ceremony. Yeah, he'd broken in the locker room, but only *after* all of that. And hopefully they didn't know about him falling apart on the other side of the door behind me and Laramie.

He's the strongest motherfucker on this team, you cretins. Who else is worthy of wearing our C?

They didn't take the bait, which was probably a good thing.

"This question is for both of you," another reporter said. "You both signed with Pittsburgh during this past off season. I want to know, if you hadn't already signed your contract when this tragedy occurred, would you still have wanted to come to Pittsburgh, knowing what happened?"

I probably let my media face slip a little, and I didn't care. Sometimes it blew my mind the shit these people would ask us. Some were just devoid of social graces, while others were clearly trying to get a reaction. I couldn't quite tell with this guy, but in the interest of not blowing up on-camera, I gave him the benefit of the doubt.

"Absolutely," I said without hesitation. "Pittsburgh was going to be my top choice if I became a free agent, and that hasn't changed in the slightest. And seeing how hard these guys are working, how much they're playing with all that heart even when they're going through hell? You have to admire that, you know? They're bound and determined to honor Erlandsson by sticking together and playing hard as a team, and I just hope I'm proving to them and the fans that I'm as committed as they are."

"Exactly." Laramie gave a sharp nod. "I mean, yeah, part of the reason I wanted to come here was I wanted to play on the same team as Leif Erlandsson. I'd always heard he was a great teammate and an awesome captain, and there's a reason he was a three-time All-Star, you know? But I also wanted to play here. With this *whole* team." He made a disgusted sound. "That hasn't changed just because the guys are going through something awful. Why would it?"

I peered at the reporter. *Yeah. Why* would *it?*

No response came, and someone else chimed in with a question about the game itself. Those could get annoying in their own right—there were only so many ways to say *"yep, we should've kept the puck away from the other guys"*—but tonight I was happy to answer them. I would talk all night long about how much we needed to improve our forecheck, how some critical turnovers could've been avoided, and how we absolutely should've taken advantage of their netminder's lack of rebound control. Anything to keep them busy and pacified while our teammates leaned on each other in private.

Eventually, Glen stepped in between us and the reporters, and he politely said, "That's enough questions."

"Are the players ready for us in the locker room?" someone asked.

Glen shook his head. "I'm afraid we're not going to allow the press into the room this evening."

Laramie and I exchanged wide-eyed glances. Shit—had things gotten worse since we'd stepped out?

There was a general mutter of irritation, and another reporter said, "This was a big night for the team after their loss. We'd like to get some comments from the players about it."

"I understand that," Glen said, completely unflapped. "But it *has* been a big night for the team. They're grieving someone very close to them, and I'm going to ask for them to have some privacy to process that this evening." He gestured at Laramie and me. "That's why these two gentlemen made themselves available for questions."

No one seemed pleased about that, but they didn't push. Probably because a few members of arena security had inched closer, watching the whole exchange with *fuck around and find out* written all over their faces.

As the reporters dispersed, Glen turned to us and exhaled, letting his own façade crack a little. "Thank you, gentlemen. I appreciate you having everyone's backs."

"Absolutely," Laramie said. "I'm happy to get in the way if they want to mess with my teammates."

"Same." I grimaced. "I can't believe they're so... blunt about asking about Erlandsson. I know reporters can be a little mercenary sometimes, but aren't there *some* lines?"

Glen's lips formed a thin, bleached line, and he pushed out a breath through his nose. "Yeah. I wasn't impressed about that. I'm going to have a talk with club management and see if I can't put out a memo barring anyone from bringing him up to players." He huffed sharply and rolled his eyes. "I've been working with the media for thirty-five years, and even I'm still surprised sometimes at how relentless they can be when they smell a story."

I made a face. Laramie just said, "Eww."

Eww was right.

We stepped back into the locker room. It was mostly quiet, now—just the sounds of people moving around and of water running in the next room. The equipment managers were wheeling out carts full of jerseys (which Laramie and I added ours to), and people were putting on sweats and T-shirts so they could go eat.

No one spoke. No one looked at anyone else. The vibe in the room was as somber as if we'd just lost game seven of the Cup final. Guys were going through the motions of their postgame routines, but all the air from our win had been sucked right out of the room.

I didn't say a word as I went to my locker stall and started taking off my own gear. I didn't blame them—I'd have been a mess, too—I just felt helpless. There was nothing I could do to make this better for anyone, and I hated that.

On the ice, Erlandsson's jersey retirement had seemed to pull together all the players who'd known him. Afterward, though, when Avery broke down, it seemed to give a lot of people the permission they needed to grieve out loud too. Now everyone was just quiet and wrung out, going through the motions like all they wanted to do was collapse on the floor and sleep.

It was a tough night, that was for sure.

I had no doubt it was hell for them, but for those of us at the edges—those of us who hadn't known Erlandsson and were still finding our place on the team—it meant more distance between us and our teammates. As Baddy and Eminem had comforted Avery, some of the other guys had choked up, and they'd leaned hard on each other. Us new guys, we did the best we could, offering support, but... what the hell were we even supposed to say? What were we supposed to do? Grieving was a complicated mess to begin with, and so was comforting someone who was grieving.

The stall next to mine was Eminem's, and he came back

from the showers as I was getting down to my base layer. His eyes were a little red, too.

"Hey, man." He clapped my shoulder. "Thanks for stepping up." He nodded sharply toward the door to the hallway. "Handling the reporters." Looking past me, he added, "You too, Laramie."

"Don't mention it." I glanced around the room. "How is, um...?"

"Calds?" Eminem pressed his lips together. "It's a rough night for him. We all knew it would be." He exhaled hard. "He didn't need the press in his face. None of us did."

"Figured as much. But he's—I mean, I don't imagine he's good. But... better than earlier?"

"Maybe?" My teammate shrugged and sighed. "I don't know how he got through the ceremony and the game in the first place, to tell you the truth. He's a lot tougher than I am, that's for sure."

"No kidding." Baddy appeared beside us. "Last thing he needs right now is the reporters all up in his business."

I swallowed, nodding silently. I was relieved to know I'd been able to help *somehow*. It didn't seem like enough, but it was something.

I glanced back and forth between Baddy and Eminem. "Listen, I didn't know him, okay? Erlandsson? But I know it's been tough on all of you. Anything I can do"—I gestured at Laramie—"anything *we* can do to take some of that off you guys, just say so."

Eminem smiled and clapped my shoulder. "You're good people, Halls. Now get your ass in the shower because you don't *smell* like good people."

That, thank God, broke through the tension, and I laughed. "Oh, come on!" I stepped toward him, arms outstretched. "Just gimme a hug!"

"Ack! No!" He ducked out of the way. "I will mace you with Febreeze! I swear to God!"

"Just one hug!"

"Screw you, Halls!"

There was some quiet laughter through the rest of the room. As I left for the showers, it had mostly died down, but at least the somber atmosphere had cracked.

It wasn't much.

But I was happy to help lift the mood a little bit.

CHAPTER 7

AVERY

BADDY

Hey, man – you good?

EMINEM

Check in and let us know if you're okay.

DAVIS

You want a lift to practice?

I exhaled into the silence of my bedroom. My face burned with embarrassment as I read message after message from my teammates. I'd just *had* to let them see me fall apart, hadn't I? Right there in the locker room, in front of God and everyone, after my first game as their captain... I'd lost it.

Oh, yeah. Captain material, right here.

Never again. Last night was a fluke. There is no way in hell I'm going to let them see me like that again. Ever.

Well. At least there hadn't been any cameras in the room except for the team reporter's crew, and they'd been summarily warned to shut it off and delete the footage. Even as I'd pulled myself together, I'd been aware that the rest of the reporters hadn't come in like they usually had.

From the murmurs of conversation around me, I gathered that a couple of my teammates had gone out into the hall to talk to the press rather than letting them in.

I appreciated that, but holy fuck, I hated myself for making it necessary. I should've been able to face the cameras and microphones myself. I definitely shouldn't have needed my teammates to step out and, well, take one for the team. I was their captain, for God's sake. *They* were supposed to lean on *me*, not the other way around.

Never. Again.

Swallowing against the bile in my throat, I wrote out a message in the Whiskey Rebels group chat rather than responding to everyone individually.

> Hey guys, thanks for the messages this morning. Last night was hard, but I'm okay. I'll see you all at practice.

Then I tossed my phone onto the nightstand, closed my eyes, and swore aloud as I kneaded my throbbing temples. My phone chirped several times with incoming texts, and I checked just in case I needed to answer any of them, but it was just teammates replying with things like *"glad to hear it, man"* and *"see you at the rink."*

Okay. That was dealt with. Now all I had to do was put my money where my mouth was. Step one, get my ass out of bed. Step two, shower. Then there'd be coffee, breakfast, and all the other parts of my pre-practice routine. I'd just have to deal with the looks of pity and concern at the rink, at least until I convinced everyone that last night was a one-time thing. Once they realized I had my shit together, everything would feel like normal again.

So just... had to get there. Put on the normal face. Be the player. Be the captain. Be okay.

Step one, get my ass out of bed.

I was just sitting up when my phone chirped again. I groaned. It was going to be like this all day, wasn't it? Or at least until I showed my face at practice in... what time was it again? I didn't even know. Probably long past time for me to be up and moving in the direction of the training facility, though.

I fumbled around for my phone, found it, then peered at the screen to see who'd texted this time.

> **RACHEL**
> Hey, hon. You okay?

Oh God. *Ouch.* Leif's widow had had to be strong for her kids last night and get through that entire memorial ceremony with all those cameras in her face, and now she was trying to comfort *my* stupid ass?

Fuck's sake. I needed to get it together, didn't I?

I swung my legs over the edge of the bed, then started typing out a response.

> I'm good. Last night was more emotional than I expected. How are you doing?

> **RACHEL**
> Good as can be expected. Do you want to come by after practice? The kids would love to see you.

I closed my eyes and pushed out a breath. Anything she and the kids needed, the answer was always a resounding *yes.* Was I strong enough for that today?

Probably not, but I was going to be, because Leif's family and our team needed me to be that strong.

> Sure. I'll text you when I'm on my way.

There. Now I was committed.

I made myself get up and into the shower. It helped, if only because the routine was familiar and comfortable. Afterward, my mind and body were both simultaneously numb and aching. I'd felt that way the morning after Leif's funeral, too, and I clung to the fact that I'd eventually broken through it.

One foot in front of the other. One day at a time. One *minute* at a time.

I'd done it then. I could do it now.

In the bathroom, I flattened my palms on the cold marble and stared myself down in the mirror. I looked like hell. The heat of the shower had only given my skin a little extra color, so I was still too pale, especially in the unforgiving vanity light. A few strands of wet hair fell over my eyes, which were surprisingly red.

Had I been crying? Hell, maybe. I'd felt a little raw in the shower, so yeah, I might've done some crying.

Good. Then it's out of my system. Time to be a goddamned grownup.

Or at least look like one.

Still holding my own gaze, I exhaled. I had to pull it together for my team's benefit. The worst part of last night was when I'd started to regain my composure, and I'd realized how many of the other guys had red, wet eyes. They'd been fine through the ceremony. They'd powered through the game. But when I'd fallen apart, I'd dragged them all down with me.

Christ. I was the most useless captain this League—this whole damn *sport*—had ever had.

I shouldn't be captain.

But if I'm not...

I closed my eyes and sighed. If I asked to be stripped of

my captaincy, I'd be failing them again. Someone else would have to step up—someone else who was *also* struggling with grief and this new normal. Or one of the new guys, like Peyton or Laramie, who'd have to figure out how to step into the skates of someone we were all grieving. That wouldn't be fair to them *or* to the team.

The C was on my jersey, and that was where it needed to stay. The Whiskey Rebels needed someone to fill Leif's role, and I was the one they'd asked to step up. So I would. I had to.

I took a deep breath. Held it. Let it out slowly.

I'd watched Leif lead this team through tough moments. Even when he himself had been struggling, he'd never let it show. Not in the locker room. Not where any camera or teammate (besides me) could see it. He'd get emotional, of course—hockey wasn't hockey if it was played without emotion—but he was always controlled and composed.

"We're all hoping for the best news about Howie," he'd told the whole team in the locker room during one intermission. *"We're all worried. But we owe it to him, to our fans, and to ourselves, to keep going. Stay focused on the game, then we can all tell Howie he owes us beers for slacking off like this."*

The laugh that had sent rippling through the room had broken the tension. As if to prove his point, Leif had gone out his very next shift and scored, giving us a lead in a tight game. We'd all been rattled after watching our teammate land badly on his head and neck, and after watching the paramedics wheel him off the ice in a C-collar, but because Leif had rallied, so had the rest of us. He'd been exactly the leader we'd needed that night.

It was only hours later—after a hard-fought win, media availability, and driving himself and me to visit Howie in the hospital—that he'd finally let the cracks show. After we'd left Howie's room, Leif had paused outside for a few deep breaths. I'd thought for a moment he might break down or start shaking or something, but no—he'd rolled his shoulders, cleared his throat, and said, *"How about we get out of here?"*

We'd gone back to my place for a couple of beers, and after he'd gotten a little bit lit, Leif had shakily admitted, *"The way he went down? That was the scariest thing I ever saw."*

And the next morning, he'd been back on the ice, practicing and chirping like nothing had happened.

I needed to be like him. Strong. Stoic. Someone the whole team could lean on.

How do I become the strongest person I ever knew when he's the person I'm missing?

A fresh wave of emotion threatened, but I tamped it down. Not now. Not when I had to get to practice and start showing this stoic side I'd never needed before.

I could grieve later. Behind closed doors. Away from the cameras, the fans, and—most importantly—my teammates. They needed a strong leader right now. They needed *me.* No one needed to know what was really going on beneath the surface.

Last night had been awful, and I hated myself for falling apart like that in front of the guys.

It wasn't going to happen again.

Convincing my teammates, coaches, and everyone else that I was okay took some serious work, but I was pretty sure I pulled it off. There were a lot of concerned looks and questions when I got to the training facility that morning. Offers of support. People asking if I was okay to practice and to play.

By the time we'd hit the ice for practice, I had everyone more or less convinced I was fine. Last night had been rough on all of us, but today was a new day. I had this.

I didn't *feel* like I had this, but I could fake it.

My other teammates were mostly falling back into the normal practice vibe. Serious focus during drills and scrimmages, but chirping and laughing in between. Concentrating on the task at hand, working hard, and all the while enjoying what we did. This was the best job in the world, and even at its most frustrating, I loved it.

Or, well, I *had* loved it.

During training camp, when everything had been new and raw, hockey had pulled my focus and kept my head above water. Over time, though, as I'd gotten back into the swing of playing, everything else had crept in again, and it didn't go away while I was skating. Not completely.

After the home opener, my concentration was a mess. It was like trying to play in ill-fitting gear—I could mostly go through the motions, but all I could think about was how uncomfortable and distracted I was.

In other areas of my life, I was slowly pushing forward. Moving on as much as it was possible to move on.

But here...

On the ice...

As much as hockey had always been my sanctuary and my escape, it was hell now. I couldn't separate hockey from Leif. I couldn't find my way back to my U16 days when I played hockey before meeting Leif. From major juniors onward, apart from that half season I'd spent in the minors after we'd both been drafted by the Whiskey Rebels, hockey just hadn't existed without Leif.

And now I was trying to focus on hockey when everything about it screamed his name. During every drill, I kept expecting to hear his voice echoing off the glass. In between, I was keenly aware of the empty space beside me where Leif would be standing, gloved hands on top of his stick while he rambled his commentary about whoever was running the drill. By the bench, every time I went to take a drink, I expected a shoulder in my back or a stick under my elbow as he tried to make me choke on my water. The laughed *"fuck you, Early!"* on the tip of my tongue had nowhere to go.

There was no hockey anymore without missing my best friend.

After one drill, while I caught my breath, I stood a few feet away from my other teammates while the fourth line took their turn. I pretended to be watching the action.

In reality…

Get a grip. Yes, he's gone, but you have to hold it together. This team is counting on you.

Every time someone glanced my way, their brow creased with concern, it galvanized my resolve to be strong for these men.

Grieve at home. You're their captain now.

Remember how much it wrecked them to see you that way last night?

I took in a deep breath of cold air through my nose and pushed it out slowly. I'd had this conversation with my reflection this morning.

Leif had still felt pain and fear. He'd still grieved. I'd played alongside him after his uncle had suddenly passed away. The grief had been palpable most of the time, but once he had on his gear, he was all hockey. All focus.

He'd done it, and so could I.

Everyone was counting on it.

I was relieved to find that getting into the right mindset for a game was a lot easier than practice. Games were far more demanding, both physically and mentally. There was a lot more at stake, and this was not the time or place to be distracted.

Two nights after our home opener, we were again playing at home, this time against Calgary. I'd felt a little wobbly during the anthems, but as I joined my line at center ice for the opening faceoff, my concentration locked into place. Though I was aware of Leif's banner high above my head, I focused on being a hockey player, and on showing my teammates that they could count on me as their captain and a top line forward.

I pulled it off, too. We won 4-2, and two of those goals were mine—a power play goal in the second, and an empty netter during the final thirty seconds. I played my heart out, and my teammates did too, and no one knew about me almost collapsing from sheer exhaustion in the showers or wiping away tears the whole way home. What they didn't know wouldn't hurt us.

I can do this. I've got this.

That held for this game and the next three. I was a mess at home, kept it together at practice, and was probably around 95% myself during games. I could work with that.

During our sixth game of the season, though, something came unraveled.

It happened during the second period. I was still out after almost two minutes; Davis and Peyton had long since gone to the bench, replaced by fresh bodies, but I couldn't get out of the defensive zone. Every time I tried to take off for a shift change, the action came my way.

I was gassed, but it happened sometimes. All I could do was hope for a breakaway or a stoppage.

What eventually came was a stoppage, but the relief was short-lived. The ref blew his whistle long and loud, not that single chirp that signaled a typical stop in play.

It only took a second for me to figure out why, and when I did, my heart dropped into my skates.

Eminem was on his side by the boards. Evan, our athletic trainer, was already hurrying out onto the ice, and then he crouched beside Eminem, touching his shoulder and leaning over him.

Panic surged through me so hard it almost knocked me off my skates. Then the Zamboni gate opened, and my stomach somersaulted. A couple members of the ice crew stepped onto the sheet with a pair of shovels and a bucket, though they hung back for now, watching where Eminem had fallen and waiting to be summoned all the way in.

That meant blood on the ice.

Oh no. Oh shit. Is he okay?

I craned my neck to try to get a look at Eminem, but Evan was mostly blocking him. Eminem was moving at least, writhing on the ice. Panic and anger twined in the pit of my stomach; which player had hurt him? Whose ass did I need to kick? And... was he okay?

I noticed my other teammates looking up. I followed their gazes, and on the screen, the replay was starting.

It wasn't even a check—Eminem and one of their

players had just collided at a weird angle, and then he'd hit the boards at an even worse one. He'd crumpled to the ice, and he was still there now.

Okay, so nobody needed his ass kicked. In fact, the other player was at his own bench, having his face checked over by a trainer. Then he was getting sent into the back, and the trainer was gesturing at his own head as another trainer nodded.

I could read between those lines—concussion protocol.

Fuck, fuck, fuck. How bad was Eminem, then?

I gnawed furiously on my mouthguard as I turned to my downed teammate. He was being helped into a sitting position now, Evan holding his arm while Mix steadied his shoulders. Blood ran down one side of his face, and it had pooled on the ice. Now it was dripping onto his jersey, staining the white red and turning the gold an ugly shade of orange.

Fuck, indeed.

I turned away, trying to keep my stomach where it belonged. I eyed the ice crew's bucket, wondering if I could get to it in time to puke.

A ripple of applause turned my head, and I blew out a relieved breath as I watched Mix and Evan easing Eminem to his feet. They paused once he was upright, Evan's hand on his chest as he asked him something. Eminem nodded slowly, pressing a bloody towel to his face.

Then they started toward the bench, Eminem a little wobbly but mostly moving on his own power. The crowd cheered and all of us banged our sticks on the ice or the boards. He lifted his head and managed a wave at the crowd, which prompted more cheering.

I exhaled as I followed him off the ice. My shift was over

anyway, but I'd been too restless and too worried to go back to the bench while he was still down.

As he continued down the tunnel with Evan, I took my seat on the bench.

"How is he?" Peyton asked over the noise. He'd been on the bench the whole time.

"I think he's fine," I croaked despite the way my heart pounded beneath my jersey. "Probably just rang his bell."

Peyton nodded. "Hope the other guy's okay too."

"Looked like they were sending him back to be evaluated for a concussion. But he was moving on his own, so..." I half-shrugged.

Another nod. Peyton shifted his attention back to the ice, where the ice crew was still cleaning up blood. He seemed reassured—confident our teammate was banged up but okay. This was, after all, part of hockey.

But I couldn't relax. I couldn't get my pulse to come back down. The jittery feeling just would not relent. No matter how much I tried to talk myself down to earth, no matter how much I reminded myself this happened all the time, I couldn't convince my heart to stop pounding.

For God's sake, players got hurt. I'd been hurt myself plenty of times. Hell, I'd been half-carried off the ice as often as I'd half-carried my teammates. It happened. And heads and faces bled like crazy; for all I knew, Eminem's visor had cut the bridge of his nose, which always looked way more dramatic than it was.

And as Evan and Mix had helped Eminem off the ice, they hadn't had that look of urgency that meant he needed to go to the hospital or anything. He'd been upright. Conscious.

He was okay.

But I couldn't shake this *oh shit* feeling. That certainty that Eminem was hurt bad.

After a few more messy shifts—I couldn't focus, damn it —the buzzer finally sounded and the period was over. Thank God. Now I could breathe, and maybe get an update on my injured teammate.

Before I'd made it two steps down the tunnel, though, Coach stopped me with a hand on my shoulder.

"Hey. Calds." He eyed me. "You've been off your game since Eminem went down. Are you all right?"

Swallowing hard and shifting on my skates, I nodded. "Yeah. Just, um..." I forced a laugh. "Just rattled me a bit. I'm good."

"You sure?"

"Yeah. Just looked scarier than it was from where I was standing." Not entirely a lie, so... fine.

Coach grimaced. "I understand that." We continued toward the locker room. "If it helps, Evan confirmed Eminem is fine. He'll be out for a game or two, but that's precaution more than anything."

For the first time since I'd seen my teammate crumpled by the boards, some actual relief rushed through me. "Good. That's good."

The biggest relief of the night? Seeing Eminem in the locker room. He'd stripped off his bloody jersey, and he was wearing flipflops instead of his skates, but otherwise, he still had on his gear. A bandage covered his nose, and both eyes were starting to turn black.

He was upright and laughing, though.

"Hey, my ass would be back out there if the trainers didn't lay down the law," he boasted. "I've played through worse!"

"Pfft." Ziggy threw a balled-up sock at him. "You just want someone to high-stick you so you can bleed all over the place and scream 'oh my God, double minor!'"

That had everyone in the room howling. Eminem turned a little red and rolled his eyes; Ziggy was never, ever going to let him forget that time in major juniors when he'd drawn a double minor after some fresh stitches had come unraveled. Everyone knew he'd already been bleeding when the other kid had high-sticked him, but boy, had Eminem sold it, and with blood on his jersey, he'd scored a game-winning goal on the resulting power play.

Yeah. Eminem was fine.

Eventually, my adrenaline would come back down, and I could chill the hell out. Right?

I wasn't going to stay like this the whole game. Was I?

Fuck. Maybe?

I snatched my water bottle off the bench and poured some down the back of my neck, letting the cold pull my focus away from my reeling mind. It helped a little, but... not much. Not enough.

Come on, come on. Get it together!

I needed to. Intermission was almost over. In T-minus six minutes, I had to be able to play, focusing only on what was happening on the ice, not in the locker room or anywhere else.

I could do this. I'd done it before, so I could do it now.

This had never been like me. Unless someone was scraped off the ice and wheeled out on a stretcher, I didn't let it rattle me. Let it piss me off, maybe, because that made me play harder and score, but this jittery *oh fuck oh fuck* feeling was new.

Why couldn't I cope with a teammate getting even slightly hurt now?

Because I'm the captain. Because I'm responsible for these men in ways I wasn't before.

That had to be it.

Right?

Because I sure as hell wasn't going to entertain any *other* explanation.

CHAPTER 8
PEYTON

I didn't know what to make of Avery. No one seemed to. Even after Eminem came back—he only missed one game— our captain was still edgy in ways that were hard to define. He socialized in the locker room and in the players' lounge, but it seemed... forced? Like it took work to laugh at things that would've had him rolling before? I couldn't quite put my finger on it.

During games, his temper flared explosively fast. He'd rarely been one to drop gloves throughout his career, but in the last four games, he'd been in two fights. Three if you counted the brief scuffle that the refs broke up before it escalated. All of those scrums had been on the heels of an opposing player committing a dirty but not overly egregious play. Slashing. Tripping. A rough check.

He'd almost gotten into it after someone slashed Davis hard enough to send him off the ice for a couple of shifts until his hand stopped tingling. Another time, a player checked me when I didn't have the puck, shoving me against the goal just right to knock it from its mooring. The refs didn't bother to call the obvious interference penalty, but they did blow the whistle because the net was dislodged. That stoppage gave Ollie, one of our defensemen, a chance to get in Avery's way and talk him down from a fight.

Throughout his whole career, even as far back as major juniors, he'd been known for having a cool head most of the time. He could lose his shit just like any hockey player, but he was extremely disciplined most of the time.

These days? Holy hell.

And judging by the worried and sometimes uncomfortable glances our teammates threw his way when he wasn't looking, I wasn't imagining anything. I sometimes caught his longtime teammates—especially Baddy and Eminem—murmuring to each other and exchanging concerned glances. The whole vibe around the locker room was that something was wrong, but no one wanted to be the one to bring it up.

I didn't know how to bring it up, if I *should* bring it up, or who I should bring it up *to*.

The best thing I could think of at this point was to defer to the men who knew him best, especially Eminem and Baddy.

Though they didn't seem to know what to do about him either. What Baddy did do was lean hard into his role as alternate captain; he stepped up and led the younger guys. I saw him consulting with Coach during practices and intermissions. Mix, the other alternate, followed his lead.

So they seemed to know something was off about Avery, but they didn't have a clue how to address it or if they should, only that they should step up.

That wasn't to say Avery wasn't doing his job as captain. Most of the time, he was exactly what a captain should be— a leader. Encouraging all of us. Guiding the young players.

Meeting with Coach on the ice and behind closed doors. He was still living up to the C on his sweater.

But there were moments when, despite his best efforts, he seemed... brittle. Distracted. Uncharacteristically volatile.

Something is wrong.

Everyone can see it.

What do *we* do *about it?*

My worries intensified on our first West Coast road trip of the season. The last week of October, we had a three-game trip playing against Los Angeles, San Jose, and Portland. That meant my *favorite* part of traveling with this sport: a long-ass flight.

Okay, it was only five hours.

But still. That was five hours of asking a plane full of hockey players to sit. I barely made it through Mass whenever I visited my grandparents. Five hours on a plane? Fuck my liiife.

Baddy, Mix, Eminem, and Avery commandeered one of the club tables for a very rowdy game of Hearts. I'd never been great at the game, and I'd found it more frustrating and annoying than anything, but it was sure fun to watch this group play.

"You're cheating again!" Avery kicked Eminem under the table, driving a yelp out of him.

"Ow!" Eminem leaned down to rub his shin. "I am not cheating! Just because you suck doesn't mean—"

"Hey, now," Mix said with a grin. "Leave his personal life out of this."

"Oh, fuck you." Avery rolled his eyes and grabbed his glass. "You're all dicks."

"That's why you love us," Baddy said, and managed to dodge a kick from Avery. "Ha! Your aim is—ow!"

Mix laughed. "His aim sucks, but mine doesn't."

"Ugh. Fuck you all."

Several of us were gathered around to watch, and we all chuckled at the interplay. Trust these four to make a game of Hearts interesting.

Baddy shuffled the deck, and he was about to deal when a flight attendant came by. Everyone ordered additional drinks, and Baddy held off shuffling until she came back with the tray of glasses and bottles.

And that was when I realized Avery was starting on his third mojito.

Alarm prickled the back of my neck. It wasn't unusual for players to drink, especially on long flights with no game or practice until the next day. But... three mojitos? Before we were even halfway through the flight? At *noon?*

As Baddy dealt the cards, he stole a glance at the drink in Avery's hand, and his jaw tightened. When Avery wasn't looking, Mix eyed the drink, then met Eminem's gaze across the table, and something unspoken passed between them. When Mix looked at Baddy, Baddy subtly shook his head, and that was that. No one said anything.

They continued their game, chirping and accusing each other of cheating even though I didn't think any of them actually were (well, Eminem might've been) and carrying on like normal. The rest of us cheered them on, laughing at the banter and reacting like a playoff crowd whenever someone started to gain an obvious lead.

Avery finished that third mojito in pretty short order, but everyone was so focused on the game and the chirping that they didn't seem to notice when he called the flight attendant over again. I cringed, though.

Another one? Dude, what the hell? You're already slurring a little bit.

To my great relief, though, he asked for water this time.

The damage was apparently done, though.

The next game, he lost one trick after another. When Avery wound up taking the Queen of Spades, Eminem whistled. "My dude. Did you forget how to play?"

Avery seemed to waver a little, and he half-shrugged. "I dunno. Maybe?"

I chewed the inside of my cheek. This wasn't good. If he was getting drunk enough to forget how to play a game he played regularly—in the middle of the day around our team-mates, no less—that seemed like a red flag to me. And quite possibly to our other teammates, who were now watching nervously, especially as the guys got down to their last few cards.

Avery lost yet another trick.

Then Baddy stiffened. "Oh, you son of a *bitch*."

"What?" Avery blinked at him innocently. "Something wrong?"

Eminem furrowed his brow. Then he groaned and sat back as he tossed one of his remaining cards into the center of the table. "Fuck *you*, Calds."

Avery smiled sweetly, tossing a five onto the pile, which currently consisted of two threes and a four. "What? Is something wrong?"

Mix muttered what I thought was some Russian profanity.

"Wait," Laramie said. "What's going on? I thought Calds forgot how to play."

"No." Eminem slapped down a ten. "He's gonna shoot the damn moon."

"Shoot the—what?" Laramie turned puzzled eyes on me. "I don't know this game. What is he talking about?"

"If you lose all the tricks," Baddy grumbled, throwing

down his second to last card. "You shoot the moon. Which means you take zero points and everyone else takes twenty-six." He narrowed his eyes at Avery. "Fucking punk."

Avery cackled, adding a Jack to the mix that ensured he "lost" this trick, too.

And on the final trick, he also lost.

His three opponents all groaned and swore, and Avery just snickered as he went for a sip from his water bottle.

I laughed along with him, but more than anything, I was relieved. Maybe I'd been worried about nothing. Yeah, Avery'd had a lot to drink, all things considered. Yet he'd remained sharp enough to not only play Hearts, but shoot the moon, something I'd rarely seen anyone do.

Okay, maybe we'd all been worried about nothing, then. Yeah, Avery'd had a lot to drink, but he was obviously still functional.

Clearly, he was fine.

Trews—Lance Trewin—was the rookie defenseman on the third D pair. He was competent and aggressive, exactly the kind of gritty, in-your-face player we needed on the blue line. He could be a real pest, too. One of those guys I was thrilled to have on my own team because he would piss me the hell off if we were on opposite sides.

He *was* still a rookie, though, and sometimes that showed. When he realized he was on the ice with some of the living legends playing in the League right now, he'd get starstruck. Not enough to throw off his game, but he'd be setting up for a faceoff and have a momentary *"oh my God, that's so-and-so"* flash across his face before he refocused. It was kind of cute, honestly, and made me nostalgic for my own rookie days.

Tonight, we were playing in Los Angeles, and as we came out for our morning skate, he stared up, awe written all over his face.

I skated up to him. "You good, kid?"

"Yeah. Yeah, I'm good." He swallowed hard, then pulled his gaze away from his surroundings and looked at me. "I used to come here to watch games when I was a kid. It's... I mean, it's already surreal to be playing in the League, but playing *here?*" He whistled low.

I bumped him with my shoulder. "Guess you made it, huh?"

He turned that starstruck look on me. "What?"

"You made it." I gestured around us. "You moved from there"—I pointed at the seats—"to here." I pointed at the ice beneath our skates, and I smiled. "That means you made it, kid. This is the top."

He stared at me, and then his smile got so big, he lit up the whole arena. "Holy shit." He scanned our surroundings. "I did, didn't I?"

"Yep." I nudged his arm. "Now warm up before Coach sends us both to the minors."

He laughed, and we both started skating to loosen up our legs.

Maybe pointing out that he'd made it into the big leagues hadn't been such a hot idea, though. As practice went on, and throughout the day as we all went through our pregame routines, his nerves were visible from space. He was jittery and anxious; hockey players were notorious for not being able to sit still, but Trews was way too twitchy.

By the time we hit the ice for warmups, I was genuinely surprised he could still skate.

That wasn't good. Especially not when he was playing *here*. He'd hate himself if he shit the bed during his Los Angeles debut.

Time to pull his attention in a different direction.

While he was doing some stretches near the penalty box, I skated up beside him. "Hey." I lowered my voice. "You want to know something about the other team?"

He turned to me, eyebrows up behind his visor. "What?"

"Number fifteen? Dodson?" I nodded as subtly as I could toward the other end of the ice. "He's *real* easy to rile up."

Trews grinned. "Yeah?"

"Mmhmm. Annoy the shit out of him, and he'll make mistakes."

"Doesn't like getting chirped at?" the kid asked. "Or doesn't like getting the puck taken away?"

"Both, but chirps especially piss him off. If you can steal the puck and talk shit at the same time, he might even break a stick over his leg."

Trews cackled. "Ooh, this is going to be fun."

I laughed and tapped his skate with my stick.

It was a strategic move, of course—Dodson really was entirely too easy to goad into making costly mistakes. It also had the other desired effect, though: as near as I could tell, Trews forgot all about the nerves he had about playing in this arena. All through the rest of warmups, he kept shooting glances toward the other team, grinning to himself. After puck drop, whenever we were on the bench, I could practically hear the gears turning in his head as he tracked Dodson's movements. If Dodson wasn't on the ice, then Trews zeroed in on other players, similar gears turning behind his wicked eyes and smartass grin.

Hell. That worked better than I'd hoped, and I filed it away for future games—when his nerves threatened to get the best of him, redirect him into ice gremlin mode.

It wasn't just keeping Trews focused, either. Dodson was, predictably, not happy about the pest chirping at him and getting in his way. Coach seemed to have caught on, too —he had Trews and his D partner, Astala, playing more minutes than usual. I mean, why not give the rookie more ice time if he's distracting the star forward enough to keep him from scoring?

About five minutes into the second period, Trews and Astala were again on the ice at the same time as my line— and Dodson's. As I was setting up for the faceoff, I did my usual glance around to make sure I knew where everyone was. When my gaze landed on Trews, I had to bite down on my mouthguard to keep from laughing. He was laser-focused on Dodson.

The puck dropped. Dodson won the draw, and he quickly passed it to one of his wingers.

Davis was closest to the winger, and he poke-checked the puck away. Not enough to gain control, but it was enough to make the winger lose possession. Perfect. Davis managed to grab the puck, and—

A whistle blew.

What the hell?

I turned around right as an official shouted, "Two minutes for cross-checking!"

"Oh, come on!" Dodson barked. "That was not—"

"You want an unsportsmanlike, too?"

That was when I realized Trews was down. He was no worse for the wear, pushing himself back up on his skates, but the wince said he'd taken a hard hit. A crosscheck, apparently, and while he was miles away from the puck.

I skated up to him as he was taking off one of his gloves. "You okay?"

He nodded and gingerly rubbed his neck with his ungloved hand. "Think I can sue him for whiplash?"

I grimaced, and I was about to make a smartass comment when the crowd started roaring in a familiar bloodthirsty way.

I spun around, and my heart jumped.

Avery and Dodson faced off amid scattered gloves and sticks, their fists up and their mouths moving, though I couldn't hear a word they were saying over the crowd. Their faces filled in the blanks, though—they were both pissed, snarling and shouting as they squared off.

It was Dodson who finally took a swing. Avery deftly avoided it, then grabbed a handful of Dodson's jersey and landed a hard hit to his face. Dodson staggered a bit—I think the only thing holding him upright was the grip Avery had on his sweater—and he managed to block the second blow. Then fists were flying, and the crowd was screaming, people banging on the glass as players tapped sticks on ice and boards.

Dodson got a grip on Avery's jersey and, I thought, his chest protecter, and he spun him around, pulling him off-balance. They both toppled, Avery landing hard on his back, which only egged on the Dodson-favoring crowd.

The refs stepped in, of course; they always did once the players went down. Someone managed to haul Dodson off Avery. Avery was on his feet in a heartbeat, still spitting nails and shouting after Dodson as blood ran down his lip and chin. I jumped in and grabbed him, pushing him back with a hand on his chest.

"Crosscheck the rookie like that again!" he snarled past me. "I fucking dare you!"

"Hey, hey." I nudged him back a little more. "Easy."

He didn't even look at me. His gaze was locked on the man he still clearly wanted to fight.

"Five minutes," the ref told him. "Cool it, or you can take a misconduct, too."

That seemed to get through, and Avery eased off a little. He was still pissed, but he pulled his attention away from Dodson. He acknowledged the ref with a nod.

There was blood on the ice, so the ice crew came out to quickly clean it up.

I turned to Avery again. "You good?"

He swallowed. "Yeah." He flicked his gaze toward Dodson again, and—shit. Avery wasn't just pissed—he was *shaking* with fury. His eyes flashed and he didn't even seem to notice the blood on his face. "Motherfucker is going to eat his teeth if he does that again."

I blinked. "I... Trews is okay. Just so you know."

Avery's gaze flicked to me again. Then he looked around, and he found Trews, who was skating alongside Astala, probably waiting for the ice crew to leave so we could resume playing.

Slowly, Avery relaxed. "Good." His shoulders dropped. "Jesus, the way he went down..." He swallowed hard and shook his head.

I just nodded, still puzzled by his reaction. It wasn't like the penalty had gone uncalled. And Trews hadn't been hurt —sore, yes, but no worse for the wear. He'd been up on his skates before Avery and Dodson had dropped gloves.

"I should..." Avery tilted his head toward the box. With a reluctant grin, he said, "Give 'em hell while I'm in there, eh?"

I laughed. "You know we will." I clapped his shoulder, and he headed for the box. Dodson got into the other one, and he seemed to have calmed down, too, at least enough that he didn't start screaming at Avery through the glass divider. A second Los Angeles player joined him to serve his crosschecking penalty.

Well, now we had a power play. I was pretty sure we could make L.A. pay for that stupid crosscheck and put Avery back into a good mood.

We did, too. L.A. didn't have a great penalty kill this year, and it only took thirty-three seconds for us to get past them and put a puck behind their goalie. That gave us a one-goal lead, too, which seemed to have Avery in better spirits when he finally left the box.

Even better, halfway through the third period, the score was 3-1 thanks to a certain rookie defenseman scoring his first ever professional goal.

"Nice one, kid!" I smacked Trews on the back. "Great place to get your first goal!"

He blinked, then looked around, and that starstruck expression from earlier came back.

Holy shit, his eyes said. *I just scored my first goal...* here.

He smiled like a kid on Christmas for the rest of the game.

CHAPTER 9
AVERY

Pulling up to Leif's house was hard.

I'd been here so many times, driving through Sewickley Heights on autopilot. I'd slept here when we'd had too much to drink or been up too late. I'd helped Leif and Rachel landscape the yard and around their pool in the back.

Today, the garage door was open, and the sight of Leif's red Porsche took my breath away. The part that made my chest hurt, though, was the vacant space *beside* the car. There was a net in the corner that we'd often dragged out to play street hockey, and some sticks and balls tucked in behind them. Along the wall were his and Rachel's snowboards.

But most of that area between his car and the wall was empty, as was the hook hanging just above the hockey net.

Leif's motorcycle was gone. So was his helmet.

Holding the wheel tight, I stared at that void, my guts roiling as I tried not to think about things I wished I didn't know.

I had no idea if Rachel had sold the motorcycle, or if it

was still where it had been parked when Leif had lost consciousness. In her shoes, I didn't know if I'd want to grab on to everything he'd ever touched and never let go, or if I'd never want to see that bike again.

I closed my eyes and exhaled, my hands aching from the death grip I had on the steering wheel.

I couldn't think about all that right now. Rachel had asked me to come over because she needed help with some things. I'd never told Leif out loud that if anything ever happened to him, I'd look after his family—why would I? We were in our twenties. Nothing was going to happen to either of us. But now that he was gone, I'd made that vow to myself that I'd never said out loud to my friend.

There was nothing any of us could do to bring back her husband and their father, but like hell was I going to add to this family's burden by being an emotional trainwreck. Even if that was exactly what I fucking was.

"Pull it together," I muttered as I shut off the engine. "Leif's family needs you."

I let that mantra beat on the insides of my skull as I got out of the car. Today wasn't about me or my grief. It was about the woman who'd lost her husband and the kids who'd lost their father.

I paused for a deep breath. Then I locked my car and walked in through the garage, ignoring the absence of that bike and the way my fingertips itched to run over the seat and the fuel tank. It had been a habit. I didn't even remember when or why I'd started doing it, and I hadn't actually been aware that I did until now when there was nothing to touch.

Jesus. Was this grief? Just getting blindsided by random gut punches over things I didn't even know I missed?

The door to the kitchen opened, mercifully jarring me

out of my thoughts. In an instant, the uncomfortably silent garage was filled with shouts of "Uncle Avery!" as the twins came thundering down the steps.

I laughed as they almost knocked my legs out from under me, and the relief was dizzying. I hugged them, and they talked over each other, wanting to drag me to their rooms or the rec room or the backyard. Kalle fell all over himself to tell me all about something he'd made in kindergarten that he wanted to show me. Linnea wanted me to take her swimming because I promised. They stared up at me with wide, elated eyes, unaware of how much they both looked like their dad. Those blue eyes. Those dark curls.

"I think that's why Rachel wants a fourth so bad," Leif had joked. *"She wants* one *of the kids to look like her."*

"Hey," Rachel had retorted, elbowing him. *"Fourth time's the charm!"*

Yep. One unexpected gut punch after another. Fuuuck.

"Come on, you two," Rachel's voice broke through the noise, "At least let Uncle Avery come in and take off his shoes. Linnea, it's too cold to swim today."

Linnea pouted. Kalle took my hand and tugged me toward the kitchen, pleading his case with his mom as we walked. Inside, Elsa saw me, and her round face lit up as she stretched out her arms for a hug.

Rachel offered a smile, obviously trying to be strong for the kids (and probably for me). She couldn't hide the fatigue and heartache, though. "Hi, Avery. How are you doing?"

"I'm all right," I lied as I hoisted Elsa onto my hip. I opened my mouth to follow up with a quip about practice or the season, but they all turned to ashes on my tongue.

"I think Coach is trying to kill us."

"You know how brutal the regular season is."

"It's tough, but I wouldn't trade a minute."

Those had all been automatic responses in the past. Today, none of them felt like the right thing to say to my teammate's grieving widow. Instead, I went with, "The season is keeping me busy."

"Yeah, I know the feeling. No hockey, but..." She gestured at the kids.

"I'm sure Coach can relate, keeping after all of us."

She managed a quiet laugh at that, and so did I.

I gently put Elsa back down so I could take off my shoes. While I did that, Rachel parked the kids in front of the TV. She and Leif had never been reliant on electronic babysitters, but they'd both freely admitted that there was no harm in *occasionally* using a cartoon to occupy the kids. I had a feeling there'd been more of that than usual lately, and I didn't judge Rachel for it *at all*.

While she got the kids situated, I poured myself a cup of coffee—they'd always insisted I make myself completely at home here—and a moment later, Rachel came into the kitchen to get one of her own.

Then, coffee cups in hand, we stepped into the dining room. Here, she could still keep an eye on the kids while we had a modicum of privacy.

"Hey," I said quietly. "Be honest—how are you doing?"

She stole a glance into the living room, then ducked back into the dining room, fully out of their sight, and let the veil drop. Her shoulders sank. Her smile fell. She seemed paler, too, though that might've been my imagination.

She set her coffee on the dining room table, and mine joined it a second later. I suddenly wasn't so sure I could stomach drinking it.

With a heavy sigh, she folded her arms loosely and pressed her shoulder into the wall beneath a wedding portrait. "It's been hard. I..." She closed her eyes and pushed out a breath before looking up at me again. "I don't know how to do this."

"I don't think anyone expects you to," I whispered. "But you know you've got all of us, right? Me, but also any of the Rebels. Even the new guys. Anything you need, anything we can do..."

Her smile returned, but it just made her look sadder and even more tired. "I know. You guys have all been amazing. Especially you." With a wet laugh, she added, "I practically have to chase all the other wives out sometimes."

I chuckled soundlessly. "Yeah, that probably gets overwhelming."

"It does. It's better than the alternative, but..." She lowered her gaze and chewed her lip. After a moment, she swallowed hard and looked up at me through her lashes. "Listen, there's a reason I asked for you and only you to come today. I... I need help with some things that I'm not ready for the rest of the wives to know about."

I raised my eyebrows. "Things you're not—" My teeth snapped shut when the piece clicked into place. I raised them even higher. "Are you...?"

She managed a smile, though it was halfhearted. "Yeah. About... My OB thinks I'm about fourteen weeks."

The flood of emotions that crashed through me were so unfamiliar, I couldn't begin to make sense of them. "Did Leif—" I put up my hands. "Shit. I'm sorry. I shouldn't ask—"

"He knew," she said softly. "We'd been trying for a while, and he was the one who actually told me to get a test." Her laugh this time was melancholy but genuine. "He knew with all of them before I did."

Oh, I remembered that much. He'd been insufferable

about it with both pregnancies. He hadn't said a word about this one, though. For a heartbeat, I wanted to be hurt by that, but he and Rachel had gone through a lot trying to have kids. That they were incredibly tightlipped about it for a while—not even telling me—really was understandable.

Rachel cleared her throat and ran a hand through her hair. "I'm not going to be able to hide it much longer. I mean, it's a good thing the weather's getting colder." She gestured at the bulky hoody she was wearing. "Makes it easy to hide things for a while. But people will know soon. I'm just... We're past the first trimester, you know? Twelve weeks is usually when we'd start shouting it from the rooftops, but I'm still just..." She trailed off as her eyes welled up.

Swallowing against the lump in my throat, I gathered her into a gentle hug, and my heart broke with how quickly and fully she sagged against me. She didn't cry—I suspected that, like me, she was overdrawn on tears these days—but she quietly collapsed against me, and I did the best I could to hold her upright.

"We've got you," I said. "The whole team is at your disposal. Babysitting, helping around the house—anything you need." I paused to steady my voice. "I know none of that fixes anything, but don't think you're in this alone, okay?"

The response to that was a ragged sigh.

After a solid minute or two, she let me go and whispered, "I feel like the worst mother ever because I'm not going out of my mind with joy over this baby. But I've spent the last two months freaking out over the slightest twinge or anything because..." She swiped at her eyes with a shaky hand. "I mean, what if I lost it, you know? It's happened before, and this baby is my last connection to Leif. So then we hit twelve weeks, and I should be so relieved and happy, but I'm just..." Her shoulders sank even more. "I'm a mess."

"No one's expecting you to *not* be a mess," I said as gently as I could. "If your feelings don't make sense—I mean, *mine* haven't made a damn bit of sense, and I didn't lose my husband or the father of my kids."

To my surprise, she gave a quiet little laugh. "I don't know." She half-shrugged, and there was a faint but unmistakable hint of her mischievous personality sparkling in her eyes. "It wasn't for nothing I always called you Leif's boyfriend."

I snorted, some warmth rushing into my face.

She laughed again, then sighed. "Anyway. It's... Things have been rough. And I'll tell people about the baby soon. Just..." She swallowed, her composure threatening to fracture again. "Not yet. Maybe once I figure out what I feel about... God, *anything*."

I hugged her again. "You've got time."

"Not much," she said dryly into my shoulder. "Hoodies are only going to do so much for so long."

"Yeah, maybe. But everyone's following your lead. Even if they can tell or they guess, I don't imagine anyone's going to ask about it or tell anyone until you do."

The sigh that came was filled with relief. "Let's hope." Then she drew back, and as she wiped her eyes again, she seemed to be pulling herself together. "I'm sorry. I didn't mean to unload on you."

"Kinda think you needed it."

"Yeah. Probably. But still." She looked right in my eyes. "How are *you* doing? And don't try to tell me you're good because I *know* you, Avery."

The sudden shift caught me off-guard, and I just barely got all my defenses back into place. Yeah, she knew me, but

I wasn't about to make a grieving widow—a *pregnant* grieving widow—shoulder the absolute emotional trash fire I was trying not to be.

"It's been hard," I admitted. "But I'm... I won't say I'm good, but I'm holding it together."

Rachel studied me, and her skepticism *almost* cracked through the façade. Much to my relief, her next question was, "How is the team doing? I, um... I haven't been watching games or keeping up on anything. I can't imagine trying to play through that."

The lump in my throat did *not* want to be ignored, but I spoke around it anyway. "It's been an adjustment. The new guys have really stepped up, and everyone else is finding their groove."

"That's good," she said softly. The corners of her mouth turned up slightly. "Having you as their captain has probably helped. The team is in good hands."

My stomach lurched at the reminder of the captaincy's pressure. "God, I hope so."

"They are." She squeezed my arm as her smile came to life a little more. "Leif always knew you'd be captain after he retired."

I laughed just to keep myself from breaking. She didn't need that.

"So what about your new teammate?" Mischief sparkled in her tired eyes. "Wasn't that the one you had a crush on?"

This time, the laugh felt more genuine, and some warmth rose in my face. "Yeah. Peyton Hall. He, uh..." I ran a hand through my hair. "He's the one I've had a thing for since... God, I don't know. A while." My humor dipped, though, and I avoided her gaze. "I... haven't really given him much thought, though. Not since..."

Rachel sighed. "I'm sorry. That really sucks."

I grunted in agreement but didn't know what to say. Uncomfortable silence threatened to set in, so I cleared my throat and gestured at the ceiling above us. "So, I'm guessing you need help setting up the baby's room?"

Rachel nodded, managing a small smile. "If you don't mind?"

"Pfft. Are you kidding?" I grinned. "So are we doing it in a Doctor Who theme?"

She groaned and rolled her eyes. "Oh my God, no."

"Oh come on! Where's your sense of adventure?"

Laughing, she said, "Jesus Christ. Just... Get upstairs."

I laughed too as she led me out of the dining room. We stopped to check on the kids—they were still happily engrossed in their show, and while we'd been talking, Rachel's mother had come in from elsewhere in the house. She offered me a taut and faintly chilly greeting; she'd never been particularly fond of me because she was convinced Leif spent time with me that he should've been spending with his wife and kids. I wasn't about to argue about it with her now, especially since I knew that Rachel vehemently disagreed with her.

With Grandma watching the kids, we went upstairs to the spare bedroom.

"The baby's going to sleep in my room as much as possible," she explained as she pushed open the door, "but this makes it easier for naps. For both of us."

I nodded. I remembered that from when Elsa was a baby; I'd asked them why they'd gone to all the trouble to set up a bedroom for her when she slept in their room.

"Because Rachel and I need to sleep," Leif had said as we'd assembled a crib. *"If the baby's having a really tough night, one of us can come in here while the other sleeps. The*

next time it happens, we switch. Or if I've been on the road for a while, she can get a good night's sleep while I handle Dad duty in the next room. We always prefer to keep the baby close, but this helps on the really fussy nights."

He'd come to many a practice or morning skate, bleary-eyed and clinging to his coffee, but he never complained, and he and Rachel had weathered all three of their newborns together.

For baby number four, I realized with a fresh pang of sadness, she'd be on her own. She had her mom here to help, and she had support from the team. But I couldn't imagine not having Dad there. I knew some of the wives, including Rachel, struggled with young kids during those stretches when their husbands were on road trips. Leif... wasn't coming home this time.

Fuck. One gut punch after another.

I shook myself and muffled a cough. "So." I looked around the room, which was empty except for some flat-packs. "How do you want to set it up?"

She gave me a quick rundown, from the paint she wanted on the walls to where the furniture should go. She tried to insist on helping, but I shooed her out.

"Not without a note from your doctor," I told her.

She giggled. "I can handle painting! It's non-toxic, and—"

"Out." I gave her a gentle nudge toward the door. "I don't want you seeing all the swear words I'm going to paint on the wall before I cover them up."

That had her laughing more heartily than I'd heard in way too long.

"Okay, okay!" She stepped out into the hall. Gesturing at my long since cooled coffee, she asked, "Do you want a fresh cup? A beer?"

Oh, God, did that beer sound tempting.

"I'm good," I lied. "When I hit a stopping point, I'll let you know, and we can order lunch."

"Please." She waved that away. "I'm putting you to work. The least I can do is make you a sandwich. Let me know when you're hungry."

"I will."

She left me to it, and I looked around the empty room.

It wasn't a huge room. Painting the walls and assembling flatpack furniture weren't exactly monstrous tasks.

But damn if it didn't all feel like I was being asked to clean an entire sheet of ice with a toothbrush.

I closed my eyes and pushed out a long breath through my nose. Time to pull it together. Rachel was dealing with far more than I was. She needed help, and she wasn't asking me to move mountains. She was just asking me to help her set up a bedroom for her baby.

Rolling my shoulders, I opened my eyes. I could do this. Nothing in the world was too much if it helped my best friend's grieving family. And like hell was I going to add to their burden by letting my own cracks show.

I wasn't okay, but for today, I would be.

As I picked up a roll of painter's tape and got to work, I reminded myself there was a brand-new bottle of vodka in my freezer at home.

All I had to do was get through today. Work on this room. Help Rachel and the kids. Pretend I wasn't this close to falling apart.

And when I got home tonight, I would drink until I couldn't remember how to cry.

CHAPTER 10
PEYTON

October and November wore on, the days getting shorter and darker as time started to blur. I'd always lost track of the calendar by this point in the season; next thing I knew, they'd be announcing it was the All-Star break, and then the trade deadline, and suddenly the playoffs would be over and I'd be wondering where the hell the season had gone. Happened every damn year.

And just like I was every year, I was startled when the announcements came out for the team's Thanksgiving get-together. It was Thanksgiving already? How did *that* happen?

This year, Baddy and his wife, Christina, were hosting. A few people had flown home last night to be with their families in other parts of the country, but most of us stayed in town.

It was always a little bittersweet, celebrating holidays with my teammates. I'd call my parents this evening, but we'd long since given up on me trying to get home for Thanksgiving. It was always such a blisteringly brief trip bookended by the most chaotic travel days of the year.

Nobody enjoyed that, least of all me. We'd have an informal Thanksgiving dinner in July when I was home, and I enjoyed that, but I still missed my family on the real holiday. Same with Christmas; I tried to get home whenever I could, but some years, the schedule was just too damn tight.

The team celebrations were always a lot of fun, though, and they were a chance for everyone to kick back and socialize without any pressure. No practices or games looming. No cameras around. We could just chill. It was good for bonding.

It was especially good for those of us who were still finding our place on a new roster. Hockey teams were always welcoming to new players, but it still took time to get in the groove with a new group. Today, Trews stuck close to me and Laramie. I got it—we were all new to the Whiskey Rebels, and the dynamic of this team was complicated. I felt bad for the kid. I was having a harder than usual time finding my place among these men; it had to be even more difficult for a young rookie who was still finding his footing as a professional hockey player. I remembered those days, and I didn't envy him being a rookie on *this* team right now.

That wasn't to say the guys were making any of us feel unwelcome. It was just a tough season for them. They were going through something I hoped I never experienced. I couldn't blame them for everything being "off."

And to their credit, they really were doing everything they could to bring us all firmly into the fold.

"You should be thanking me, kid." Eminem slung his arm around Trews's shoulders as we watched some of the guys shooting pool downstairs. "When Pittsburgh traded for me, they *also* got a second-round draft pick." He smacked the kid's chest. "Guess what they used to draft you?"

Trews laughed, and his blush was kind of cute. "Where did they get you and the pick from?"

"Edmonton." Eminem grimaced theatrically. "You wouldn't want to go there, my friend."

"Oh, shut up." Willie threw a Dorito at Eminem. "You loved it there."

"I did, but I'm not there now." Eminem shrugged and tossed the Dorito in his mouth. "Without me, who'd want to play there?"

We all groaned and laughed, rolling our eyes.

The attention turned back to the pool game, which was currently a game of eightball rife with relentless shit-talking. Mix had Ziggy on his heels, and even though a number of their chirps were in Russian, the rest of us were still thoroughly entertained by the resulting expressions and middle fingers.

Shortly after Ziggy beat Mix, I headed upstairs with Laramie and Trews to refresh our drinks. The hallway between the kitchen and living room was mostly empty, and the three of us paused there just to have a break from the noise.

I took advantage of the quiet moment and said to Trews, "So, aside from Eminem's bullshit about his trade landing you here—how are you liking it?"

"I do like it." Trews sipped his drink. "Pittsburgh is nice. The guys are great." He glanced toward the living room where several of the guys were watching football, then turned to me again. "Is the weird vibe just me, though? Like is this..." He chewed his lip.

I shook my head slowly. "It's not just you." It was my turn for a glance down the hall. "But with everything they've had thrown at them..."

Trews exhaled. "Yeah. Seriously." He grimaced. "I can't

even imagine. My teammates in college—they were like my brothers, you know?"

"Yeah. I know exactly what you mean."

"I think they're killing it, all things considered," Laramie said. "I'd be on the ground."

I nodded. "Me too. It'll probably get better after this season, but it's gonna take time."

"Still," Trews whispered. "I don't know how they've made it this far."

Laramie and I both nodded, murmuring our agreement.

We headed back down to the basement to rejoin the guys playing pool. Trews continued to stick close, and I didn't mind. Along with Laramie, we made the rounds through the party. There was the pool table in the basement, kids playing in the backyard, football on in the living room, and people shooting the shit and munching on snacks in the kitchen and family room.

I sucked at pool. I could do all kinds of shit I was ridiculously proud of on ice, but knocking balls around on felt? Yeah, no. Not my forte *at all*.

The rookie, however, turned out to be quite the pool shark.

"How did you *do* that?" Baddy squawked after Trews potted the eight ball. "That's—is that even possible?"

"Of course it's possible," Avery said with a laugh. "If you actually know how to shoot, which he does. You?" He made an exaggeratedly apologetic face and shrugged. "Well..."

"Fuck off, Calds." Baddy rolled his eyes. "Act like you can get through a game without scratching when you try to sink the eightball."

Avery scoffed. "That happened *once*."

"Yeah, last time we all partied and you played *once*."

Avery flipped him off.

Trews grinned in that way he did when he was about to go full ice gremlin. "You want to play, Calds?"

"Ooh, you're asking for it now." Eminem slapped Avery on the back. "Come on, Captain. Put the rookie in his place."

Avery laughed and shrugged. "You putting money on me?"

Eminem scoffed. "No. Because you'll lose on purpose just to be a dick."

"What?" Avery put a hand to his chest. "I would never—"

A chorus of coughed "bullshit, bullshit," rose around the room.

Avery huffed. "You know what? You guys are all assholes." He looked pointedly at Trews. "You sure you want to play me?"

Trews was *beaming*. "Hell, yeah. Let's do this."

Watching Avery play pool with Trews was entertaining as all hell, but it was also heartbreaking in a way. Yeah, he was trash-talking like everyone else, laughing at jokes and giving Trews a run for his money on the table.

But there was a pall over him that was impossible to miss. He reminded me of someone trying desperately to have a good time while an injury was too sore to ignore. Even his most full-throated laughs were followed by that subtle deflation, like someone who'd forgotten for a moment or two about the awful spasm in his back or the relentless ache in his knee. The way his expression turned flat, or—when he seemed really sure no one was looking—he let the hurt show through.

That was tough to watch.

I nudged Mix, who was standing beside me, and nodded toward Avery. "Is he okay?"

"Hmm?" Mix peered at Avery. Then he sighed and took a pull from his beer. Speaking just loud enough for me and no one else to hear, he whispered, "He and Early always played pool at team events."

"Ooh. Fuck."

Pursing his lips, he nodded, but he didn't say anything else. I supposed he didn't need to.

That had to be rough as hell, being reminded at every turn that his best friend was gone. I saw it in him today. I saw it in the locker room and on the ice. Sometimes even during games, when he'd get that distant look in his eyes before shaking himself out of it and refocusing.

The weirdest thing was that throughout the day, even as a new member of the team, I was aware of Leif's absence myself. It was hard not to notice despite never having known him. Most people were in happy, festive moods, but I didn't miss that occasional dip in conversation—the awkward pause as if someone had said something that poked at everyone's wound, or when they'd dart helpless, pained glances toward Leif's widow or Avery. It was impossible not to notice when someone was telling a story, and then they'd reach the part that included Leif and suddenly get that panicked, *"oh damn, did I just kill the mood?"* look on their face.

Shortly after people had started arriving, Rachel had, rather than making a big announcement, quietly told a few of the wives she was expecting. Word got around quickly, of course, and more than once I heard people offering her congratulations, the exchanges tinged with visible sympathy and pain. Everyone told her emphatically that if she needed help with anything to give them a call; she was still part of the Whiskey Rebel family, and everyone was eager to step up. She clearly appreciated it, but it must've been a gut punch every time. A reminder that there was a need for that help. A reason why they had to remind her she was still part of the family.

A reminder of why that was even a question.

———

Despite it being almost December, the weather wasn't bad, the chill demanding jeans and a light jacket at most. Especially as the packed house grew stuffier, Trews and I moved outside for some fresh air while Laramie stayed by the pool table.

The air was cold, but it didn't have the bite of a midwestern winter like I'd grown up with in Omaha, never mind the two seasons of major juniors I played in Quebec or the years I'd spent in Detroit. Today reminded me a little of the chill of a practice rink—comfortable and familiar.

We joined some of the guys and the wives on the back deck. Below us, Avery and Ziggy were kicking a soccer ball around in the yard with several of the kids, and I... couldn't help staring.

This was the first time since I'd come to Pittsburgh that I really saw Avery relaxed and smiling. He and Ziggy were chirping each other, but they were mostly encouraging the kids, and they cheered them on every time one got the ball into one of the two hockey nets on the grass.

When one of the younger kids tripped and fell, Avery helped her up and dusted her off. He didn't fall all over himself and freak out that she might've been hurt—just made sure she was okay and got her smiling again before any tears could start. Within seconds, they were back to their game, the little girl trotting after the ball and giggling with Avery right on her heels.

Oh, fuck me—*that* was the version of Avery that had made coming to Pittsburgh extra appealing. Relaxed. Laughing. So adorable with kids that it made my insides go all gooey. I'd seen so many videos of him with young fans or with the Make-A-Wish kids, and he was always ridiculously cute with them.

Today, the transformation was jaw-dropping. It wasn't just that his face lit up when the kids wanted to play—it was like he came alive. Yeah, he'd chirped along in the basement while we'd played pool, but there'd still been that sad edge to his mood. Now that he was outside with the little ones, he seemed to have shaken off everything else.

Maybe in another time and place, I could have acted on this attraction. Nobody cared anymore if players were gay or if teammates dated. It just wasn't a big deal.

But there was no chance of something happening between me and Avery. Not even if this attraction was mutual, which it probably wasn't.

As the informal soccer game wore on, I realized Leif's widow was watching, too, a serene smile on her face.

She turned to me. "Oh. I don't think we were ever really introduced." She offered her hand. "I'm Rachel Erlandsson."

"Peyton Hall." I shook her hand gently, not quite sure what to say.

"How are you liking it here?"

"It's been good so far." I laughed. "Not as cold as Omaha or Detroit, so..."

She laughed too. "The milder winters are nice, that's for sure." She gestured at the kids playing with Avery and Ziggy. "Are any of them yours?"

"No. No. I'm... It's just me."

"Gotcha. Well, the little one out there is Elsa, my youngest." She nodded toward the yard. "The two brunettes are also mine. Kalle and Linnea."

I realized then that Elsa was the girl Avery had helped up earlier.

"They're cute," I said. "Looks like they're having a good time."

"They always do." She laughed softly. "And they'll probably sleep *hard* tonight. Playing like this always wears them out."

I cocked a brow. "The kids? Or...?" I gestured at Ziggy and Avery.

She giggled softly. "Well, the kids. They're always exhausted after spending time with their uncles." She quirked her lips. "The guys probably sleep pretty hard, too."

I laughed. "Yeah, my nieces and nephews wear me out. Maybe that's the secret to getting everyone to sleep on road trips." I nodded toward the soccer game. "Turn them loose with some kids until everyone passes out."

"You're not wrong. They always—" She caught herself, and her voice hitched a little. She cleared her throat, then said, with a smile that seemed ever so slightly forced, "They always wore their dad out."

Shit. All roads led to him, didn't they? I couldn't blame her at all; it just had to be hard, having a casual conversation and slamming face first into your grief.

"I bet," I said quietly. "My brother has Irish twins. One's three, the other is two. He's always passed out on the couch even before they go to bed."

That brought a hint of life back to her expression, and she smiled with a touch more feeling. "I can imagine. A pair of toddlers? Been there, done that." She grimaced and crossed herself, and we both laughed.

I wasn't sure what to say after that.

Fortunately, we were interrupted by Baddy letting us all know it was time for dinner. There was a veritable stampede of children onto the deck and into the house, with Avery and Ziggy following at a more subdued pace.

"They didn't wear you out, did they?" I asked them.

"What?" Avery scoffed. "Of course not." He smacked Ziggy's arm. "I was just hanging back in case this old guy collapsed or—"

"Oh, fuck you, Calds." Ziggy shoved Avery, knocking him right into me.

I caught his arm and shoulder, and I laughed. "Whoa, easy there."

Avery laughed. "I'm good. I'm good."

As he righted himself, he met my gaze, and for a split second, we both froze. My pulse sped up. I had no idea what I was seeing in his stunning hazel eyes—what thought was crossing his mind and giving him pause—only the words that slammed into my own consciousness:

Holy shit, you're gorgeous up close.

Mercifully, he broke eye contact and cleared his throat. "Come on. We better find seats before they start putting people on the floor."

"On the floor?" I huffed. "What kind of uncivilized Thanksgiving is this?"

"Eh," Avery said over his shoulder as he headed inside. "Baddy's hosting. We have to keep our expectations low."

Something flew at Avery's head, though he deftly avoided it. A dinner roll, I thought. That was followed by, "I heard that!"

"I wasn't trying to be quiet!" Avery fired back.

I just chuckled, my heart still pounding for reasons I didn't want to think about right then.

Despite the huge house, space was a little limited with this many people and their families, and several of us did end up in the living room, which was fine. The dining room table was designated for the kids, and there was a longer table for most of the adults. Some of the parents had worked out a system where three would sit with the kids for a while, then trade with three others and rejoin the adults. I thought about offering to help, but they seemed to have it down to a science, so I left well enough alone.

Those of us who didn't fit at the table loaded our plates and settled onto the couch and chairs in the living room. Baddy's wife provided TV trays for anyone who wanted them, and there was the coffee table and end tables. Most of us just perched our plates on our laps.

I sat on the end of the couch with Mix in the middle and Ziggy on the other end. Baddy took one of the recliners; he and Eminem were swapping kid table detail, so at some point, Eminem would come in and take that spot. Trews and Laramie sat on the floor and put their plates on the coffee table.

In the recliner kitty corner to me, his plate on his thigh and his other leg slung over an armrest as if he'd been thrown into the chair, was Avery. He picked up his beer off the coffee table. "Hey, Mix." He tilted the bottle toward our teammate. "Tell the new guys about that prank we pulled on you when you were a rookie."

Laramie straightened a little, clearly interested.

For his part, Trews looked justifiably alarmed.

Mix sighed, jabbing his fork into a green bean. "You really want me to tell new guys what an absolute bag of dicks you are?"

"Pfft." Ziggy tilted his beer bottle toward me, then Laramie and Trews. He said something to Mix in Russian, which got a grunt and a shrug that I thought translated to, *"okay, fair point."*

"Hey." Avery lobbed a bean at Ziggy's head. "How about sharing with the whole class?"

Ziggy threw it back. "I said, 'You don't think they know by now? They're not stupid.'"

Laramie, Trews, and I all nodded, and I was a little too enamored with the wicked laugh from Avery. He was gorgeous to begin with, but he'd been so sad and distant since training camp, his stunning smile far too rare. Whenever one broke through, it messed with my pulse.

Thank God, none of them noticed me staring at him. Or nearly dropping the plate I was carefully balancing on my lap.

That was just what I needed—to mop up my Thanksgiving dinner off Baddy's carpet while the whole team realized I'd been ogling our captain.

While I regained my dignity and equilibrium, Mix put his beer bottle down and sighed. "These assholes. When I came to Pittsburgh, I lived with Sigayev." He tipped his head toward Ziggy. "Because my English was..." He furrowed his brow, then turned to Ziggy, who said something to him in Russian. Nodding sharply, Mix said, "My English was less good." He narrowed his eyes at Avery. "And *that* asshole..."

"What?" Avery snickered. "I didn't do anything!"

"Bullshit." Mix rolled his eyes. To us new guys, he said, "He had Willie write everything on whiteboard in French. And then he paid Coach—the one we had back then—to start practice in French."

Laramie groaned. "Oh, God. My team did that to me in major juniors."

Trews shot him a look. "Didn't you play in Quebec?"

"Yeah, but still." Laramie shrugged. "My French sucked."

"At least you knew a *little* French," Mix muttered. "Me?" He tsked and shook his head. "All I know is French curses."

At that, Laramie brightened. "Well, yeah. That's the important shit!"

Mix laughed. "Russian curses are better."

Trews frowned. "*I* don't know any of those."

"What?" Ziggy straightened. "How are you in this league, and you don't know how to swear in Russian?" He waved a hand and didn't wait for a response. Thumping the end table with his finger, he said, "Time for you to *learn*."

And just like that, he and Mix were off and running, filling the rookie's head with Russian profanity. Laramie listened intently, too; he hadn't picked up nearly as much as I had during major juniors.

As I sat back and watched the interplay, laughing at Trews and Laramie sounding out the new words, I sensed someone watching me. I turned and met Avery's gaze. He jumped a little, as if he hadn't expected to get caught, and he flicked his eyes back to our teammates. After a second or two, he cautiously looked my way again.

I hesitated, then offered a small smile.

When he returned it...

Oh, fuck me.

I didn't want to read anything into it, so I didn't. I refused to interpret that mischievous little sparkle in his eyes as anything other than amusement over our teammates discussing Russian curses.

But as I turned my attention back to the swearing lesson, my pulse pounded in ways it had no business pounding. Suddenly I was in that same place I'd been when I'd first signed with Pittsburgh, wondering how I would ever concentrate with Avery Caldwell on the ice beside me.

He wasn't flirting, Peyton.

He's just being friendly, and he's laughing at all the Russian talk.

Get a grip.

I chanced another look at him.

Busted him looking right back at me.

And when he pulled his gaze away this time...

Oh, fuck me again.

He blushed.

CHAPTER 11
AVERY

I had never been more relieved to drop onto a hotel bed.

Not after those long-ass flights to the World Cup and to the Olympics. Not after crossing countless time zones and—on occasion—the goddamned International Date Line. Not after yet another game followed by a flight during a grueling playoff series.

After tonight's game (well, technically last night now, since it was after two in the morning, but whatever), we'd flown from Pittsburgh to Detroit, which was only about an hour. It was hardly the longest night I'd had since I'd started traveling with a hockey team back in my U10 days, but holy shit, I was relieved to be here. Alone. Behind closed doors.

Lying back on the bed, still wearing my suit, I scrubbed my hands over my face and exhaled. I was exhausted, and it had little to do with the intense grind of a game we'd played just a few hours ago.

I'd done one of the intermission interviews. Before the game, Falon had interviewed me as well, since we'd been playing New York, one of our longstanding rivals. There'd been fans outside after the morning skate and again braving the cold outside the hotel tonight, and I'd smiled for all of them as I'd signed autographs, taken selfies, and chatted with them about hockey. During our flight, I'd handily beaten both Eminem and Peyton at rummy, then joined in cheering on Baddy and Ziggy as they'd played Mario Kart on the charter jet's big screen.

It was all a perfectly normal part of the regular season, but I was absolutely drained. I had been all season, and that had only gotten worse since Thanksgiving at Baddy's house almost three weeks ago.

Closing my eyes, I rubbed my forehead with the heels of my hands. I'd spent that whole day putting on a show. I'd spent every day since putting on another one. That day, it had been *"easygoing, celebratory Avery who doesn't die a little inside every time he looks at his best friend's kids or widow."* Every goddamned day after, it had been *"relaxed but focused Avery who's dialed in on this morning's prac- tice,"* followed by *"happy and fun Avery who's keeping morale up and spirits high because losing one game doesn't mean we'll lose the next one."*

Then we'd had an intense homestand of nearly back-to- back games, and now I was alone in this hotel room, and for a little while at least, I could finally fucking breathe.

Well, I was *allowed* to breathe anyway. I wasn't so sure how capable I was.

Suck it up, Calds. Have a drink, go to sleep, and be the captain you're supposed to be.

Ugh. All of that sounded like a lot of work.

The drink part sounded pretty good, though, so I pushed myself up off the bed. I didn't dare touch the mini- bar; I'd indulge sometimes, but I didn't want to do it often enough to catch the travel coordinator's notice. Instead, I took my shaving kit out of my suitcase and dug around to find two plain plastic bottles that looked like they contained shampoo or something.

I unscrewed the cap on one, and my mouth watered. The plastic didn't do much for the taste, but I wasn't in this for the flavor. I just wanted to throw back what amounted to two shots of good, strong bourbon.

I made a face as it went down, almost gagging on the plasticky taste combined with the burn of the alcohol. Maybe I needed to get some glass bottles to take with me. But... no. Those would be too obvious if someone searched my bag. The opaque blue bottles with *"shampoo"* and *"conditioner"* written in Sharpie wouldn't pique anyone's interest the way a glass bottle full of suspiciously dark liquid would.

I'd just have to live with the taste.

It wasn't enough to give me more than a very, very mild buzz, even with the remnants of my in-flight drinks still keeping my head light. Hopefully it would be enough to let me sleep, though, because I couldn't risk having any more than this. Not when I had to be at the team breakfast at oh-fuck-thirty, and not when I had to skate a couple of hours later.

This would have to be enough.

I went through the motions of getting ready for bed, then climbed under the covers.

Tomorrow, I'd practice with the team. After that, I'd go golfing with Eminem, Ziggy, and Baddy. The weather was promising, and getting out there for eighteen holes would be good for me. It always was.

Tonight, I would sleep. If nothing else, being this exhausted would knock my ass out, and maybe I'd even get lucky and not dream.

Tomorrow, I'd be Avery Caldwell, captain of the Pittsburgh Whiskey Rebels. I'd golf with my friends. I'd play hockey with my team.

Maybe everyone would believe I was okay.

Maybe even me.

That scream.

That heart-wrenching scream.

Lying there in the dark, drenched in sweat and breathing hard as the dream slowly faded, my ears still rang with that awful sound. My chest still hurt, that impossible mix of being cavernously empty because my heart had just been torn out and feeling like it was about to explode from all those excruciating emotions.

Some part of me tried to reassure myself it had been just a dream, but the worst part was... it *hadn't* been just a dream.

Tonight, sure. Tonight, I hadn't been there in that waiting room. Tonight, I hadn't listened to a doctor calmly and professionally tell everyone our lives would never be the same.

Tonight, I hadn't heard Rachel scream like her soul had just been ripped out of her body.

But all that had been real. And every damn night, it happened again and again.

It would get better eventually, right? Farther away?

Maybe.

But not tonight.

Golfing out here with the guys had sounded like an amazing idea. Just the change of pace I needed to jar me out of the funk I was working so hard to keep out of everyone's sight. There were few things that couldn't be helped by a little fresh air—even when it was cold—and some shit-talking over eighteen holes.

But I may not have thought it through today.

We'd played here every time the Whiskey Rebels were in Detroit. Every year I'd been with the team. It was a tradition, even when the weather was awful. One I looked forward to whenever we were in town.

And like everything in my goddamned world, it reminded me of someone who wasn't here anymore.

On the way out to the course with Baddy, Eminem, and Ziggy, I forced those feelings as far beneath the surface as they would go. Through the first three holes, I refused to acknowledge the long past conversations that insisted on echoing through my head as I followed this familiar path.

At the fourth hole, though, Baddy turned to me, a grin on his face, and he started to speak, but then clearly caught himself.

"Hey do—" He froze, going full-on deer-in-the-headlights. Recovering quickly, he cleared his throat. "Do you remember the time we were out here and it started storming?"

I forced the most genuine laugh I could muster. Yeah. I remembered. But I had a feeling his mind really had gone to the same place mine had.

"For fuck's sake." Leif had thrown up his hands and scoffed. *"What is it with you and this course?"*

I'd flashed him a huge grin. *"What? It's not my fault you always go a million over par on this—"*

"Bite me," he'd muttered. *"I think we should take away*

your handicap when we play here, because you always beat the shit out of all of us on this course."

"He's not wrong," Baddy had said. *"Did you come out here last night and make some kind of sacrifice? You never play this good!"*

"Oh, kiss my ass." I'd rolled my eyes. *"I play just fine!"*

Leif had huffed sharply. *"You never play this good, Calds. Never. I think Baddy's on to some—"*

"Calds?"

Baddy's voice. In the present. The here and now.

I shook myself and turned to him. "Hmm?"

All three of my teammates were watching me, the chirping and competitiveness gone from their expressions.

"You okay?" Eminem asked. "You kind of..." He waved a hand in front of his face.

"I'm good." I laughed and poked him with my club. "Just doing the math to figure out how far over par you are."

He huffed and rolled his eyes. "Eat a dick."

"Math?" Baddy tsked. "Bro, you have a smartphone." He held his up and jiggled it. "Use the calculator when the numbers are that big."

That earned him a smack across the shin from Eminem's five iron, and he yelped and hopped.

"You deserved that," Eminem muttered.

That seemed to make them all forget I'd spaced out, and I did nothing to remind them of it. As we continued down the green, he and Baddy kept bitching at each other like they always did when we golfed while Ziggy egged them on. I threw in my two cents now and then, too, just to keep them off the scent that my mind was elsewhere.

My mind *was* elsewhere, though. Everything about this day had Leif written all over it, and it hurt. We'd played in this city. We'd golfed on this course. Ziggy wouldn't even be here, soundly beating all three of us, if things had been different.

If things were still the same.

How much longer until I get used to this?

That didn't even seem possible. Leif was too indelibly imprinted on too many parts of my life to just be... gone. There was no getting used to that

Ever since the night he'd died, I'd had a few sharp, shameful moments of wishing I'd never met him.

Of course I didn't wish that at all. I was a better man for having known him, and my life was a million times better for having him in it. But goddamn, when his loss was this close to the surface—when it was this unavoidable—never knowing him at all sounded like fucking *bliss* because it would mean I'd never had him to lose.

Right now was one of those moments, and I hated myself for it, which made me feel even worse.

I shouldn't have come here.

I didn't know if I meant this golf course or this city—not that I had a choice about coming to the city—only that being anywhere but here was incredibly appealing.

My teammates had already caught on that I wasn't in a good place today, though, and I didn't want them to worry. They needed to trust that I had my head together enough to play hockey and to be their captain.

So, I forced myself to focus on our golf game, and I forced myself to join in with the banter and snarking even though I wasn't feeling it at all.

By the time we reached the eighteenth hole, the sun was starting to set. Made sense—it felt like we'd been out here for hours and hours. Except then I realized it was only like 4:30.

We hadn't been out here forever. It was just late November and the sun went down earlier.

"You think that's dark early?" Leif had given a haughty scoff. *"Try living somewhere the sun doesn't come up at all this time of year."*

"Oh, fuck off." I'd shoved him. *"Your hometown doesn't get the polar night, you drama queen."*

"Hey! I had family in Kiruna!"

"Uh-huh, and you only visited them every other year, so you didn't live there. Shut up."

At least this time, I snapped out of it before any of the guys noticed, and I managed to stay in the present as we headed into the clubhouse. We grabbed dinner there, since they had a great restaurant, and then we Ubered back to the hotel. There, some of our teammates were, predictably, hanging out in the bar, so naturally, we joined them.

I had to resist the urge to pound my mojito like a shot while gesturing at the bartender to start making me another one. Not here. Not in front of my teammates.

I sipped it, willing myself to drink slowly no matter how bad I wanted to get fucked up. When I made it the bottom of the glass, I casually ordered a whiskey on the rocks. A double. If I couldn't throw it back like I so desperately wanted to, then I could at least make it strong enough to pack a punch.

It was getting the job done, too. As the evening went on, I had to work harder to follow the conversations around me, and not just because the bar was so loud. It started with my teammates who had strong accents—Mix and Ziggy, mostly, but also Astala, who was Finnish, and Willie, who was Quebecois. After another round, even the Americans and Anglophile Canadians started making less and less sense.

Yes. God, yes. More oblivion. Less clarity. Hell yeah.

At some point, as I was getting into my... hell, I didn't know how many I'd had at this point, but I was only partway through my current drink. Anyway, the guys were starting to settle up their tabs and peel away. A few sips later, only Baddy and Mix remained besides me.

"Morning skate comes early." Eminem clapped my shoulder. "You heading up soon?"

I gestured with my glass. "Gonna finish this first. I'm right behind you."

He arched an eyebrow. "You sure?"

"Yeah." I grinned. "You want me to let this go to waste? That's alcohol abuse!"

He considered me curiously for a moment, then chuckled, smacked my shoulder again, and left with the rest of the guys.

I closed my eyes and exhaled. I was finally alone except for the bartenders and the ghost of my best friend. I couldn't shake him off. Not here. We'd played on that golf course. We'd drunk in this bar. Leif's name was all over this city. All over my *life*.

I couldn't even look at my gorgeous new teammate without thinking about the man who'd bet me a hundred bucks and three steak dinners that we'd hook up. At least Peyton hadn't joined me and the guys in the bar tonight. I'd probably do or say something stupid.

I took a deep swallow from my drink, begging it to take me closer to the oblivion where Leif had never existed and I could actually be sane.

God, I miss you, Leif.

Apparently this was the ugly side of having such a close friend. Everywhere I went was stained with his memory. With his *absence*.

I needed to sleep. We had our morning skate, and we had tomorrow night's game.

First, I needed to spend some time forgetting why this place hurt so damn much.

So I finished my drink just like I'd told Eminem I would.

And then I ordered another double.

CHAPTER 12
PEYTON

"Are you ready to play against your old team?" Dad asked.

I shrugged, trying not to jostle my phone, which I was using to FaceTime him as I stood outside the hotel doors. "It'll be kind of weird, not gonna lie." I grimaced. "Hopefully the fans don't boo me."

"Eh, they know how it goes. It isn't like you get to dictate trades."

"Still. Sometimes they don't like seeing us in rival jerseys."

"I'm sure they'll get over it." Dad grinned. "Score on your old boys a few times. It'll make you feel better."

I laughed. There honestly wasn't much that a few goals couldn't alleviate. "We'll see. And I had lunch with some of the guys this afternoon. It was good to see them, you know?"

"I bet. No hard feelings, then, huh?"

"Nah. They get it." I chuckled. "Jantzen wanted to know if Coach Tabakov is really the hardass everyone says he is. I said, 'No. He'd probably be all over *your* ass for dicking off, but for those of us who actually work...'"

My dad barked a laugh. "That sounds like you."

I just snickered. We moved the conversation away from hockey, and he caught me up on everything happening back home. Mom was on a trip with some of her friends, so it was just him for the next week or so; no wonder he'd wanted to talk almost every night this week. We FaceTimed a lot anyway, but he got a little stir crazy sometimes when Mom wasn't there. And although Mom hadn't had a relapse in years *and* her sponsor was on the trip with her, I knew he still got nervous when she went away. So even when I was ready to faceplant into bed, I always had time for my night owl father.

I didn't mind. Being away from my family had been my norm since major juniors, and even now, well into my professional career, it was hard sometimes. We'd been through hell as a family, and by some miracle (and thanks to a lot of therapy for everyone), we'd come out of it closer than ever. Despite the geographical distance, and I was glad we'd kept up that closeness after all this time.

It always did make me a little homesick, though. After we'd ended the call, I promised myself—same as I always did—that I'd head back to Omaha the minute the season was over. Maybe Dad and I would finally rebuild his shed like we'd been meaning to do for the past like five years.

Probably not, I thought with a chuckle on my way back into the hotel. *We'll put it off and put it off, and the day we decide to do it, it'll rain. Same as every year.*

God, I missed my family.

As I crossed the hotel lobby, I glanced toward the bar to see if any of my teammates were still hanging out. It was late, so I wasn't surprised that they'd all cleared out.

Wait. No.

Not all of them.

I did a double take and realized I recognized the man hunched over a glass at the bar.

I checked my phone. It was almost 1:30. Breakfast started at 7:00. Buses would start leaving for the arena at 8:30.

I hesitated outside the bar. I wanted to go crash myself —I was exhausted—but my gut told me it wouldn't be a bad idea to check on my teammate.

Pocketing my phone, I strolled into the bar and up to Avery. "Hey. You're still awake?"

He turned to me, a few strands of dark hair falling over red, exhausted eyes. Then he shrugged. "Just having a nightcap."

Was that a slur, or was I imagining things? Hell, tired as I was, I'd probably started slurring myself.

He patted the barstool next to him. "Have a seat. I'll buy a round."

I hesitated, scanning the bar. There was no one from the team in here. No players. No staff. I didn't need or want a drink, but I also had a feeling I shouldn't leave my captain alone right now.

I took the offered seat. "Just water for me. We have to be up in a few hours."

"We do?" He took out his phone and fumbled with it, then peered at the screen. Sighing heavily, he dropped the device on the bar, letting it clatter loudly beside his glass. "Shit. Night got away from me."

I chewed the inside of my cheek. Nightcap, my ass. Avery did have a slur going on, but that wasn't the only thing that suggested he'd had too much. His gestures were heavy and clumsy, and when he'd checked the time on his phone, he seemed to be having trouble focusing his eyes.

He could drink like any hockey player, and he usually held his liquor well. Not like this.

I tried not to drum my fingers nervously on the bar. "You good tonight, Captain?"

The wince was subtle, but it was there, though he quickly covered it with a laugh before sipping his drink. "Just too wound up to sleep. You know how it goes."

"Uh-huh. I do." I shifted in the barstool. "You, um... You planning on...?" I gestured toward the elevators.

Annoyance flickered across his face, sending a ripple of panic through me. Shit, had I overstepped? But before I could back pedal, he released a resigned sigh. "I should get some sleep." He threw back the remainder of his drink, and the ice cubes clinked as he put the glass down beside his phone. Then he gestured for the bartender, who brought him his check.

Well, at least he was calling it a night now rather than later. The bar would be closing in the next half hour or so, but that meant he still could've squeezed in one more drink before last call. With as much as he was struggling just to sign the credit card receipt, one more drink could've spelled disaster.

"All right." He put the pen down on the receipt and pushed it away. "Let's get out of here."

I managed a quick smile and got up.

Then Avery went to stand, but his balance wavered. Badly.

I grabbed his arm and put my other hand on his chest to steady him. "Whoa. Hey. You sure you're all right?"

He laughed, gripping the back of the barstool for support. "Should've watched that first step, I guess."

I raised my eyebrows.

"I'm good." He smacked my arm, casually brushing my

hand off his chest in the process. "C'mon. Let's get upstairs before—" He made it two steps this time before he staggered to the side.

Without a word, I slung his arm around my shoulders and wrapped mine around his waist. He muttered insistence that he could walk just fine, but he was leaning heavily on me, so I listened to his body instead of his mouth.

We both probably looked drunk as hell, staggering across the lobby toward the elevators. Fine. I just wanted to make sure Avery got back to his room, ideally in time to sleep this off and absolutely before someone else from the team saw him.

God, please don't let anyone be filming us.

The last thing either of us needed was this ending up on the internet.

Fortunately, the lobby was pretty deserted and I didn't see any phones pointed in our direction. I didn't think anyone even noticed us, honestly, aside from a desk clerk who glanced up at us before returning her attention to her computer monitor.

Not a moment too soon, I poured us into an otherwise empty elevator. "What floor are you on?"

He didn't answer immediately.

"Avery? What floor—"

"Ninth." He tugged something free from his pocket and glared at it, then nodded sharply. "Yeah. Ninth."

Well, that was a plus—he had his keycard with him. I hadn't even thought to check, and I really didn't want to have to ask the front desk for another key to his room.

I jabbed the button for the ninth floor. My room was on the eighth, but I'd get there after I knew Avery was safely in his.

Avery made a half-assed effort to free himself from me,

but as soon as I loosened the arm around his waist, he faltered. He caught himself with a hand flat on the mirrored wall, leaving a handprint on the otherwise clean glass.

"Shit," he muttered. "They mix 'em *strong* in this place."

I huffed a laugh, but I didn't buy it. Yeah, some of the hotel bartenders could have a heavy hand, but one drink—no matter how strong—wasn't going to turn a pro hockey player into... *this*.

The elevator stopped. I let Avery try to take a couple of steps on his own, then just quietly caught him again and hauled him out of the car. "What room?"

"Nine twenty—uh..." Avery turned over the keycard's envelope. "Oh. Nine-twelve."

I grunted in acknowledgment and steered us toward that room. There were voices behind some doors. Familiar voices. TVs, too. Some of our teammates and likely staff members were still awake.

With each step I took, half-dragging him down the hall, I silently begged every door to stay shut.

Luck or some deities were on our side tonight, because we made it to room 912 without incident. One tap of the keycard, one click of the lock, and we were home free.

I guided him into the room and nudged the door shut behind me. Then I helped him to the king-size bed and eased him down on its edge. "There we go." I tried not to sound relieved as his weight slid off my shoulders. Not because I couldn't hold him up—I just hated the responsibility. The absolute certainty that I was going to take a bad step and let him fall.

Now he was safely in his room and on his bed.

Avery wavered a little, then seemed to steady himself,

and he clumsily loosened his tie. "Uh, thanks. I guess I'll... see you at breakfast?"

I nodded. "You good for the night? I don't know if I should leave you when you're..." I trailed off, wondering why I was trying to discuss this with someone who was that drunk.

"I'm fine." He slid the now undone tie off his neck and let it fall onto the comforter beside him. Gazing up at me, he grinned. "I'm *fine*, okay?" He pushed himself slowly to his feet, pausing to make sure he had his balance. As he unbuttoned his jacket, he added, "I'm not—I'm good, okay?"

I tried to keep my skepticism out of my expression, but I doubted I succeeded.

Avery rolled his eyes and shook his head. "I'm *good*." He shrugged off his suit jacket, and there went his balance again.

Without thinking, I grabbed his shoulders to steady him. "Whoa, easy."

"I'm fine!" He tried to take another step as if to prove it, and that... did not end well. He toppled into me, sending me back against the TV stand. By some miracle, I didn't hit the flatscreen behind me, though it wobbled precariously. It didn't fall, and I managed to steady both Avery and me. Again.

He grabbed the edge of the TV stand for some extra support, and we locked eyes. For a moment, we were both still, my heart absolutely slamming into my ribs as we stood there, neither of us apparently quite sure how to disentangle ourselves.

"Um." I swallowed. "Maybe you should sit down again. Have some water before—"

His weight shifted, and I moved to catch us both again when—

Avery kissed me.

Just... out of nowhere, his mouth was against mine.

For a couple of seconds, I was frozen, disbelieving that Avery Caldwell—the man I'd wanted since forever—was kissing me.

But then the astringent taste and fumes of strong booze nearly made me cough. They also reminded me why we were here.

Avery wasn't kissing me. A version of Avery who was so shitfaced he couldn't walk was kissing me.

I put my hands on his shoulders again and—carefully but firmly—pushed him back a step. He didn't protest. If anything, he looked a little confused. By my rejection? By the fact that I was here at all? Who knew. All I knew was that I needed to get out of this room and away from him as quickly as possible. He was way too drunk to know what—or who, let's be real—he was doing, and I didn't fool around with people who were intoxicated.

I guided him back a couple more steps until he hit the bed. Then I pressed down on his shoulders, and he sat again.

Releasing him, I said, "Let's get you some water."

He nodded, looking a little dazed.

I scanned the room. This hotel, like so many others, had a pair of complimentary bottles of water on the dresser. I grabbed one and broke the seal, which took some work because holy shit, my damn hands were shaking.

"Okay, this should help you sober up." I turned to hand him the bottle, but halted.

He'd lain back across the bed, and he was already out cold. Passed out? Asleep? Well, unconscious one way or another.

"Christ," I muttered, and then took a swig from the bottle since it wasn't like he'd be drinking it any time soon.

I studied him as I tried to figure out what to do next. I couldn't just leave him like this. What if he had alcohol poisoning or something? What if he got sick while he was still lying on his back?

I could text one of the trainers or the team doc. Except... damn it. No. That could get him disciplined by the club. If nothing else, it would humiliate him, but it could also hurt his career. His place on the team.

Standing there in Avery Caldwell's room at almost two in the morning, listening to him snore as he lay sprawled in his expensive suit...

I had no idea what to do next.

CHAPTER 13
AVERY

Oh God. I feel like hammered shit.

My head. My stomach. My burning throat. Did I mention my head? Because holy *shit*, my *head*.

And it couldn't really be 6:30. I had to have messed up when I set my alarm, and now it was shrieking in the middle of the night for some reason. It wasn't even daylight yet!

Wait, was it *supposed* to be light yet? This was winter so...

"Goddammit," I croaked, and I felt around until I found my stupid phone on the nightstand. The screen was blurry as hell, but I managed to find the button to turn off the alarm. Then I closed my eyes and let the silence soothe my head for a minute or two.

I needed to reset my alarm, though. I did have to be up at 6:30 if I wanted to get to breakfast on time *and* get on the bus for the morning skate.

I fumbled with the phone again, and then squinted my aching eyes at the screen until the numbers came into focus.

6:31.

Are you kidding *me?*

How the hell was it already time to get up? And how the hell was my room this dark?

I lay back and rubbed my throbbing forehead. Today was going to suck. I'd already been up to puke twice, and I wasn't sure that was over yet. I had no idea how I was going to get food down my throat, never mind keep it there. Practice? Then play a game? Fuck me.

I wanted to just go back to sleep and stay that way until my hangover was gone. Besides, maybe if I fell asleep now, I could slip back into that dream. The one where, instead of Rachel releasing that distraught scream over and over, Peyton had been in here with me.

God, I wish that kiss had been real.

Clarity knifed its way through my miserable haze. I replayed that moment in my dream when I'd finally worked up the courage to kiss Peyton.

My dreams were vivid, but not *that* vivid. I could have some pretty intense sexual dreams, but I'd never felt the softness of a guy's lips or the scuff of his beard when I'd kissed him in a dream. Only...

Only in real life.

I stared up at the darkened ceiling as horror curdled alongside the nausea in my angry stomach. That was also when I realized I wasn't naked or in gym shorts the way I usually slept. This shirt... these pants...

I'd lost my jacket and tie at some point, but this was the suit I'd been wearing last night. Wearing to the bar. Where I'd been drinking. And I didn't remember leaving the bar to come back to my room. Except I very vaguely *did* remember—

Oh, fuuuck.

That kiss *had* been real, hadn't it?

So had his startled expression, and he hadn't been startled like someone who'd been pleasantly surprised by a kiss. In the moment I hadn't understood a thing I'd read on his face, but now I could see—hell, I could *feel*—the *WTF?* and not in a good way.

"You've got to be kidding me," I gritted out, rubbing a hand over my face as a third trip to heave in the bathroom threatened to happen. No, that kiss couldn't have been real, though. Right? Because I distinctly remembered it happening in here. In my room. Why would Peyton be in my room?

Yeah. Why would he?

He hadn't even been at the bar with me and the guys last night. Some of our teammates had come and gone, but Peyton hadn't been there. I'd have noticed if he was, because I *always* noticed when he was nearby.

So no, there was no way he'd wound up in my hotel room last night.

The fresh nausea steadily receded. I was working myself up over nothing. It was a dream. Period. I'd had a few drinks last night, passed out in my clothes, and then had a stupid dream about kissing Peyton and him clearly not being into it. Blame the booze. At least I hadn't had that awful recuring nightmare again—mission accomplished.

I swallowed a few times to be sure whatever remained in my stomach stayed put. Then I carefully got up, indulging in a groan when that made my head throb more.

A hot shower and a little too much ibuprofen helped. So did a bottle of water.

Hadn't the cleaning staff left *two* bottles, though? Because I could've sworn there were two when I checked in, and I hadn't touched either of them.

A moment later, I found the second bottle—empty in the trash.

No idea when I'd drunk that one, but okay.

I pulled on a pair of sweats and a hoodie, made sure I had my phone and keycard, and took my pounding head downstairs for breakfast. That weird-ass dream had mostly faded along with the worst of my headache, though it pecked at me a little, too. Mostly because I wished it had actually happened.

The part where Peyton and I kissed, anyway. Not the part where he'd pushed me away. That had sucked.

But if he kissed in real life the way he had in that dream?

Oh my God. Yes, please? Where do I sign up?

Then I walked into the hotel's banquet hall for breakfast, and when my gaze landed on Peyton...

Ooh shiiit. Last night *hadn't* been a dream, had it?

Because that would explain why Peyton jerked his gaze away from mine and buried it in his breakfast. His breakfast, which he was barely picking at. It would explain the sudden color that rose in his face.

Well, this would be fun to sort out.

For the moment, there was nothing I could do or say. Not in front of our teammates. Instead, I did the best I could to act normal: I got some coffee, loaded my plate, and joined my usual group of guys.

My ass had barely hit the chair before Peyton got up.

"I need to go pack," he muttered. "See you guys on the bus."

He didn't wait for a response. He bused his dishes, and then he was gone.

Well... shit.

"What was that all about?" Eminem asked.

"Hell if I know," I lied as I dug into my food. "Were you telling stories about Baddy's cooking again?"

"Hey!" A grape flew across the table and bounced off my forehead. The impact didn't help my headache, but I laughed and played it as cool as I could.

"What?" I asked innocently. "If you told him about that time you tried to make lasagna, I don't blame him for leaving."

That had everyone at the table nodding and murmuring in agreement while Baddy crossed his arms and huffed. "Fuck you, Calds."

I snickered. "But I'm not wrong."

"*Fuck. You.*"

At least that pulled everyone's focus away from Peyton's sudden departure. Everyone except me, anyway. The chair he'd abandoned may as well have been a flickering fluorescent light for all I could ignore it. The only thing that kept me shoveling food into my face was the need to keep up appearances. I didn't want anyone catching on that something was off between me and Peyton.

Especially if it was "off" the way I thought it was.

Christ, what had happened? I didn't remember a goddamned thing except being in the bar and then dreaming—or not—that Peyton and I had been kissing.

It took so, so much work not to visibly cringe every time I thought about that, and I couldn't *stop* thinking about it. When it had just been a wild dream, it had made me shiver because holy hell, I wanted that man.

Now that I knew it was real, I just wanted to crawl into a hole and die. Was there any coming back from this? Was Peyton angry? Embarrassed? Reporting me to the team right the hell now for sexual harassment?

Fuck. Fuck, fuck, *fuuuck*.

He and I needed to talk about this, and we needed to do

it soon. Straighten things out as best we could. Do whatever damage control I needed to do.

I ate as much as I could stomach, plus a little more just to sell my teammates the story that I was fine, perfectly fine, and had no earthly idea why Peyton had bailed the second I'd sat down. Then I casually left the banquet hall and headed upstairs. I had to resist the urge to sprint out of the elevator and down the hall, especially since some of my teammates were out and about.

Act casual. Don't let anyone suspect anything.

Finally, I was in my room. Now...

Now I just had to figure out what the hell to do.

Sitting on the edge of the bed, I chewed my lip and debated what to do next. We had to talk. We didn't have a lot of time before we needed to be on the bus, but we needed to clear the air before we had to be on the ice together. If we were off during practice, that could throw off the whole team and screw us for tonight.

I grabbed my phone, pulled up his contact, and sent him a text.

> Did something happen last night?

It seemed like a cowardly approach, but I wasn't sure what else to say. Asking if I'd kissed him would make things supremely weird if I hadn't. Telling him we needed to talk would just put him on edge.

As I stared at my stupid message, the word "Read" appeared underneath it, sending my heart into my throat. Then the three dots appeared, and I held my breath.

Peyton started and stopped typing a few times. Finally a message came through.

> We should do this face to face. I'll be up
> in 5.

My stomach knotted. Then it tightened even more when I realized he hadn't asked which room was mine.

Because he already knows.

I tossed my phone aside and buried my face in my hands.

Oh my fucking God.

I was still self-flagellating when there was a quiet knock at my door. I opened it, and all I had to do was make eye contact, and I knew which of my low-resolution memories were dreams and which had been very, very real. The uncomfortable expression. The renewed color. The way his eyes flicked away from mine.

I let him in and shut the door behind us. We stood in awkward silence for a long moment, several feet of space between us. He was by the TV stand, and my skin crawled; that was where it happened, wasn't it? I'd grabbed him and kissed him right there, pushing him back against—

Fuuuck.

Shoulders dropping, I looked away from him. "I'm sorry. Let's just get that out of the way upfront. I... Jesus." I raked a hand through my hair. "I am so sorry. I don't even remember everything, but I remember enough, and I want to say I don't do shit like that, but obviously I do."

"I get it." Peyton's voice was even. Not hostile, but not overly warm either. "You were pretty drunk, so you weren't yourself."

My face burned even hotter. I was glad he understood, but I couldn't say I felt any better. "I'm sorry." I didn't know what else to say.

"I know." He finally looked at me, his expression soft. "I need you to level with me about something."

I swallowed. Oh God, he was going to make me admit it out loud, wasn't he? Tell him how much was the alcohol and how much was real? I didn't even know how to answer that. I mean, I knew what the answer was, but how could I phrase it so things didn't get any weirder between us?

"You don't usually drink that hard," he said quietly. "Was..." He studied me, furrowing his brow and tilting his head a little. "Was there something making you drink like that?"

Oh. Hell.

I tore my gaze away from his and folded my arms tight across my chest. Couldn't he have asked about the kiss instead? Because I wasn't ready to talk about this. Not with him. Not with anyone. Not *ever*. "It was just a bad night."

"Yeah, I got that. But what was—"

"Leave it alone!" I snapped, meeting his eyes again.

He jumped, eyebrows climbing as he showed his palms. "Hey. Take it easy. I'm not interrogating you. I'm just saying, if there's something going on—"

"I had too much to drink and I did something stupid. I'm sorry for that. That's all there is to discuss."

I didn't expect—or understand—the hurt in his expression.

Was there something else? Something I was missing?

Cautiously, and without the anger in my voice now, I asked, "What, um... What all happened last night? Because my memory is..." I tightened my arms and shifted a little. "I don't remember much."

Peyton took a deep breath. "You were in the bar by yourself. I asked if you were heading up, and you realized what time it was, so you closed your tab and..." He waved a hand. "Anyway, when you tried to get up..." He chewed his lip.

There was a dreamlike memory that might've been that moment. Something about standing up and the whole room spinning until strong arms helped me upright.

"I got you back to your room," he said quietly. "Then you, um..." His cheeks were bright red and he refused to look at me.

"Jesus," I whispered. "I am so sorry."

"I know you are." He hesitated, then managed to reclaim eye contact. "I know it wasn't, you know, you. But *something* was going on last night."

I could read between those lines. He didn't mean something was going on between us. Something had driven me into a bottle, and he was worried about it.

Christ. I knew I should've gone up to my room to get drunk.

I sank onto the edge of the bed and rubbed the back of my neck. "I'm fine."

Why did I have a sudden sense of déjà vu? As if I'd been sitting right here, Peyton looming over me while I told him that same damn lie?

This time—somehow I was sure it hadn't played out this way last night—he sat beside me, keeping a few inches between us. I couldn't look at him, but I could feel him watching me intently.

"What's going on?" he pressed gently.

"I'm *fine*," I insisted.

He studied me for a painfully long moment. "Does this have anything to do with Leif?"

I flinched, my throat suddenly tight with the immediate threat of tears. *Absolutely not,* I told myself. Peyton was already too aware that I was a mess. He didn't need to see the waterworks too.

"It was a rough night." I stared at the floor as I spoke. "It's been hard, you know? I'm good most of the time, though." *Liar, liar.* I took a deep breath, then turned to him. "I just had a bad night. And morning. But I'm fine."

"You're fine." There was a hard edge to his voice now.

I bristled. "Yes."

"Everything is under control." Sarcasm didn't drip off his words—skepticism did. "You just... got shitfaced by yourself last night, in a hotel bar, and then—"

"I got drunk," I snapped. "Okay? Is that what you want to hear? It happens. But that doesn't mean I've got a problem or I'm out of control. It was *one* night."

"Yeah, you keep saying that, but nobody gets fucked up alone on a road trip when they're—"

"I'm sorry, am I not allowed to fuck myself up when we're not playing?" I glared right back at him. "*You* drink when we—"

"I don't get blackout drunk the night before a game," he threw back. "What would've happened if I hadn't wandered into the bar last night? Huh? How exactly were you getting back to your room?"

I hated myself for not having an answer to that.

Peyton watched me with a look of anger and... was that disgust? I couldn't read his expression, never mind his thoughts, but the way he was staring at me made my skin crawl. It made me want to puke just thinking about how last night had gone down.

Way to go, Calds. Blow any possible shot you ever had with this guy and *fuck things up with a teammate. 10/10, genius.*

"It was a bad night," I gritted out, masking my embarrassment with anger. "I appreciate the help getting back here, and I'm sorry about—" I shook my head. "I'm sorry about what happened. What I did. But it was just a bad night, all right?"

He still held my gaze. Still radiated anger, disgust, and God only knew what else. I was about to try again, but he spoke first. "We need to go." He got up and headed for the door. "The buses are waiting."

And then he stalked out before I could say another word.

CHAPTER 14
PEYTON

There was nothing in the world quite like trying to practice with a linemate I didn't even want to look at.

We had to look at each other and communicate—there was no avoiding it in this sport—but we only did as much as we absolutely had to. Throughout the morning skate, our interactions were as sharp as our skate blades and as cold as the ice beneath us.

I felt bad for Davis. It probably wasn't pleasant for any of our teammates, but our third linemate had to be feeling the worst of it. Whenever we weren't skating, he was stealing wary glances at the two of us. More than once, he either stood or sat between us, as if casually making himself into a barrier in case we were thinking of throwing gloves.

I didn't want to fight Avery. I was pissed at him, sure, but at most, I wanted to grab his shoulders, shake him, and talk some goddamned sense into him. I wanted him to understand what he was doing to himself and what he was going to do to this team.

But as my dad always said during the worst days of my mom's addiction, denial wasn't just a river in Egypt, and

Avery sounded like he was neck deep in it. Dad had told me addicts needed to hit rock bottom before they were willing to do anything about it. Before that... well, there wasn't much anyone could do.

After watching Jeff Richards hit rock bottom and keep on digging, though, I was scared for Avery. Scared that his rock bottom was well below what the League and the team would tolerate. I wanted to believe he could recover like my mom had, but what if he crashed and burned like Richards?

I stole another glance at Avery. Then I scanned the other faces on the ice.

Do any of you see what I see?

You all know him way better than I do.

He won't listen to me, but maybe he'll listen to one of you.

Was this what people meant when they felt like they were screaming in the middle of a crowded room and no one could hear them? Not that I was exactly saying or doing anything, but I was sure, all the way to my bones, that if I tried to draw anyone's attention to what was going on with Avery...

Shit. What the hell do I do?

Well, for the moment, I practiced with my teammates. I tried to focus—I really, really did, because hockey wasn't a sport you could play on autopilot. I was too distracted, though. Too focused on Avery.

I can't fucking take this.

After a light practice with the whole team, Coach turned it over to the power play coach for some special teams work.

The top power play unit went up against the top penalty kill until Davis managed to squeak the puck past

Ziggy and into the goal. While we caught our breath, the second units were up.

I took advantage of the moment and skated up to Avery. "Hey."

He turned frosty, slightly-red-around-the-edges eyes on me, and his jaw worked.

I dropped my voice a little. "You good?"

"I'm fine," he snapped just loud enough for me to hear. "Leave it alone, all right?"

Yeah, I hadn't heard that before from people who were trying to hide serious problems.

"Look, I'm just—"

"Leave it alone." And then he was gone, skating away to join Eminem and Mix at the other end of the zone.

I sighed, letting my shoulders sag beneath my pads. Jesus Christ.

Davis appeared beside me, and he glanced in the direction our linemate had gone. Vice low, he asked, "Everything cool with you and Calds?"

I tongued the backs of my teeth. "It's fine."

The upward flick of Davis's eyebrow called bullshit on that bald-faced lie. I felt guilty for it, too; I was feeding him the same line Avery had fed me. But what else could I say?

"It's fine," I repeated, and then gestured at our teammates who were finishing up the drill. "It's almost our turn."

Davis scowled, but right then, our power play coach blew the whistle, and we had to set up to run through the drill.

Avery and I exchanged glances. Even in that moment, that brief glimpse of his face, his expression seemed to vacillate between frosty anger and a plea. As if he were still pissed at me, but he was also begging me to—what? Not tell anyone? And which part did he want me to keep secret?

The part where he'd kissed me? Or where I'd had to half-drag his drunk carcass up to his room? Both?

I didn't even know. And I hated lying to our teammates, whether outright or by omission, but what else could I do? I couldn't break Avery's confidence. If I let it slip what happened last night, he could wind up seriously disciplined. It could permanently damage his reputation with the club and around the League. What if I was wrong and last night really had been a one-time thing? Because people had rough nights sometimes. People drank themselves senseless and did stupid things, and then moved on with their lives without issue.

At least, people did that who weren't clearly trying to pretend they weren't in emotional hell.

I couldn't get my head together. All through practice and my pregame routines, all through warmups that night, I was on another planet, distracted by my linemate who was also someplace else. That... did not bode well for a good game. When two of the top three forwards aren't functional, things tended to go awry.

And it just had to happen in front of my old teammates and fans, didn't it?

Though I'd been excited to go to Pittsburgh, I'd known I would miss my old teammates. Seeing them yesterday had been bittersweet. Taking the ice opposite them tonight... that was harder than I expected.

Like, a *lot* harder.

Not because they targeted me. Not because the fans booed every time I touched the puck. Not because it was just alien and weird to be on the opposite side of men who'd been my friends for so long.

No, the worst part was how bad I ached to put on a Detroit sweater again. It was how much I regretted coming to Pittsburgh, and how I wished I could go to the home locker room during intermissions instead of the visitor room.

More than I'd ever thought I would, I wanted to come back to Detroit and stay here. I wanted to go back to that familiar locker room where I knew what little drama there was, and where I knew the guys well enough that if someone went off the rails, I could *act*. I wouldn't just sit back and second guess myself.

Here in this locker room, on this team I'd been so excited to join...

I'd never felt more helpless or alone in my life.

I did mercifully get a break from all the tension between me and Avery, and that break came in the form of going home for Christmas.

A week after that incident in Detroit, I stepped off a plane in Omaha, got into a rental car, and drove out to my parents' place just over the state line in Council Bluffs, Iowa. They'd moved about five years ago; Dad said he didn't want to deal with the big yard anymore, but I'd always wondered if they'd just wanted to get away from the bad memories in my childhood home. There'd been some rough years in that place.

Now, they were in a split-level gray house with a somewhat smaller yard. It required a hell of a lot more work than the old one, though, especially after a tornado had ripped through the area. Dad never complained, which made me think the move had definitely been less about yardwork and more about ghosts.

As sad as I'd been that they'd sold my childhood home—there were, after all, good memories there, too—I liked the new place, and I liked the fresh start it had given everyone. Plus they had two guest rooms, so my sister and I could both stay at the house when we came to town. My brother and his family lived locally, and when I arrived the day before Christmas, my parents' house was loud and raucous. I never thought two kids—my three-year-old niece and two-year-old nephew—could make that much noise, but hoo boy, they could.

"Of course they can," Dad had mused last year. *"They're Halls."*

He had a point. There was a reason my siblings and I had been shoved into every sport imaginable as kids, and it wasn't in the hopes of scholarships or pro careers. My parents had just wanted to wear us the hell out.

It was good to be home. Good to see my family. Good to have a break from hockey even though I loved the sport.

Getting some space from Avery and *That Incident* was a relief, too, but that didn't mean I could shake it off completely. All through Christmas Eve, I felt like Avery had looked during Thanksgiving—mostly in the moment, but constantly tugged back to the apprehension and worry as if they were relentless physical aches.

It didn't help that I couldn't look at my mom without remembering everything we'd all gone through. Though she was sober now, and our family and my parents' marriage was long since back on the rails, there was no hiding how the years of heavy drinking had ravaged her. She was four years younger than my dad, but looked at least a decade older. She always seemed tired, which was apparently from all the problems she now had with her liver; there was probably a liver transplant in her future. Seeing her that way had always been heartbreaking, and it had also been a stark reminder of how close we'd come to losing her.

I couldn't look at her without thinking of how much worse Richards had to be by now, and that made me worry more about Avery. I just couldn't do a damn thing about him, which frustrated me, and...

God, this is going to drive me insane.

On Christmas Eve, my mom, brother, and sister-in-law were in the rec room trying to wear out the kids so they'd sleep and let Santa come. My sister had gone to bed, so Dad and I ended up alone in the living room, drinking coffee and enjoying the quiet while it lasted.

"So." Dad grinned. "How is everything in Pittsburgh?"

"It's..." I dropped my gaze and chewed my lip.

Dad's tone shifted to one of concern. "I thought you said you liked it there."

"No, no, I do. It's..." I sighed and looked at him again. "The guys are great. The city is great. But... I mean, you remember what happened before the season started, right?"

"*Ooh.* Yeah." He exhaled. "Those boys must be having a hell of a time with that."

"They are. Especially Avery Caldwell."

Dad cocked his head. "He's your linemate, isn't he?"

"Mmhmm. And the thing is, Erlandsson was his best friend. They were tight. And he's..." I hesitated. "He's not taking it well."

"I don't know if there's a way to take something like that well. Someone that young..." He trailed off.

"I know. What worries me, though..." I swallowed as I tried to put my thoughts into words. "Well, I mean, I think he's trying to bottle it up. Like, *literally* bottle it up."

Dad grimaced. "So he's drinking it away."

"I think so? I mean, a lot of the guys drink, you know? And I have no idea how much he drank before."

"Do your other teammates notice it?"

"I... maybe? Like I've seen them giving him looks sometimes, and they seem kind of worried about it, but no one says anything." I scratched the back of my head. "Maybe I'm just hyperaware of it."

"That's possible," Dad admitted. "Something like that—you're always going to notice it, even when it's not out of control."

I met his gaze. "Does that happen to you, too?"

Sighing, he nodded. "It does. I know not everyone has the same problem your mother does, but—well, I guess it's like someone who's had a housefire getting jumpy whenever they see a lit candle. It probably won't fall over and catch the place on fire, but you're sure gonna keep an eye on it in case is does."

"Yeah. Yeah, that's exactly what it feels like." I drummed my nails on the armrest. "And then there was what happened to Richards, and..."

Dad gave a soft, sympathetic laugh. "Between him and your mother, I don't blame you for being jumpy about people drinking."

"Especially someone who's going through something like Avery is. But, I mean, how would I even know if there's a problem? For all I know, he's coping with his grief and just has some tough moments here and there, but the drinking isn't an issue."

"It's possible. But the cracks will show eventually. If he's got a problem, he'll try to hide it, but he can't hide it forever. No one can."

I studied him. "How long did it take for the cracks to show with Mom?"

Dad sighed, shaking his head. "I don't know. I really don't. Mostly because I couldn't tell you how long they'd been showing before I finally started making myself notice them." He sat back, his gaze turning distant. "I still tell myself all the time things would've been a whole lot different if I'd stepped up sooner."

My stomach wound itself into an uncomfortable ball. "You didn't know how to handle it. You'd never done it before."

"No, but I knew something was wrong. I shouldn't have let it hurt you kids and our marriage for as long as I did before I stepped up."

My chest tightened. I always hated when he blamed himself for all the damage Mom's alcoholism had done, but it was even harder to stomach now. I didn't want to have that regret with my teammate. At the same time, though, I didn't want to jump the gun and see something that wasn't there.

"What do I do?" I asked.

Dad looked me in the eyes. "Right now, the best thing you can do is keep an eye on him. Look for those cracks. If they start showing... Well, you're a smart man. You do what you think is best, whether that's talking to him or going to your coaching staff." He reached across and gripped my wrist. "And remember, he won't like you. He won't be happy about it, and if shit starts falling apart, he might just blame you." Squeezing my wrist, he added, "Hold the line. You got it?"

Swallowing hard, I nodded. I remembered all too well the fights my parents had had in the wake of Dad finally putting his foot down. I remembered how much she'd blamed him, threatened to leave him, screamed at him.

Eventually, she'd begged his forgiveness. Then ours. She'd gone through rehab and come back to us, and though she'd had a couple of relapses, they'd been brief and relatively minor. As far as I knew, she'd been sober for at least the last four or five years.

There'd been history there, though. All the years married to my dad. All those years as our mom. I didn't have that history with Avery. A years-old crush and a few months as teammates didn't make for any kind of sturdy foundation. If I intervened and he didn't take it well, there was no guarantee he and I could salvage anything because there wasn't much to salvage.

Still, I was haunted by the darker years of my childhood and by watching a substance abuse problem destroy a teammate back in Detroit. If it became clear that Avery truly did have a problem, I'd take him hating me over the alternative.

"I got it," I told my dad. "I'll hold the line."

CHAPTER 15
AVERY

I had hoped that the brief holiday break would give both Peyton and me a chance to forget what happened in Detroit.

No such luck.

I knew the instant I walked into the locker room for our morning skate that he hadn't let it go. He met my gaze, then quickly dropped his and refused to look my direction again. *That* boded well for a pleasant practice.

Though I wasn't much better off, to be honest. The best parts of my whirlwind trip back to Abbottsford had been the annual tradition of getting hammered with my cousins on Christmas Eve. My dad, brother, and I had all shuffled downstairs on Christmas morning, eyes barely open as we sucked down coffee and tried not to collapse beneath the weight of our hangovers. That had been about twelve blissful hours of not caring about anything, followed by several hours of wondering if my head might explode. By the time I'd sobered up enough to care about much, I was jumping on a plane and heading back to Pittsburgh.

Now I was back here. Back in Pittsburgh. Back in the Whiskey Rebels' locker room.

Back in the place that reminded me of Leif and back in the crosshairs of my linemate's icy contempt and relentless pity.

For the millionth time, I wished I'd just gone up to my room in Detroit and gotten trashed in peace. I never got that drunk in public, and the fact that it was Peyton who'd seen me? Fuuuck.

Putting on my gear took more work than it should have. Even pulling on my base layer was a struggle because my hands were shaky and sweaty, and my mind was just... not here. It didn't help when Peyton got up and clomped out of the room toward the sheet. Was I imagining the extra sharpness in his steps? The anger in his gait?

Maybe. Maybe not. Did anything make sense anymore?

I sighed as I dropped onto the bench and started putting on my shinpads. I hated the mixed bag of bullshit that set up shop in my brain every time I looked at Peyton. Every time I thought about him, honestly, but especially when I looked at him. When we were in the same room, the same plane.

The same *bar*.

I cringed inwardly. That night he'd taken me back to my hotel room weighed miserably on my shoulders, the humiliation burning in my chest. I hated the shame that burrowed behind my ribs whenever he asked me if I was okay, or when he looked at me like he *wanted* to ask because he suspected something was wrong.

Oh, there *was* something wrong, but he'd never understand. Nobody would. They'd all think I was a mess—mostly because I *was* a mess—and then they'd know I wasn't worthy of a Whiskey Rebels sweater. Especially not one with a C on it.

And the mess just got messier the more I thought about it, because sometimes he'd catch my eye, and an entirely different but equally unpleasant feeling would sweep through me: how much I wanted him.

God, he was so damn hot. Of course I'd always loved the way hockey players were built—lean, sculpted muscle was my absolute catnip. Peyton was on the broader end of the spectrum for guys in our sport; he wasn't built like a football player or anything, but his shoulders were a little wider, and his hips and thighs—oh my God. The things a man could do to me with a physique like that? Jesus Christ, I hadn't been laid in way too long, and I'd have chewed off a limb to have someone like him take me for a ride.

But every time that zing of attraction took hold, it was followed immediately by an avalanche of embarrassment and self-loathing. Yeah, he was hot as hell, but in what universe would he be even slightly interested in me after what had happened in that hotel room? Even if he'd been totally onboard—both into me and game for hooking up with a teammate—I'd seen to it that that ship sailed, sank, and vanished through a wormhole. Snowball's chance in hell didn't begin to describe the odds of Peyton ever laying a hand on me.

Damn shame, too, even in those moments when looking at him had rage flaring in my chest.

As I continued gearing up, all those conflicting thoughts colliding inside my head, Leif's voice came to the surface: *"A hundred bucks plus three steak dinners on the road says you screw him before the season's over."*

Fuck.

I wasn't sure if I wanted to cry or throw up. Maybe both.

But I couldn't. Sometimes I did one or the other, but right now, I had to put on my gear, get on the ice, and convince everyone who was looking that I still had any business on this team.

No, I wouldn't be losing that bet, and not just because the man who'd offered the wager wasn't here to collect. There was no way Peyton wanted a piece of me now. Early on, I'd caught him stealing glances at me, and there'd been that glimmer of hope that the attraction was mutual.

One drink too many, though. One stupid, drunk mistake in a hotel room.

And now I had to keep playing alongside the man my best friend had bet would be in my bed before the season was out, knowing that *at best*, Peyton looked at me with pity. That didn't bode well for teammates, especially linemates, and it definitely didn't pave the way toward anything sexy or affectionate.

One minute I hated him for what happened that night and everything he said after. Couldn't he have just left me to drink myself stupid in peace?

The next minute, though, I hated myself. Why hadn't I just stayed in my damn room? So what if I'd already gone through the minibar? I could've ordered more booze. Hell, I could've DoorDashed more.

But no, I'd taken my ass down to the bar, and Peyton hadn't been able to just walk by and leave me alone, and now...

Now we could barely look at each other.

What the hell was I supposed to do about *any* of that?

My focus sharpened when I went out for warmups that night. We were playing in Boston, and these assholes had knocked us out of the playoffs last year. It hadn't been pretty, either; things had gone all right for the first two games of the series, but then they'd started injuring our players. They'd been out for blood, and they'd gotten it, with the refs only calling some of them as minor penalties instead of ejecting players and fining or suspending them. It was a shitshow and a half.

By the fourth game, three of our forwards and two defensemen were down with head injuries. In games five and six, we lost both goalies. The next thing we knew, were in an elimination game with five kids from the farm team skating, our third-string goalie in the net, and a nineteen-year-old backup goalie who'd never played at this level before, never mind in the playoffs.

They'd wiped the floor with us.

Now we were healthy and out for redemption. And revenge. Revenge was definitely on the list.

They weren't just going to roll over and take it, though. As soon as the puck dropped, the game turned physical. Hard checks. At least three or four crosschecks that didn't get called.

Okay, fine. If the refs weren't going to call penalties—prison rules!

A defenseman tried to poke-check the puck away from me. I slammed him hard into the boards—not high, not dangerously, but definitely enough to leave him in a heap while I continued into the offensive zone. A minute later, someone slammed Davis into the boards, which resulted in a brief scuffle, but no gloves came off and no whistle was blown. Boston snagged possession and broke away, and Davis wisely ditched the scrum to help us on defense. Then during a commercial break, Astala and someone from Boston started yapping at each other, which led to them dropping gloves. The video must've been hilarious for people watching at home—two players going at it while the ice crew skated around them with their snow shovels.

After sitting for five minutes, Astala and the other guy came out of the box during another stoppage, and there was still two and a half minutes to go in the first period.

The fans were getting their money's worth, that was for damn sure.

The second period started much the same way. Lots of checking, pushing, shoving, and crosschecking. And we were moving the puck around and getting scoring chances during that, too. We'd come out of the first period with a 2-0 lead, thanks in part to Ziggy standing on his head, and now we were as determined to make it 3-0 as Boston was to get on the board and catch up with us.

Seconds after yet another faceoff, a whistle shrieked at the same time there was a ripple of shock from the crowd.

Oh, no. What now?

I turned, and the panic that tore through me almost knocked me off my skates.

Blood pounded in my ears, the only sound in the otherwise silent arena.

Someone was down, one of our guys and an opposing player crouched beside him as Trews waved to our bench for help.

Oh. *Shit*.

I skated closer, and just before Evan got to him, I saw the number on his sleeve.

Nineteen.

Peyton.

Evan crouched beside him. Peyton was moving, at least;

hands and feet, which was always a good sign. He was on his side, though, curled in on himself. That could mean any number of things. Head injury? Ribs? Wind knocked out of him?

Evan still had his towel over his shoulder, so no blood. A good sign, but it also left a lot of questions.

Come on. How bad is he?

Please get up, Peyton.

Please, please get up.

I didn't think my heart had ever beat as fast as it did in that moment, and it was only when my vision started darkening around the edges that I realized I'd forgotten to breathe.

Shit. Shit, I needed to pull it together. There was nothing I could do to help Peyton, and falling to pieces myself wouldn't help him or anyone else.

I skated in some small circles, ostensibly to keep my legs loose. Mostly I just needed to move. I couldn't stay still and watch Evan tending to Peyton.

I didn't watch the replay. I wanted to know Peyton was all right, but I didn't want to watch the slow-motion video of whatever had happened. Judging by the collective gasp that went up... No. No, I did *not* need to see that.

I took some slow, deep breaths as I skated, trying to calm myself the hell down. Injuries happened all the time. Guys went down all the time. This was just one of those things that came with hockey. Sure, I always worried when it was one of my guys—hell, I worried when it was an *opposing* player—but this season... fuck me. The second a Whiskey Rebel went down, I was a panicky mess on the brink of hyperventilating.

Get a grip, Caldwell. What the hell?

I had to get a grip. Had to pull it together. Nobody

needed to see a player, never mind the team captain, falling apart just because someone got hurt.

You're the captain, Calds.

Show the guys, the fans, and the damn cameras *that you can handle this.*

I could handle this. I'd handled it for years. Why couldn't I calm myself down this time?

Right then, just like they had the night Eminem had gone down, the crowd started applauding and all the players started tapping their sticks. I turned, and sure enough, Peyton was slowly being helped to his feet.

He waved to the crowd, but he didn't straighten all the way up. He stayed doubled over, and Davis and Trews each held one of his arms as they slowly led him off the ice.

Then he and Evan disappeared down the tunnel.

Now everyone was setting up again. Time to get back to hockey.

At least Coach called Davis and me back to the bench, sending out the third line in our place. Sitting there, still trying to get my head together, I watched Mix win the face-off, and the action continued like normal.

Like goddamned normal.

While Peyton was back there. Being evaluated? Getting on an ambulance? What the hell?

I *hated* that, when an injured player disappeared and we all had to carry on like normal. It was too damn distracting. How bad was it? Was he on the way to the hospital? Or was someone just going to give him some ice and call it good?

Could someone please tell me before I had to concentrate on hockey again?

Maybe I should've watched the replay after all. Maybe I should've—

"Hey. Calds." Davis bumped me with his shoulder. "You still here?"

I shook myself. "Yeah. Yeah, I'm, uh..." I exhaled. "Do you think Halls is okay?"

"I'm sure he is. He's probably in a world of hurt, but he'll be fine."

I raised my eyebrows. He raised his.

Gesturing at the Jumbotron, he asked, "Didn't you see the replay?"

"No, I..." I swallowed. "I didn't see it."

"Oh. Yeah, it was ugly." He nodded toward someone on the ice. "That asshole Larsson hit him in the crotch."

I reflexively pressed my legs together. "Shit."

"I know, right?" Davis shuddered. "Dude better hope Halls is done for the night, or he's going to get his ass beat."

"Maybe he still should," I growled.

Davis grunted.

I found Larsson on the ice again and tracked him as he tried for a scoring chance. Yeah, odds were good that he was getting a beatdown tonight. Since the refs hadn't bothered to call a penalty—well, that was where the rest of us stepped in to police ourselves.

Before this game was over, someone in black and gold would make sure Larsson thought twice before hitting a man in a tender spot again.

"Calds." Coach caught my arm just before I stepped into the locker room for the second intermission.

I halted. "Hmm?"

He glanced around to be sure we were alone. Then he inclined his head and looked me right in the eyes. "You've never been like this. I've seen you bounce right back and play after someone's left in an ambulance, but lately, every time someone goes down..." His brows knitted. "What's going on?"

I avoided his gaze, which wasn't easy when it was boring into me like that. "I'm... I'm good. It just stresses me out, you know?"

"I know it does. But we have to be able to play through it, and you've never had a problem with that."

I finally met his eyes, and the subtle softness in his brought a lump into my throat. He didn't ask it out loud, but I heard it like the goal horn had just sounded:

Is this about Leif?

Christ. Everyone thought I was hanging by a thread because of that, didn't they? And why shouldn't they? After the way I fell apart at the home opener—yeah, I'd be questioning it too.

"I'm fine," I insisted, ignoring the way my voice tried to crack. "I just—I feel a lot more responsibility for the guys now, you know?" I tapped the C on my chest.

Coach glanced at the letter, and his lips pulled tight. I didn't think he believed me. I didn't even know if I believed me. It was just the only explanation that made any sense.

He sighed. "I saw the way you were looking at Larsson during your shifts." He shook his head. "*Don't*, Calds. Just don't."

There was no point in playing stupid or arguing with him. I knew what he was saying—do not get into a goddamned fight tonight. Which... fair. Coach wasn't one of the old-school coaches who liked a lot of fighting and physicality. He wanted some grit, of course, but he was more focused on things like precision in offense and defense. Fights didn't score points.

They could turn the tide sometimes and shift the team's attitude. Shake up the crowd and give them a bloodthirsty vibe that could help drive us offensively.

But not every dirty play warranted a retaliatory fight, especially because the resulting penalty could be costly.

So... fine.

"Okay," I said. "I'll... I won't fight him."

Coach nodded sharply. Then he tilted his head toward the locker room, dismissing me.

When I stepped into the room, I finally let go of a relieved breath.

Not only was Peyton upright and moving, he was pulling his gear back on. He wasn't standing completely straight—there was a subtle hunch to his posture—but he clearly intended to return to the game.

I'd known he wasn't seriously injured. Getting hit down south hurt like a motherfucker, but didn't *usually* mean major damage. If I had to guess, he'd be sending a hand-written thank-you and an expensive bottle of wine to the company that manufactured his athletic cup.

I clomped over to his stall. "Hey. You really coming back next period?"

"Of course." He met my gaze with a startled expression, as if he were surprised I was talking to him. Which... okay. Fine. But then he shook it off and flashed me a grin. "They'll have to work harder than that to put me on the bench."

Rolling with the *this is fine, everything is fine* vibe, I raised my eyebrows. "I don't think I'd challenge them to do *that* harder."

He winced, and I thought he shuddered. "Yeah. Fuck that." He tugged at his sleeve. "But I want to beat them, and I want to score on them."

Okay, yeah, that sounded like a hockey player. We all played through all kinds of injuries; as long as we weren't bleeding everywhere or didn't have a concussion, no one would stop us.

Though we all had our limits. I'd probably still be curled on the ice in a fetal position after an injury like that, but clearly Peyton was more angry and determined than anything. More power to him.

I clapped his shoulder gently. "Well, let's get out there and get you that goal."

He flashed me a lopsided grin that made my spine tingle, and he held up his fist. "Let's do it."

I bumped his fist, then went back to my own stall to cool off and hydrate. And maybe catch my breath from talking to him about something other than the things we were both avoiding talking about.

Was that hope I was feeling? Hope that maybe we could put that night behind us and act like teammates again?

God, please... Because I don't know how to fix this other-wise, and I don't know how to handle the awkwardness.

I'd roll with it for now. Act like everything was normal, interact with him like any other teammate, and see if he followed suit. Sometimes that was all it took, especially among guys who didn't have a clue what else to do.

After intermission, we headed back out onto the ice.

Peyton was walking (and then skating) a touch gingerly, but he was holding his own. Probably best not to make him sprint more than necessary, though.

I skated up to Davis as we all warmed up again. "Hey. Let's keep the breakaways to you and me." I tipped my head toward Peyton. "Maybe not have him doing the longer sprints?"

Davis's eyebrows shot up. Then he glanced toward Peyton and nodded. "Okay. Yeah. Yeah, we can... That makes sense." He turned to me again. "So you guys are cool now?"

I shrugged that away as if there'd never been any question. "We're fine."

He eyed me skeptically but didn't push the issue.

Shortly after that, it was game on again, and I had to admit, it was probably just as well Coach had warned me off fighting Larsson. Because I *really* wanted to fight Larsson. Every time I so much as glimpsed his number, his name, or his stupid face, I saw red.

I was on thin ice with Coach, though. He didn't like how much I'd been fighting lately, or how many penalties I'd been taking, and that conversation outside the locker room had been about more than just dispensing some justice on Larsson.

Fine. *Fine.*

I wouldn't throw gloves with Larsson. I might check him. Maybe even risk a crosscheck just to get my point across. Absolutely chirp the shit out of him. One way or another, this game wasn't ending without him knowing damn well he'd screwed up.

In the end, I didn't lay a hand on Larsson.

Trews, however, checked him hard into the boards. Harder than necessary, yes, though not what I'd call dirty.

It pissed off Larsson something fierce, and he punched Trews.

The whistle blew before anyone could drop gloves. Larsson not only got a penalty, he got a double minor, since it was deemed unnecessary roughness. Maybe they thought the blood was enough to warrant the extra penalty. Maybe they were just as fed up with Larsson as the Whiskey Rebels were.

It was also possible they thought putting him in the box for four minutes would be enough to let us all simmer down enough that we didn't kill him.

Either way, he was mad, Trews was fine, and we extended our 3-0 lead to 5-0. That last goal? A beautiful top shelf from Peyton, with an assist from Trews.

Perfect.

CHAPTER 16
PEYTON

We'd played in Boston tonight, but now we were back at the hotel instead of heading to the airport. The original plan had been to fly to Buffalo right after the game so we could play there the day after tomorrow. Unfortunately, Buffalo was getting hammered with "don't even think about flying in here" weather, and the hotel in Boston had been able to accommodate us for another night, so... here we were. Tomorrow afternoon, assuming the weather let up, we'd fly to Buffalo, but for now, we could just chill in the hotel bar.

Chill. Yeah, right. There was nothing "chill" about a hockey team still vibrating with excitement after a decisive win.

"To owning Boston on their own ice!" Eminem said, holding up glass.

"Cheers!" We all clinked our glasses and bottles together, then took deep pulls from them.

"All hail Ziggy!" Baddy added. "Third shutout of the season!"

Everyone roared, and Davis slapped our big goalie on

his narrow shoulders hard enough that Ziggy almost choked on his beer.

"Hey!" Ziggy elbowed him in the pec. "Don't spill my fucking beer!"

"Well, protect it." Davis grinned wide. "That's your job!"

Ziggy just groaned, gave Davis a shove, and drank his beer.

I was sitting on Davis's other side, across the long table from Avery and Eminem. The mood in the hotel bar was raucously happy—we'd shut out Boston 5-0, which the guys were saying felt like repentance after Boston had knocked Pittsburgh out of the playoffs last season. I hadn't been part of that, but Boston had swept my team, kicking our asses 3-1, 8-4, 4-2, and that incredibly embarrassing 6-0 just before the playoffs. They were a good team—had made it to the Eastern Conference Finals and barely lost that series—and it always felt good to hand them their asses.

Granted they were missing two of their top six to injuries, had lost their star left winger and one of their tandem goalies to free agency, *and* there was a nasty stomach bug running through their locker room, so they weren't exactly playing at their normal caliber.

Still, a win was a win, a shutout was a shutout, and beating Boston was always sweet, so... bottoms up.

Of course, I could've done without getting my ass knocked around. I was still hurting from that in places nobody wanted to be hurting, and my teammates didn't even give me shit about it. There was a little grumbling about how the other guy should've taken a penalty, but that was it. Maybe the refs hadn't seen it. Maybe they just didn't think it should be illegal to hit a guy between the legs with a stick. I didn't know. I hadn't really been paying attention to much of anything in the minutes after that except how bad it hurt and how close I'd been to puking.

In the locker room, Evan had assured me there was no shame in sitting the rest of the game. I wasn't injured per se, but I didn't imagine anyone would've judged me if I'd said, *"Fuck this, I'm going to go ice my balls for the next few hours."*

That was still an option now. The dull ache below my belt was unpleasant to say the least, and the queasiness hadn't fully abandoned ship. Fortunately, I knew that would ease up on its own. *Un*fortunately, I knew that from experience.

Despite the relentless ache and nausea, I sipped a Coke in the bar with my teammates. I was too wired after the game to go to sleep, and I enjoyed the camaraderie, especially after a win.

"C'mon, Halls," Eminem said. "At least let us buy you a drink. Feels like we owe you after you took one of the team."

Half the guys at the table squirmed uncomfortably— probably sympathy pain.

"I'm good." I raised my Coke. "You guys can buy on a night when I feel like getting trashed."

"Usually I'd say it's a one-time deal." Eminem shook his head. "But if I took one to the nuts like that, I'd expect all you assholes to buy me drinks *and* dinner for the rest of the season. So... deal."

There were some grunts and nods.

"Is that all it takes to get free food out of you guys?" I grinned. "Well, damn. It's almost worth it."

That got some laughs. And some more squirming.

Right then, a server came by to check on us, and a few people ordered another round.

Including Avery.

The glass in his hand wasn't even empty yet, but the way he gestured with it as he and the server exchanged a few words, he was definitely ordering another.

Wasn't that like his third or fourth?

It's none of your business, Peyton. Ignore it.

But then my dad's voice said, *"Hold the line, Peyton."*

Fuck my life.

I'd been too young to notice the signs of my mom's drinking—or, well, too young to realize what they'd meant—but they were so obvious in hindsight.

It was during my second season as a pro that I'd seen those signs again in someone else. Richards had been as slick as my mom about dismissing hangover symptoms as allergies or a difficult night sleeping. Like her, he'd gaslit people around him into believing, *"No, I'm still working on the same beer you saw me drinking an hour ago,"* when it was actually his fourth or fifth. The times they did drink to excess in front of people, they still insisted it wasn't a problem. Mom had been "working nonstop for weeks on end" and *"just needed to cut loose for once."* Richards had scoffed that *"you'd be getting this shitfaced too if your ex-wife just told you she's going for full custody."*

I'd accepted everything they'd said right up until they'd hit rock bottom. Dad had told Mom it was either rehab or divorce. Richards had spiraled down and down and down as his messy divorce progressed, and after his ex-wife had been granted full custody, he'd wound up in the hospital with alcohol poisoning.

Mom had eventually recovered, and she'd even stayed married to my dad. Richards's story had gone from bad to worse. The team had given him much the same ultimatum my dad had given my mom—player assistance program or a terminated contract—and he'd responded by getting a DUI.

After his contract was summarily terminated, he wrapped his car around a lamppost. He'd survived, but any hope of ever playing hockey again was dashed thanks to his injuries, and then came the painkiller addiction.

I had no idea how or where he was now.

And every time I thought of him, I was almost overcome with guilt. Could I have stepped in sooner? Could I have noticed *something* and told *someone* and maybe gotten him help before things had gotten so far out of hand? I'd had more therapy to cope with that guilt than I'd had to deal with my mom's alcoholism, and that was saying something.

Now here I was, sitting across from a man who was waving the same flags Mom and Richards had waved, and I was paralyzed. I didn't know what if anything I was supposed to do.

As surreptitiously as I could, I studied Avery. Was I just jumping the gun because I knew he had a *reason* to dive into a bottle? Was everything about him and his drinking perfectly normal, but I was edgy because of my past experiences and because I knew he was grieving?

What the hell do I do?

As the server came back and placed the glass in front of Avery, my stomach somersaulted. It wasn't like I'd never been around hockey players getting drunk. Hell, I'd done it myself plenty of times, especially when we had a light schedule the next day, though I wasn't above showing up hungover-but-functional to practice.

Avery started to take a drink, but he glanced my way, then did a double take and locked eyes with me. "What?"

Oh, shit. Was I wearing my worry on my face?

"Uh." I cleared my throat and shook my head. "Nothing. I was—"

"If you've got a problem, Halls," he said with sudden anger. "Just say it."

I blinked. "I didn't say a—"

"Yeah, your face said it out loud." He slammed the glass down on the table, sending some drops flying onto his hand. "Do you think I need a babysitter or something?"

"What? No! I—"

"Then why are you side-eying every goddamned thing I drink?" He picked up his glass. "If you've got a problem, just fucking—"

"I don't have a problem with anything," I snapped. "But if you're so damn defensive just because I looked at your drink, then maybe—"

"Oh, get wrecked." He took a deep swallow from his glass. He grimaced as the alcohol went down, then glared at me again, renewed fire in his eyes. "If you've got something to say, then either say it, or fuck off so the rest of us can—"

"Hey! *You* came at *me* sideways, not the other way around, so—"

"Whoa, hey guys," Baddy said, alarm written all over his face. "Everybody chill out, okay?"

"I'm chill!" Avery said, the faintest hint of a slur in his voice, and he flailed a hand toward me. "You want someone to chill, talk to—"

"Hey, hey." Eminem slung an arm around Avery's shoulders and gave his chest a firm pat. "C'mon, Calds. Take a breath, all right?"

Beside me, Davis nudged me with my elbow. "Might not be a bad time to call it a night."

I didn't get the feeling he was trying to boot me out, just do damage control like Baddy and Eminem were. And he was getting up too, so he was probably going to leave with me.

I didn't argue. I pulled a ten out of my wallet and tossed it on the table; it would more than cover my soda and tip. Then I left with Davis, pretending not to notice Avery's angry voice calling out something at my back. At least my heart was pounding too hard and the bar was too loud for me to make out the words. The drunk anger was more than enough.

Davis and I walked in silence across the lobby. Thank God, there weren't a lot of people out and about this time of night, and we didn't have to wait for an elevator.

As the doors closed us inside, I sagged against the wall and scrubbed a hand over my face. "Jesus H. Christ."

"Calds?" Davis asked.

I nodded and turned to my teammate. "Not gonna lie— I'm worried about him."

"Me too," Davis admitted. "He hasn't been himself since..." He winced and shook his head.

Yeah, I could put those pieces together. "It really messed him up, didn't it? Losing Early?"

Grimacing, Davis nodded. "Yeah. Fucked us all up, but Calds?" He whistled. "Not gonna lie—I was surprised he even made it to training camp. I was sure he was going to take a leave of absence or something."

Right then, the elevator stopped, and we stepped out into the hallway, but neither of us continued toward our respective rooms.

Gaze distant, Davis said, "Sometimes I think he'd have been better off if he'd taken some time. But then I think about how much hockey and being around the team helped me after the funeral, and... I mean, it's probably the only thing that's kept him upright, you know?"

I nodded slowly. "I think it's the only thing that kept a

lot of you going." I hesitated, then added, "To tell you the truth, I don't know how any of you have managed."

"We have to," he whispered. "Early's gone, but we still have contracts and fans. And the alternative is just sitting at home thinking about how much it sucks that he's gone." He worked his jaw for a moment, then cleared his throat, and his voice was a little threadbare as he said, "Early would want us to keep going."

I nodded again, unsure what to say.

Davis sighed, and his shoulders dropped as he gazed back at the elevator doors. "He'd want us to keep going... but man, what happens if someone *can't* keep going after that?"

He didn't have to specify which someone he meant.

And I was glad he apparently didn't expect an answer out of me.

Because I had no idea.

CHAPTER 17
AVERY

I'd give Coach Tabakov credit—he was discreet.

I mean, I liked him anyway. He was a great head coach, and we'd all thrown him a party when the GM had extended his contract for three more years. The man knew hockey, and he knew how to coach.

But I'd always particularly liked that he preferred the *"praise in public, criticize in private"* approach to things. If the whole team was a mess, he'd dress us down right there on the ice during practice or in the locker room during intermission. If the problem was with one player, though, it was always behind closed doors. I knew for a fact he'd addressed things with my teammates, but I never knew when or where it happened.

And when he sat down for a face-to-face with me, it was always with as little fanfare as possible. A text message. Catching me when I was alone in the locker room. Joining me while I walked around the ice level before a game.

Today, as I was finishing up breakfast, he came by where I was sitting and tapped his knuckle on the table. "Chat with me before we get on the buses, Captain."

The "Captain" was, I guessed, a way of letting my teammates at the table know this was business as usual. He and I had one-on-ones all the time now that I was captain, and he'd done it with Leif, too.

From the way my teammates focused on their breakfasts and didn't look at me or Coach... I had a feeling the subterfuge didn't work this time.

"Yeah, Coach," I said. "I'll, um... I'll be done here in a couple of minutes."

He gave a sharp nod and left.

Eminem, Baddy, Ziggy, and Davis didn't look up from their food. They didn't say a word. In fact, none of us had said much since we'd sat down—the whole banquet hall was unusually quiet—and I didn't think it was just because we were all nursing hangovers. The awkward near-silence was uncomfortable as all hell.

So was the fact that Peyton hadn't joined us like he usually did. He was a few tables over, back resolutely turned to me, having a hushed conversation with Laramie, Trews, and Astala. Even the guys at other tables who hadn't been at the bar last night had clearly picked up on the vibe in the room; they exchanged *"WTF?"* looks and peered at the rest of us with uneasy eyes.

This was my fault.

Peyton's too, for silently judging me across the table. What was his problem, anyway? But I should've dealt with it privately. Going off on him in the bar in front of our teammates—not my best moment as the Whiskey Rebels' captain.

Suddenly my own breakfast was even less appetizing than it had been when I'd sat down.

"I'm gonna go pack," I muttered to my silent teammates. No one tried to stop me, and I got up to bus my dishes.

I wondered if I imagined the collective relief in the room as I was walking out.

I texted Coach to let him know I was heading back up to my room and would meet him in fifteen minutes.

As I was riding the elevator up, my phone pinged.

COACH

Come to my room. 1122.

My stomach somersaulted. That sounded... ominous. And why was he only calling me in and not Peyton? Yeah, I was the captain, and yeah, I was the one to go off half-cocked in the bar, but it wasn't like I'd been pissed at the wall.

Maybe they were going to have a talk in private some other time. I just hoped this wasn't all falling on my stupid shoulders.

On the eleventh floor, I found Coach's room and tapped on the door. He let me in without a word.

His things were already packed. His suit jacket was draped over the handle of his carry-on bag, and as he started tying his tie in the full-length mirror, he said, "Have a seat, Calds."

I took one of the chairs by the window.

Coach finished tying his tie. Then he came over and took the other chair. There was a small round table between us, and he rested his hand on it, drumming his fingers as he studied me. "I heard about the incident in the bar last night."

I flinched and broke eye contact. "Yeah. I, uh..." I scratched the back of my head. "It wasn't a good night. But I'm okay now."

"Are you?"

I chanced a look at him. "You don't think I am?" All

right, that was a stupid question. As much as I'd been trying my damnedest to keep anyone from noticing that I was far from okay, they weren't stupid. And I wasn't as slick as I needed to be. Especially when I was drunk.

"I, um..." I dropped my gaze again. "I shouldn't have had that much to drink. It, um... It won't happen again."

"That's what I'm worried about," he said gently. "That it *will*."

"It won't," I insisted. "One drink when I'm out with the guys and that's it." I shook my head. "I just... got a little carried away last night."

"I'm not as worried about the drinking."

I searched his eyes. "You're not?"

Coach shook his head. "Hockey players drink. It's..." He waved his hand. "As long as none of you are driving and it's not affecting your health or your hockey, I don't care if you drink."

"Oh." I supposed that made sense. I'd seen Coach get absolutely smashed at parties before, and once in a while, he'd gotten a little loud and rowdy when we were celebrating a win. If rumors were to be believed, he'd been a legendary party animal during his years as a player. So... yeah, I didn't imagine he cared too much if we drank.

"My concern," he went on, "is that altercation between you and Hall."

I stared at the floor as heat rose in my face. "Yeah, that was..." I didn't know how to explain it away.

"It's not *just* that," Coach went on. "You're not yourself lately." It wasn't an accusation. I kind of wished it was, though; if anything, the words were wrapped in concern, and I couldn't deal with that right now.

"I'm fine," I told him, but the words limped out of my mouth.

"You're not. Calds..." He sighed, shaking his head. "I know losing Erlandsson has been hard for you. It's been hard on everyone, but especially you. We can—"

"I can still play hockey," I snapped. "And I can still lead this team."

Coach's eyebrows rose. The skepticism bit right into my ego, but even worse was the expression that asked which of us I was trying to convince.

Dropping my gaze, I pushed out a breath and rubbed the back of my neck. "It's been tough, okay? I won't pretend it hasn't. It's..." Damn it. I was not going to cry. Not right here in front of my coach, least of all while I was trying to convince him I had any business wearing a Rebels' jersey, never mind the C.

Coach leaned forward a little, and his voice was still full of concern and empathy. "No one's saying you can't play or that you can't lead. But you're struggling."

I had to work so fucking hard not to lose it, gritting my teeth against that lump in my throat and fighting the waver that wanted to creep into my voice. It didn't help that my head was still throbbing and my stomach was still unhappy. Because I was hungover. Because I'd had too much to drink last night. Because...

I closed my eyes and sighed. Who was I even kidding?

"I *am* struggling," I admitted, meeting my coach's gaze again. "I can't... I mean, everything I do, everywhere I go—I just see Leif everywhere." I swallowed hard to push that lump out of the way. "Moving forward—it's hard."

"I know." His voice was soft, as was his expression, and he studied me for a painfully long moment. "There is— listen, no one is going to push you this way, so if you don't want to, then..." He showed his palms. Lowering them, he continued, "If a change of scenery is what you need, I don't think anyone will hold it against you."

"A change of—" My spine straightened. "You want the team to *trade* me?"

"No," he said quickly. "The fans, the front office, the coaching staff, your teammates—we would all be more than happy to have you retire as a Whiskey Rebel."

I inclined my head. "But...?"

"But if going somewhere else is what you need to take care of yourself..." He gave an apologetic half-shrug. "That *is* an option."

As much as being reminded of Leif at every turn was painful, the thought of leaving this team—leaving the city and my teammates—was a gut punch.

"No," I gritted out. "No, I don't want to leave Pittsburgh *or* the Whiskey Rebels." I rolled my shoulders and sat up straighter. "I'll be fine. Yes, it's hard right now. This new normal—it fucking sucks, and I don't know how to get used to it. But I'm not leaving." I swallowed again. "Not unless the front office makes me leave."

"They won't." He sounded very, very certain. "None of us want you to leave. But we also know you're going through hell after losing someone who was like a brother to you."

That almost made me break down right there in Coach's hotel room. I had to choke back the emotions, and I swore I almost choked *on* them.

I'd already lost Leif. I couldn't lost this team, too. The Pittsburgh Whiskey Rebels were my *life*. Plus they were depending on me. They were going through hell, too. I needed them and they needed me, goddammit. Yeah, trades and free agency happened, and a lot of players ended up on multiple teams in their careers. It was always a possibility.

But as long as I had any say in the matter, I didn't want to go anywhere.

Don't cut me off from the only connection I still have to—

"I don't want to leave this team," I ground out.

"Then you won't," he said without hesitation. "It's only an option if it's what you need to take care of yourself. I'm not telling you this because I want you to leave—I'm telling you because I want you to know that if you *need* to leave, no one in Pittsburgh will hold that against you."

"I don't," I whispered. "I think it's the only thing keeping me sane."

From the subtle arch of his eyebrow, I suspected he was wondering how much *anything* was succeeding in keeping me sane these days.

"I'll be fine," I insisted. "Last night—it was a bad night. I got carried away and lost my head. But I'm focused and committed to this team."

Coach nodded as I spoke. "And what about the situation with Halls?"

I winced. "I, uh... I should talk to him."

"Is there a problem there that I need to know about?"

"No. No, it was just..." I sat back and huffed a dry laugh. "I was just drunk off my ass last night, and he was in the wrong place at the wrong time." I shook my head. "I'll sort it out with him." I wasn't looking forward to that conversation—groveling was not my strong point—but it was my responsibility. I had to unfuck everything from last night.

Coach watched me a moment longer, then sighed. "This team needs you, Calds, but we need you to take care of yourself, too. All right?"

"I will." I wasn't sure if I was lying. "Last night—that won't happen again." That was the truth; I would make sure I didn't screw up like that again.

Or like the night Peyton had half-carried me into my hotel room. The night I'd drunkenly kissed him. Ugh. Jesus. I was lucky he hadn't gone to the front office over that—the getting blackout drunk on a road trip and the drunk, unprovoked kiss. I'd have been screwed if he had.

Yeah. Definitely had to make things right with him. *Stat.*

"I'll talk to Peyton," I assured Coach. "And I'll be fine."

He studied me like he wasn't sure if he should press, or if he should just let me have enough rope to hang myself. Then, with a long-suffering dad sigh, he said, "All right. But come talk to someone—anyone—if you need help. Please?"

"I will."

He let me go after that, and I hurried toward my own room, praying none of my teammates happened into the hall until I was safely inside.

Someone must've been listening, because the hallway remained deserted long enough for me to let myself into my room.

I didn't have a lot of time to put on my suit, pack up my things, and get my butt downstairs to board the bus.

Still, I leaned against the door for a moment and closed my eyes.

The conversation left me rattled on a lot of levels. I'd worked hard to keep my emotional shit out of my teammates' sight, and I was pretty sure I'd mostly succeeded. The drinking, though—Christ. I *needed* the alcohol to cope with Leif's absence. It was the only thing that was remotely effective at numbing me—the only thing that wasn't on the banned substances list, anyway—but I'd let myself get out of control last night. Too much to drink in public and in front of my teammates. That *couldn't* happen again. Fine. I could always DoorDash some booze to the hotel if I couldn't sleep.

And when I was at home? Well, I could have all the oblivion I wanted without anybody noticing.

I opened my eyes and stared up at the ceiling as I continued leaning on the hotel room door. Coach's comments about sending me to another team had left my blood cold. I didn't think the possibility of a trade was a threat from him, but it *might* have been one from the front office. It felt a whole lot like he was gently presenting it to me so I'd get my head out of my ass, but it had come down from the powers that be as *"Tell Caldwell to either get his shit together, or he'll be wearing a different sweater."*

I didn't have a no-trade or no-move clause, and it wasn't hubris to believe at least half a dozen teams in the League would offer up a whole pile of assets for me. I was a veteran player but still young. My stats, even in this shitshow of a season, put me in top ten lists for points, goals, assists, and plus/minus differentials. I wasn't too shabby defensively, either. For the same reasons Pittsburgh had repeatedly said they wanted to keep me (I was eligible to sign an extension after next season), they could dump me in a hurry if they decided I was becoming a liability. Ideally (for them) before my off-ice issues started showing themselves during games.

I had to get my shit together, and fast.

Step one, get my ass downstairs and don't miss the bus.

I pushed myself off the door and started peeling off my hoodie.

As I changed clothes, I walked myself through everything I needed to do so I didn't wind up on the trading block. Focus on hockey. Stay upbeat around the team so they didn't feel like they had to walk on eggshells or handle me with kid gloves.

No more drinking with the team, either.

And I should probably do something about Peyton before tomorrow night's game.

CHAPTER 18
PEYTON

What was I supposed to do now?

I'd heard that old cliché of the tension in a room being so thick you could cut it with a knife, but experiencing it for real at this morning's team breakfast had been something else.

The usual banter and chirping had been MIA. Some of the guys had exchanged looks now and then like *"what the hell do we do?"* I'd felt like a kid in junior high, avoiding Avery's table, but what else was I supposed to do? Sit with him and see if he was still as pissed as he'd been last night?

Laramie and Ollie hadn't been there last night, but after I'd told them about it, they'd both insisted it would blow over.

"Two of the guys on my last team almost got into a fist-fight over something," Laramie had whispered in the near-silent banquet hall. "And Calds is a good dude. He probably just got wasted and went off on you."

I'd grunted and continued picking at my eggs. "Yeah. Probably." I hadn't believed myself. I also hadn't looked to see if any of my teammates were any more convinced than I was.

Now I was back in my room, packed and ready to head downstairs to get on a bus to the airport. Normally, I'd go down now and mill around with the guys in the lobby or chill with them on the bus. Maybe sign things for fans who'd gathered outside, which they often did.

This time, I lingered in my room.

I wasn't sure I could face my team after last night. Breakfast had been excruciating, and now I'd have to get on the bus and on the plane with them. What was I supposed to do when that was unavoidable? Especially when Avery joined us? We could avoid each other to some degree, but sooner or later, we would have to be in the same room. The same bus. The same plane.

The same line.

I closed my eyes and scrubbed a hand over my face. How the hell did we go back to normal after last night? What was I supposed to do? Because what happened at the bar—that was my fault. Avery's too, but I was the one who'd pushed him when he'd clearly wanted me to back off.

I should've backed off. At the same time...

I stared up at the ceiling as I gnawed the inside of my cheek. Hockey players drank. Some more than others. There were a few among us who didn't, but a hockey player drinking was about as shocking as a sailor drinking. Especially when we were chilling out on a night when we didn't have practice or a game the next morning, sometimes we drank.

But every time Avery had taken a sip—and God help me, every time he ordered another round—I'd gone back to that night in Detroit. To him drinking alone late at night, so hammered he couldn't even walk, and then he'd...

I winced and sighed.

That had happened *once*. I hadn't seen him do anything else alarming or stupid, drunk or otherwise, since.

Still, last night...

Something was wrong. I could feel it. I hadn't wanted to give him shit or piss him off—I wanted to help him. I wanted to stop him from self-destructing the way he was apparently determined to do. Or maybe I'd just been jumpy after how trashed he'd been in Detroit. It was possible that had been a one-time thing, and now Avery could drink like the rest of us without issue.

Why couldn't I convince myself that was the case?

And what could I even do if he *was* self-destructing and his drinking *was* becoming a problem?

I could get the hell out of Pittsburgh.

That thought made my stomach wind itself into knots. I didn't want to leave, least of all when this team was already struggling to hold itself together without Erlandsson. I didn't want to do that to these men.

But did I want to continue having a front-row seat to their captain pretending he wasn't being ripped apart by grief?

Part of my contract had included a no-move clause, but I could always waive it and request a trade. I knew for a fact there were three other teams who would salivate at the chance to snatch me up, and two of them had some assets that would make a trade worthwhile for Pittsburgh. If I wanted out of Pittsburgh, I could be gone before the week was over.

Maybe I needed some outside advice. Fortunately, for all I still felt isolated and alone on this new team, I did have people I could reach out to elsewhere. I pulled up the League app and checked where Vancouver was playing right now. Fortunately, they were at home, which meant it was early yet, but knowing him, he was awake. If I was lucky, I'd catch him before he left for practice.

> Hey, do you have a few minutes to FaceTime?

The response, thank God, came through quickly in the form of a FaceTime request. I accepted, and the face of my ex-boyfriend, Dan, appeared on the screen. His hair was wet and spiky like he'd just taken a shower, and he had on a hoodie. Judging by the background, he was in his kitchen.

"Hey," he said. "What's up?"

"Just..." I chewed my lip. "There's some shit going on here—on my new team—and I don't know who else to talk to."

Concern pinched his brow. "Yeah? What's up? I thought you were liking it there."

"I am. The team, the city—it's all great." I rubbed my forehead and sighed. "But there's—I mean, you heard what happened, right? During the off season?"

Dan exhaled. "I definitely heard. I can't imagine playing through that."

I nodded. "It's been hard on all of them. How they've made it this far..." I trailed off, shaking my head.

"I bet. So why the SOS, though? I'm guessing there's something more going on?"

"Yeah. There is." I gave him a brief rundown, trying to tread carefully and avoid crossing the line between filling him in and gossiping. I trusted Dan, though; he was a steel trap, and even two years after we'd split up, he was still my closest confidante. There was no one else I could talk to about this so candidly without worrying it would turn into rumor fodder or something.

After I told him about what happened last night, Dan blew out a breath. "Shit. Yeah, that doesn't sound good."

"No, it's not. And like, I don't think it's... I mean, this isn't a locker room cancer situation like what happened with you and Miceli."

Dan made a face, probably at the reminder of that toxic asshole who'd plagued his old team for three long seasons. "Definitely not. Sounds like Caldwell is a good guy and a good player. He's just fucked up after losing his friend. Shit, I don't know if I'd even be able to play through that. Trying to be captain on top of it?" He whistled and shook his head. "No way."

"Right? Same." I kneaded the back of my neck. "But what do I do? All of us who didn't know Erlandsson are trying to carry the team as best we can. Keeping morale up, playing hard—all that shit. But off the ice... I don't know what to do."

"I'm not sure there's much you *can* do, baby," he said softly. "I know you—you want to help people. You want to fix things. That's not a bad thing, you know?" He grimaced apologetically. "But I'm not so sure this is your problem to fix."

"What about the shit between me and him?" I protested. "Half the team saw that all go down last night, and..." My shoulders slumped. "Am I supposed to just hope they forget about it?"

"I mean, kind of? Teammates clash sometimes. It happens. If it was just a one-time thing, then it might be a little awkward for a while until everyone accepts that it's not going to happen again. Then things will go back to normal, you know? Or, well, whatever qualifies as normal on a team that's going through what they are."

I deflated, leaning back against the headboard. "I just

feel like I should do... I don't know. Something? Just quietly letting it fade away doesn't seem like the right thing."

Dan smiled fondly. "Of course it doesn't. That's not you. But the best thing in this situation might be to leave well enough alone." He paused. "Unless it really seems to be festering and causing issues, I'd follow your teammates' leads. Caldwell's, but also the rest of the guys, you know? If last night seems like water under the bridge for them, then let it go."

He was right. I knew that. We'd had conversations like this before when I'd been freaking out that something had permanently disrupted a team dynamic. Dan was always confident that it would work itself out, and it usually did.

I swallowed. "What about what happened with Caldwell before? With him being drunk, and..." I chewed my lip. "I don't know. It seems..."

"Bigger than it probably is?"

The heat in my face was undoubtedly visible on the screen, and I gave a little self-deprecating chuckle. "Yeah. Probably. Maybe I'm reading more into it than there was."

And why was that thought disappointing? The last thing I wanted was someone throwing themselves at me when they were drunk. But Avery Caldwell kissing me, drunk or not, had ignited some hope I had no business having. Was there an attraction there? Or had he just been so shitfaced he'd have moved in on anyone?

"Whatever you're thinking," my ex said softly, "you're probably overthinking it."

Sighing again, I nodded. "Probably. Yeah. But what else is new?"

He chuckled, though he sounded more fond than anything. Sobering a little, he said, "Right now, like I told you, I'd just leave it alone and follow your team's lead. If they seem like they're letting it go, let it go. And Calds? If it was a drunken mistake, he's probably hoping you'll forget it."

"True." Again with that weird disappointment. "Okay. So. I'm overthinking things, and I need to follow everyone else's lead. I can do that."

"I know you can. And being this worried about it—that's not a bad thing, you know. You care about people. Especially teammates." Dan smiled as he half-shrugged. "Even if you can't solve everything for everyone, the fact that you care this much is good, you know?"

I managed to smile back. That was again a conversation we'd had before, and he always seemed to know when I needed to hear it. Not being able to fix something was frustrating, and sometimes I needed to hear that not everything was mine to fix. One of these days, maybe that would stick. In the meantime, I was grateful I had Dan to gently remind me.

"All right," I said. "I'll keep all that in mind. I should let you go, though. Thanks for talking to me."

"Any time. You know that." He glanced at something off-camera before meeting my gaze again. "I should run—I have practice."

"Me too. Buses leave soon for the airport."

"Okay. Travel safe."

"I will. Thanks again."

After we ended the call, I closed my eyes and leaned against the headboard. I did need to leave soon, but a few minutes to get my mind back on the rails wouldn't be the end of the world.

Dan was right about everything, and I knew it. Still, the thought of waiving my no-move clause needled the back of my brain. Maybe everything going on wasn't my problem to fix, but that didn't mean I needed to stick around and watch my teammates struggle. Or watch one teammate in particular who might or might not have been self-destructing.

I wanted to be there for these men. Be a team player. Be a supporter while they tried to play through their grief. Be Avery's teammate and linemate and *not* be a source of anger and frustration for him.

But I had to take care of myself, too. Watching him hurt like that—it hurt *me*. Sitting back and letting it happen, accepting that I couldn't do anything to fix it or even help him...

Much more of that, and this team was going to have *two* players in uncontrollable downward spirals.

I hated admitting it. I hated thinking it.

But the truth was, if only to protect my own sanity...

Maybe I couldn't stay on the Whiskey Rebels.

On the team's charter jet, I stowed my carry-on and took my seat. Closing my eyes, I debated if I wanted to eat something once we were in the air. I'd barely touched my breakfast, and I wasn't used to going this long without eating anything substantial.

As Dan had suggested, I studied my teammates' vibes to see they handled things going forward. If they were acting like everything was normal on this flight, then maybe I could do the same, including unwinding my stomach so I could eat.

So far, the vibe was subdued but not overly tense. I'd seen Avery chatting with Ziggy and Baddy on the bus as if nothing unusual had happened last night or this morning. He and Eminem had been chirping about something on the way through the airport. By the time we'd been about to board, I'd started to convince myself things were tilting in the direction of normal.

Right up until Avery and I had made eye contact across the airport lounge.

We'd locked eyes for all of a second or two, and in an instant, his expression had shifted. He'd been laughing at something Baddy had said, but his humor had vanished and he'd looked away from me.

I had no idea if he'd bounced back after that; I hadn't dared look his direction.

Now that we were on the plane, I closed my eyes and listened to my teammates settling in all around me. They were getting back into the usual groove of chirping, challenging each other to card or video games, and sneering over the awful officiating that had apparently happened in the Seattle-San Jose game last night. Everyone on the plane sounded like things were back to normal.

Maybe I just needed to follow suit. I wasn't sure how—last night prodded at me like a piece of gear pressing into a bruise—but if they were all moving on, then I needed to do the same. I needed to listen to my ex, listen to my teammates, get a goddamned grip, and—

"Mind if I sit there?"

My eyes flew open at the sound of Avery's voice. I thought he must've been talking to someone else, but no, he was standing over me, a bag strap on his shoulder and an uncomfortable look on his face.

He wasn't hostile. No anger in sight. If anything, he seemed a little sheepish.

"Uh." I pulled my legs back. "Yeah. Sure. Do you want the window or the aisle?"

"Window is fine." He slid in between me and the seats

in front of us. Fortunately the charter jets had leg room like commercial business class, so it wasn't a tight squeeze for him at all. After he was situated, he turned an uneasy look on me. "Let's, um... Let's wait until we're in the air."

Chewing the inside of my cheek, I nodded. I could read between the lines—he wanted to talk, but he wanted to wait until the noise of the plane gave us some relative privacy.

Thank God, we didn't have to wait long. He'd been one of the last to board, and minutes later, we were taxiing. After takeoff, with the steady, familiar roar drowning out most of the conversations around us, he turned to me.

"Look," he said. "I'm... sorry about last night. I shouldn't have gone off on you like that."

"Oh. Uh. Yeah, it's... It's fine." I shrugged. "It happens."

"It shouldn't, though," he said quietly. "I bit your head off over nothing. I'm sorry about that."

I wasn't convinced. That he was genuinely apologizing, yes, but that it was nothing? Not so much.

"It's all right," I said. "Are you... Are you good, though?" That seemed like a stupid question, because no matter how much he tried to pretend he was good... he wasn't. He absolutely fucking wasn't. I just didn't know how else to press the issue without setting him off.

He avoided my gaze. "Like I said, it was a bad night."

"Last night isn't what I'm worried about," I whispered. "It's... There's also that *other* night. In Detroit."

Avery's jaw worked.

"I'm not being judgy, okay?" I said even more quietly. "I may be new to the team, but I can still support my teammates, you know?" I took a breath. "If there's something you—"

"I'm good." He said it firmly, but he didn't quite snap, and then he turned dog-tired eyes on me. "Look, last night was a bad night. Detroit... same thing. I've been fine the rest of the time, though, you know?"

I pressed my lips together. Oh, he gave the *appearance* of being fine most of the time. Well, *some* of the time. Put him on the ice, and he was almost good as new.

I didn't know if anyone else could see what I did. Ever since that night I'd half-carried him out of the bar, though, the cracks had been impossible to miss. I wanted to believe him that those two nights were flukes, but I couldn't lie to him. I couldn't lie to myself.

Apparently seeing the uneasy skepticism in my expression, Avery sighed. Voice quieter—almost pleading now—he said, "Last night and in Detroit—I'll be the first to admit I fucked up, and I *got* fucked up, and..." He waved a hand, then let it drop into his lap. "I own it, okay? But it won't happen again. I promise."

I wanted to push. We both knew there was more going on than those two nights. Right? Or was I seeing something that wasn't there because of what I'd missed in the past?

I couldn't say. What I did know was that if there was a problem, and if I wanted to help him—truly be the support he needed—then I needed to take my cues from *him*. Not from my past or my assumptions. Avery wasn't my mom, and he wasn't Richards.

Getting us back on the rails as teammates was a start. After that, I could keep an eye on him and see where things went.

So, I nodded. "Okay. We're good."

Avery studied me uncertainly, then let a small smile crack through. "Okay. Okay, good." For as much as he'd been trying to bullshit me and everyone else that he was all right, the relief in that moment did seem genuine. As if he'd really been upset about his behavior last night and the way things had been off kilter between us.

A metallic rattle pulled my attention to the front of the plane, and I realized the flight attendants were starting to bring food and beverages to our teammates. I gestured at them and asked Avery, "Should we get something to eat?"

He glanced in the same direction, then nodded. "Yeah. We should. I, um..." He laughed a little sheepishly and rubbed the back of his neck. "Kind of didn't eat much this morning."

The words *"same here"* stopped at the tip of my tongue. I didn't need to give him another reason to beat himself up. Instead, I went with, "I wasn't impressed with that hotel's eggs. You'd think they a swanky hotel could do better than a *plane.*"

Avery's laugh was tired but real, and I pretended my pulse didn't skyrocket at the sight of him not just smiling, but relaxing. He nodded toward the flight attendants. "To be fair, charter jet food isn't exactly the same slop they serve in coach."

"You're not wrong," I said, chuckling.

When the flight attendants reached us, we both ordered breakfast. One of them asked Avery what he wanted to drink, and he started to respond, but hesitated. His eyes flicked toward me, and then he cleared his throat and asked for orange juice.

My heart sank.

He wanted a drink, didn't he? A stiff one? But he wasn't going to order it now. Not in front of me, not after the conversation we'd just had.

So what's going to happen when you're alone?

Because that was the other side of my worries about

him. It wasn't just that he'd had too much to drink at the bar last night and in Detroit.

You're going to be careful around us.

But what's happening behind closed doors?

I let that go for now, though. He obviously wanted to smooth things over between us, and so did I. If I started pointing out the signs he wasn't hiding very well, he'd just started hiding them better, and things would get tense between us again.

As we moved on to lighter subjects, as our breakfast came and we chatted about the upcoming game, it was all still there in the back of my mind. It was like watching someone play when I knew the trainers were begging him to take it easy on an old injury—when I knew it was only a matter of time before something gave, or until a hard check or an unfortunately aimed puck made their worst fears come true. It was painfully obvious what was going to happen, and there was nothing anyone could do except cringe while we watched him barrel toward the inevitable.

The best I could do right now was be his friend and teammate. Be someone who was safe instead of adversarial.

And hope like hell he asked me or anyone else for help before it was too late.

Things were better after we had that talk. Our teammates picked up on the changed vibe between us just like they'd picked up on the tension, and by the time we were at the next day's morning skate, everything seemed close to normal. The team breakfast was as full of chatter and chirping as usual. Avery was his usual self at the table, on the bus, and on the ice.

To any casual observer, nothing had ever been amiss.

I didn't feel good about it, though. For all he'd assured me those two nights were isolated incidents, it was only a matter of time before it happened a third time. I knew it. I could *feel* it. I'd known it since we'd had that conversation on the plane, and every day that went by only made me more certain that the inevitable was coming.

No matter how much I pretended not to notice them, the signs that he was drinking were still there.

The first game after our talk was a grind, but that had less to do with interpersonal differences and more to do with Buffalo being pissed off about losing two nights ago. We were, despite the bump in the road thanks to Avery and me, still flying high from stomping Boston into the ground, and Buffalo was determined to knock us down a peg. The game ended in a 4-3 overtime loss. Not ideal, but a point was a point.

We'd gone home after that. Several of the guys were going to dinner at a steakhouse in Wexford, and they invited me along. Baddy and Eminem had both seemed surprised when Avery didn't join us, and then they'd gotten worried. Like... really worried.

Baddy had nervously excused himself to step outside and call him.

"I think they all have a little PTSD," Laramie had whispered to me. Gesturing at Ziggy, he'd added, "He told me the night Erlandsson died, he was supposed to have dinner with them. Didn't show up, didn't answer his phone... and then his wife called."

"Oh, shit," I breathed. "Yeah I think that would mess me up, too."

Laramie nodded solemnly. And now that he mentioned it, the only guys who seemed on edge—fidgeting in their chairs and flicking their gazes in the direction Baddy had gone—were the ones who'd been with Pittsburgh when their captain had died. Trews, Laramie, and I were all new acquisitions.

Conversation at the table was subdued, especially for a bunch of hockey players, until a few minutes later when Baddy returned. He was chuckling, which instantly put the whole group at ease even before he said, "He's good. Dumbass just fell asleep and forgot."

That had everyone laughing, and the relief was palpable. Nothing was wrong. Avery was fine. We'd see him at practice tomorrow.

Everyone at the table was relaxed and chill after that except for me. It was entirely possible he *had* gone home, fallen asleep, and forgotten about dinner plans.

The problem was that it was *also* possible he'd been drinking.

When he showed up to practice the next morning with faintly red eyes and that telltale miserable expression of someone fighting off a hangover...

Shit. This wasn't good.

There were other incidents, too. Some subtler than others.

Like three nights later after we'd finished our postgame media availability. One of the things about hockey was that it had a lot of very specific and strong odors. It was always easy to pick out anyone who was new to a hockey locker room—from partners to reporters—because the faces they made when they hit that wall of funk were hilarious. The rest of us were used to it because it came with the territory and it permeated everything. It was just part of hockey.

When a *different* smell joined the mix, though, even if it was relatively faint, it could rise above the miasma simply because it was unusual. Like that one reporter who'd always come into our locker room in Detroit wearing some kind of cologne that made my eyes water whenever he stood too close to me. Or that time one of my teammates was playing his thousandth game, and he had a bouquet of flowers to give his wife during the pregame ceremony—I had no idea what kind of flowers they were, only that the smell permeated the room and lingered for hours after.

On this particular night, as I was heading out of the showers, I passed Avery on his way out, and the scent—even though it wasn't terribly strong—stopped me dead in my tracks.

Alcohol.

I shook myself and continued into the showers. Maybe it was aftershave or something? Rubbing alcohol? He couldn't possibly be drinking here. Was he actually sneaking booze with him into the shower so he could drink without anyone noticing?

Or am I just projecting because that's exactly what Richards did?

That must've been it. It had to be.

But then I joined my teammates in the players' lounge for food, and as I walked past him with my loaded plate... there it was again. We all ate and carried on and talked about the game and an upcoming game, and everything seemed normal.

Was I the only one who noticed?

And was I just imagining things?

Because Avery seemed perfectly sober and coherent. He was laughing and chirping with the guys, but there was nothing unusual about him.

Nothing except that faint smell.

That might not have even been alcohol.

But I was pretty sure it was.

To anyone else on the team, to the fans, to the media, Avery seemed perfectly okay. Everyone had moved on from that night in the hotel bar, and Avery and I didn't speak of the *other* night in the *other* hotel bar. Everything was normal. Everything was fine.

But Avery *wasn't* okay. I could feel it to my core, and I couldn't make myself believe it was just because I'd watched two people drown in bottles before him. The signs were there. He was doing everything he could to hide it—everything he could to pretend he was back to normal despite the jersey hanging in the rafters above our home ice —but I could see it. I could feel it. I could smell it.

He was *going* to crash and burn sooner or later.

And I had no idea what any of us could do to stop him.

CHAPTER 19
AVERY

I held it together—or at least kept it out of sight—until January 14.

We had a game that night, and I both loved and hated PR for the tribute they did for Leif's birthday. It was an emotional night for all of us, and it didn't help that Rachel—now visibly pregnant—was there with the kids.

It was amazing, and it was exactly what Leif deserved, and I was glad to see the family.

But holy shit. Putting on the happy, professional face, being the captain, being a hockey player, being me—that had all been exhausting already. That night, it was like our home opener all over again. Too much emotion. Too much hurt.

Worse, we were in a four-game losing streak, and even our efforts to play well on Leif's birthday couldn't stop us from extending that to five.

Afterward, I didn't fall apart in the locker room. I kept my media smile firmly in place, and I didn't let my voice shake through my postgame interviews. Not even when they asked about life after Leif. I'd gone through the motions of showering, getting dressed, eating with my team-mates, and signing autographs on the way out of the parking garage, and I'd stayed smiling and stoic the whole time. Anyone got a photo or a video of me, they'd see nothing but the usual Avery Caldwell.

Then I drove home on autopilot and poured booze down my throat until I didn't feel anything anymore.

Practice the next morning... yeah, that didn't happen.

My alarm went off like usual, but by then, I'd already been up for fifteen minutes, heaving my guts out and wondering if my skull was going to explode. God knew if Coach Tabakov bought my excuse about being sick, or if he saw right through to how hungover and fucked up I was after last night. He didn't give me any grief over the phone, though. I'd probably hear about it tomorrow.

Honestly? I couldn't bring myself to care. I felt too awful to give a shit about anything.

Sitting back against my bathroom wall, I let the cold marble cool my throbbing head while I waited to see if my stomach was done punishing me. I'd been doing so damn good lately. Games, interviews, just... existing—everyone, including Peyton, had been acting like everything was normal with me, so I'd obviously been keeping the cracks hidden. I was damn good at hiding the red in my eyes when-ever I came to a practice or joined my team for breakfast in a hotel. I knew how much I could drink in front of my team-mates before they'd worry—less these days, thanks to Peyton making them all scared I was drinking too much—and then I'd retreat to my room and drink some more by myself. I knew *exactly* how drunk I could get to numb myself for the night and still pass for functional the next day.

But last night...

Last night, I hadn't cared, and now I was paying for it.

And I didn't care all that much about that, either. The only thing I could bring myself to care about right now was how much my head hurt and how much I desperately wanted to be numb and distracted. Once this hangover was gone, I was heading back into a bottle and I wasn't sorry.

Not just a bottle, though. Not this time. Getting drunk and oblivious like I had last night wasn't going to be enough this time.

Tonight, I wanted to be so drunk that I was oblivious to everything except a hot man banging me senseless. I didn't even care if the sex was good. I just wanted to get dicked down until I was trembling and aching in all the right places and numb as hell in all the others. I hadn't had sex in months—not since before all this pain started—and now I wanted it.

A club. I'd hit up a club, get good and fucked up, and then get, well, good and fucked.

Would I be able to practice tomorrow morning? Eh. That sounded like tomorrow's problem.

I went upstairs, showered, and started putting myself together for a night out. It felt weird, getting ready to go clubbing, and not just because I hadn't set foot in a club in ages. There was no tingle of excitement. No anticipation of a fun night out and maybe an even more fun hookup. It reminded me of heading to the emergency room with an injury—just trying to get there and get this over with before the pain got the best of me.

I took an Uber into downtown Pittsburgh, and I had the driver drop me off a couple of blocks over from the club. I was out and everybody knew it, and hockey players didn't get recognized as much as football players and A-listers, but I still felt weird about my driver letting me out in front of a gay nightclub. Did it make sense? Hell, did anything in my world make sense these days?

Eh. Whatever.

I walked the rest of the way to the club. I'd checked online that they were still open, and I was pleased to see the information had been correct. Clubs came and went sometimes, and I'd pulled up to some that had gone under but hadn't updated their online info yet. Or they rebranded, changing everything but their name, for better or worse.

This place was exactly as I'd left it. Same garish green-and-yellow neon signs outside. Same bead curtain between coat check and the lounge area. Same long bar tended by incredibly hot men.

In fact, I was pretty sure that blond at the second station had spent his break blowing me in the alley behind this place a year or two ago before we'd gone back to his apartment after his shift. From the way he grinned when our eyes locked—yep, that was him. Talented mouth, too; maybe I'd have to see if he was busy after his shift.

I wasn't so sure if I wanted to wait that long, though. I was on a mission tonight that didn't lend itself to hanging around until the place closed. Though if he had a break coming up...

Nah, even that wasn't what I needed. I wasn't here for a blowjob or a quickie.

I did get a drink from him, though, and we exchanged a few flirty looks. I tipped him well, and he leered at me in a way that made me think maybe I *could* wait until the club closed.

Maybe. If I didn't find someone interested in a hookup before then, I was all his.

For now, step one—get *hammered*.

One cocktail and three shots in, I was feeling good

enough to hit the dancefloor. Well... "good." I was getting to the point I had to stop and think about why I'd been so miserable earlier, so that meant I was on the right track. One more shot, and I was among all the men dancing to a song I probably could've identified sober. Eh. Whatever. It had a good beat.

I wasn't the only one here on the prowl, either. It was easy to spot the guys who were here for more than just dancing; it wasn't a predatory look per se, but it kind of was. That expression and body language that said this dancefloor wasn't their final destination for this evening. The way their eyes raked over other men's bodies. The touches that were clearly more than just a means of making contact while dancing. That blissed-out look of a man who was almost hypnotized by another's scent and body and hands.

I made my way from one to another, slipping away between songs to throw back some more alcohol. My thoughts were getting hazy and the floor was tilting a little, so... perfect.

At some point, I found myself pressed up against a redheaded guy who looked at me and touched me like he wanted to devour me. As we danced without a sliver of space between our bodies, he slid his hands up and down my back, over my ass and hips—anything he could touch, he did, though he kept his lips just out of my reach. He didn't strike me as someone who wouldn't kiss me—some guys didn't kiss hookups—but rather like he was teasing me.

I'll kiss you, this closeness said, *but not here. Not now.*

God, I wanted his mouth.

I wanted *him.* He was taller than me by an inch or two, and built thick and broad, not lean like a hockey player. He had gorgeous eyes, too, and a sexy-ass smile that made me wonder what else that mouth was capable of.

That mouth that kept hovering just out of my reach.

Needed to do something about that. Like *now*.

We couldn't hear a damn thing, but there were ways to communicate without speaking. A head tilt toward the back of the club accompanied by an inquisitive eyebrow lift. A grin and a nod in response. A hand on the small of my back, leading my weaving ass off the floor and through the crowd and into the back and—

He had me up against the wall, his tongue in my mouth and his hard-on grinding on mine. He kissed deep and hard, almost bruising my lips, and I gripped the front of his shirt to beg him for more. I couldn't hear either of us moaning, but I could feel the thrum of his voice, and oh, yeah, he was into this. So was I.

He broke the kiss and nipped the side of my neck. Then he found his way to my ear. "I wanna bend you over and pound you."

I bit my lip, whimpering as my knees went slack. "Ooh, yeah."

A low growl vibrated beneath the bass, and he rutted harder against me. "I'm gonna take you home, and I'm gonna—" He cut himself off by kissing me again, even more greedily and forcefully than before. My knees and spine had turned to liquid; if not for him pressing me up against this wall, I'd have melted to the floor at his feet.

And then he could just get down and fuck me right there.

Somehow I knew that wouldn't happen—that this wasn't where we'd end up screwing—but the thought drove me on. I slung my arms around his neck and opened to his kiss. Holy fuck, I wanted—

Out of nowhere, a memory flashed through my hazy mind of how Peyton's mouth had felt against mine.

Of that dreamlike, drunken kiss I barely remembered and we both regretted.

For Christ's sake. No. Don't think about that right now.

Peyton isn't here. This guy is here. I'm here. And I—

Do I even want to be here?

Hands slid down between my back and the wall, and then gripped my ass firmly and pulled me harder against his erection. He ground hard against me as we kissed. Sloppy. Messy. Frantic. Primal.

This was exactly what I'd come here for. This man was a forceful, greedy kisser, exactly what I wanted tonight.

Exactly what I *thought* I wanted.

There was nothing unattractive about this man, but did I actually want him? Did I actually want sex with anyone?

I...

No, I kind of didn't.

And now that I was on that bullshit train of thought, I was suddenly raw in ways I didn't need to be in a club. Apparently I wasn't drunk enough. Except...

Ugh. No. Getting more drunk seemed like a bad idea. I didn't even know why. I was just sure that more alcohol would only make things worse.

I can feel worse than this? How? That doesn't seem possible.

The stranger bumping and grinding against me, getting so hot I wouldn't have been surprised if he came in his tight pants, was suddenly unwelcome. He wanted to have sex with me. I'd wanted to have sex with him, but now even making out with him made my skin crawl. Getting naked? Getting fucked?

Oh, hell, no.

I didn't even know why. Was it the alcohol coming back to haunt me? Too much too fast?

Shit, I had no idea.

I put my hands on the guy's chest and nudged him back. He resisted a little, but then took a step and grinned expectantly.

Oh. Did he think...?

I swallowed the bile rising in my throat, and I shook my head.

His expression suddenly darkened. "What the fuck?" His voice barely carried over the music.

"I can't."

"What?" He scoffed and cupped my dick, which was still hard, through my pants, making me gasp. "Feels like you can do just fine. And you don't even need to be hard while I'm—"

"No." I shook my head as I batted his hand away. "I—think the booze is making me sick." Eh, close enough.

He arched an eyebrow. Then he rolled his eyes. "Whatever. You're a little bitch."

I blinked. "I—"

"Fucking cocktease," he muttered, and he stalked back toward the dancefloor.

I stood there stupidly for a moment, wavering badly on my feet.

I almost slept with that guy?

I almost slept with that guy.

Holy shit, I should not *be here.*

I really did feel sick right then, but I didn't think I was going to throw up or that it was the alcohol. Not entirely, anyway. Slumping against the wall, I tried to will my heart to slow down from the sudden panic. Somehow I was still teetering precariously on that knife's edge where I was lucid enough to know I was drunk enough to do something I'd regret. Somewhere in my liquor-soaked mind, I held on to a sliver of awareness that said I was too fucked up to get any *more* fucked up.

One more drink...

One more deep, alcohol-flavored kiss...

And I would absolutely do something I shouldn't.

As raw and drunk as I was right then, that something was probably going to be *"hook up with a stranger and start sobbing while he's railing me."* Because in that moment, I couldn't see myself getting through sex without breaking down. Or getting through anything.

I almost had sex with that guy.

If I'd had one more drink, I'd have done it.

God. What was wrong with me? What was I doing?

I needed to get away from here.

I stumbled my way back toward the lounge and somehow got through the crowd along the edge of the dancefloor. I made it to coat check, found my claim ticket in my back pocket, and took my jacket.

The sharp bite of the January wind brought me a couple of degrees closer to sober. I needed to get home, but... how?

I was too hammered to drive. No doubt about that. And my car wasn't here anyway.

Uber? Lyft?

Oh, yeah, that was exactly what I needed—some driver to see me like this. They all had dashcams now, didn't they? If someone uploaded the video of me drunk—especially drunk and crying, since that was a definite possibility—then I'd never survive the humiliation.

Okay, no Uber. No Lyft.

I leaned against the cold brick wall and struggled to focus my eyes as I thumbed through my contacts. There had to be someone I could text or call to come scrape up my stupid drunk ass.

Baddy? Eminem? Ziggy?

I could text Coach. The thought made me cringe with preemptive embarrassment, but he had always told us—just like our parents had as teenagers—that we could call him any time if we were too drunk to drive. He'd lost a friend in high school to a drunk driver; he took it *very* seriously.

But could I ever look him in the eye if I took him up on that offer? Probably not.

I kept scrolling.

Willy. Astala. Trews.

My heart jumped into my throat.

Peyton.

I stared at his contact.

Did I want him to see me like this? Absolutely the fuck not.

On the other hand, he *had* seen me like this. Of everyone on the Whiskey Rebels, Peyton was the only one who knew what a mess I was. The only one who'd seen me fall the hell apart. I wouldn't be showing him any train-wreck he didn't already know about.

I closed my eyes.

Did I have any other options? It was a safe bet that any shot I ever had with him was dead and gone, and had been since the night he'd collected me from the bar. He already knew how pathetic and messed up I was. So... what did I have left to lose?

Queasy with shame, I tapped his contact.

> Any chance you can give me a lift home?

CHAPTER 20
PEYTON

AVERY

Any chance you can give me a lift home?

To say the text startled me would be an understatement. As much as Avery and I had tried to iron things out, the air between us hadn't been the same. Now he was texting me? Jesus, how many of the other guys weren't responding or weren't available that he had to resort to reaching out to me?

Either way, I was up off my couch and heading for the parking lot even as I wrote him back.

On my way. Where are you?

He responded with the name of what looked like a club and a downtown address. I punched it into the GPS, then told him I'd be there in about twenty minutes. No response, though he did read the message.

There was a good chance I'd be there in less than twenty, and not just because traffic was light at this hour. I had no doubt he was drunk, but was there more going on?

Did something bad happen? Why did he need me of all people to come get him at 12:30 in the morning?

I tapped my thumbs on the wheel as the engine whined, and I prayed there weren't any speed traps between here and there. I needed to get to that club immediately and make sure Avery was okay.

I doubted he was okay. I just didn't know how bad he was.

After the tribute to Erlandsson on his birthday last night, I'd known it was only a matter of time. Oh, Avery had tried to hide it. He'd tried to stay strong, and he'd played his balls off the whole night. In the locker room, he'd been his usual chatty, chirping self, even if he'd been bummed by the loss, but I'd seen right through it. I'd seen how much he was forcing it; how the fatigue would crack through when he didn't think anyone was looking.

Or maybe I was projecting because I was so convinced he had a problem. Maybe I saw something that wasn't there, and he was just being responsible tonight and getting a ride because he'd had too much to drink. Maybe he'd gone with someone and they'd bailed, so he needed a Plan B. Maybe it was a *complete* coincidence that this was just hours after he'd missed practice this morning. After he'd allegedly been sick.

I wouldn't know until I got there.

So I floored the gas and got there as fast as humanly possible.

I drove up to the front of the building first just to make sure I knew where it was before I went and parked. I fully expected to then go into the club and find Avery a stagger-ing, slurring mess like he'd been that night in the hotel bar.

To my surprise, though, he was waiting outside, leaning against the wall and looking at his phone. When I pulled up to the curb, he glanced up, and he immediately pushed himself off the wall and crossed over to the car. As he moved, he was definitely intoxicated, but he was more or less steady on his feet.

As he dropped into the passenger seat, he didn't look at me. "Thanks. I, um... I really appreciate it."

"Don't mention it." I pulled away from the curb onto the mostly deserted street. As I eased to a stop at a traffic light, I turned to him. God, it was mind-blowing how someone could look so good and so terrible at the same time. The snug jeans and dark blue shirt clung to his sculpted body like a dream. He'd styled his hair into an artful version of the messiness that was usually left after he took off his helmet. That man had come here looking to get laid, no doubt about it.

But his face... Jesus Christ, he just looked *lost*. He stared straight ahead, his beautiful eyes dim and his shoulders slouched a little beneath his jacket.

"You okay?" I asked.

When he spoke, somehow his voice came out both flat *and* slurred. "Yeah. I'm just too drunk to drive."

I chewed the inside of my cheek, alternately glancing at him and looking for the freeway onramp. Once I was accelerating onto I-279, I asked, "Why *are* you this drink?"

I braced for him to snap at me and tell me to mind my own damn business. Instead, all I got was a tired, "I'm just in a bad space tonight. I—" He cut himself off, and I was about to press for more, but then he murmured, "I came here because I didn't want to be alone."

My stomach dropped. Oh, shit. He'd been drinking and trying to hook up while he was depressed. That had a habit of not ending well.

Avery exhaled. "What?"

"What?"

"You've got that look on your face." He twisted toward me, leaning against the door, and the words came out sharp-edged this time: "Let me guess—you're worried about me, and you think I'm a jackass who can't hold his liquor."

It took a lot of work to keep my voice and expression neutral. "I just want to make sure you're all right."

The laugh that escaped his lips was near-silent, but still dry and caustic. "I haven't been all right since August."

Ooh. I wasn't surprised—I'd known Leif's death was at the root of most everything going on with Avery—but I was startled to hear him make the connection. Or at least acknowledge it.

Pressing back against the seat this time, he chuckled, but it was a heartbreakingly brittle sound. "Christ. Leif is probably laughing his ass off somewhere right now."

I glanced at him. "Why's that?"

"He was *so sure* I was going to end up hooking up with you." Avery pressed his elbow beneath the window and rubbed his forehead. "Bet he never thought I could blow it like this."

I damn near swerved. What the hell? Was I hearing what I thought I was hearing? Or was it just wishful thinking? He was, after all, drunk.

Just like he'd been in Detroit. When he'd kissed me.

Kissing me once was a drunken lapse in judgment. Blurting out that he thought he'd blown it with me—that he'd thought there was anything to blow—was a pattern.

Was...

Was Avery Caldwell into me the way I was into him?

I chewed my lip, driving silently for a mile or so. Then I decided, what the hell, and I said, "You haven't blown it."

"Hmm?"

I glanced at him, and I found him watching me, brow furrowed as if he were struggling to understand me. Facing the road again, I quietly repeated, "You haven't blown it. With me."

"I..." The leather seat creaked as he shifted. "I haven't?"

"No. You're..." I tapped my thumbs rapidly on the wheel. "I like you, Avery. A lot. And yes, I'm attracted to you. I... have been for a long time. And I still am."

The response to that was silence.

Long silence.

Conspicuously long silence.

I hazarded a glance at him.

And then my heart dropped—he was asleep.

Probably passed the hell out.

I laughed to myself and shook my head as I kept driving. Eh, maybe it was just as well. This probably wasn't the best time or place to be pouring my heart out to him. Now was definitely not the time for us to be doing anything about this apparently mutual attraction.

I'd just... wanted him to know. I couldn't completely explain why. Because he'd been so heartbreakingly vulnerable in that moment? Because he was just so deep in depression and despair that I wanted to give him hope of *something?*

I didn't know.

But it didn't matter anyway.

Because he was passed the hell out beside me.

CHAPTER 21
AVERY

The pounding headache and churning stomach weren't unusual. Lately, they'd been constant companions more mornings than not, if not *quite* this viciously.

The shame, though—that was new.

As I sat back against the cold bathroom wall, hoping I was done getting sick, I couldn't even put my finger on why I was so excruciatingly ashamed, only that I was. Or why my skin crawled beneath the club clothes I was still wearing.

I groaned into the silence and kneaded my temples. I must've done something awful while I was drunk. Hopefully no one had videoed it. That club had a no-camera policy, so there was that.

The club. Right. I was dressed like this because I'd been out drinking myself numb while I looked for someone to drill me into oblivion.

I knew immediately I hadn't been laid. I may or may not have remembered anything that happened, but my body made it pretty clear that there hadn't been any sex last night. No telltale aches or twinges. And... somehow I just knew. My memory of last night was piecemeal, with lots of drinking, dancing, and some kissing, but that was as far as it had gone. That wasn't a blank spot in my memory—it hadn't happened.

So what *had* happened?

I wasn't going to figure that out until I'd had a shower and some coffee, so I hauled myself onto my feet, flushed the toilet, and stripped out of my clothes. Then I dragged myself into the shower, which helped a little. Coffee would help a lot more.

In a pair of gym shorts and an old tank top, I managed to get my stupid ass down the stairs... only to very nearly tumble off the bottom step.

From my couch, Peyton watched me. He was *also* still wearing what he'd had on last night, minus his shoes.

How do I know what he was wearing last night?

That answer came fast—he'd picked me up at the club. I didn't remember how he'd known I needed a ride, or if he'd just shown up and taken me home, but I knew I'd come back with him.

But why the hell was he still here?

"Uh. Hi." I cleared the last step. "You're still—You stayed over?"

He nodded, pushing himself to his feet. "Didn't seem like I should leave you alone."

I died a little inside. "Do I even want to know why?"

Peyton's laugh was soundless and gentle. "Pretty sure your hangover is a clue."

"Yeah, I know I got drunk. But..." I grimaced. "What did I *do?*"

"I don't know." He slid his hands into his pockets and shrugged. "You texted me and asked me to pick you up. So I did."

That wasn't the whole story. I could see it in his eyes and the way they couldn't quite stay on mine.

I avoided his gaze. "Do you, um... Do you want some coffee?"

"Yeah. Sure."

We silently moved into my kitchen. At least coffee didn't require too many brain cells to make. I was too hungover for anything more complicated than working a Keurig, and *way* too distracted by my unexpected houseguest.

With coffee cups in hand, we returned to the living room.

The living room where Peyton had slept. After bringing my ass home from... wherever I'd been.

I surveyed the couch. He'd used the afghan that had been draped over the back, and he'd arranged some throw pillows for his head. Fresh guilt twinged in my stomach; how much of a mess had I been last night that I'd let him sleep like that?

"Sorry," I murmured as I sat on one end of the couch. "I, um... I should've put you in the guest room, or..." I shook my head and stared into my coffee.

"It's all right." He shifted a little, and I winced when I realized he was twisting a crick out of his back. God, he must've been miserable; this couch was comfortable for watching movies and stuff, but it wasn't great for sleeping on. I hadn't been too worried about that when I'd bought it, because... guest room.

Jesus. I was seriously batting a thousand when it came to this man.

I swallowed some coffee and made myself look at Peyton. "Any chance you can fill me in on last night?"

I fully expected an eyeroll and a scoff, followed by some

comment about what a trash fire I was. Except that wasn't really how Peyton rolled; I was probably just projecting because... Well, because I was a trash fire, and I didn't imagine I was fooling anyone about that anymore. Least of all this man.

Peyton took a sip of his own coffee. "Like I said, you texted me and asked me to come get you. From a club."

"Oh God," I croaked. "And I don't remember much of it, so I must've been shitfaced."

"You were," he acknowledged gently. "But you weren't... I mean, you were drunk. But you weren't, like, belligerent or anything."

"I guess that's a plus." I pinched the bridge of my nose and sighed. "I'm sorry. I appreciate you coming and getting me. But... I'm sorry."

"Don't be. Better than driving yourself."

"Yeah." I dropped my hand into my lap. "I... kind of remember not wanting an Uber driver or something to see me like that, either."

Peyton held my gaze. "How much *do* you remember?"

A lot that I didn't need him to know about, but I didn't say that. Bits and pieces of last night were coming back, though. "I just remember dancing at the club, and then feeling like I didn't want to be there anymore." I shook my head. "The rest..."

Peyton leaned forward to put his coffee cup on a coaster. As he sat back, he wrung his hands in his lap. "I remember it a little more clearly."

My stomach dropped. I wasn't sure I wanted to know, but as I put my own coffee cup down, I asked anyway: "What do you remember?"

"You told me you were too drunk to drive, and to be at the club." He swallowed. "When I asked why you were that drunk, you said you'd come to the club because you didn't want to be alone. You said you were in a bad space, so hooking up didn't seem like a good idea."

Well, at least I hadn't been completely out of my head. "I... kind of remember that, now that you mention it. Not wanting to be alone, but being in a bad space." I let my shoulders drop. "Last night was a bad night. I definitely shouldn't have been drinking. I'm just glad I wasn't stupid enough to go home with someone."

I shuddered at the thought, vaguely aware that that possibility had been on the table at some point. I couldn't remember a specific face—faces?—only that something had definitely happened. Something that had to do with this skin-crawly feeling the shower hadn't been able to wash away. Good thing I'd come to my senses, and despite the humiliation of facing Peyton now, thank God I'd thought to text Peyton. And that he'd been willing to come get me.

I turned to him, furrowing my brow. "You didn't have to stay the night."

He shrugged and picked up his coffee for a quick sip. As he put it back down, he said, "I was worried. I... I mean, I didn't think you'd had enough to have alcohol poisoning or anything. But I felt weird about leaving."

Renewed shame twisted behind my ribs. "Was I that bad?"

Another shrug. "Might've been a little jumpiness on my part. I... worry about people when they're drunk, especially if they're not in a good place mentally." He turned a sheepish look on me. "I didn't want to intrude or stay when I wasn't invited. I just... wanted to be sure you were okay."

"No, it's fine. Probably for the better anyway." When alarm registered in his expression, I quickly added,

"Because I was obviously a mess. You couldn't have known how bad I was."

That seemed to assuage some of his worry. "You're good now, though?"

Oh, wasn't *that* a complicated question?

"Well, I'm not drunk anymore." I grimaced as I brought up my coffee for another swallow. "I feel like shit, so I'm..." I wanted to say this would probably keep me from getting drunk again any time soon. I wondered if he would believe that any more than I did.

"I have a question," he said, voice still soft. "Just... yes or no, okay?"

I gritted my teeth as I put my coffee cup down. "Okay."

He studied me for a long, painfully silent moment before he whispered, "Last night—was that about Leif?"

The dam didn't break this time.

It *shattered.*

The sound of my best friend's name, wrapped in genuine concern from someone who'd apparently seen right through the mess I'd been last night, smashed all the defenses I'd been holding up for too damn long.

Crying sucked under the best of circumstances. When I was already hungover and miserable, it fucking hurt.

But I'd have been lying if I said it wasn't a million times easier when Peyton collected me in his arms and started stroking my hair. As miserable as I was, as bad as I was hurting, I *reveled* in being wrapped up in strong arms that held me together even while I broke apart. Gentle fingers stroked my hair. Soft words propped me up almost as much as his solid frame.

And for the first time since my best friend's widow had collapsed in my arms, I leaned on someone else. I let the grief and the guilt and all those other awful feelings crash over me, same as I had so many times, except I didn't have to hold myself up. I didn't have to care about pulling it together and hiding all the evidence before showing my face to other people, because the jig was up now. Peyton knew what a mess I was, and he was just holding on and letting me fall apart the way I'd so desperately needed to for so damn long.

After I had no idea how long, I finally collected myself and sat up. Peyton kept a hand on my shoulder, studying me with an expression full of nothing but gentle concern. No judgment. No *Jesus fuck, man up already*. When he was apparently sure I could hold myself up, he withdrew his hand, but he didn't slide away from me. There was plenty of room on this couch for us to put some serious distance between us if he wanted that. He stayed where he was, though.

I was a goddamned mess. It took a couple of tissues to take care of that, and a swig of cooling coffee helped, too.

"Damn it. I'm sorry." I sniffed as I wiped my eyes with a badly shaking hand. "I'm such a trainwreck."

"You're not," he whispered, and he didn't sound the least bit judgy. "I get the feeling you've been holding all that in for a long time."

"I have to."

"Why? It's not healthy."

I shook my head. "Doesn't matter. The team needs me."

"Yeah, and you need them, too." He held my gaze. "I've watched you, man. You've been holding up everyone and letting the whole team grieve. We can do the same for you, you know."

Shaking my head, I clenched my jaw. "No. If I fall apart, the whole team falls apart."

Peyton arched an eyebrow. "Okay, but if you *need* to fall apart, then—"

"I won't. I got into my own head, and I guess it was bothering me last night."

"And today." It didn't sound like an accusation, but it was close. He touched my forearm. "I know you're trying to be the captain of this team and hold them all up. But you're human. And from what I've heard, you were closer to Leif than anyone else on the team. Of course losing him will hit you harder."

My throat tightened as tears threatened again. "They need a captain. They need me to be—"

"You're *human*, Avery," he said again. "There isn't a single person in that locker room who wants you to carry all of them at your own expense. No one is expecting you to shoulder all that grief *and* pull the entire team."

I am, I wanted to say. I needed to do both of those things. "If I buckle, where does that leave the team?"

"Do you think we could hold our own if you were out with an injury?"

I chewed my lip. I wanted to tell him it wasn't the same thing. But... it kind of was. Players went down all the time. Whether a guy was hurt, sick, suspended, or at the hospital with his laboring wife, the gap he left was the same. No matter what, it would be next man up. Someone would come up to fill his vacancy on a line or a D pair, or the backup goalie would take his place, and someone else would be called up from the minors to fill his space. The game would go on. Yeah, it was hard to lose someone, especially someone who played as many minutes as Peyton or I did—as many minutes as Leif had—but the sport stopped for no man.

"You could play without me," I said. "I just... I don't want to put the team in that position." Before he could protest and insist it wasn't my responsibility, I whispered, "God, I hate this." I wiped a hand over my face. "I don't even... I can't blame it all on grief. I don't think."

"What do you mean?"

"I mean I—maybe it *is* because of Leif? I don't know. But I'm a panicked, nervous wreck every goddamned game now. Every time someone gets hurt or goes down—like when Eminem collided with that other player, or when you..." I closed my eyes and exhaled before looking at him again. "Whenever something happens, I freak out."

"I've seen you get upset," he admitted. "But you usually snap back to having a cool head."

I let my shoulders sag. "Because I bust my ass to make sure everyone *thinks* I have a cool head. But the reality..." I didn't even know how to explain it. How to describe that surge of anxiety every time one of my teammates so much as winced in pain. Or the flash of anger every time an opposing player crosschecked one of my guys, or boarded him, or did anything that could cause an injury. Even the normal shit that happened every damn game. How it all fucked me up long past the moment of impact, sabotaging my concentration and even keeping me awake in bed hours later.

Everything fucked me up. *Everything* made me panicked or angry or...

Pressing my elbows into my thighs, I leaned forward and rubbed my eyes with my thumb and forefinger. "God, I am such a mess."

Peyton was silent for a long moment. When he spoke, his voice was gentler than I'd ever heard it before, which honestly said something. "Listen. This isn't me judging you or calling you weak or any of that shit. I'm speaking as your teammate and as your friend, okay?" When I met his gaze, his forehead creased. "I think you need to get some help."

I straightened. "What kind of help? Like a shrink?"

"Therapy, yeah." He half-shrugged, and his tone was cautious as he softly added, "Rehab, too."

Bristling, I glared at him. "I'm not an alcoholic."

"I don't think you are. But I do think you've been self-medicating enough that you're hurting yourself." He chewed his lip. "I think... Look, I'm not an expert, okay? But if you keep going the way you're going, I think you're going to *become* an alcoholic." Rage surged up in me, and I was about to lash out defensively, but he softly added, "Because that's what grief does to people sometimes, you know?"

I froze, mouth open, but the words lodged in my throat.

"It's nothing to be ashamed of," he went on. "You've been through hell. You're still going through it. Honestly, I don't know how you've kept yourself upright this long."

The fury was suddenly gone, replaced by that ever-present lump in my throat. "I don't think I've been holding myself as upright as you think."

"If it were me," he said dryly, "I'd be in a fetal position somewhere."

I slouched back against the couch. "I can't do that, though. The team... The fans..."

He studied me, brow pinched. "But what about *you?*"

I couldn't look at him. There was no room for me. No room to let myself crumble the way I wanted—needed—to crumble. My voice was brittle as I whispered, "There are too many people depending on me." I closed my eyes, surprised my back didn't ache from the weight of everyone —my team, our fans, my best friend's widow, their kids...

"You know," Peyton said softly, "just because millions of people rely on a bridge every day doesn't mean it won't collapse when it goes too long without repairs."

I met his gaze.

He moved a little closer to me, eyes locked on mine. "Avery, you've been trying to hold up this entire team while you're falling apart. Let us carry the team while you take care of yourself. Let *us* carry that weight while you take care of yourself." He put his hand on my forearm. "Let *us* take care of *you*."

My throat constricted, and I avoided his gaze.

"I get it, okay?" he said. "We—men—we're supposed to be strong and stoic. Letting our emotions out is supposed to be weak, but it's *not* weak. And the thing is, even if it *was* weak, no one's expecting you to be *this* strong."

God, I was so done crying. Today. At all. I was just so done with tears.

At least I didn't completely unravel this time. I wasn't so sure I had it in me to fall apart like that again. Peyton rested a hand on my shoulder as I collected myself, and when I'd more or less regained my composure, he asked, "You all right?"

"Not really, no." Why was it so liberating to say that out loud? "But I think... I don't know. I think I needed that more than I realized. And what you said..." I managed something that I hoped resembled a smile. "Thanks. I needed to hear that."

His smile was soft. Far more sweet and endearing than I deserved.

I sniffed and wiped my eyes. "I think you're right, too. About the drinking and—yeah. I can't keep doing this to myself." I pushed out a ragged breath. "I should talk to the front office about the player assistance program."

Peyton exhaled hard, and I didn't think I was imagining the sheer relief rolling off him. "I can go with you if you want," he said softly. "If you need some moral support."

"But you need to get to practice." It was still early yet, but in another hour or two, he'd have to start getting ready.

"I'll talk to Coach," he said. "This seems more important."

I studied him. "Why are you doing this for me? After I've been such a dick to you, and…" I trailed off, not sure how to finish.

Peyton was quiet for a long moment, staring down at his own hands. "To be fair, I might've come on a little strong about the drinking."

"No, you didn't." I rubbed the back of my neck. "You were right. Yeah, I was pissed about it, but now…"

He shifted a little on the cushion. "I could've been more…" He chewed his lip, then sighed and shook his head. "I don't know. I do jump the gun about stuff like that, though." The distant look in his eyes gave me pause.

"Is there a story there?"

Peyton swallowed. Then he rolled his shoulders and reached up to scratch the back of his head. "My mom—she had a drinking problem. A bad one."

"Oh. Shit."

"Yeah," he whispered. "She's better now. She's been through rehab and all that, but I mean, the damage is done. She has a ton of health problems now because of it, and I know she feels guilty about the strain her addiction put on all of us." He turned to me. "And one of my teammates drank himself right out of his career."

My breath hitched. "Really?"

Pursing his lips, he nodded. "Jeff Richards."

"Ooh. Yeah, I remember he..." I tilted my head, trying to remember what I'd heard about Richards. "He lost his career over it?"

"In the end, yeah. It was pretty messy." Peyton sat back against the couch and blew out a breath. "I don't even know where he is now. Or... *if* he is."

A chill shot right through me. Of all the things Peyton had said to gently nudge me toward rehab, I was pretty sure that one was the swift kick in the ass I truly needed.

What if I'd lost control before someone had scraped me up? What if I'd managed to get deep enough into a bottle that I completely screwed over not only my team, but myself? Alcohol poisoning. A car accident. Hadn't Richards's drinking problem been piggybacked by an opioid addiction? How bad could *that* have gotten?

Cold water slithered through my veins as the truth hit me in the chest:

What if I'd been so far out of control that my teammates had to grieve another player?

While I'd buckled under the pressure of being their captain after we'd lost Leif, it had never dawned on me what it might do to them if they had to bury another captain.

"Shit," I whispered, reaching back to rub my neck with both hands. "I fucked up bad, didn't I?"

"No, you didn't." The *"not yet"* went unspoken, but I heard it just the same.

"I would have, though." I sat up again, facing him even though meeting his eyes filled me with renewed shame. "If you hadn't been here, no one else would've stepped in."

"You don't know that. I'm probably more tuned into it than most people, so I picked up on it right away. But someone would've noticed the cracks sooner or later." He looked right in my eyes. "I know you were trying to keep it out of everyone's sight, but you can only do that for so long."

I wanted to be embarrassed by that, but I think I'd hit embarrassment saturation at that point. And if anything, gratitude hit me. That despite all my efforts to hide what was happening, I would've failed eventually. That I'd had someone on my team—on my line—who knew the subtle signs to watch for so I didn't have to hit rock bottom first.

I pushed out a ragged breath. "I guess I'm lucky Pittsburgh signed you."

He laughed quietly. "It worked out, didn't it?"

"Yeah. It did. In fact..." I took a deep breath. "You want to hear something crazy?"

Peyton watched me with a mix of caution and curiosity.

My voice shook, but I managed to get the words out: "One of the last conversations I ever had with Leif was about you."

"It... It was?"

I nodding, staring down at my hands. "He knew I had a thing for you. Had for a long time. So when we found out your were coming to the team..." I laughed almost soundlessly. "When I kissed you in the hotel... Yeah, I was drunk. I don't even remember it all that clearly." I made myself look in his eyes. "Just... don't think being drunk was the only reason I came on to you like that."

He stared at me, his expression unreadable. "Oh."

Shame and embarrassment coiled in the pit of my stomach, and I dropped my gaze again. "I'm sorry. For what happened in the hotel, and for bringing it up now. I..." I laughed as I raked a hand through my hair. "I don't even know why I told you that."

"It's okay," he said. "Because..." He shifted a little,

suddenly flustered in a way I couldn't quite understand. "Listen, to put it bluntly, the feeling's mutual."

My head snapped up, which didn't do much to ease the throbbing inside my skull. "It is?"

"Yeah. I was... Coming to Pittsburgh, I was really excited to be on your team. And not just because of the way you play hockey."

I blinked. "Seriously?"

A blush rose on his cheeks as he flicked his eyes away and nodded. "Yeah. And it's... That hasn't changed, you know?"

"Not even after I've made a complete ass of myself?"

"You haven't, Avery." He met my gaze again. "You've been going through hell. I'm not holding it against you or judging you for it."

"But I..." Heat rushed into my face. "God, I blew it, didn't I? With everything I—"

"No," he whispered. "You didn't blow it."

I searched his eyes, disbelieving there was any coming back from the last several weeks. And yet at the same time, I had an odd sense of déjà vu. As if we'd had this conversation already. Or at least brushed up against it. Last night, maybe? Christ, I could only imagine how *that* had gone.

"You didn't blow it," Peyton said again. "But you need to focus on you right now. Not the team, and not... whatever this is."

I swallowed. Well, at least he tried to let me down easy. I could read between the—

"If there's something here"—Peyton gestured at himself, then me—"it'll keep, okay? I'm not going anywhere. I'll still be here as your friend and your teammate while you're getting through this. The rest? We can figure that out later."

I blinked. "We can?"

"Of course we can. There's time. I was attracted to you before I came to Pittsburgh, and I still am. I can wait."

I had no idea how to process that. After all the reasons I'd handed him to wash his hands of me and decide I wasn't worth a damn, he was still here. He was going to help me get into rehab and therapy. And somehow, he still thought there was potential for something to happen between us. Something good, rather than all the recent bullshit.

The thought of waiting, though, didn't sit right. I was suddenly antsy and nervous, filled with a sense of urgency I'd never experienced before—a panicked feeling like it was now or never. If we didn't do this now, then we might never get the chance.

It only took a moment for those pieces to click into place:

If we didn't do this now, then there was a possibility one or both of us could be gone.

Because I'd lost someone who'd seemed like a permanent fixture in my life. I'd taken for granted that Leif would be there—that night at the bar, later that month at training camp, and well into the rest of our careers and into our retirements.

What if something happened to Peyton?

My throat was getting tight again, and I had to swallow hard. "Oh God. I think I *do* need therapy."

He furrowed his brow. "Why's that?"

"Because I want to jump into this right now. I'm terrified to not do it right now because..." I had to grit my teeth to keep from choking on my own words. "I don't know how to make plans for the future when I'm still trying to get used to someone being gone the way Leif is."

Christ, that sounded so stupid and pathetic. I wasn't the

first person in the world to lose someone. They figured it out. Why the hell couldn't—

"That makes sense," Peyton said softly.

"It does?" I laughed halfheartedly. "Because it makes sense in my head, but when I say it out loud..." I flailed a hand.

"It does," he confirmed. "My therapist once told me that happens sometimes when someone gets slapped in the face by their own mortality. Suddenly nothing is guaranteed anymore, so they're in a hurry to do everything before time runs out."

"Oh. That... Shit, yeah, that makes sense." Then I studied him. "You have a therapist?"

"Had one." He gave a quiet, self-deprecating laugh. "Isn't it obvious?"

Now that he mentioned it, yeah, it kind of was. As dialed in as he was about things like this, it made perfect sense now that he'd been to one.

"Sounds like it was good for you," I whispered. "I kind of don't want to sit down and dissect everything going on..." I gestured at my head. "But maybe it's what I need."

He put a hand on my arm. "It's worth a try."

I nodded slowly. Nothing else was working, that was for sure. Especially not drinking myself numb.

The thought made me wince, and I sighed. "The player assistance program—do you know how that works? Will they suspend me?"

"I don't know," he admitted. "But I mean it—I'll go with you to talk to the front office about it." He gave my arm a gentle squeeze. "You don't have to do this alone."

The lump again rose in my throat, but it wasn't from crushing grief this time. I covered his hand with mine.

"Thanks. I'll, um... Let me get dressed, and we can go to the training center."

Peyton nodded, then looked down at himself. "I should probably grab a change of clothes, too. Maybe a shower?"

"Right. Of course. Why don't we go back to your place, and I'll call the front office while you're getting dressed?"

"Sounds like a plan."

CHAPTER 22
PEYTON

In the locker room before our morning skate the next day, and with the press outside, Coach Tabakov broke the news to the team. When he said out loud that Avery was going into the player assistance program, it was like a shockwave going through the locker room.

"Holy shit," Baddy said. "I didn't even know he was..." He trailed off, looking dazed.

"It's because of everything with Early, isn't it?" Willie sounded pained. "Calisse, I should've known he was struggling."

"He's coming back, though, right?" Eminem asked. "They're not going to put him through rehab and then waive him or something, are they?"

Coach shook his head. "He's not going anywhere. The front office has been very clear that he will not be traded or waived, and they still have every intention of negotiating an extension when that time comes."

The response to that was a collective sigh of relief that I wished Avery could've heard.

"His captaincy is up to the." Coach sent a

sweeping look around the room. "We can have three alternates, or we can choose a new cap—"

"Like hell," Eminem said. "Calds is our captain. Full stop."

Nods and a murmur of "yeah" and "damn right" went through the room, which brought a small smile to Coach's lips. I had a feeling he'd known that would be the response.

Admittedly, I wanted to argue that maybe we *should* pick a new captain. Not to punish Avery, but to take off the pressure we never should have piled on his shoulders.

I kept that to myself, though.

"He'll stay the captain, then," Coach said. "During his time in the program, though, he won't be playing or practicing with the team." Faces fell and expressions shifted to dismay and anger, but Coach put up a hand. "It's a requirement, and it's also to make sure he can focus on taking care of himself. But no one—not him, not the team, *no one*—is making any noise about him leaving the Whiskey Rebels."

"Good," Ziggy said emphatically. "Because we'd fucking riot."

More nods and sounds of agreement went around the room, and I couldn't help smiling. I wished Avery could've been a fly on the wall for this.

Eminem glanced around before looking at Coach. "Is this like when Ricky went through the program a few years ago and he couldn't come to games and we couldn't talk to him?"

"Absolutely not," Coach said without hesitation. "Calds is *not* suspended. He hasn't broken any rules. None of this is disciplinary from the League or from the club. This is a player asking for help, and he's getting that help. He can't practice or play with the team until he's reactivated, but he *can* still come to games and team events, and you're all welcome and encouraged to keep in contact with him."

That seemed to be exactly what everyone needed to hear, and the collective relief was palpable. I'd already known that part from being there when Avery discussed the situation with Coach and the club, but it was still comforting to hear it. It was even more comforting to realize the rest of the team *wanted* that contact with him.

Do you have any idea how much support you have, Avery?

Probably not. He'd been so far down, so lost in his own grief and his growing addiction that he'd likely felt completely alone and isolated. Hopefully by the time he came out of this, he'd understand just how loved and supported he really was.

"While Calds is out," Coach went on, "it's our job to hold down the fort. Keep playing. Keep collecting points and aiming for the playoffs. It's been a difficult year for this team, and both the fans and the front office know what we're up against. But we can still take it one game at a time. Keep playing. Keep doing what we do best. We can carry Early's memory with us, and we can stay strong as a team while Calds is getting help."

Everyone nodded solemnly.

"We can win for Calds," Eminem said. "Win tonight and break our losing streak—the better we can do while he's out, the less pressure there will be on him."

I actually choked up a little as my teammates nodded and murmured "yeah" and "we've got this." For all Avery had convinced himself he had to carry the entire team, they were rallying around him, ready to play like hell so he wouldn't feel like he had to rush back before he was ready.

"That's the attitude we need." Coach gestured over his

shoulder at the locker room door. "Step one, practicing before tonight's game. We're going to keep it light this morning. Let everyone process. But we've got a game tonight, and we need to *focus*. Got it?"

Nods all around.

He was true to his word, too—we did practice, but he didn't work us hard. Light drills. Some special teams, which was crucial today because Toronto had the number two power play in the League. Their penalty kill was nothing to sneeze at either; our best bet was to stay out of the box and keep the game five-on-five as much as possible.

After about thirty-five minutes instead of the usual hour, he dismissed us to cool down and head for the locker room.

On the way up the tunnel, I heard Baddy telling Eminem, "We should hit Calds up to go golfing. When the weather's not shit."

Eminem nodded. "Good call."

I didn't hear the rest of their conversation, but it was a relief that they were already trying to keep Avery close.

"Hey. Halls." Davis appeared beside me. When he stopped, I did, too.

"What's up?" I asked.

He glanced around, then looked up at me. "This was you, wasn't it? Getting Calds into rehab?"

I chewed my lip, not sure how much to divulge.

Sighing, Davis shook his head. "You don't have to say yes Just—whatever you did, I'm glad you did it. Because I was worried about him."

"Me too," I admitted quietly. "I was afraid he'd..." I trailed off, not sure how to word it, and a little afraid that saying it out loud would manifest the worst.

He's in good hands now. He's in rehab. He'll be fine.

Davis glanced toward the locker room again, then met my gaze. "Listen, I was really happy when they signed you over the off season, man, but—" His voice cracked, and he cleared his throat before he tried again. "Now that I know you saved our captain?" He swallowed hard as he clapped my shoulder. Then he continued into the locker room without another word.

I was grateful he hadn't said anything more.

The guys had been through enough today without seeing me fall apart too.

Avery sat on his couch and studied me as I took a seat in one of the recliners. Grimacing, he asked, "So... How did they take it?"

"Honestly?" I smiled. "I wish you could've seen it."

His eyebrows climbed almost to his hairline.

I told him what our teammates had said, and the parts they'd been most concerned about. "As soon as Coach said you're not suspended and we're encouraged to keep in contact with you, everyone started talking about going golfing with you or dragging you out to eat."

Avery wrinkled his nose. "Oh God. Don't tell me I'm going to have to fend off Baddy and Eminem trying to take me golfing."

"What? I thought you liked golfing."

"I do, but those two..." He groaned theatrically and flailed a hand before letting it fall to the cushion beside him. "Oh my God."

"Yeah? Do tell?"

"Eh." He shook his head and managed to laugh. "There's a lot of stories to tell."

I shrugged. "I've got time." I'd need to head home at some point for my pregame nap, then to the arena, but I still had a couple of hours yet. Something told me that stories about golf course shenanigans would be easier for Avery to handle right now; he was still brittle and ashamed after his talk with the brass.

He pursed his lips, gaze turning distant for a moment. Then he chuckled. "There was one time we were golfing in —I want to say Vegas? Might've been Arizona. All the dry states look alike after a while."

I snorted. "Yeah, they kinda do."

"Right? Anyway, wherever the hell we were, Eminem brought a box of those prank golf balls?" He groaned and rolled his eyes. "The ones that explode when you hit them, or they're weighted weird so they don't go where they should."

"Wait, those are a thing?" I laughed. "Really?"

"Ugh. Yes. And the ones he got—they're almost impossible to tell apart from the real thing." He picked up his drink and muttered, "That was the longest eighteen holes I've ever played."

"Yeah, I bet. Did they bring the real balls too?"

"Oh, they did. Though..." He snickered. "Baddy thought it would be funny to mix them all into the same bucket, so then they were getting the prank ones, too. Eminem was doing pretty well that day, but then he got one of the exploders, and it fucked him all up."

"You know, I never could quite reconcile hockey players with golf," I mused. "Because it just seems so sedate and mellow, and every hockey player I know gets bored if he has to sit still for two minutes."

Avery chuckled. "I know, right? But put a bunch of

pranksters and shit-talkers out there, and it ends up being a lot of fun."

"I believe that."

He laughed again, but it faded, and from the shift in his expression, some less pleasant thoughts were creeping in.

Eyes distant, he whispered, "Leif got his best ever score that game. The prank balls didn't throw him off at all, and even without his handicap, he blew all of us out of the water." Watching his fingers play with the hem of his shorts, he said more to himself than me, "Golfing without him has been really weird."

"I'm sure it has," I said softly.

He shifted his gaze in the general direction of his garage, and he sighed. "His clubs are still in my trunk."

I jumped. "They are?"

His Adam's apple bobbed as he nodded. "I should give them back to Rachel. But I didn't want to upset her, and..." He shook his head. "I always kept them in my car when we were both in town during the off season. Since he usually took his bike when we golfed." He moistened his lips. "Including the last time."

My stomach somersaulted. "Shit. That's..." What the hell was I even supposed to say?

Avery cleared his throat and shook himself. "I'm sorry. I'm... I didn't mean to bring that up." He sighed. "It's amazing how everything kind of leads back to it, you know?"

"You two were close," I said quietly. "I can only imagine how many things remind you of him."

"It's a lot. It's... God, I still don't know how to do this."

"Do you think the therapists will help?"

"I do, yeah. They're assigning me a counselor who specializes in grief. I'll have an addiction counselor, too, but the grief counselor—she's the one I'm really hoping will help." Avery sighed again, suddenly looking utterly exhausted. "I don't know how much anyone or anything can help, but I hope she will."

"I hope so too."

"At least make me less of a mess," he muttered. "The team needs me to have my head together."

"Don't worry about us. We're all worried about *you*."

Avery winced. Exhaling, he leaned forward, hanging his head so he could rub the back of his neck. "I hate that I'm worrying them. They've got enough on their plates, you know? They lost Leif too."

"They did. But everyone knows you two were closer than anyone." I paused, then gently added, "They're all supporting you. I promise."

"I know. And I appreciate it." He was quiet for a moment before softly admitting, "I thought they'd be pissed at me. For bailing on them."

The temptation to reach over and knead his neck for him was almost irresistible, but I folded my hands tightly in my lap. Touching, even platonically, would only complicate everything we'd temporarily shelved.

"They're not pissed," I told him. "They're worried about you. They want to support you any way they can. But they're not pissed."

He pressed an elbow into his thigh and rubbed his eyes with his thumb and forefinger. "I hate being this much of a mess, though. They should be able to focus on hockey. Not... Not picking up my goddamned slack."

"Avery. Go easy on yourself. This is no different than if you were out with an injury."

He lifted his gaze to meet mine.

"Would you feel like a failure if you were out because

you'd torn your ACL or got a concussion or something?" I asked. "Because it happens to all of us."

Chewing his lip, he sat back against the sofa. "I usually do feel like I'm letting everybody down when I'm hurt. That year I broke my collarbone in U16..." He frowned and shook his head.

I studied him. "Okay, but if someone else went down, would you be upset at them?"

"Not if they got hurt," he said.

"What if they needed help with some mental health?" I pressed. "Didn't Conway take half a season off for his mental health?"

Avery opened his mouth like he was going to insist that was different, but he stopped himself. Staring down at his wringing hands, he quietly admitted, "Yeah. He had some real bad depression." He pushed out a breath. "God, we were worried sick about him the whole time he was gone."

"Okay. Well. That's where the team's at right now. They're not mad at you. They're not freaking out, thinking they're going to fall apart without you. They're just worried about you." I paused, then quietly added, "We all are."

He wiped a hand over his face. "I was trying so hard to carry the whole team. Then I just..." He sat back, dropping his hand to his thigh. "Now I'm leaving them in a lurch."

"You're not," I whispered. He turned skeptical eyes on me, so I went on, "This is a *team* sport, Avery. That means if somebody's out for some reason, we all step up. If a team falls apart because they lose one player, or they're upset at that player for being out and letting them all down?" I scoffed. "Then they're just slacking off and expecting that person to carry them. A team like that *deserves* to lose."

He blinked.

"We're going to keep moving forward," I said, "same as

we would if you'd broken your leg or went down with a concussion. And yes, it *is* the same thing."

He stared at me, mouth still open with what was probably a protest.

"Mental health is important too," I went on softly. "We're all really good at ignoring it, but it's important. And I can't imagine *anyone* thinking less of you because yours took a dive after you lost your best friend."

Avery pressed his lips together and stared down at his hands again. When he finally spoke, his voice sounded hollow: "It's been a lot harder than I thought it would be."

"I don't think anyone's ever prepared for something like that."

He shook his head slowly, eyes distant. He was quiet for a moment, then ran a hand through his hair and pushed out a breath. "Thank you, by the way." He looked at me with tired eyes, and he managed a small smile. "I'm sorry you ended up with so much of this on your shoulders. I have no idea how to make it up to you, but…"

"Don't worry about it. I'm just glad you're taking care of yourself."

"I'd like to tell you that was inevitable," he said softly. "Maybe it was. But you shoving a mirror in my face got me to get help before things got out of hand. So… thanks for that. And I'm sorry I put you in a position to need to do it, but I'm still grateful you did."

My voice threatened to get thick as relief and too many awful memories piled on. Too much guilt—what if I'd done something for Richards? I couldn't change that now, though. I could just be glad I'd stuck to my guns this time.

"You're my teammate," I said softly. "And my friend."

Avery flinched. "Teammate, yeah. I, um… I don't think I've been that great of a friend, though."

"You had a lot on your plate. I don't—"

"No." He shook his head sharply. "I was an asshole to you. Plain and simple. I'm just incredibly lucky that you're the kind of person who doesn't throw up his hands and say, 'You know what? Fuck you.' So... thanks for that." He swallowed hard. "And I'm sorry again. For all of it."

"I know," I whispered. "I never doubted that."

He studied me for a moment, some unspoken thought pulling his eyebrows together. Then he tilted his head back against the cushion and sighed. "Losing Leif—that was hard. Still is. But this? It's fucking hard as hell too."

"Going to therapy and rehab?"

He nodded slowly, as if the movement took all the energy he had left. "My first session with a counselor is tomorrow. I'm, uh... I'm not looking forward to it."

"You haven't talked to anyone yet?"

"I have." He opened his eyes and stared up at the ceiling. "But that was just an intake evaluation. Figuring out what I need, how much if a mess I am..." He wiped his hand over his face again. "Tomorrow, we start digging into the hard stuff."

I watch him, not quite sure what to say. Finally, I went with, "Do you want me to come by tomorrow?"

He met my gaze, surprise registering in his expression. "You don't have to."

"I know. But maybe it would help to see someone who's just going to chirp and tell you the latest locker room gossip."

The laugh that tumbled out of him was soft, but it gave me a rush I couldn't quite explain. As if it was a good sign, and also because it was a glimpse of that smile that always made me dizzy.

"Locker room gossip and chirping are always good," he

said, still chuckling. "If, um... If you want to. I don't know what kind of headspace I'll be in, but I won't say no to the company."

"All right." I nodded sharply. "I'll text you after practice is over. See where you're at."

"Okay." He swallowed. "I think my appointments and crap are over at like four. There's..." He groaned and rolled his eyes. "There's a lot tomorrow. They said the schedule will be lighter going forward, but it starts out with a *lot*."

"I bet."

Silence hung between us. I was still treading cautiously here, trying to figure out where to step. After a moment, I asked, "Are you coming to the game tonight?"

Chewing his lip, Avery shook his head. "Not... Not yet."

"The guys would love to see you," I whispered.

"I know." He didn't look at me. "And... tell them I said thanks for the support. Because it really means a lot. But it's..." His jaw worked for a few long seconds before he finally said, "I'm not ready to face them."

I wanted to tell him he had nothing to worry about. If anything, the guys would hug him until he couldn't breathe.

But in his shoes, maybe I wouldn't want to face the team, the fans, or—God forbid—the cameras. Maybe he still needed some time to get his head around things.

I reached across the space between us and touched his arm. "No one's going to pressure you, okay? But when you're ready, everyone will be happy to see you."

He looked at me through his lashes, and he let a tiny smile come to life. "Thanks. It... That really means a lot. Just, um... Tell them I appreciate the support? And that I'll come to a game soon?"

"I will. I promise."

CHAPTER 23
AVERY

The hardest part of this whole player assistance program thing was being away from my teammates.

Peyton came by a lot, and we texted. I texted with some the guys, too. They kept asking me to come to practice and hang out, or come to a game, or go golfing, but I just... couldn't Even facing Peyton was hard, and he'd seen me at my absolute worst. The other guys hadn't, and I didn't want them to. I wasn't even sure I'd be able to look any of them in the eye when I was done with the program and back on the ice. That was a bridge I'd cross when I came to it. Right now, I was too damn embarrassed to see anyone except that stubborn son of a bitch who kept coming over. Which I appreciated. Even if I sometimes wished he wouldn't.

The program itself was less terrible than I'd convinced myself it would be. The therapists were great, and as much as I didn't like the idea of sitting in a room and making myself vulnerable with someone, it *was* doing me some good.

It helped that I'd managed to avoid the group therapy sessions. I'd told the people in charge that, with my high profile, I wasn't comfortable opening those wounds in front of other people. No matter how confidential they were on paper, I just wouldn't be able to relax knowing someone else *could* repeat something I'd said.

After my second solo session with Shannon, the grief counselor and the therapist I saw most often, I'd admitted the deeper truth: "I'm having a hard enough time saying any of this out loud. The thought of doing it in front of a room full of people—even four or five people—makes me literally sick to my stomach."

I'd cringed, fully expecting Shannon to shake her head apologetically and tell me that I really did need to do it, high profile be damned.

Instead, she'd given a subtle nod and told me, "If a form of therapy gives you that much anxiety, then it's probably going to hinder your recovery more than it'll help it. If you decide later that you feel comfortable with it, that's something we can revisit down the road."

I'd actually wavered a little, caught off guard by the comment but also by the alien sense of relief that followed. I'd piled so damn much on my own shoulders—so much more than I'd realized—that I wasn't used to what it felt like when someone else took some of that weight off.

So... no group sessions, and no guilt over avoiding them.

I also saw a substance abuse counselor three times a week. He was confident that I probably wouldn't relapse with the drinking. Given the totality of circumstances, he didn't think alcohol would be a serious problem for me going forward. Yes, I'd been self-medicating from the grief and trauma, but even as I'd begun the painful prospect of unpacking all that, I hadn't felt compelled to drink.

"We'll still approach this as an addiction," he'd assured me. "It can be an insidious thing. Someone who's used opioids after an injury can become addicted even after they're not in pain anymore. The same can happen after using alcohol to numb emotional pain following a traumatic experience. So we'll take this as seriously as we would a well-established, long term addiction, and you'll always have access to any of us should you relapse or think you're going to. But I'm confident."

"What happens if I do relapse?"

He'd offered a gentle smile. "Honestly? Most people do at some point. We do everything we can to avoid that, of course, but the reality is that it's very common. It's not a failure of the person or of the rehab—it's just a setback that we can work through."

"So... like when an injury is healing, and then I push too hard and hurt myself again?"

"Exactly. There's no shame in it. We'll do everything we can to help you, and we'll give you all the tools we can to prevent a relapse. But if it happens, then all isn't lost."

As determined as I was to never relapse, I appreciated that.

"Does this mean I can't drink at all?" I'd asked another day. "Like, socially?"

"We'll figure that out over time. Some people do find they're able to drink socially without relapsing. Others..." He'd shaken his head. "For some, they can't control the compulsion to *keep* drinking or to get drunk, and it's too destructive for them. I've also had some patients who found the process of quitting to be so miserable that just thinking about having to go through it again makes them abstain."

Something told me that last one would be me. The withdrawal had been relatively mild compared to the dire warnings they'd given me, but it hadn't been a picnic. As much as I'd enjoyed drinking with the guys, I couldn't even think about having a drink right now without imagining that miserable handful of days.

Maybe I'd just be better off not drinking. Especially since the only time I really missed it was when the grief was hitting hard, like during a particularly intense therapy session or when I was trying to sleep. If the only time I wanted to drink were the times I needed to self-medicate... yeah, maybe avoiding it altogether wouldn't be such a bad idea.

Today was one of those days when a drink sounded good. Probably because my therapy session was scratching closer and closer to the bone. The thought of stepping behind closed doors, opening up a bottle, and falling the hell apart was more appealing than it should've been.

Shannon studied me for a long moment. "I'd like to know your thoughts about something I've been noticing during our interactions."

"That I'm a trainwreck?" I asked dryly.

"No. I'm sure you feel like one—that's more normal than you might think."

I wasn't sure if that was supposed to be comforting or not.

She went on, "You've spoken a lot about wanting to keep not just your substance abuse, but your grief out of your team's sight."

Shifting uncomfortably, I stared down at my hands and nodded. "They already saw me collapse once. They don't need to see that again."

"Did they respond negatively to it?"

"Not..." I chewed my lip. "I mean, they didn't get mad at me or anything? But I could tell it messed with all their heads. Seeing me lose it like that. I'm the *captain*, you know.

They're all struggling with what happened to Leif. They need *someone* in the room to keep it together."

"Do you think they expect that someone to be the person who was closest to Leif?"

The sudden lump in my throat almost made me choke. "I... I don't know. But I also... I mean... I shouldn't be this much of a mess. Not just in the locker room or in front of my teammates, but—I mean, Leif was my *friend.*"

Shannon tilted her head slightly as if she were trying to read me. Something she was scary good at doing most of the time. "Leif *was* your friend," she acknowledged. "So everyone—yourself included—should fully expect you to be grieving."

"But this hard?" I hated how my voice shook. "It's been *months* and I feel like it's still the night he died." Those last two words slammed into my chest, and I had to close my eyes and pull myself together.

"You feel like you should be back to normal by now." It wasn't a question. I almost took it as an accusation, but rewinding it in my head—no, it was just a gentle observation. I *wanted* it to be an accusation. I *wished* it was. Wasn't that what I deserved for being such a broken mess?

"I feel like I should be..." I chewed my lip as I gathered both my thoughts and my composure. "Like, Leif was my best friend. We were really, really close. But the way I've been since he died—" I sniffed and swiped at my eyes. "Should I be *this* much of a mess over him?"

Shannon was quiet for a moment. "Do you think you shouldn't be?"

"I think it would make sense if he'd been my boyfriend or a family member or something, you know? Rachel—of *course* she's struggling. She lost her husband. Her kids lost their dad. I lost..." I had to fight back the lump in my throat, not that it helped much. "I lost my friend."

Again, she was quiet, this time as if she expected me to continue. When I didn't, she asked, "Am I understanding that you think you shouldn't be grieving this much for someone who wasn't a family member or a romantic partner?"

"Exactly," I whispered.

She nodded slowly, then folded her hands on her tablet. "I have to say, Avery, this is one of those unfortunate areas where society has failed everyone. Especially men."

I blinked. "You—wait, what?"

"In our culture, we're expected to mourn different people in different ways. And to some extent, we do. You might feel sad over the death of a colleague you didn't know well, but you won't grieve like you would if you'd lost a spouse or a sibling."

"Right," I said, nodding but still not sure where she was going.

"When we lose a friend—whether because they've passed, moved away, or there's been a falling out that ended a friendship—I think we're often blindsided by just how hard that grief hits. And people around us often don't expect it either. They don't honor it or know how to deal with it." Shannon sighed. "Probably because another area where our society often falls short is when it comes to non-romantic and non-familial love."

I tilted my head. "What do you mean?"

"The bond of friendship can be as important as a romantic or familial one," she went on. "People love their friends, but we don't realize or acknowledge *how much* we love them. And then when they're gone... we don't know how to grieve that love, and the people around us don't know how to support us through it. Thanks to toxic masculinity, that problem is even worse for men—you're not allowed to acknowledge how much you love your friends when they're here, and you're certainly not allowed to when they're gone."

My throat was getting tight again, and I swallowed hard. "So this... It's normal?"

"Very," she said softly. "We don't know how to love people who aren't our families or partners. Or, well, we do, but we don't know how to express it or to grieve it. And it's not just how we love and grieve people. I have a lot of clients who sit right where you are, sobbing their eyes out and feeling like failures or like there's something wrong with them because they're grieving a pet. Our society unironically calls dogs 'man's best friend,' but then they wonder why someone is an emotional mess after their dog passes away." She folded her hands on top of her notepad. "We're much the same with our human friends. We form very, very close bonds with our friends. We love them far more deeply than we say out loud. It's not at all uncommon for people to refer to their friends as being like siblings."

I swallowed. "Like me and Leif."

"Exactly. That isn't just something people say—there are people with stronger bonds with their friends than with their siblings. But we expect them to grieve a lost sibling far more than we allow them to grieve that close friend." She paused, pursing her lips. "I worked with a veteran several years ago who struggled because he'd been granted permission to take leave from a deployment to attend his brother's funeral. He wasn't overly close to his brother, but they had a good relationship. Then he deployed again, this time into a warzone. When his best friend was killed right in front of him, he didn't even have the chance to watch the casket get loaded onto a plane, never mind attend the service or take some leave to deal with his grief."

"Holy shit," I whispered. "He just had to... keep on fighting after that?"

Shannon nodded. "Obviously there was a lot of trauma there relating to being in a combat zone, but the absence of time and space to properly grieve his friend played an enormous role in his struggles. And I think, in a way, you're having that same difficulty."

I shifted uncomfortably and avoided her gaze. "Except I've *had* time and space. My team, everyone around me—they've been supportive."

"Mmhmm. They have. But how much time and space have you allowed *yourself*?"

I jumped like she'd kicked me. "What?"

"You lost your best friend, Avery," she said softly. "Suddenly and tragically. But you've been berating yourself for grieving too much. You're surrounded by love and support, but have—"

"I saw how it affected my team when I fell apart though," I said shakily. "That night in the locker room—our home opener—I'm supposed to be their *captain*. I can't—I can't just fall apart on them."

"Could that mean you weren't ready for that kind of pressure?" Her voice was full of nothing but kindness. No judgment or condescension. "That maybe you still needed time to sit with your feelings and let yourself grieve your friend?"

It took a *lot* of work to swallow. "They needed me."

"And I think you needed them too," she said. "You told me they supported you that night, didn't they?"

Wincing, I nodded. "They shouldn't have had to."

"But they did."

"So which is it—was I not ready to be there? Or was it okay because I had my team's support?" My shoulders dropped. "God, it doesn't even matter. I shouldn't have put that on them."

"It could mean both," she said evenly. "They're not mutually exclusive. Maybe you needed more time, but maybe you also needed their support. But I think more than anything, you needed to be gentle with yourself. Give yourself the extra time if you needed it. Let yourself lean on the people who care about you. You can only knuckle through the grief for so long before it's going to drag you back down and *make* you face it."

I closed my eyes and exhaled. This was the most brittle and raw I'd been in one of our sessions. I hated it, even if I knew it was—somehow, probably—what I needed.

"I have a question for you," Shannon said. "And you don't have to answer me out loud. I just want you to think about it."

I met her gaze warily. "Okay...?"

She looked me right in the eyes. "My question, Avery, is what do you think would happen if you let yourself grieve your friend as fiercely as you loved him?"

And just like that... we scraped bone.

From somewhere deep inside came a surge of renewed pain that was almost as intense as it had been at the hospital and at Leif's funeral. As if there'd been this reserve of grief simmering just out of my reach, and now it bubbled to the surface in a single scalding deluge of loss.

Crying had become such an irritating, frustrating thing —something I was so sick of doing because it felt about as useful as tripping over my own skates. This time, it was different. Even as it all came down on me harder than it had in a long time, even as it seemed to tear apart all the walls I'd been trying so hard to rebuild, it was... cathartic? Cleansing? I couldn't find the word because I couldn't find any of them. There wasn't much I could do in that moment except let the loss of my best friend shake me apart all the way down to my core.

Feeling all of this fucking sucked, but it was also like I'd been trying to stop an avalanche with my bare hands, and now I wasn't fighting it anymore. Now I could just... let go. Breathe. Sob. Hurt. And it turned out that surrendering to the avalanche was a lot less painful than trying so hard to hold it back.

I was grateful that Shannon just pushed the tissue box closer. She didn't say anything. She didn't try to tell me this was good and it was healthy. She didn't try to get me to man up (not that she would have, but none of my thoughts made sense right then, so whatever). She just let it all crash over and through me.

I wadded up some tissues to wipe my eyes and my face. It didn't do much good, but it was something to do with my shaking hands. Falling apart like this, it hurt like hell. I wanted to be angry she'd ignited this, but I also wanted to drop to my knees and tell her how grateful I was that she'd given me permission to break like I hadn't realized I needed to.

Little by little, I composed myself again. I was still shaking all over, my eyes still burning from tears, but I could finally catch my breath.

I half-expected Shannon to ask me how I felt, or to say... I don't know. Something. But she just watched me silently, her expression gentle and without any judgment or surprise.

When I finally managed to speak, I almost choked on my words: "Does it ever get better than this?"

"It does," she said. "I won't tell you that it'll ever go away. You'll never be who you were before you lost Leif." She shook her head. "When you lose someone you loved that much, there will always be a piece missing."

My eyes stung again, but I didn't fall apart. I took a moment to make sure I was going to stay together, then cleared my throat. "So it's just... It'll always hurt."

"To some degree, yes. You'll always miss him, Avery, and you'll always grieve for him. Our society has this idea that grief is a process, and once it's over, it's behind us, but that's not how it works. It *is* a process, but it isn't one that *ends*. Not entirely." Her smile was faint and reassuring. "Over time, though, you'll be able to remember him and be happy that you had him in your life even while you're sad that he's gone."

My chest tightened. I missed being able to reminisce about him almost as much as I missed him.

"It'll always hurt," Shannon said softly. "But it'll hurt *less*."

Closing my eyes, I nodded as I pushed out a long breath.

Not very long ago, the thought of carrying all this grief for even a moment longer had made me want to lie down and give up. Today, though, as my hands still trembled and my eyes still stung, the thought of missing Leif forever wasn't as excruciating anymore. It would be a long, long time before thoughts of my best friend turned bittersweet, but I could finally believe that time would come.

I hurt a lot more now than when I'd walked into Shannon's office today, but there was hope around the edges. Opening up that wound I'd been ignoring, grieving him in the way I'd desperately needed to but didn't know how—it hurt like hell, but there was relief there too. That sense that there was no shame in having this pain and in needing to feel it this hard.

"I'm so glad I had him in my life," I said shakily. "I really am. It just... I miss being able to think about him without..." I gestured at the tear that had slipped down my cheek, then wiped it away. "I guess that's the price of having someone that amazing."

"It is," she said, her voice still gentle and soothing. "And as a society, we're not supposed to feel this way over losing a friend. Men especially aren't supposed to. But we do—including men—and sometimes the best thing we can do is give ourselves *permission* to really love and grieve our friends."

I nodded slowly, swallowing against the ache in my throat.

This was hard. It hurt.

But for the first time since August, even as I hurt worse than I had in months, I could finally believe there was life after this.

After that therapy session, I went home and slept for three blissfully dreamless hours. I did that a lot after my sessions; they were cathartic and draining, and sometimes I just needed to faceplant for a while. I didn't usually sleep *quite* this hard afterward, but I'd been utterly drained.

A long nap, some lunch, and a few stupid internet videos later, I left the house again, but not for therapy or rehab. Though ice time *did* kind of feel like unofficial therapy. I'd been staying conditioned as much as I could both on and off the ice, and though the club had explicitly said I was not barred from being around the team—something that happened during suspensions—I hadn't been able to bring myself to join them. I still felt weird about everything. About leaving them high and dry. About everyone knowing I was in the assistance program. The thought of facing them, never mind joining them on the ice, made my stomach turn.

But Peyton had already seen me at my worst, so I felt okay about being around him right now. And he was willing to skate with me—he'd offered several times—so why the hell not? Though there was no game tonight, the team had practiced this morning, so this would be a light session, but that was fine.

Walking into the facility, I was still wrung out from therapy. It had been a good session, though. A hard one, but a good one. It had left me raw in ways that didn't feel great, but I knew would help me heal. It was a little like having surgery to correct an injury—it sucked in the moment, and it wouldn't fix everything overnight, but it *would* make things better with time.

"I don't even know if I have the energy to skate today," I'd told Shannon at the end of our session.

"It's okay if you don't," she'd said. *"But from what you've been telling me, I suspect you'll feel better after you've done some skating."*

We'd see, wouldn't we?

Right now I had that feeling like the last thing in the world I wanted to do was skate or even work out. It felt a whole lot like arriving at a physical therapy appointment, knowing damn well that even if it was good for me, it was going to suck from start to finish.

But this wasn't physical therapy, and I knew from experience that once I hit the ice, I'd shake that off.

When I stepped into the locker room, it was almost deserted.

Almost.

Peyton looked up from lacing his skates, and those blue eyes almost had me stumbling even before that brilliant smile came to life. "Hey. How's it going?"

"It's, um..." I dropped onto the bench by my stall. "I miss hockey, if that tells you anything."

He chuckled, unaware of how gorgeous he was. "You're a hockey player. If you're not on the ice, you miss hockey. Full stop."

I laughed. "Okay, yeah. You got me." Sobering a little, I looked down as I untied my sneakers. "It's been harder than when I've been out with an injury though, you know? Because, like, when I'm hurt, I can feel it. I can't skate. I can't play. Fine. This time?" I shook my head as I toed off one shoe.

"I get that," he said softly, all the teasing gone. "I'm always climbing the walls during the off season."

"Right? Especially when the playoffs are still going. So there's still guys playing hockey while I'm not."

"Exactly!" He laughed again. "Like when a *certain team* eliminated mine in the second round two years ago."

I lifted my gaze, and I wasn't at all surprised to see him shooting me a playful but pointed look. "What?" I shrugged innocently. "It's not my fault you guys couldn't get anything past Ziggy."

"Ugh. Fucking brick wall." He huffed with mock annoyance as he got up from the bench. "Not gonna lie, though—I'm much happier playing on his team than against it."

"Tell me about it." I stood and peeled off my hoody and T-shirt. "When we signed him, I was so damn relieved."

"They're extending him, right?" Peyton sounded genuinely concerned. "We're not going to let him become a free agent, are we?"

"Are you kidding? I don't think there's anyone on the roster Gary *wouldn't* trade in order to free up cap space to pay Ziggy whatever salary he wants."

"Smart man."

"I know, right?" I was about to say our GM was a damn wizard, having not only snatched Ziggy during an absolute steal of a trade four years ago, but signing Peyton this past summer. I... didn't want the air to get awkward between us, though, and if I started fanboying him—well. Some things were just better left unsaid, at least for now.

"So." Peyton picked up his stick and gloves. "Down for some one-on-one?"

I laughed. "Well, it isn't like we have enough for a full scrimmage, so..."

I regretted that as soon as I said it, because he raised his eyebrows in that way that told me exactly what was coming next.

"I can talk to the guys," he said. "I'm sure they'd be happy to join us. Not today, but..."

Avoiding his gaze, I shook my head. "I'd... just some one-on-one will be good for—well, for me. You've been practicing with..." Fuck. Why was I rambling? I cleared my throat. "The other guys—not yet. Maybe down the line a little."

Please don't push, please don't push, please don't push...

He didn't push.

"Okay." He nodded and collected his gloves and visor off the bench. "I'll meet you out on the sheet."

And then he was gone.

Alone in the locker room, I exhaled, relieved he'd let the

subject be. Truthfully, I did want to skate with my other teammates. I wanted to be back on the ice with the whole team, caught up in chirping and practicing and running those annoying drills that our coaches dreamed up. Sometimes the way I missed my teammates seemed to cut almost as deep as the way I missed Leif. These men were my family, and being isolated from them sucked hard.

But the shame of collapsing so hard that I drowned in a bottle...

The humiliation of failing them as not only their teammate but as their captain...

No. I wasn't ready to face them. Not yet. Not until I was firmly on my own two feet and they could be confident I wouldn't let them down again.

Well, that was another goal to set my sights on. Get my shit together so I could be with my teammates again. So I could be with my *family* again.

Resolved to do exactly that, I put on my gear and headed out to the ice to skate with Peyton.

CHAPTER 24
PEYTON

After I'd finished warming up, I was still alone on the ice. For a few minutes, I skated lazy circles and fired a few pucks at the net, all the while glancing toward the chute for Avery.

Was he bailing? Had he decided not to do this after all?

Because he'd looked rough when he came into the locker room. I'd seen him a few times after his therapy sessions, and they obviously took a toll, but today? Jesus. He looked like he was hungover, jetlagged, or even recovering from the flu or something. All three at the same time, honestly.

Damn. Maybe this hadn't been a good idea. Maybe I should've hung around the locker room for a few more minutes. Feel him out. See if he really was up for—

Clomp clomp clomp.

The familiar sound of someone walking in skates yanked my attention back to the chute, and I was glad no one but me could feel or hear the way my pulse surged.

Avery paused to put his water bottle in one of the racks

by the bench, then glided out onto the ice as if he'd never been away. He had on a gold practice jersey with no name or number, and a white helmet, same as he would for any practice, but he looked as hot to me as when he skated onto the ice for a game. His focus was sharp. His dark hair curled around the edges of his helmet. The way he moved... God, he was mesmerizing.

He hadn't missed a step, either. He moved a little slower than he usually did, even during practice, but he was as precise and confident as ever.

His earlier fatigue seemed to be gone, too.

Sometimes that was all it took—getting into hockey gear and hitting the ice. There was something almost magic about it. I'd dragged myself to training facilities in the past, sure I would rather be run over by the Zamboni than practice, but once I was on the ice, I was good.

That must've been the case for Avery, because holy shit, he was a different person now that he was skating. As he warmed up, he picked up some speed, too. Not full speed—this was a light, unofficial practice, after all—but definitely not beer league speed either. When he fired a shot at the net and missed, the puck cracked against the boards loud enough to echo through the whole rink.

Watching him like that, I was lucky I didn't lose an edge. This version of him—this loose, effortless version—was the Avery I'd drooled over for years. I'd loved watching him play hockey from the moment he'd made the Whiskey Rebels' roster, and the more I'd seen him in interviews and hype photos, the more I'd watched him as more than just a hockey player. He was my absolute catnip—addictive to watch on the ice, jaw-droppingly gorgeous off the ice, and with a beautiful smile and a wicked laugh that made my brain short circuit.

And right then, while I was distracted by how much I wanted him, I didn't realize he was skating toward me. Not until he skidded up next to me and showered me with ice crystals.

Eh, a cold shower was a cold shower.

I laughed as I dusted myself off. "Dick."

"What?" He graced me with that wicked laugh. "You could've moved."

"Yeah, yeah." I flipped him off. "You want to practice or not?"

"I've been practicing. I was just waiting for you to join me."

Rolling my eyes, I muttered, "For God's sake." I grabbed a puck on my stick. "Let's do this." I paused. "Or we could make it a challenge."

He grinned. "Go on."

Pretending that grin wasn't going to be my undoing, I said, "Get out the goalie practice pucks."

Avery guffawed. "Bro, we are not playing with white pucks. Fuck that."

"What? Why not?" I tapped his skate with my stick. "Where's your sense of adventure?"

He narrowed his eyes. Then he shrugged. "You know what? Fine. You talk a good game." He gestured toward the locker room. "Go get us a white puck."

"Yeah? You in?"

"One-on-one, white puck, first to five?"

"You got it." I skated toward the bench. "Be right back."

Of course now that I'd dropped the gauntlet, I wasn't quite sure where the white pucks actually lived. I'd only ever seen the goalie coaches bring them out a few times (usually to a chorus of cursing from Ziggy and Laramie), but where did they actually get them *from?*

I didn't want to go rifling through the equipment managers' bins, and I didn't know if Ziggy would text me back in time (wasn't he golfing this afternoon?). I could check one of the cabinets where we kept pucks, though, since they might—

Ah. Jackpot.

I grabbed a couple of the diabolical discs out of the bucket. They were off white, and they were hard as hell to see on the ice. Great for honing a goalie's ability to track a puck.

And also great for a couple of skaters who were just fucking around on the ice.

"Jesus Christ." Avery's voice echoed off the rafters. "Did you have to Amazon Prime them?"

"I had to *find* the damn things." I tossed them onto the ice, sending them sliding toward him. "They're hard to see!"

Avery caught one on his stick. "I saw this one just fine. Don't know what your problem was."

"Yeah, yeah." I joined him on the ice. "I'm hearing a lot of talking, but I'm not seeing any—"

He whipped past me, hip checking me and protecting the puck all the way. "Sorry, what was that?" He called over his shoulder. "I didn't hear you!"

I laughed as I skated after him. "You're an asshole!"

Avery cackled, then slapped the puck into the goal and pumped his stick in the air.

I just rolled my eyes and collected the puck from the back of the net. "That was a cheap shot."

"Pfft. You let your guard down." He skated up and skidded to a halt, showering me with ice crystals again. "The commentators would've had a field day with that."

"I stand by what I said." I brushed snow off my face and jersey. "You're an asshole."

"Yeah, but I'm also one goal ahead of—hey!"

I charged toward the other goal, the puck on my stick, and it was my turn to cackle as he cursed at my back.

He almost caught me, though; I was halfway across the offensive zone when he tried to poke check the puck away. He came close, but I managed to shoulder check him off me and score.

"One-one!" I pumped my fist. "Kiss my ass, Calds!"

Still laughing, he knocked his shoulder into my back, and I whacked his shin with my stick.

"Fine, dickhead." He huffed melodramatically. "We're tied. Still first to five?"

"Sounds good." I dug the puck out of the net. "Too bad we don't have someone to drop the puck for us. We could actually do a faceoff."

"Yeah, but what fun is that? I suck at faceoffs, and besides..." He swiped the puck off my blade and took off. "We don't need them!"

I rolled my eyes again. I shouldn't have even been surprised.

Avery edged me out 5-4, but it was close.

By the time he potted that last goal, we were both drenched in sweat, and I was exhausted like I'd just played thirty minutes in a real game.

"You know," I panted as I skated up beside him. "This was *supposed* to be some friendly one-on-one. And *some* of us had practice this morning."

The innocent look he shot me was too damned cute. "It was friendly, wasn't it?"

"Uh-huh. I think I'm gassed, though."

"Me too, now that you mention it."

We started toward the bench and the water bottles we'd left on top of the dashers.

After I'd taken a drink, I poured some down the back of my neck. "Do you, um, want to grab some—" I glanced at the clock on the scoreboard. "Okay, it's a bit late for lunch, but maybe an early dinner?"

Avery looked in the same direction, then shrugged, and when he faced me again, his smile could've melted the ice beneath our skates. "Yeah, I could eat. Got anywhere in mind?"

There was a restaurant right beside the training center that players and staff alike frequented, but I had a feeling that might be a little high-profile for him right now.

"Well." I hesitated. "I was planning to cook tonight, since I don't have to be at the arena. You're welcome to join me?"

Surprise flickered across his face, and for a moment, I was sure I'd overstepped. We were on strange ground and had been for a while, and I didn't want to complicate that any more than we already had.

But then he smiled. "I didn't know you cooked."

Some warmth rushed into my face as I half-shrugged. "I won't be competing on *MasterChef* any time soon, but I can hold my own."

"Well, now I'm curious." He tipped his head toward the locker room. "Shall we?"

I tried not to think about why my heart sped up as we headed off the ice. Over my shoulder, I asked, "Do you like salmon?"

"I love salmon." He paused to deposit his stick on the rack. "Can I bring something?"

The words *"maybe a bottle of wine or something?"* very

nearly flew from my lips. I caught them, though, and went with, "I didn't have anything planned for dessert. If you want to grab something sweet..."

"I can do that. If I had more time, I'd make something, but storebought will have to do."

As I stepped into the locker room ahead of him, I glanced back. "You bake?"

He grinned and puffed out his chest. "I'll have you know I'm an exceptionally mediocre baker."

I barked a laugh. "What exactly qualifies as 'exceptionally mediocre'?"

"I can hold my own without burning anything," he explained as he pulled off his helmet. "And most of what I make is pretty good. But nobody's ever going to ask me to make a wedding cake again."

"Again?" I cocked a brow as I took off my own helmet. "Is there a story there?"

"One I'll tell you over dinner, yes."

"Deal."

With post-practice plans established, we started stripping off our gear. We undressed with all the unselfconsciousness of guys who'd been in hockey locker rooms since we were kids.

Usually there were a lot of people getting in or out of gear, though. Or at least a lot of people and activity. I couldn't remember a time when it had been just me and one other person without any other noise or movement around us.

Especially when that one other person was someone as intensely attractive as Avery Caldwell.

I was not ready for the work it took to keep my gaze from accidentally landing on him. I wasn't going to perv on him or anything, but without any other distractions, it was easy to absently let my focus snap on to him. Just like when we'd been on the ice, it took work not to zero in on him simply because he was the only one there, and then *keep* staring because he was so... damn... *hot*.

I seriously did not need an eyeful of that man's bare shoulders. Or six-pack. Or ass. Or package. Or...

Goddammit, he was so sexy.

But this was the locker room, not a nightclub. He was my teammate, not a potential hookup. No matter how much I wanted him—oh my God, I wanted him—this was neither the time nor the place.

It was especially not the time. He was up to his neck in trying to get a handle on his grief and his drinking, and getting involved with anyone—especially a teammate— would only complicate things.

As I headed for the showers, it wasn't lost on me that he'd gone out to get drunk and get laid the night he'd had me come get him from the club. Were hookups a normal thing for him? Or had that just been part of his self-destructive pattern? Not that I thought hookups were self-destructive. I was hardly above them, even if I hadn't had the time, energy, or inclination to get laid since I'd come to Pittsburgh. But hookups *could* be self-destructive the same way drinking *could* be.

And was it even my business? Yes, I was concerned about him, but the way my stomach curdled when I thought about him firing up Grindr or Tinder while I was on the road... that was not concern.

Am I... jealous? Of someone who might not even exist?

I mouthed a few curses as I let the shower's hot spray rush over my neck and back.

What is wrong *with me?*

Nothing I needed to be thinking about now, that was for

sure. I'd come here today to help Avery get back on the rails. After this, we'd have dinner so we—

Oh my God. I'd invited him to my place for dinner.

Squeezing my eyes shut, I hung my head to let the water rush over my hair. What was I thinking? I'd barely been able to skate when it was just him and me on the ice.

Well, there was no turning back now. I'd find a way to not make an ass of myself tonight, and hopefully I'd be able to focus well enough to cook. I could play hockey while I was distracted. Cook a salmon without scorching it? We'd find out.

By some miracle, I managed to finish my shower and get dressed without embarrassing myself. Avery was a few steps behind me, and he sat down to put on his sneakers just after I'd finished tying mine.

"Before we go," he said as he leaned down to tie one, "I think I'm going to go grab a cup of coffee."

"Mind if I join you?"

When he glanced up, his smile was a little tired but adorable nonetheless. "Not at all."

Why was that making my stupid heart do stupid flippy things? God, I was stupid.

After he'd put on his shoes, we strolled out of the locker room to the training center's lobby. This area could be absolutely crawling with people if there was a tournament going on, or when fans crammed into the stands to watch training camp. Today, the schedule was pretty quiet, so there were only a few people milling around out here. There was a signup table for skating and hockey lessons, and a handful of parents waited with their kids in tow. The coffee stand had two people in line, and I thought I saw someone wandering into the Rebel Wear store, which sold jerseys and other team-branded items for fans.

"It's so weird when it's this quiet," Avery murmured as we got in line. "It's like when I come here to practice during the off season." He huffed a laugh. "I keep expecting to see a tumbleweed roll through."

I chuckled. "No kidding. And it was crowded as hell earlier."

"Was it?"

I nodded. "Big turnout for practice."

"During the week?"

"Yeah?" I shrugged. "It happens."

He grunted in agreement. Some weekday practices were a ghost town. Some were, well... not.

Avery opened his mouth to say something, but before he could, there was a shrill, "Mom! Look! It's Peyton Hall!"

We both turned toward the voice and found a mom wrangling four kids, the oldest of whom couldn't have been more than twelve. One of the younger ones pointed at us and bounced.

"Justin," the mother scolded. "It's rude to point!"

"Sorry." He lowered his hand. "But it's—Mom! That's Avery Caldwell!"

Beside me, Avery tensed.

"It is! It is!" One of the boys ran toward us. "Can we get pictures? Can you sign something for us? Oh my God, I can't—"

"Stephen," the mother said patiently but firmly. "Let's be polite."

The kid backed off, but excitement still radiated off him.

With the other three kids in tow, the mom came closer, and she shyly looked at Avery and me. "I'm so sorry. They're big fans, but we don't have anything for you to sign. Would you mind if I go grab a couple of jerseys?" She gestured toward the Rebel Wear store. "I don't want to keep you, but they would love to have some Hall and Caldwell autographs."

Avery and I exchanged glances, and we both shrugged.

He smiled. "Sure. We're not going anywhere." He motioned toward the coffee stand. "We're just waiting for some coffee."

"Okay." She sounded relieved. "Five minutes—I promise." To her kids, she said, "Come on, let's go get a jersey while they get their coffee!"

The kids all went wide-eyed with excitement, and they sprinted across the lobby to the store with Mom following.

When we were alone again, Avery patted his pockets, then turned an alarmed look on me. "You don't have a Sharpie, do you?"

"I..." I patted my own pockets. "Shit. No."

He chewed his lip. "I've got one in my locker." He fished out his wallet and handed me a ten-dollar bill. "Can you get me a regular coffee?"

"Of course. Yeah."

Then he was gone, jogging back toward the hallway that led to the locker room.

By the time I had our coffees, Avery still hadn't returned. I found a chest high table, put the cups down, and set about polluting mine. I couldn't quite remember if Avery liked cream or sugar in his, but the stand was only a few feet away, so I figured he'd get whatever he needed.

I had just put the lid back on my coffee cup when the smallest of the woman's four boys sprinted up to me holding a jersey that was almost as big as he was. He was almost to me when he skidded to a halt, his smile vanishing in favor of worry, and he looked around. As his mom and siblings caught up, he gazed up at me, eyes wide and sad. "Is he gone?"

"No, no!" I put my coffee cup down beside Avery's. "He just went to get a marker so we can sign your stuff. He'll be right back!"

Relief took over the kid's expression, and he clutched the jersey close to his chest.

A second later, though, his face lit up again. "There! There! Mom, look!"

I turned, and sure enough, Avery was jogging back, two Sharpies in his hand. As he gave one to me, he looked at the mom and kids, and he sounded slightly out of breath. "Sorry about that. Couldn't remember where I'd left them."

"Oh, it's okay!" The mom was beaming. "They're so excited to meet you both, and I really appreciate you guys going to this much effort." To her youngest, she said, "A.J., can you give him the jersey to sign?"

The boy gazed shyly up at Avery for a second. Then he thrust the jersey at him. "Can you sign it? Please?"

Avery seemed surprised, but he recovered quickly. "Sure. Of course." He crouched and gave the kid a bright smile before he took the cap off the marker.

Then he paused, peering at the jersey. The kids and their mom exchanged uncertain looks.

Trying to keep the moment from getting awkward, I gave him a playful nudge with my foot. "A-V-E-R—"

That did the trick. Avery burst out laughing and smacked my thigh with the back of his hand. "Shut up." Then he carefully scrawled his autograph on the number.

I chuckled, relieved the tension was broken, and returned my attention to signing the other jersey.

After that, their mom asked if we minded doing photos, which of course we didn't. We posed for a handful with the kids, who had huge smiles as they held up their newly signed jerseys.

As soon as the photos were done, one of the older boys looked at Avery. "Hey, do you know when you'll be back?"

"Stephen!" their mom whispered. To Avery, she said, "I'm sorry."

"It's fine," Avery said with his media smile in place, and he looked at the boy. "I'm not sure when I'll be back, but I'm hoping it'll be before the playoffs."

Both of the older boys' faces lit up.

"Yeah?" the oldest asked. "So you'll be back this season?" He shoved his brother. "I told you!"

"Whatever!" The other kid shoved him back. "You didn't know either."

"Boys," their mom growled.

Avery just chuckled. "I'll be back this season."

That seemed to make their day even more than the photos and the signed jerseys.

The kids peppered us both with questions, and then their mom told them it was time to go. To us, she said, "Thank you both. I think you just made their whole week."

"Ours too," I said, and I meant it.

That earned us another bright smile from Mom, and then she herded the kids out toward the parking lot.

When we were alone again in the lobby, Avery picked up his coffee and took a drink, but his expression was distant.

"You good?" I asked him. "When you took the jersey, you seemed a little..." I didn't know how to describe it.

Avery gazed in the direction the family had gone. "I guess..." He chewed his lip. "I don't know. It kind of blew my mind that she actually went and dropped almost three hundred bucks on a Caldwell jersey."

"A Hall jersey too," I said. "I don't know if you noticed, but they were even more excited to see you than me."

He stared at me with wide eyes.

"When you were in the locker room," I said, "the little one looked like he was about to cry because he thought you'd left."

Avery's lips parted and his eyebrows climbed even higher. "He... He did?"

"Yeah." I gave him a nudge. "You have fans, you know. A lot of them."

"I..." He glanced toward the parking lot, then dropped his gaze. "I guess. I mean, know I had fans. But with me being out, and everybody knowing why..." He trailed off as some color rose in his cheeks.

I put a hand on his shoulder. "They're not going to bail on you because you needed help. Yeah, everyone knows you're in the player assistance program, but they also know you lost someone really close to you." I gave his shoulder a squeeze, then let him go. "They've got your back, same as we do."

He straightened a little. "Really?"

"Hell yeah. I mean, on the last road trip, me and Baddy stopped to sign for some fans outside the hotel in Tampa. Lot of them were asking about you."

Avery blushed again. "They were?"

I nodded. "Uh-huh. They wanted to know how you were doing. If we thought you'd be back this season." I smiled. "Some of the kids waiting outside of practice the other day told us to tell you they're already making signs for your first game back."

"Holy shit," he murmured.

"I'm serious," I said softly. "The fans miss you, and so do we."

Avery winced and dropped his gaze. "I feel like I let everybody down."

"You didn't. And nobody feels like you did."

He gave a quiet, bitter laugh. "Tell that to the commenters on social media."

"Pfft." I rolled my eyes. "I don't suppose you've read the comments by other people shutting those assholes down, have you?"

From the sheepish shrug, he had. He probably just hadn't let himself believe that he had more defenders than detractors.

"There will always be people who hate some of us," I said. "Hell, Ziggy's first in the League for shutouts this season. Every time there's an article mentioning him, though, there's a handful of people who have to pipe up and talk about the bad season he had a couple of years ago and how he needs to be traded."

Avery laughed, wiping a hand over his face. Then he reclaimed his coffee cup. "Yeah. That's true. Haters gonna hate."

"They are. The vocal minority assholes online are going to be vocal assholes no matter what. But the fans—" I gestured with my coffee cup toward the parking lot. "The real fans who actually come to games and understand that we're as human as the next person—*they* support you. *They* matter."

He studied me uncertainly, but after a moment, the tension in his neck and shoulders started to ease. "Maybe. It's just hard to hear them over the haters, you know?"

"You could start by not reading the comments," I said dryly.

That made him laugh for real. "Okay, okay. You're not wrong."

"Of course I'm not." I nodded toward the other end of the building. "Now how about we get out of here so we can eat something?"

Avery's stomach growled audibly. So did mine.

We both chuckled and headed for the player parking lot.

When Avery pulled out of his parking space, he smiled and waved, and then he was gone.

I indulged in a relieved sigh. I had no doubt rehab was tough on him, and being away from the team and the fans was even tougher. That was the thing about hockey—it became a player's entire world, and being separated from that world and the people in it was devastating. I'd been suspended for two games during my second season, which meant I couldn't even communicate with my teammates for five days. No practice, no travel, no meals, no games—they couldn't even include me in the group text. That had been the longest five days of my career. I'd literally changed how I played after that to avoid another suspension just because I didn't want to face another separation from my teammates, and I hadn't had more than a double minor penalty since.

Avery could at least communicate with us, interact with us, and come to team functions.

Though he hadn't been coming to any games or practices. The guys kept asking me about him because I was the only one who'd seen him in person since he'd started in the program.

Maybe I could coax him into playing with me and some of the other guys. After that, maybe a game. It would probably be good for him.

As I left the parking lot, I mentally strategized how I could persuade him to be around the team more. I didn't want to coerce him into something he didn't want to do, but maybe if I got him to see that it would do him good? That the guys wanted to see him and weren't angry with him?

I'd work on it.

Maybe tonight over the salmon dinner I was making for the two of us.

CHAPTER 25
AVERY

I stopped at a small bakery on the way to Peyton's and picked up a fruit tart. Then I continued to his apartment in Cranberry.

I was a little surprised when I pulled into the complex, because this was where the team set up newly acquired players. I'd lived here myself for a season before I bought the place I lived in now.

It made perfect sense that Peyton was here, of course. Somehow, I'd just forgotten that he was a new arrival. He'd only been with the Whiskey Rebels since the start of this season, but it felt like he'd been here all along. Like he'd become as much a fixture as Coach or Ziggy.

I wasn't sure what that was all about, but whatever. I pulled into a parking space, grabbed my phone and the dessert, and headed upstairs.

When he opened his door, my heart did a little flutter. I *did* know what *that* was all about. And now I was going into his place? Just the two of us?

Not something I needed to think about right now. Not at all.

"I picked up a tart," I told him after I'd taken off my shoes. "It has fruit on it, so we can gaslight ourselves into thinking we're eating healthy."

"Gaslight, hell." Peyton waved that away. He took the tart and led me into the kitchen. "I practiced twice today. I would video myself eating an entire half gallon of ice cream, send it to Coach, and dare him to bitch about it."

I laughed. "I mean, I can video that if you want." I held up my phone. "If you really think—"

"Yeah, no. I don't need his disappointed dad look at practice." Peyton rolled his eyes. "He's weaponized that look, I swear."

"Don't most head coaches?"

"Yeah, but Tabakov is just..." He whistled, shaking his head.

I chuckled. He wasn't wrong. At his invitation, I took a seat in one of the barstools at his kitchen island while he went around the other side, presumably to continue cooking.

"If you think that dad look is brutal," I said, "wait until we get blown out. One of those really bad losses where we're *all* fucking up and the internet goes nuts that we're a disaster?" I grimaced. "Every team has at least one a season, and Coach's 'I'm not angry, I'm just disappointed' face is *legendary* after those."

"Oh God." He opened the fridge and slid the tart box onto a shelf. "I'm not looking forward to seeing that."

"Neither am I. Mostly because it means we had a blowout loss. Those are the *worst*."

"Aren't they?" He started to shut the fridge. "Do you want a beer or some—" He stiffened. "Shit. Sorry. Habit. Do you, uh... I have coffee, soda, water..."

"I'm good, thanks. And, um... don't worry about it." I

absently turned my phone between my fingers just to give my hands something to do. "I really don't want people acting different around me."

"No, I get that." Peyton rubbed the back of his neck. "I just... I know you're trying to..."

"It's fine. Don't worry about it." I gestured around us. "So they're still putting new players up here, eh? I used to live two units over, one floor down."

"Apparently, yeah." He rolled his shoulders, seeming relieved by the subject change. "I can see why they use it. It's not bad. Quiet. Nice units."

"You thinking of getting another place? Or staying here?"

"Don't know yet." Peyton looked around, then shrugged. "It's small, but I like it. And I mean, it's just me. I would kind of like to get a dog at some point, but only when I have a yard."

"Oh man, me too. I have the yard, but I'm gone too much, so it doesn't really seem fair, you know?"

"Exactly. That's why I didn't get one in Detroit. I had a housemate for a while, and I thought about it, but..." He trailed off, shaking his head.

"A housemate?" I asked. "Or...?"

Peyton was entirely too cute when he blushed. Shaking his head, he laughed. "Just a housemate. I know, I know, I heard all the rumors too, but it wasn't anything like that."

"So everyone was convinced it was because the only reason a gay man would live with another man is if they're banging."

"Exactly." Then he flashed me a wicked grin. "You want to hear something the press never figured out?"

I sat up a little. "Do tell."

"The whole time they thought Baldwin and I were

screwing because we lived together?" Peyton laughed. "I was *actually* dating Dan Carter."

"You—are you serious?"

"Mmhmm." He turned and rattled around in the fridge before coming back to the island with a Pepsi in hand. As he popped the tab, he said, "I still don't know how we managed to keep it under everybody's radar."

"No kidding. Weren't you guys flying back and forth? Oh, wait, he was in..." I quirked my lips. "Was that while he was still playing for Chicago?"

Peyton took a swig of soda, then nodded. "The long-distance thing wasn't too bad. Chicago to Detroit..." He shrugged. "We drove to see each other. Sometimes we'd meet halfway if it was a short trip, like if one of us had a game the next day or something."

I grimaced. "What about morning skates?"

He groaned. "God, those were some *early* morning drives. We'd spend the night together in a hotel, then be on the road by six to get back to our respective cities in time to practice. My pregame naps were lifesavers on those days."

"Yeah, I bet." I studied him. "How long did you guys... uh, date? Hook up?"

"We dated." Peyton leaned under the island and pulled out a metal pan. As he started taking stuff out of the fridge, he said, "It was serious for a while. We talked about coming out as a couple. Getting a place to live during the off season. Then he hit free agency, and Detroit made him an offer."

"No shit?"

He nodded. "At first, it sounded perfect. We'd finally be in the same city, and we could actually spend more time together." His face fell as he started cutting some cherry tomatoes, and he shook his head. "But then we realized... we'd be in the same city. We'd actually spend more time together. And that's kind of when we figured out we weren't in it for the long haul."

"Oh. That sounds tough."

Peyton half-shrugged. "It wasn't fun, that's for sure. But it worked out all right. He got a better offer in Vancouver anyway, and we're still friendly. We talk all the time, and we usually grab a beer or something when our teams play against each other."

"That's good. He always seemed like good people."

Peyton's soft little smile had no business turning my insides to liquid, but there it was. "Yeah, he's a good guy." He groaned. "I *hate* playing against him, though. Jesus Christ."

I burst out laughing. "Okay, I'm glad you said it, not me. I'm sure he's a nice enough dude, but he is a brick fucking wall."

"Ugh. Right?" He rolled his eyes. "He shut us out like three times when we played against them." Bringing his drink to his lips, he muttered, "Dick."

I snorted. "Yeah. God. What a jerk, playing lights out for his own team."

"Seriously." Peyton huffed. "Anyway, we're good now. It wasn't a bad breakup or anything, and we make better friends than boyfriends." He paused, looking a little sheepish. "Friends with occasional benefits, anyway."

"Oh really?" I grinned. "So you guys still hook up?"

"We... Well, not recently. But for a while, we'd go on the odd 'let's go on vacation together during the off season and get laid' trip."

"So, all the fun of going on a trip with a boyfriend, but without all the potential drama?"

"Basically." He winked. "Plus it means we're two-thirds

of the way to a threesome if we decide we want to have one, so..."

I barked a laugh. "Ahh, so slutty travel buddies." I raised my drink in a mock toast. "I can respect that."

I could. I really, honestly could.

And I was absolutely *not*...

Not at all...

Not in the *least* fucking bit...

...*jealous.*

Peyton turned out to be a fantastic cook. I could hold my own in the kitchen, but no salmon I'd ever prepared came out as perfect as this one. He'd also made salad and risotto to go with it, both of which were amazing as well.

I suspected he'd intended to have some wine with dinner, too. There'd been a bottle of white on the counter, but at some point while he'd been cooking, the bottle disappeared.

As we ate, I gestured with my fork at his glass, which was three-quarters full of Pepsi. "If you'd rather have wine, it really doesn't bother me."

"I..." Peyton chewed his lip. "That's good to know, I just... I don't know." He picked up some salad on his fork. "It didn't feel right, drinking in front of you while you're still going through the program."

My face heated as I picked at my salmon. "I appreciate it. I do. But... really. It's fine." I sighed. "Honestly, the alcohol hasn't been that much of a problem. I was self-medicating, yes, but... Well, it's like you said—I'm not an alcoholic, but if I'd gone on like that much longer, I would've been one."

He swallowed. "I'm glad you're doing it, then. The program, I mean."

"Me too."

We held each other's gazes, and the moment threatened to get painfully awkward.

"So, um." I cleared my throat and focused on my food. "How has practice been going?" Not the smoothest change of subject ever, but thank God, Peyton ran with it.

"Good. It's good. The penalty kill isn't doing so hot, so Coach has us doing a ton of special teams work."

My head snapped up. "What's going on with them?" I paused, then sheepishly added, "I, um... I haven't been watching the games much." Much? More like *at all.* Being away from hockey and my teammates hurt, and I was afraid to hear what the commentators were saying about me.

Peyton cut off a piece of salmon with his fork. "It's hard to say what the issue is. They've been doing exactly what they're supposed to do, so—I don't know, maybe the other teams have just figured them out? Whatever the problem is, they've allowed six power play goals in the last four games."

I winced. "Ouch."

"Yeah. The second unit has been especially rough, but honestly, I think it's just lack of experience. Both the power play and penalty kill have been shuffled around a bit because we're down some players, so we've got some guys up from the farm team, and..." He waved his hand. "They're young, you know?"

My stomach somersaulted. "A couple of players missing from the power play." I nudged my food with my fork. "Including one who's in rehab."

Peyton jumped as if he'd forgotten I was one of the missing players he'd been referring to. "Avery." He shook his head. "This isn't on you. We're also missing Willie because he has the flu, Mix was down until yesterday with the same, and Lavoie is probably done for the season because of his elbow."

"So it's the worst possible time for me to be—"

"Don't do that to yourself," he said gently. "We're holding the line. The penalty kill's struggling right now, and we've had some tough losses throughout the season, but we're doing all right in the standings. We're still in the playoff conversation." He gave his head another shake. "We've got this while you recover, same as we've got it while Willie and Mix recover."

Half a dozen arguments flew to the tip of my tongue. *They're sick and injured—I'm not. I should've held on until the rest of the roster was healthy. The team shouldn't have to do all this extra work because I couldn't keep it together.* I could hear my therapists' voices in the back of my mind, reminding me I wasn't being selfish or neglecting my team. I could hear my coach and GM telling me they supported me and wanted me to take care of myself. I could hear everyone and their mother reassuring me that this wasn't weakness or failure. It was grief, plain and simple, and I was doing what was best for myself *and* the team by addressing it.

"Avery," Peyton said again. "We've got this. Everyone's working hard and stepping up to the challenge, and you're going to come back in a few weeks as an even better version of yourself." He smiled. "It'll all be worth it."

I exhaled. "God, I hope so. I guess it's good I've been practicing." I frowned as I scratched the back of my neck. "Not sure how long it'll take to get my timing back once I'm with the team again, but..."

"Well, we don't have to *just* practice one-on-one."

I locked eyes with him.

Peyton stared at his plate and half-shrugged. "The other

guys—if you want to skate with more than just me, I know I can get some to join us. Eminem and Baddy would definitely be down."

"They..." I sat back in my chair, and I somehow I managed to whisper, "Really?"

"Absolutely. They all miss you. Every time we have a team meeting, someone's asking about when you'll be back."

"They do?"

He nodded, and he smiled. "The only reason I didn't tell them we were skating today was I wasn't sure how you'd feel if a bunch of them stuck around to see you."

My throat tightened around my breath. "You think they would have?"

"I'd bet money on it."

"Whoa."

Voice softer, he said, "They want to see you. I know they do. But it should be on your terms—that's why I didn't tell them. So they wouldn't catch you by surprise."

I stared down at my food. I missed my team so damn much. I wanted to see them so, so bad. And holy shit, I wanted to believe that they missed me and wanted to see me too.

But I was still convinced that they resented me for leaving them in a lurch mid-season. It was impossible to imagine the kind of warm welcome he was suggesting.

"I'm serious, Avery," he said gently. "Next time we skate, let's see if some of the guys will join us. I can guarantee they will."

The thought of practicing with my friends again filled me with both a sense of dread and a deep, painful longing. I cringed at the idea of looking them in the eyes again; no matter how much Peyton assured me they had my back, and no matter how much they'd been texting me to try to get me to golf with them, I was embarrassed and ashamed of what I was going through. It didn't matter how much people reassured me that this wasn't a failure or a character flaw, it still felt like one, and I didn't want to see their pity or their derision.

At the same time, just thinking about hitting the ice with Baddy, Eminem, and some of the other guys... God, it made my chest physically ache. I'd always been restless when I was rehabbing from an injury, eager to get back out there and skate, and now—I mean, fuck. What was stopping me except pride?

I took a deep breath and met Peyton's gaze again. "They really want to practice with me?"

"All of them," he said without hesitation.

My heart pounded as I weighed my options, hemming and hawing between hiding away with my bruised pride and stepping back out into the camaraderie I'd been missing so much.

Finally, I nodded. "Yeah. Yeah, let's do it."

And nothing galvanized my decision more than the way it made Peyton smile.

God, yeah.

Let's do this.

CHAPTER 26
PEYTON

We had practice the next morning, and before I left for the rink, I sent out a group text.

> Hey guys, if anyone wants to get in a bit more ice time, me and Calds have the rink from 3-4. More the merrier.

The responses started almost immediately.

BADDY

Today? Hell yeah I'm there.

EMINEM

Count me in

> Yeah today

MIX

Full-contact or?

WILLIE

Got plans with the kids, but LMK about next time!

BADDY

Calds is there, Mix. You know it's gonna be full contact.

MIX

Fuck yeah. I'm in.

LARAMIE

What's the plan? Scrimmages or what?

Depends on how many of you assholes show up.

MIX

Think Coach will go easy on us if we tell him we're skating with Calds after?

COACH

No.

EMINEM

Wait who TF added Coach to the group chat?

BADDY

There's an adult in here? WTF?

COACH

Sounds like someone wants to bag skate.

EMINEM

(crying emoji)

BADDY

(halo emoji)

COACH

(eyeroll emoji)

When I showed the exchange to Avery in the parking lot before our ice time, he stared at it with wide eyes.

"Whoa," he murmured as he scrolled through the

lengthy conversation. "They're... Are they really *all* coming?"

"I know Baddy, Eminem, Mix, and Laramie will be here. Some of the other guys had stuff going on, but they said to keep them in the loop if we do this again."

He fixed that wide-eyed stare on me as he handed back my phone. Then he looked around the players' parking lot behind the training center, and he shifted from surprised to a little crestfallen. "Well, their cars aren't here, so..."

I clapped his shoulder and gently steered him toward the building's entrance. "We're early. Give them time."

Boys, you better come through.

Sure enough, about twenty minutes later, the door banged open and voices filtered up the hall.

"—swear to God, if you do that again," Baddy was saying to someone, "I will put ghost pepper sauce in your jock."

"Dude, that's messed up." Eminem's voice, followed by what sounded like a smack. "You touch my jock, and you'll be wearing it on your face."

"For fuck's sake," Mix said. "Now you're just making it kinky."

That prompted groans, and a second later, the three of them strode into the locker room.

Instantly, their eyes lit up.

"Calds!" Baddy crossed the room, arms out. "Holy shit, I've missed skating with you!"

Avery laughed as he accepted the hug. "Just stay away from my athletic cup, all right?" He slapped Baddy's back. "You fucking sadist."

"He's just happy there's someone here who skates slower than him," Eminem declared.

"You know what?" Avery released Baddy and mock-punched Eminem's shoulder. "Fuck *you*."

"Not my type, Calds," Eminem said with a snicker even as he stepped in to hug Avery. "*Not* my type."

"Pfft. Whatever. I told you you could top if—"

"Shut up."

They laughed and shared a quick embrace, and Avery did the same with Mix. About the time they were finishing up greetings, more footsteps came up the hall, and we were joined by Trews, Laramie, and Marts—Antoine Martel, one of the fourth line forwards.

"Ooh, Laramie's here!" Mix grinned. "We've got a goalie!"

"Aww, damn it." Baddy huffed. "I wanted to play goalie."

"Dude, no." Avery shook his head, and he held his hand up just slightly above his own head. "You must be at least this tall to tend the net."

That earned him a sneaker tossed at his chest, which he caught. Laughing he tossed it back, and the bantering and chirping continued.

As I put on my base layer, I mostly sat back and watched the interplay, relieved that so many of the guys showed up. More followed, too, including Ziggy, which meant we now had *two* netminders. By the time I was lacing up my skates, we had enough players for a three-on-three scrimmage with a couple of people rotating in from either bench.

Before long, we were all out on the ice, warming up and firing pucks at the boards and the nets. There wasn't a coach, ref, or reporter in sight (though we all knew to assume there was a camera on us at all times), so we could relax a little, and we played like we often did when we were winding down after practice. We goofed off. We committed in egregious but not dangerous penalties, like when Eminem dragged Laramie out of the net by his blocker so his team could score. Or when Mix deliberately upended Baddy into the opposing team's bench when the puck was miles away from either of them. Or when Trews knocked Marts's helmet off during a faceoff. Nobody was really keeping score beyond *"you tripped me, now I'm going to trip you."*

I didn't think I'd ever laughed this hard during a practice—well, "practice"—in my entire life.

The best part, though?

Watching Avery laughing his head off. He was skating freely and easily, smiling like I hadn't seen since I'd come to Pittsburgh.

He wasn't magically cured or back to who he'd been before losing Leif, but at least for this perfectly chaotic hour on the ice, he seemed truly, genuinely *happy*.

And me? I was lucky I could skate. Yeah, I'd had a crush on him since forever, but seeing him like this reduced me to that hormonal teenager who forgot how to think when he saw an attractive guy. Today, Avery was every bit the man who'd made my heart skip whenever his face had appeared in a promo or when I'd skated opposite him during a game. Flushed with exertion, drenched in sweat, alternately laser-focused and laughing so hard he almost fell off his skates—he was just so... so...

Oh my God, you're beautiful.

I had to tear my gaze away before I fell off my own damn skates.

Fuck me. I had it so damn bad for this man. Having a crush on him had been one thing. Getting closer to him, seeing him vulnerable, being the one he reached out to when he hit the wall—he'd become so *real* and so *human*, and I was just so ridiculous for him now.

How was I going to stay sane when he made it through rehab and the League reactivated him? When I had to play beside him after he'd risen from his own ashes and made the comeback I knew was inevitable?

I had no idea how I was going to process all that without losing my mind.

I just knew in this moment, as I watched him getting a taste of the life he'd have again after he recovered…

…that I couldn't fucking wait.

CHAPTER 27
AVERY

I didn't think I'd ever had more fun on the ice than I did that afternoon. Coach would've been rolling his eyes so much he'd have given himself a monster headache, but everyone had a blast.

After convincing myself the guys would handle me with kid gloves or resent me, I couldn't even describe the relief that came from skating, screwing off, and laughing so much my face hurt. They didn't treat me any differently. They didn't side-eye me or make backhanded remarks about keeping things going while I got myself together. Which... that wasn't how any of them were, so I shouldn't have been surprised. I'd just created this narrative in my head that they'd all hate me or pity me.

Created this narrative in my head? Good God, I've been going to therapy too long.

I was a little disappointed when our informal practice ended. It had been so much fun, I wasn't ready for it to be over.

That disappointment was short-lived, though.

"We're gonna do this again, right?" Eminem asked. "When do you guys have the ice again?"

Peyton looked up from taking off his shinpads. "When do you want to do this?" He jerked his chin toward the door. "I can talk to the rink before we leave and nail down a time."

Just like that, everyone was debating when to schedule something. Texts went out to some of the guys who hadn't been able to come today. The team was leaving for a four-game road trip after tomorrow night's game, but there were some days after they came back that would work for everyone.

"What about you, Calds?" Baddy turned to me and gestured with his phone. "What's your schedule like?"

I swallowed. "Uh. I usually have—" I hesitated. Even though these men all knew what I was doing these days, I felt weird saying it out loud. "My appointments are usually over by about noon."

He nodded sharply. "Okay, so let's see if the rink is available on Tuesday and Thursday at like two?"

I watched the continued conversation, still a little dazed that they were doing this. Then again, we were all rink rats, so it didn't take much arm-twisting to get us to come skate. So... that was probably all it was.

Except as we were all heading out to our cars afterward, Eminem suddenly grabbed me and pulled me into a fierce hug.

"It was good to skate with you, man." He slapped my back. "Been worried about you."

I froze for a second before returning his embrace. "Thanks for coming." As he released me, I realized some of the other guys were watching us. "Thanks to all of you. This was really great."

"You know we got you, Calds." Baddy slung an arm around my shoulders. "And who's gonna miss a chance to knock you into the boards without getting in trouble?"

I laughed and gave him a shove. "Too bad you're too slow to get that chance, right?"

"I'm not too slow!" He scoffed.

"No, but you were taking a nap at the bench when—"

"Oh, fuck you," he muttered as the rest of the guys laughed. "Next time we'll dump *you* in the bench."

"No," Mix said with a smirk. "It's way more fun to toss you back there."

The banter went on like that for a minute or two, and then the guys continued toward their cars. I leaned against mine as I watched them go.

Then I turned to Peyton, who'd lingered. "You were right. I didn't think they'd want to see me, but..." I shook my head.

He smiled, which made me warm all over. "Sometimes you just have to see it to believe it." Gesturing at his car, he added, "You want to grab something to eat?"

Now that he mentioned it, I was starving. Not surprising after a satisfying workout like that. "Sure. Yeah. Do you, um, do you want to come back to my place? I don't cook as well as you do, but I can order something."

Fuck me, that smile.

"Sure. Meet you there?"

"Sounds great."

An hour or so later, we were lounging in my living room with some Thai food.

"Holy shit," Peyton said after a few bites. "Is this place always this good?"

"Every time. I can't even eat crab rangoon anywhere else anymore."

"I don't blame you. Damn. I thought the place near my house had good pad Thai, but this?" He whistled and shook his head. "Seriously good."

"Mmhmm. There's an Asian fusion place closer to you that does Thai really well, too. But I usually get Phở there, so..." I shrugged. "I haven't had their Thai in a while."

"Yeah?" He cocked a brow. "So they have good Vietnamese?"

I nodded. "Mix and Baddy say their sushi is some of the best, too. I swear they can each blow like a hundred bucks apiece on sushi at that place, and it's not that expensive."

Peyton laughed. "I probably could too, if it's that good. But if they've got good Phở..."

"Best I've had since I came to Pittsburgh."

"Well then." He nodded sharply. "Sold. I want to try it!"

I grinned. "When the team's back in town, we should go. I won't have to ask any of the other guys twice."

"Perfect."

The conversation fell into a comfortable lull as we continued eating. Truthfully, I was kicking myself for suggesting we get the rest of the guys to come with us to that place. I wanted to go there with Peyton. Just Peyton.

Buuut that felt a little too much like a date. Two dudes could go out to dinner without it being a date, even if they were both queer, but he and I were on some weird ground. We'd both admitted to some mutual interest, and even though I was still convinced I had blown any chance I ever had with him, I wanted to tread carefully. Both on that off chance I still had a shot with him, and also because I liked this friendship we'd slipped into since I'd started getting my shit together. I didn't want to ruin either of those things.

So... we'd go to the restaurant as a group. Keep things relaxed. Pretend I had more of a shot with Peyton than Vegas had of ever making it past the first round of the play-offs. Better to have him as a friend than a teammate who wouldn't even make eye contact with me.

After a while, Peyton broke the silence. "So, um..." He sipped his drink. "Feel free to tell me if it's none of my business. But... you're doing good these days? I mean, the assistance program and all—is it helping?"

I nodded. "Yeah. It's been hard. Some of my therapy sessions lately have been rough. But... I get through it." I loaded some risotto onto my fork. "Probably a lot of hard things I needed to hear. And say."

"Yeah?"

I took a bite of my pad Thai. After a sip of water, I explained some of what Shannon had told me recently about grief, and how it was especially difficult for men in this society. "We're not supposed to be emotional. And we're sure as shit not supposed to be this emotional about someone who isn't family or a partner, you know? So I guess I just..." I sighed. "I guess I just didn't know how to be as fucked up over Leif as I am."

I cringed—God, that sounded so pathetic.

But Peyton was nodding as I spoke. "I've heard that. It's all stupid anyway—how men are and aren't allowed to have feelings, never mind show them. But yeah, now that you mention it—I've never imagined trying to handle losing a friend."

"I didn't either. I always kind of figured with stuff like this, you just do it, you know? Grief is what it is. But it turns out if you put up enough mental walls..." I laughed bitterly. "It's possible to fuck up grieving."

"You're not fucking it up," Peyton said softly. "You've just never had to do this before."

"There is that. This isn't the first time in my life that someone's died. Just... the first time it's been someone I was this close to."

He winced. "I can't even imagine how hard that is."

"You don't want to," I whispered, shivering as some of those awful emotions tried to claw their way to the surface. Shifting in my seat, I stared down at my food. "Things like today, though—it helps. A lot. Being around the guys—I think I needed that more than I realized."

"I bet," he said softly. "I think it was good for them, too. For all of us."

I met his gaze again. "You do?"

He nodded. "The guys really are pulling for you. They've been worried about you. Seeing you on your feet, skating, being yourself?" Another nod. "Yeah, I think that's good for all of us."

I had no idea what to say to that.

"In fact..." He hesitated.

I lifted my gaze to meet his.

Peyton chewed his lip, then took a deep breath. "Come to tomorrow night's game. We're about to hit the road for a few games, so it'll be good for the team—really good for them—to see you there before we go. It'll be good for morale." He paused, brow pinching. "And I'm no expert, but I bet it'll be good for you, too."

I chewed the inside of my cheek. He'd been honest with me—sometimes brutally honest—from the start. He wouldn't blow smoke up my ass now. That just didn't seem like him.

I fidgeted. "You don't think it'll be a distraction? I don't want to throw the guys off right before—"

"Not at all." He sounded confident. "Trust me. It'll be a good morale boost." He paused. "And not just for the team."

I couldn't explain the rush of warmth. Maybe because he saw right through me and knew that visit would be good for me? Or maybe because I thought he might be referring to himself? Both?

Either way, I couldn't say no. I'd been dreading the first time I saw my teammates playing without me, but now...

"All right." I smiled. "I'll be there."

I had some second thoughts about going to the game, but Peyton was holding me to it. In fact, I'd offered to drive him to the arena since he and the team were heading to the airport right after the game. So now I *couldn't* bail.

I mean, I could. I knew he'd let me off the hook without any protest, and it wasn't that big of a deal for someone to drive himself on a travel night. But I wouldn't let myself out of it now, so... whatever.

In my bedroom, I tugged at my tie and looked myself up and down in the mirror. I'd been wearing suits to games since forever, and it hadn't been all that long since my last game. Still, it felt weird tonight. Like being in the wrong skin.

Like I don't belong there.

I pushed that thought down. No, I *did* belong. My stint in the assistance program was a setback, like an injury putting me on LTIR. I'd come back from those just like I'd come back from this.

I just wondered how many games it would take before

this newfound imposter syndrome went away. Before I felt like I was worthy of a Whiskey Rebels' sweater, never mind one with a C on it.

That thought gave me pause.

Maybe the C is the problem. Maybe I can't handle the captaincy.

Maybe I needed to talk to Coach about that. Talk to the guys about relinquishing the C and letting someone else take the reins.

That was a conversation for another day, though; the whole point of tonight was for me to show my face. Be a morale boost for the guys so they could head out on their road trip without worrying about me. I didn't imagine any of them were losing much sleep over me, but Peyton insisted it would be good for them, so... I was doing this.

I gave myself one more long look in the mirror. Straightened my tie. Took a deep breath.

Then I headed downstairs, got in the car, and drove over to Peyton's place.

As he came out of his apartment, some of my tangled-up thoughts faded away. What could I say? It was hard to hold on to a negative thought when that man was coming down the steps in a dark blue plaid suit that fit him like a damn dream. He just looked so fucking good.

Any chance we can go inside for a little while? Maybe get a head start on your pregame warmups?

The ridiculous thought made me chuckle, so at least I was smiling when he got in the car. That meant he wouldn't catch on that I'd been mentally spinning out and reconsidering my place as the team's captain. Perfect.

As he pulled on his seat belt, he met my gaze, his own smile lighting up the whole world. "Ready for this?"

"Of course." I started backing out of the parking space. "Isn't like I've never been to a hockey game."

"Okay, true. But you know what I mean."

I did. As I shifted gears and headed out of the lot, I was grateful that I had the road to hold my attention. I wasn't sure I could handle seeing the scrutiny that I could feel coming from the passenger seat.

"It's... weird, I guess?" I tapped my thumbs on the wheel. "It's one thing to show up when I'm on LTIR or something. This is different, you know?"

"I get it. But it's really not as different as you think. I mean, one of my teammates a couple of years ago took a leave of absence to deal with his mental health. Bad bout of depression, I think it was."

I nodded slowly. "Oh, yeah. I remember that. Hayes, wasn't it?"

"Yep. And the thing is, we all knew he was struggling. When it finally came out what was going on, nobody gave him shit. It was like, oh, okay, *that's* what's happening."

I swallowed. "And when he came back—did things change? With him and the team?"

"No. He was still Hayes. Same as ever. Some of the guys who were closer to him than me, they'd check in on him more. Make sure he was doing all right. But otherwise, it was no different than if he'd been out with an injury."

God, I wanted to believe that would happen this time, too. I understood that mental health was as important as physical health, but not everyone applied that in practice.

I squirmed a little as I pulled onto the freeway. "There are definitely some fans who aren't happy about it."

"You've reading social media comments again, haven't you?"

"Against my better judgment, yeah."

"Fuck 'em," he growled. "They're keyboard warriors. Haven't you seen the way they talk about all of us?" He scoffed and I glanced his way in time to catch him rolling his eyes. "Remember all the crap they say about Ziggy? And come on, these are the same assholes who criticized Matt Conley for being off his game last year during the Cup final, even *after* they found out he'd been playing through a core muscle injury, a broken finger, and two fractured ribs."

I grunted in agreement, because, well, he did have a point. Every year, it came out that some players had knuckled through incredibly painful injuries during the postseason. And every year, there were jackasses on social media who'd call them "soft" or "weak" because their play had suffered. I knew they were full of shit then. Why was I listening to them now?

"Is it stupid that I'm afraid I'll get booed once the fans see me again?"

"It's not stupid," he said. "But I think you're going to be pleasantly surprised."

I glanced at him again. "Yeah?"

Peyton gave my forearm a squeeze. "You'll see."

At the arena, we parked in the players' lot and headed inside. All the anxiety and uncertainty wound itself into a tight ball of bullshit in the pit of my stomach, but I mostly ignored it. I'd seen some of my teammates yesterday, but not all of them. None of the staff or coaches, either. Definitely none of the fans.

Nervous? Me? Yeah, just a little.

Still, I stayed in step with Peyton as we headed for the

locker room. In the hallway just outside the door, Falon, our team's reporter, did a double take when she saw me.

"Calds? Oh my God!" Her high heels clomped on the concrete as she trotted across the hall to hug me. "It's so good to see you!"

I smiled, hugging her back. "It's good to be here."

Even if I'm a nervous fucking mess.

Drawing back, she locked eyes with me. "You know, the fans would love to hear from you." Gesturing over her shoulder to where her cameraman was arranging his gear, she added, "Any chance you'd be interested in a quick interview?"

I gulped. "Um."

"It's okay if not," she said quickly. "But I think everyone will love to see you. There's so many rumors swirling, I think this will put some of them to bed."

"Rumors?" My spine straightened, and I glanced back and forth between her and Peyton as panic surged up in me. "What kind of rumors?"

"People speculate," she said. "When they hear player assistance program, they assume the worst."

I groaned. "Of course they do."

"Not like that," Peyton said gently. "She means they're worried. So many players disappear from sight when they go into the program, so no one knows if they're getting better or if they're in really bad shape, like, physically."

I swallowed. Truthfully, I couldn't argue with that; I'd worried and speculated about other players who'd gone into the program. The way they abruptly vanished, sometimes not even posting on social media for months, left us all concerned about just how bad their situation might be. Sure, there was gossip and judgment, too, because people could be assholes and God knew men's mental health was badly stigmatized.

But hockey was a tightknit community. We looked after our own. For every judgmental asshole, there were ten more quietly waiting for some kind of update so they could breathe again, knowing the player would be okay.

I'd been one of the guys who worried, and not because I thought someone was a loser or a trainwreck. I'd never thought someone was weak or a wuss because he struggled with mental health problems and/or addiction.

Was it really such a stretch to imagine people had the same concerns about me?

"Okay," I whispered. "Yeah, I... I can do an interview."

"All right." Falon smiled. "Let me get Jim and the camera set up."

As she walked away, Peyton turned to me. "Are you sure about this?"

"Do you think I shouldn't?"

"I didn't say that. I just want to make sure you're okay with it."

I gave it some careful thought, then nodded. "I'm good."

"Okay. Do, um... Do you want me to stay out here with you?"

I checked my phone and shook my head. "No. You need to start your pregame routine." I smiled, and hopefully it was reassuring and didn't look at all panicked or anxious. "I'll be fine."

He studied me, chewing his lip. Then, "Okay." He clapped my shoulder. "I'll be in there when you get done."

He headed into the locker room, and I took a moment to steel myself before I joined Falon and her cameraman.

"Tell me honestly before we turn on the camera and

microphone." She inclined her head. "Do you want to discuss why you're in the assistance program?"

I again gave it some thought before I nodded. "Yeah. I think it would be good for people to hear it."

"Okay. This is a recorded interview, okay?" She gestured at the camera. "Anything you want us to cut out, say so."

I nodded again. Live interviews could be stressful as all hell, and I had trust issues with some reporters who insisted they'd edit based on our requests. Falon was good to us, though. As the team reporter, she had to have our trust; if she did one of us dirty, then everyone would likely clam up around her, and she'd find herself out of a job.

I didn't think she was the type to do that anyway. Either way, I was glad we weren't doing this live.

I took a deep breath. Then I let her know I was ready, and a moment later, the camera was rolling.

"I'm here outside the Whiskey Rebels' locker room," she said to the camera, "and joining me is a surprise guest—Pittsburgh's captain, Avery Caldwell."

The cameraman backed up a little, probably to bring me into the frame, and I smiled. I was used to being in front of those giant lenses and microphones, but it was a little nerve-racking this time.

"Now, Calds," Falon said, "you and the team recently announced that you are in the League's player assistance program. Can you talk about why you entered the program?"

I nodded. "I think everyone knows what happened to Early before the season started. And me and him—we've been close since major juniors, so I took it hard. I took it *really* hard." My throat was getting tight, but I was not breaking down in front of a camera, damn it, not even when

I knew this could be edited. So, I barreled on. "The truth is, I wanted to move on faster than I was ready to. I felt the pressure to be captain, and to keep..." I shook my head. "I put too much on myself. And when it got to be too much, I started drinking to deal with it. So... that's why I'm in the program."

"For alcohol?"

"For..." I pursed my lips. "Kind of? The alcohol was a bandage over something I needed to deal with. The hardest part of the program hasn't been giving up the alcohol—it's dealing with the stuff underneath."

"The grief for your teammate?"

"The grief for my best friend, yeah." I cleared my throat. "At the end of the day, I just had to step back, take care of myself, and let myself grieve the way I needed to. The way I wouldn't let myself in the beginning."

"And is that going well?" Falon raised her eyebrows, and I got the sense she was asking from both a journalistic place and a genuine, personal place.

"It is, yeah. It's hard. I'm not going to pretend it isn't. But I think that was one of the things I had to make peace with—that losing someone like Leif is hard, and I shouldn't expect myself to be okay overnight. So this whole player assistance program thing—it hasn't been about alcohol at all. It's about learning to be good to myself and give myself room to feel pain. You'd think that kind of pain comes whether you let it or not, but it turns out..." I trailed off into a half shrug.

"That's amazing." She sounded sincere, as if she were really saying that to me and not just to the camera. "So the program has been helpful for you—that's great to hear."

"It has been." I had a flash of memory of the shame I'd felt when I'd made the announcement, and of the times I'd seen other players looking humiliated as they too entered the program, and some determination surged inside me. "If there's one thing I hope fans and players alike can take away from my experience, it's that there's no shame in asking for help. It's hard, admitting you've got a problem—whether it's with drinking or with something up here." I tapped my temple. "But man, things get a million times easier when you realize how many people are pulling for you and how much help is really available."

"Excellent point," Falon said, nodding as she spoke. "Those resources are available, and there's no shame in using them."

"Exactly. And..." I hesitated, making sure my voice was going to stay steady. "If you know someone who's struggling, reach out to them. They might reject it at first. They might be in denial and they might get hostile toward you. But it makes a big difference, knowing someone gives a—knowing someone cares." I swallowed. "I don't even want to imagine how far down the rabbit hole I'd have gone, and how much I'd have destroyed my life, my career, and my body if Peyton Hall hadn't been incredibly persistent. I owe him more than I can ever repay."

Falon asked me a few more questions about how I was doing, and then she smiled as she asked, "One last thing—do you think Whiskey Rebel fans will see you play again this season?"

I returned the smile, and I meant it as I said, "I'm very optimistic."

"Good. Everyone in Pittsburgh and in the League is in your corner, Calds, and we're looking forward to seeing you in black and gold again."

She did the usual signoff so the network could transition

back to the commentators when the interview as actually broadcast, and the interview was over.

As soon as the camera was off, Falon stepped closer and hugged me again. "I'm so sorry you've been struggling. I knew you had to be having a hard time, but I didn't realize it was this bad."

I returned the unexpected hug and chuckled softly. "It probably wouldn't have been quite as hard if I hadn't been so stupid and stubborn about it."

"Nah." She let me go, and as she pulled back, she met my gaze. "Nobody wants to feel that way, and I mean, I've been covering hockey for a long time. I know how close you boys get." She gestured with her microphone at the locker room door. "You're not the only one who's had a tough time."

I grimaced. "I just hope it hasn't been harder on them, watching me collapse like this."

"No. Quite the opposite, from what I've seen."

"Yeah?"

"Yeah. You remember what happened after the home opener?"

I shuddered. "I wish I didn't."

"Right, well, I know it wasn't fun for you, but I think it did your teammates more good than you might think."

"It—" I blinked. "It did?"

"Well, yeah. Especially the younger guys. They're all trying to be tough and pretend nothing affects them, but then when they see you buckle under it, they realize it's not just them, and it's okay to hurt that much." She squeezed my arm. "I know you're afraid everyone thought you were weak or that you let them down, but you couldn't be more wrong."

My throat constricted around my breath. It hadn't

occurred to me that the rest of the team might be struggling the same way I was—not sure how to grieve or how to release some of those unfamiliar and horrible emotions. All I'd imagined was them keeping their game faces on while they held me up, the whole time thinking they could never look at me the same again. Or that they'd overestimated my ability to lead this team.

"I didn't think about that," I admitted. "I thought..." The words stuck in my tight throat.

"These men love you, Calds." She gave my arm another squeeze before letting go. "From what they've said to me, they've been in awe all this time that you stayed upright as long as you did, and that when you hit your breaking point, you didn't completely crash and burn." She smiled. "You're tougher than you think, hon, and everyone in there"—she nodded toward the locker room—"knows it."

I swallowed past that obnoxious lump. It was hard to believe that, but I'd learned that I was wrong about a lot of things over the past few months. There was no reason to think this couldn't be an exception.

"I should go in and see them," I said. "Before they have to have their game faces on."

She nodded and left me to it, heading down the hall toward the ice, probably to set up by the bench for rink-side interviews during warmups.

Alone in the hallway, I paused for a moment to steel myself. I had no reason to believe my intrusive thoughts were right when they'd been wrong about so many other things.

Finally, I took a deep breath.

Then I pushed open the door and stepped into the locker room.

CHAPTER 28
PEYTON

I was looking down and pulling on my shinpads, but I still knew the instant Avery walked into the room.

"Captain!" Baddy called out.

"Holy fuck, it's Calds!" That was Ziggy. I think. Might've been Mix—they sounded almost the same when they were being exuberant.

I lifted my gaze, and my heart flipped. I'd seen (and ogled) him in that suit when we'd driven in, but the way he was smiling right then... oh my God. He'd been so damn worried about how our teammates would receive him, even the guys who'd played with us yesterday, but all that worry had vanished. He was smiling like I hadn't seen since I'd come to Pittsburgh. A little startled, a lot relieved, and genuinely happy. He'd probably missed this place and these men, and I knew he'd worked himself up, thinking the guys wouldn't want to see him.

Sometimes it was good to be wrong, and from the way he smiled and chirped in between hugs, he didn't mind at all that he'd been wrong.

I wasn't at all surprised—not by his reception, not by his

reaction. Yeah, he'd played with some of the guys yesterday, but he was clearly still tied up in knots thinking he'd failed us or that we'd all give up on him. As the guys said hi to him and hugged him and caught up with him, I hoped that chipped away at his uncertainty. Especially the guys who hadn't been able to join us yesterday; if I had to guess, he'd worried they hadn't *wanted* to join us.

You're wrong, Avery. So, so wrong. Everyone here loves you.

Just having him here brought a whole new vibe into the locker room. For all he'd been afraid he would bring us down, his presence injected more enthusiasm into everyone than I'd felt in a while. Everyone had been so worried about him, and all the guys who'd known Erlandsson had been floundering in their own grief.

Tonight, though, Avery was here, and this was the most upbeat the team had been since I'd arrived in Pittsburgh.

If we could carry that onto the ice, Chicago wouldn't know what hit them.

As we all geared up and Avery wandered the room, chatting with teammates, his gaze landed on Eminem, and his smile faltered. I suspected he'd noticed the A on our teammate's jersey. Some guilt clouded his expression. Probably because he felt bad that someone else had had to step up while the captain was out.

I wanted to remind him that this was no different than if he'd had to bow out of a game with an injury. There was no shame in it, and no one held it against him.

Baddy beat me to the punch, though. I didn't hear what he said at first, except when he finished with, "Man, we've got you." He clapped Avery's arm hard enough to almost knock him off his feet. "You know we'll keep the team going while you get better."

Avery managed a smile. "I know. I have total faith in all of you." He smirked. "I mean, maybe not you, but—"

"Oh, fuck off." Baddy shoved him. "Dick."

Avery just snickered.

I continued putting on my own gear, relieved someone had derailed his melancholy train of thought.

We went out for warmups, and on the way back in, I saw Avery and Coach having a hushed conversation. Then, after Coach had given his usual pregame speech, he said, "Before we go out there, your captain has a few things to say."

Avery had been leaning against the wall by the door, and he took a deep breath before joining Coach in the middle of the room. It was a solid minute before he spoke, but not because of nerves or anything like that—it was because that's how long it took for all of us to stop cheering for him.

When we finally settled, he cleared his throat. "Listen, guys, I know it's been a tough season. Nobody ever expects to start a season the way we did, and no one would've held it against us if it didn't go well. But everyone's been playing hard, and everyone is proud of all of you." He tapped his chest. "I'm especially proud of how everyone has kept yourselves upright even after I..." His voice wavered a little, and he had to clear his throat again. "I *will* be back this season, but even while I'm not playing, I'm still your captain."

That prompted even more cheers, and I thought Avery might've choked up a little. By the time we'd again quieted, he'd reclaimed his composure.

"This will probably go down as one of the hardest seasons the Whiskey Rebels have ever faced," he went on. "I *hope* it's the hardest season we ever face. You guys lost your captain, and then you lost another captain temporarily, but you're still in the playoff conversation and you're still holding yourselves up." He gestured sharply toward the locker room door. "Let's have another good game tonight."

The locker room was nearly as loud as a playoff crowd in the arena. Guys got up to high-five and hug Avery before they headed out to the ice.

I paused on my way and clapped his shoulder with a gloved hand. "Great speech, Captain."

He laughed softly, and... was that a blush? He smacked my shoulder. "How about a goal from the top line tonight?"

I saluted him. "You got it."

Then I continued out to the ice, my own enthusiasm ticked up a few notches by Avery's speech. There was also a pang of sadness in my chest; it was amazing how he could be so empathetic and understanding toward the team, but he beat himself up for struggling with the very same thing.

How do we show you that you're just as strong as the rest of us?

Well, that was for after the game. Right now, I had to focus on hockey. Which... turned out to be harder than I expected. Avery was worried about being a distraction instead of a morale boost, and in that moment... he might've been right.

Not for the whole team, though—just my dumb ass.

How was I supposed to play hockey after seeing him smile like that?

All I knew was that I was *going* to figure it out, because we were *not* losing tonight. Not with our captain here in the arena. He needed to see for himself that we could hold it together without him; yes, he was important to us, and yes, he was a crucial part of this team, but he needed to know that it wasn't on him to carry us. He could take time to recover from this, same as he could an injury or an illness, knowing we wouldn't crumble without him.

And that meant I needed to keep my head together no matter how much I wished he and I could be alone somewhere instead.

My distraction notwithstanding, the enthusiasm Avery had infused into the team worked wonders. From the first faceoff, we *dominated* Chicago. We made rush after rush into their zone, racking up shots on goal like we were shooting fish in a barrel. By the first intermission, we had two goals while Chicago only had two shots on goal, both of which Laramie had stopped with ease.

The second period started to get chippy. They were getting frustrated, and I suspected their coach had reamed them out during intermission, so they came out swinging.

That didn't go well for them.

Less than ninety seconds in, one of their defensemen was heading to the box for tripping Eminem. The resulting power play goal put us up 3-0, and that led to one of their forwards losing his cool and slashing Davis.

I'd give their penalty kill credit—they managed to break away and make a valiant run into our zone for a short-handed scoring chance. Mix and Baddy were hot on the guys' heels, but they weren't quite fast enough. The forward's shot went right through Laramie's five-hole into the back of the net.

Shame the play turned out to be offside.

The crowd was thoroughly pleased at having Chicago's lone goal knocked off the scoreboard, and Chicago's players were *pissed*.

There were two ways an angry team could play. One, they'd focus hard on hockey and channel all their fury into breaking through the opposition's defenses to score. Two, they'd get so mad they lost track of what they were doing, and they fell apart.

Chicago was a mix of the two. Their top line was focused and solid, and they very nearly got a couple of shots past Laramie. The second D-pair kept their heads together, too, and they wouldn't let us near their goal for anything.

The rest of the team, though? They were a mess. More interested in checking and trying to start fights than, you know, scoring.

Fine by us. None of them could successfully goad a Whiskey Rebel into a fight, and three of their attempts at checking or provoking turned out to be penalties—one boarding, two interference—which led to two more power play goals.

5-0 with six minutes left in the second? I couldn't argue with that.

During a commercial break, the crowd suddenly started roaring. I looked up from an iPad, figuring I'd see Avery in the owners' box on the Jumbotron.

It wasn't him in his seat, but it *was* him, standing outside the locker room with Falon. I couldn't even hear what he was saying because the crowd was going absolutely wild. The roar quickly shifted to a chant, and soon the whole arena was shaking with, "Caldwell! Caldwell! Caldwell!"

The interview went away, and then the camera showed what I'd expected—Avery sitting up in the owners' box. He looked dazed, staring around wide-eyed and slack-jawed.

As soon as he appeared on the screen, the chant intensified. Every fan was on their feet, and when Avery shakily rose and waved, I thought they were going to blow the roof off the place. They were already excited over this blowout of a game, and seeing Avery in the building had them screaming like we'd just clinched the Cup.

I didn't blame them one bit.

It was during the second intermission that I finally found out what he'd said during the interview. Several of the guys were huddled around an iPad, and when I craned my neck to see, I realized that was what they were watching.

"I don't even want to imagine how far down the rabbit hole I'd have gone," he was saying, "and how much I'd have destroyed my life, my career, and my body if Peyton Hall hadn't been incredibly persistent. I owe him more than I can ever repay."

My breath lodged in my throat. Fuck. I didn't think... Holy shit.

Before I could even get my thoughts in order, Eminem reeled me in tight and slapped me on the back. "We all owe you, man."

"No, you don't."

"We *do*." He pulled back and put his hands on my shoulders, looking me dead in the eye. "You saw something we didn't. We all knew he was in bad shape, but whatever you did—he's getting help." His voice actually wavered a little as he added, "We're gonna have Calds back because of you."

"He's right." Baddy looked at me with the most serious expression I'd ever seen on him. "This could've gotten real bad if it wasn't for you."

I could barely breathe, but I managed, "I'm just glad he'll be okay."

"He will." Baddy clapped my shoulder. "And we *all* owe you for that."

They didn't, but I didn't argue. I couldn't. Not when I was getting this choked up.

It didn't matter who or why.

The bottom line was that Avery was going to be okay.

Avery came down to the locker room after the game, and he was going to need to dry clean that suit after being crushed in hugs from everyone in sweaty gear. He didn't seem to mind. He was smiling more easily now; I hadn't even realized how much tension he'd been carrying in his neck and shoulders until it had relaxed.

How much have *you been piling on yourself, Avery?*

And now I was going to be gone for a few days? Shit. I trusted him to take care of himself, especially now, but I'd still worry myself senseless if I couldn't see him or talk to him.

Who was I kidding? I'd worry, but I'd also miss him like crazy. I wasn't even gone yet and I already missed him.

I've lost my damned mind, haven't I?

Probably, yeah.

I finished showering and getting dressed, and I ate with Avery, Baddy, Eminem, and some of the other guys. Then Coach was shooing everyone toward the bus so we could head to the airport.

I admittedly dawdled a little. Though I was usually one of the first on the bus because I was always afraid of missing it—lesson learned in my youth days—I hung back, and I was rewarded with Avery walking out beside me in an otherwise deserted hallway.

Near the door to the parking lot, we stopped. I had no

idea what to say. The urge to wrap him up in a hug was almost irresistible, but I held back.

Finally, I said, "By the way, that was a great interview."

Avery laughed as he slid his hands into his pockets. "Yeah. I didn't realize they were going to play it during the game." He snorted and added, "Not that anyone heard it."

"Eh, not when it was played on the Jumbotron, no, but I bet half the stadium downloaded it so they could hear it."

"Oh God," he groaned. "I don't even remember half of what I said."

I chuckled. Interviews could be like that sometimes—the camera and microphone were still intimidating after all this time, and more often than not, I'd walk away from an interview wondering what I'd actually said. Or, as much as I hated to admit it, cringing because goddammit, I really said *that?*

"The interview was fine," I told him. "Trust me."

"I hope so," he whispered.

"It was. And I'm also I'm not surprised everyone went nuts when they saw you."

Avery's laugh was silent but genuine. "*I* was surprised!"

"Not me. Not at all."

"Yeah, well. Either way, thanks for making me come tonight." As soon as the words were out, he winced, and color bloomed in his cheeks. "For fuck's sake. Thanks for getting me to come *to the game.*"

I snorted. "Yeah, I figured that was what you meant."

He facepalmed and groaned. "Open mouth, insert skate."

You can open mouth, insert something else if you want.

I cleared my throat as some heat rose in my own cheeks. "It's all good." I sighed. "Too bad you won't be able to come to the next few."

Avery frowned. "Yeah, I know. How long is the road trip again?"

"Four games," I said. "I... can't remember how many nights. You know how it is—they all kind of bleed together."

"Yeah." He laughed. "They kind of do." He locked eyes with me, and then, to my surprise, he wrapped me up in a tight hug. "Kick some ass out there for me, eh?"

I laughed, closing my eyes as I returned his embrace. "I will. I promise." As I let him go, I added, "You can text me any time, you know. Or FaceTime if you need it."

He studied me as if he wasn't sure he'd understood me, or if he worried I didn't mean it.

"Seriously," I insisted. "I can't always be on my phone because..." I gestured around.

"No, no, I know." He slid his hands into the pockets of his trousers. "Trust me. I get it. You need to focus on hockey."

"Not 24/7, though. So... if you want to chat..."

God, that man's smile was going to be the actual death of me.

"I might take you up on that," he said softly. "But either way, I'll see you in a few days."

"Yeah. See you in a few days."

Our eyes locked, and my pulse ticked up. The impulse to step in and kiss him was almost overpowering.

Not here, though. Not now.

"If there's something here," I'd told him, gesturing at each of us, *"it'll keep, okay? I'm not going anywhere."*

Trust my own words to come back and remind me to settle down. We'd get there. Avery still had a big hill to climb, and anyway, if we gave in to that kiss right now, we'd just have the whole damn road trip to lose our minds over being apart. I wasn't sure either of us would get through that in one piece.

So I just hugged him again. "I'll see you soon."

"You will. Now go get on the damn bus before they leave with out you." He gave me a playful shove. "I'm not driving your ass to the airport."

I laughed and let him go. "You're such a dick."

He shrugged unrepentantly. "You knew what this was."

Yeah, I did. And damn, it was good to see his snarky side coming out again.

I was going to miss that over the next few days.

CHAPTER 29
AVERY

I'd been out with injuries a few times in my career, including two stints on LTIR and a one-game suspension that I still maintained was complete bullshit. It all came with the territory of a sport like this.

The part I'd never been able to get used to—staying home while my team went out on the road. I could handle being alone during the off season or on days when we didn't have games or practice. There was just something about being *here* while my guys were out *there* that drove me fucking nuts.

And this time was so much worse. I spent the whole first morning wondering why I was so out of sorts, but then I got a text from Peyton and it all made sense. The text itself was benign; he was telling me Eminem was cheating at Hearts again, which... no shit.

But suddenly the pieces connected. My team was gone, and so was Peyton.

God, I missed him.

Texting wasn't enough. FaceTiming wasn't enough. I wanted him *here*. I wanted to be *there*.

Why, Avery? So you can pine after him when the best you can ever hope for is maybe a pity fuck?

Ugh. God. Yeah, I'd just embarrass myself, wouldn't I?

I was suddenly restless. My house suddenly seemed too big and quiet. I needed to get the hell out of here and be somewhere besides alone with my thoughts. Especially my stupid thoughts about a teammate who'd scraped me up off rock bottom, and who'd politely insisted I hadn't blown my chance with him even though—let's be real—I'd blown my chance with him.

Most of my social circle was on the road right now, so my options were limited. The gym, maybe? A good workout was always a nice distraction.

Except I'd worked out this morning before therapy. Damn it.

I scrolled through my phone in search of someone to hang out with, and when I landed on Rachel's contact, I had a direction. After texting back and forth a bit with her, I went over to help her out with some projects around the house. Those would definitely keep me busy.

She let me in and offered a hug, which was getting more difficult now that she was like eight months along. "Come on in. I'll get you some coffee."

"Don't worry—I can work the coffeepot."

She waved that away and led me into the kitchen. I didn't argue as she made me a cup, but I did worry when, after she'd handed it over, she leaned on the counter and rubbed her back gingerly.

"You okay?" I asked.

"Yeah. Yeah. Just..." She pointed emphatically at her belly.

I grimaced. "How, um, how are you feeling these days?"

She blew out a breath. "I'm just trying not to think

about how much worse it's going to get, and I keep reminding myself this heartburn isn't forever."

"Heartburn?"

Pointing at her belly again, she muttered, "Comes with the territory."

"Oh, man. That sucks."

"Eh. At least this won't be a summer baby." She made a face. "Being pregnant when it's that hot is the *worst*, especially with twins."

I grimaced. "I can't imagine."

"You have no idea. Let's go sit."

I followed her into the living room and took a seat on the couch. It took her some work, but she settled into the recliner, and she sighed with relief as she put up her feet.

I winced sympathetically. I'd never envied my friends' wives as they'd gone through the latter stages of pregnancy. They always seemed perpetually uncomfortable.

"I was an absolute baby when I had knee surgery," Astala had once said. *"But I had painkillers, and it really only hurt when I moved. She can't get anywhere close to comfortable at all, she can't take a damn thing, and she still has six weeks to go."* Shaking his head, he'd added, *"I'd be lying on the floor and sobbing."*

"I don't know how she does it," Baddy had said another time. *"I'd rather have a puck knock out half my teeth than go through that."*

When a reporter asked Eminem if he changed his newborn's diapers, he'd looked her dead in the eye and said, *"I'd have changed his diapers no matter what because I'm his dad. But after I watched my wife power through that pregnancy from hell* and *an emergency C-section? I'll walk barefoot over Legos to change him so she doesn't have to lift a finger."*

Rachel's first two pregnancies had been pretty rough, too. The twins had been as difficult as carrying twins apparently was, plus the morning sickness that had put her in the hospital for a few days. With Elsa, she'd also been sick, and it hadn't let up after the first trimester; she'd still been green around the gills right up until the end. On top of that, sciatica had had her in near constant pain for like five months.

"I don't know how she does it," Leif had told me more than once. *"She's stronger than I am, that's for sure."*

I didn't think he or anyone else had ever imagined she'd have to be *this* strong, though.

From the looks of it, the gods had scrounged up enough mercy on her not to make her as physically miserable this time around. Uncomfortable, yes, but she looked a million times better than she had with the previous two. She'd been through enough in the last year; a relatively easy pregnancy seemed like the *least* the universe could do for her.

Give this woman a break, all right?

I sipped my coffee. "So where are the kids?"

"Out with my mom. The twins' class had a field trip this morning, and then she took them all to get lunch and to run around at the park." Rachel blew out a breath. "She's been a godsend, let me tell you."

"I bet."

Our eyes locked, and I suspected she had the same thought I did in that moment—whenever he wasn't on the road, Leif always took the kids out to play and burn off energy. He was an amazing father, and he also made sure his wife regularly got breaks for hours at a time.

I cleared my throat. "So, anything you need taken care of?" I gestured to encompass the house and the sprawling yard. "I'm all yours for the day."

"There isn't a lot that needs doing, to be honest," she said. "I've had more help than I know what to do with."

"Yeah?"

"Oh yeah. The team has been amazing." She smiled, absently resting her hand on her belly. "Eminem and Baddy have been doing a ton of yardwork. I mean, not that much needs to be done this time of year, but they've trimmed back some of the trees and the rosebushes. Ziggy put up the Christmas lights, and Eminem took them down. You've all been such a huge help."

"You know we're always here," I said. "Anything you and the kids need."

Her smile turned a bit sad, and she nodded. "I know. Believe me, I appreciate it. The wives even threw me a little baby shower. I don't need a thing—we held on to everything from the other babies—but it was nice, you know? That they're thinking about me?"

"Of course they are. You and the kids are family."

"I appreciate that," she whispered. "And I hope you don't mind me having you over just for some company."

"Not at all. I was, um... I was getting a little stir crazy myself, so let's call it you scratching my back and me scratching yours."

She laughed and seemed to relax a bit. Knowing her, she both loved and hated everyone fussing over her. Maybe fussing over me gave her something else to focus on.

"I'm glad you've had a lot of help," I said. "You know the team is always here, no matter what."

"I know. And I appreciate everything everyone has done." She paused. "Between you and me, though, some-times... Sometimes all the help makes it worse."

"How do you mean?"

"Because it's like this constant reminder that Leif is

gone. I love everyone on the team and everything they've done. But it's like... *Leif* should be trimming the rosebushes. *Leif* should be putting up the Christmas lights. Someone else doing those things just..." Her chin quivered and she put a hand to her lips as her eyes welled up. "It just means he's really gone."

"I'm sorry," I whispered, because I had no idea what else to say.

"God—grief and pregnancy hormones are such a bullshit mix." She sniffed as she wiped her eyes. Then she cleared her throat and met my gaze. "So how has the program been?" Her brow pinched. "If you don't want to talk about it, that's okay; I'm just worried about you."

I recognized a subject change when I heard it, and I didn't mind the topic, so I rolled with it. "It's been good. I was afraid it would be awful, and it's had some pretty tough moments, but... it's been good."

"And you're..." She hesitated, eyebrows up. "You're doing better?"

"I am." I absently traced my finger around the rim of my coffee cup. "It's been... It's been hard, but yeah, I think I'm doing better." I leaned forward to set the cup on a coaster. "Digging into the feelings and shit?" I blew out a breath.

Rachel winced. "I should probably talk to someone, too. I'm just not sure I'm ready."

"That's okay. I wasn't either, but I fucked myself up drinking, so..."

"Well, I'm glad you got help sooner than later, then." She offered a faint, sad smile. "The team is here for you too, you know."

"Touche," I said with a soft laugh. "Yeah, I know they are. I'm just glad one of them gave me a shove before I dug myself in too deep, you know?"

Rachel held my gaze, and a little smile started to form. "Hall?"

I tilted my head. "Hmm?"

"It was Hall, wasn't it? Peyton Hall?"

I sat up a little. "How'd you guess?" But then I caught up and leaned back against the cushion. "The interview. Right."

Rachel shook her head as her knowing smile curled her lips. "No. I did see the interview, but... let's just say that part didn't surprise me at all."

"It didn't?"

"No. I started coming to some practices and games after Christmas, just to be around everyone and because the kids wanted—anyway, I've seen the way you two interact."

I slouched and exhaled. "That wasn't pretty for a while."

"It wasn't, but I could tell by the way he was looking at you that he was concerned."

I avoided her gaze as warmth rose in my face. "Yeah. He was. And I was... God, I was such an asshole to him about it, too."

"I doubt that," she whispered.

"No, I was. I was absolutely a—"

"Avery." Rachel shook her head. "I've snapped at my mom about things I don't even care about. I have to be so careful around the kids because sometimes I just get so angry I can't see straight, and I don't want to take it out on them." Her eyes welled up as she added, "It's grief, honey. It makes everything messy, including us."

"Isn't that the truth?" I scratched my neck. "What sucks is I had a thing for him, and..." Renewed heat rushed into my cheeks. "I think he had one for me too."

"Oh, I know you were into him." She giggled. "Leif thought it was adorable how you crushed on him."

I rolled my eyes and laughed. "Of course he did." My humor faded. "I'm pretty sure I messed it up, though."

"Do you really think so?"

I took a deep breath and told her the story. I didn't gloss over the ugly parts, either. The night Peyton had poured me into bed in the hotel. How I'd kissed him. Asking him to come get me from the club. Waking up to find him in my living room because he hadn't wanted to leave my pathetic trashed ass alone.

By the time I'd finished, I was queasy with embarrassment. "He *says* I didn't blow my chance with him, but..." I groaned and covered my face with both hands. "There's no way he wants anything to do with me after this."

"Sweetie." Rachel reached over and touched my arm. "If you blew it with him over that, then he wasn't worth getting together with anyway."

I lowered my hands and met her gaze. "What do you mean?"

She gave my arm another squeeze before leaning back in her chair and folding her hands on top of her belly. "You didn't do anything wrong, Avery."

"You didn't see how things went with Peyton."

Her lips pulled tight. Then she shook her head. "Whatever it was, he doesn't seem to be holding it against you." Before I could protest, she barreled on, "You've gone through something awful—you're still going through it—and you needed help." She shook her head. "I mean, do you think I screwed up by forgetting to register Elsa for Pre-K next year? Or getting behind on some bills because I was so overwhelmed I lost track of everything?"

Mute, I shook my head.

"Right. It's grief. It's going through hell. If Peyton is a good guy—and I think he is—then he'll see that you aren't a bad person. You're just hurting."

I had to swallow hard to keep my emotions in check. It was bad enough she of all people was comforting me this much; she didn't need to help me stop crying, too. When I was sure my voice would hold, I said, "I can't imagine he found any of it *attractive*, though, you know?"

She shrugged. "Then he doesn't deserve you."

"Is it stupid that I still want him even if he doesn't?"

Rachel laughed softly. "No. It isn't. Emotions aren't rational, and everyone has loved someone who didn't deserve it. But I don't think that's what's happening here."

"Maybe," I conceded. "But I mean, I *was* an asshole to him. Even if it was the grief and the alcohol talking... it was still *me*." I half-shrugged. "I can't really blame him if he can't look at me the same way, you know? Or if he doesn't find it attractive."

She seemed to consider it. "Maybe? Even if he isn't interested in anything like that, though, he seems to be a really good friend."

"He is. I just wish I could be around him without kicking myself for fucking up a chance at anything else."

"Eh, give him time. And give yourself time. He might surprise you."

I nodded but said nothing. As much as I desperately wanted to cling to that glimmer of hope she was offering, I couldn't make myself believe it. No matter how much Peyton may or may not have been interested in me before, neither of us could change what had happened. I didn't blame him if he couldn't look past it.

But I could sure hate myself for it.

Rachel gazed at me sadly. "I wish I'd known you were struggling so hard."

I was shaking my head before she'd finished. "You didn't need that."

"I didn't need to find out you were suffering in silence, either," she said pointedly.

"Okay," I admitted. "Fair. I just..."

"You didn't want to burden anyone else."

I blinked.

She laughed softly and patted my arm. "I know you." Her smile fell. "You should've told me you were having such a hard time. Sweetie, you know we all would've been there for you."

"I was trying to be there for *you*." I swallowed hard. "And the team—I'm the captain now. They don't have Leif anymore, so someone had to take the reins and be strong."

She stared at me as if she could barely understand what I'd said.

"What else could I do?" I whispered. "I couldn't—"

"Avery. Honey." She took my hand. "If things had been reversed—if Leif had lost you instead of the other way around—don't you think he'd have been a mess, too?"

It was my turn to stare at her.

"But he was always..." I swallowed. "He was the one who kept the team together."

"And he kept me and the kids together, too. He was strong as hell, no doubt about that. But he was human, too." She chewed her lip. "Remember a couple of seasons ago when you hurt your neck?"

I shuddered. That was a night I *wished* I could forget. The crunch when I'd landed. The way everyone had frantically held me still, ordering me not to move until they'd stabilized my neck. How much it had fucking hurt, and how we couldn't tell if I'd lost feeling in my left leg because of spinal damage or if the position I'd been in had just cut off circulation.

In the present, I cleared my throat. "Yeah. Of course I remember."

"Okay. Well. So do I." She locked eyes with me. "And I remember my husband being an absolute mess because his best friend had been stretchered off the ice on a backboard, and we still didn't know if you were okay."

My heart dropped into my stomach. I vividly remembered Leif being worried sick and rattled after our other teammate had taken a similar fall. For some reason, it had just never occurred to me that he'd been that much of a mess—or more of one—when I'd been hurt.

She wasn't finished yet, either. "He made Coach Tabakov and half a dozen other people promise to call the *minute* they heard how you were. And you know what happened when they called?"

Swallowing hard, I shook my head.

Her eyes started to well up for a third time. "As soon as he heard that you were okay, and that you were probably going to be on LTIR for a while but you'd be back—" She put her hand to her lips, and when she continued, her voice shook. "The only other time I've ever seen him that relieved is after things got scary with me and the twins in the delivery room."

My lips parted.

"He was human, honey," she said. "He loved you like a brother. If he'd ever lost you, he'd have been a broken man for a long, long time." She squeezed my hand again. "None of us were ever going to judge you for falling apart when you lost him."

Speaking of falling apart...

I was so damn tired of crying, but this time... God, just like it had been in my therapist's office and with Peyton, it was cathartic. It wasn't that crushing grief that had become a constant companion. As Rachel pulled me close and let me literally cry on her shoulder, it was like a long overdue release of things I'd stupidly held on to for too damn long. It didn't matter how much I'd let out in therapy, there always seemed to be another reserve of heartache to tap into.

"I'm sorry," I whispered. I didn't even know if I was apologizing for keeping all this from her, or for leaning on her of all people when she had to be struggling even more than any of us. Both, probably, since I *was* sorry for both.

"You don't need to apologize," she said softly, stroking my hair. "I don't have a monopoly on grieving for Leif."

"Still." I let her go and wiped my eyes. "I should be supporting you, not leaning on you."

She was already shaking her head. "No. We can be there for each other."

I knew better than to argue with her, so I nodded. "Okay. But... tell me if it's too much, all right? I don't want to make things worse for you."

Her smile was sad but sincere. "You're not. I promise." Before I could ask if she was sure, Rachel sat up a little, wincing as she rubbed her back. "Ugh. Being pregnant is *not* for wimps."

I chuckled, both at the comment and because I was relieved we were shifting gears. "No kidding. Are you okay? Do you need an icepack or—"

"No, no." She huffed sharply. "I just need it to be my damn due date so I can serve an eviction notice."

"You're almost there. Only, what, three or four more weeks?"

She shot me a glare. "There's no such thing as 'only' three or four more weeks of... *this*."

Showing my palms, I said, "Fair enough."

She laughed, then glanced toward the kitchen. "Do you want something to eat?" She smiled sadly. "And don't tell me you're not hungry. You're a hockey player—you're *always* hungry."

I laughed, and it felt good, especially because it made her laugh, too. "Yeah, you got me." I took out my phone. "Why don't we order a pizza or something?"

She made a face. "Ugh. No. Just the *thought* of pizza makes me gag right now."

"Seriously?"

She gestured at her belly.

I scoffed. "That kid is going to be *born* grounded."

"You have no idea." She picked up her own phone off the end table. "What about Thai? Does Thai sound good?"

"Thai always sounds good. And I guess as long as the kid lets you eat Thai, we can reduce the grounding to two months instead of three."

She scoffed. "Please. This child is making me hate garlic. He'll be lucky if he's ungrounded before kindergarten."

I arched an eyebrow. "He?"

Some pink rose in her cheeks, and she smiled. "Yeah. We found out last week."

I managed to smile, too, pretending not to notice that pang of renewed grief beneath my ribs. "That's awesome. Congrats."

"Thanks." From the way her smile faltered, she had a similar feeling—that awful twinge that came with remembering Leif wasn't here.

They were having another baby boy... but Leif wasn't here.

The team won a game... but Leif wasn't here.

We were ordering Thai from the best restaurant in Sewickley... but Leif wasn't here.

Rachel put her phone aside and pushed out a ragged breath. "This isn't how it was supposed to be. I'm just... I'm glad Leif knew. About the baby. But it's hard because he doesn't know..." She trailed off as tears spilled over her lashes.

I slid closer and wrapped my arms around her, trying like hell not to choke on my own emotions. "I know it's hard. I'm sorry."

She held on and trembled, crying silently against my shoulder for a moment. "God, I'm sorry." She pulled back and wiped her eyes with a shaky hand. "Everyone keeps telling me this will get better, but..." She shook her head. "Damn hormones."

"I don't think it's the hormones," I said gently. "I'm sure they don't help, but like I just told you, I've been a mess, too, and I'm not pregnant."

Rachel met my gaze, her eyes red and wet.

I clasped her hand in mine. "You just saw me fall apart, and believe me, it's not the first time that's happened. One of the things my therapist keeps telling me is that even though society doesn't acknowledge it, losing a close friend can hit *almost* like losing a partner, you know? It's not romantic love, but it's love, and it fucking hurts." I gently tightened my grasp o her hand. "Losing him has wrecked me in ways I never imagined it would. If it's fucked me up this much as his friend—if it's going to have me breaking down and crying at the slightest provocation—then of *course* it's going to make a mess of his wife."

Her shoulders slumped and some more tears fell. For a heartbeat, I was afraid I'd said the wrong thing and made it worse, but then she gripped my hand tighter and whispered, "I think I needed to hear that." She swiped at her eyes again. "I feel like I should just snap out of this and go back to normal, or that everything I feel is just hormones, but it's..." She covered her mouth as she started to cry again. "I lost my husband."

I pulled her back into my arms and tried to hold myself together. Hearing and feeling her cry like this was absolutely heart-wrenching. Even more than when I'd had my own breakdown a moment ago. It reminded me of that day when I'd lost it in Shannon's office; I just hoped this was because she'd also realized it was okay to feel what she felt and grieve Leif as hard as she loved him. Society didn't understand friends grieving like this, and friends didn't always know how to do it; maybe spouses didn't know how either.

After a long moment, Rachel started to quiet, and I whispered, "I'm sorry," because I didn't know what else to say.

"Don't be." She drew away and reached for the tissues on the end table. "I think it's what I needed to hear."

"I know the feeling. My therapist and I had a similar conversation." I wiped my own eyes. "We're always trying to be stronger than we are."

"God, isn't that the truth?" She handed me a tissue, which I took gratefully. "Grief is bullshit."

I laughed through my tears. "It really is. What the fuck."

She laughed, too. "I want to speak to a manager."

I snorted. "Right?"

We both chuckled and dabbed at our eyes.

Sobering, I said, "Listen, I don't..." I hesitated, gnawing the inside of my cheek. Then I met her gaze. "I don't want to pour salt on wounds or anything. But I have some things of Leif's. I, um... I want to give them back, but if it's easier for me to hold on to them for now, I can."

Renewed pain flickered across her face. "What things?"

I couldn't begin to explain why my voice tried to crack as I whispered, "His golf clubs."

Her features threatened to crumple too, but she rallied and cleared her throat. "God, I totally forgot about those." She rolled her shoulders. "I think his brother might like to have them."

"Okay. I'll—" I stopped myself before I said I'd go out to the car and grab them. I didn't want to explain to Rachel that it was still in my trunk. I didn't want her to figure out that they'd been there since August. That no one had moved or touched them since he'd put them in there beside mine. That moments after he'd put the clubs in the place they still were today, he'd ridden out of the parking lot on his bike, and I'd never seen him again.

I shifted a little and coughed to get my breath moving. "I'll bring them by next time."

Her sad smile made me glad I'd kept that card close to my vest. It seemed like such a small, inconsequential thing, but if there was one thing I'd learned in the months since we'd lost her husband and my best friend, it was that *nothing* was small or inconsequential.

"Thank you, Avery," she said. "And... thank you for being here. I hate that you're grieving too, but it's nice to not be alone."

"Yeah. It is."

Her words brought me up short, though. It hadn't

occurred to me that she might feel alone in this. It made perfect sense—it just hadn't crossed my mind.

Unaware of my brain catching on her comment, she rolled her shoulders and pushed out a breath. "On that note, how about we order some food? Because if we're going to be sad, we should at least stuff our faces with good Thai food."

I laughed. "That is some sound logic." I picked up my phone. "Your usual?"

"Yeah." She paused, wrinkling her nose. "Zero star spice, though."

I raised my eyebrows. "Seriously? You don't want that crazy five-star shit you always order?"

"Oh, I do." She scowled and pointed at her belly. "He, however, does not."

I blinked. Then I shook my head, and as I opened the app, I muttered, "That kid is grounded until *high school*."

Rachel laughed with some actual feeling, and it was the best thing I'd heard all day.

CHAPTER 30
PEYTON

Road trips were a normal part of a hockey player's life. From the time we started playing above local peewee leagues, traveling to games was as normal as lacing up our skates. Buses, planes, hotels, restaurants—it was as much a part of the sport as the ever-present funk of hockey gear.

But two games into this four-game road trip, I was restless. Hell, I was *homesick*. Not for Nebraska or Iowa, though, and not for Detroit—for Pittsburgh.

For Avery's place.

For Avery.

We'd played tonight in Denver last night and then flown to Vegas, landing at around two in the morning. I'd slept, I'd practiced with the team, and now I had a little time to myself before a team meeting this afternoon.

If I was smart, I'd spend that time getting caught up on some sleep.

If I was smart, and if I wasn't so damn restless that I couldn't sit still.

Restlessness came with being a hockey player—most of us were incredibly wired and constitutionally incapable of being still for very long. I was probably on the calmer end compared to some of my past and present teammates. I'd played with some guys who were so full of energy all the time, they practically vibrated when they had to sit for any length of time. Today, I was pretty sure I could give most of them a run for their money.

Lying back on my hotel bed, I swore aloud and rubbed my eyes with the heels of my hands. Restlessness was normal, but I didn't recognize *this* feeling. It didn't make sense. From the moment I'd boarded the bus at the arena and watched Avery walk back to his car, I'd felt…

Untethered? Was that the word? Close enough.

All because I was away from Avery. Why was I such a damn mess for him? Yeah, I'd had a crush on him before coming to Pittsburgh. And then there was that period where everything between us had felt like a powder keg getting ready to blow, and not in a good way.

But ever since he'd gone into the program…

Ever since we'd started spending so much of our available time together…

The itch to text him or FaceTime him had me squirming on the bed. I needed to see his face. Talk to him. Even get a few lines of text from him. *Something.* I couldn't make sense of it, but I also couldn't ignore it.

Eh, fuck it. What was stopping me from reaching out to him? What was the worst that could happen?

> I'm chilling at the hotel for a bit. FaceTime?

He wrote back almost immediately.

> On my way home right now. Give me 20 min?

Take your time.

Even as I wrote the words, I silently pleaded with him to step on it. I felt ridiculous and stupid and more than a little pathetic, but what could I say? I wanted to see his face, even if it was on a screen.

About fifteen minutes later, he sent the FaceTime request, and I was a little embarrassed by the intense relief that rushed through me when he appeared on my phone. He was lounging on his couch, I thought, his hair wet and stringy as if he'd recently showered.

"Hey, sorry." He smiled as he tucked his arm behind his head. "You caught me on the way out of the training facility."

"Oh yeah? Skating?"

"Not today. I needed to get out of my home gym, so I was working out there."

"Ah, okay. I don't blame you—that facility is nice."

"Right? It was great before, but after they renovated it a couple of years ago?" He whistled. "I spend more time there than in my home gym."

"I don't blame you. You don't have to clean or maintain any of the equipment there."

"That's a very, very nice bonus. Is that why you use it all the time too?"

I shrugged, neither confirming nor denying, and I was rewarded with an adorable laugh.

"It kind of felt like the off season today," he said after a moment. "Usually there's trainers and teammates around, but today..." He shook his head.

"At least then you didn't have to worry about anyone forgetting to rack their weights." I narrowed my eyes. "Unless you're the one who doesn't rack his weights."

"What? Me?" He put a hand to his chest and batted his eyelashes. "I would *never*."

"You better not," I muttered. "Ugh, the other day, someone must've leg-pressed every forty-five-pound plate in the building. Did they take them off the machine? *No*."

"For fuck's sake." Avery tsked. "They probably left crotch sweat all over the seat, too."

I made a face. "Eww, I didn't even think of that. It was dry by the time I got to it, but... eww."

He laughed. "You'll think about it next time, won't you?"

I gave him the finger, which only made him laugh harder.

The conversation continued in that vein for a while, mostly just shooting the shit over whatever, before I had to log off so I could head to the team meeting.

"It was good to talk with you," Avery said, and he sounded like he meant it. "We should do this again."

The excitement that swelled in my chest caught me off-guard, and it also didn't surprise me at all. Of course I wanted to talk with him again. I just hadn't expected to be so enthusiastic about it.

"Sure! Yeah!" I smiled. "We're on a pretty tight schedule, especially with two back-to-backs, but definitely."

He smiled too, and was he... relieved? Because he sure sounded like it as he said, "Okay, great! Just, you know, text me when you've got time, and we'll get on chat."

"Perfect. We'll talk soon."

As much as I didn't want to end the call, I needed to, and a moment later, we did. Though I was supposed to be heading down to the team meeting, I lingered in my room for a moment, still lying back on the bed as I replayed our call in my mind.

We hadn't talked about anything substantial. It was just chatter about our days and the training facility's gym and superficial things like that.

But the relief settling into me went so much deeper. As if talking to him at all, regardless of what it was about, soothed my soul.

Was that all I needed? To just spend some time talking to him and seeing his face, even if we were just shooting the breeze?

Maybe it was. All I knew was that after our call, I didn't feel so scattered anymore. That untethered feeling was... not gone, but better.

I wiped my hand over my face, then stared up at the ceiling, Avery's soft voice still ringing my ears like a roaring crowd after an overtime win. Talking to him helped, but it also didn't. I was even more restless now. And I had to go to a meeting? And concentrate? And then come back and try to sleep at some point? When I wanted to be on FaceTime with him for another hour or three? How?

I sighed into the stillness. I was such a damn mess. For all I tried to gaslight myself into thinking I didn't know why, I knew exactly why.

I wanted Avery.

I wanted him on the ice with me. On the bench with me.

In this goddamned *bed* with me.

"Fuck my life," I said aloud. Now was so not the time. He needed to focus on his therapy, his recovery, and his grief. He needed to concentrate on getting back up to speed so he could play hockey again. The last thing in the world he needed was to stumble into anything with me, whether it was for sex or... more than sex.

I squeezed my eyes shut. Fine, we wouldn't hook up or

get together, but could I at least see him? Like, in person instead of a twenty-minute FaceTime call?

Christ. Is it time to go back to Pittsburgh yet?

I'd been on some long road trips during my time as a hockey player. Some much longer than this one.

But I didn't think I'd ever been this homesick in my life.

"Tough game, eh?" On my screen, Avery offered a sympathetic grimace.

I sighed, settling back on the hotel bed. "I take it you watched?"

"Yeah. I was helping Rachel with the kids today, and we decided to watch the game before I headed home."

Jealousy flared in my chest, and I couldn't quite explain it. I loved that Avery was spending time with Leif's family, and they probably appreciate his company and his help. It was a *good* thing. It was probably great for his recovery to not be alone, too. Plus, I mean, Avery and I weren't together. I had no claim on him. And I was pretty sure he was gay, not bi, so Rachel wouldn't be on his radar even if she had any interest in dating this soon after losing her husband.

Am I just stupid? Is that the issue?

I tamped that weird feeling away. "How is she doing?"

Avery half-shrugged. "I mean, she's struggling, but all things considered, she's doing good. We took the kids to the science center this afternoon, which was a lot of fun." He chuckled. "They passed out the minute we put them to bed."

"I bet they did," I said with a laugh that hopefully didn't sound as forced as it was.

Seriously, what was wrong with me?

Besides the fact that I wish I could've been there.

Ah. *That* was it. I wasn't jealous or territorial like someone who thought his boyfriend was interested in someone else—I was jealous that she got to see him at all.

I fucking *missed* him.

I cleared my throat. "How are the kids?"

"They're good. I think... I mean, they're so young, they don't completely understand death, you know?"

"Oh, that's rough."

"It is. The twins *mostly* get it, I think. But sometimes Elsa asks when her dad's coming home, and that just..." He pushed out a breath. "That hits right in the feels."

"Yeah, I bet. Poor kids. That's gotta be rough on their mom, too."

"It is. And she's holding it together as much as she can, but she's been having a tough time." He sighed. "I don't know how she does it, honestly—handling all of this on top of taking care of three kids with a baby on the way. Just a day of helping her wore me out."

I grimaced. "She's tougher than I am, that's for sure."

"Right? I mean, it's not like she had a choice, you know? I'm sure she'd rather not be handling it." His expression turned even sadder, his gaze a bit distant. "I know I'd rather not, and I don't have it half as hard as she does."

"I can only imagine."

Silence fell between us that I had no idea how to fill.

Fortunately, Avery got us back on the rails and moving in a different direction.

"So how was Coach after the game?" He grimaced again. "He must've been *thrilled.*"

I made a face, though I was relieved at the new subject even if tonight's performance made me cringe. "Ugh. I swear that's the worst part of losing—the disappointed coach speech afterward, and you were right about how awful it is from *this* coach."

He laughed. "That bad, eh?"

"And this was the third loss in a row, so..." I exhaled.

Avery frowned, his expression full of both worry and guilt, and I didn't need to be mind reader to know where his thoughts were going.

"Don't put this on your shoulders," I said softly.

He looked at the camera again. Then he laughed. "Why am I not surprised you can see right through me?"

"Nah." I shook my head. "I'd probably be feeling the same way."

His eyebrows flicked up. "Really?"

"Well, yeah. You're not the only one who feels like he's letting the whole team down when he's benched. Every time I've been out and my team has lost, I've beaten myself up over it for days after."

"But there's eighteen skaters on," he said. "Even if you go down in the middle of the game, that leaves seventeen to get the job done. It's not on you."

I inclined my head and arched an eyebrow.

He held my gaze. Then he chuckled. "Okay, okay. Point taken." Sighing as his smile fell, he sat back. "I really want to get back out there. Not because I feel like I need to take charge and get the team back on track—I just miss it. Even the losses, you know? I'd rather play a losing game than not play at all."

"I know exactly what you mean."

He shifted a little, as if he were as restless as me. Being a hockey player, he probably *was* that restless. "I thought going to therapy and dealing with all that shit would be the worst part. And that part's hard, don't get me wrong. But not playing hockey?" His shoulders sagged. "It fucking sucks. Even when I can still practice a little. Especially when the team is struggling and there's nothing I can do to help."

"You've *been* helping. Coming to games, practicing with the guys—it helps keep everyone's spirits up more than you probably realize."

"But tonight..." His expression turned pained.

"You know damn well we could've lost catastrophically with you, too. It wasn't your absence that lost tonight—it was us falling apart."

"Still."

"Look, I know you're having a tough time, but don't shoulder this too. And you'll be back playing hockey again before you know it, and we'll be glad to have you. But the most important thing right now is taking care of you. The team? We can hold the line." I paused. "Well, most of the time, but losing streaks happen even when players aren't missing, so..."

He laughed. "Yeah, they do. God, that one we had last season?" He rolled his eyes and groaned. "Thank God Vegas had that fourteen-game losing streak, or we'd have had the biggest one for the season."

"I remember that. What was it, twelve games?"

Rolling his eyes, he nodded. "Twelve very long and frustrating games, yeah." He grinned. "And yet you still signed with us, you fucking masochist."

I snorted. "Not like I had much choice. And anyway, I seem to recall you guys also had a couple of solid winning streaks last year, so I'll take my chances."

"Fair enough. Detroit held their own last year, too, didn't they?"

"We did. If I'd stayed, I think I'd have been happy, but it probably was time for a change of scenery."

"I know how that goes."

I eyed him. "Says the guy who's still with the same team that drafted him."

"Yeah, but I was seriously considering leaving after my entry-level contract was up. I liked the team, but the coaching was..." He wrinkled his nose.

"Ooh, that's right. You guys had John Robinson, didn't you?"

He rolled his eyes and groaned. "God, I hated that guy."

"Really? Was he actually as bad as people say?"

"He..." Avery quirked his lips. "I mean, there are definitely worse coaches out there. There was one in my division in major juniors who was a real piece of work. Robs? He was just... He was one of those old-school coaches who was old school for the sake of being old school."

"Oh, Jesus." I rolled my eyes. "So, an absolute hardass who thought everyone was getting too soft?"

"Exactly. He'd yell and scream because that's what old-school coaches did, not because it was actually effective." Avery sighed. "The thing is, he was pretty good when it came to strategy, and his systems were good. If he'd chilled the fuck out a little, he'd have been fine. But he was so determined to be a drill sergeant on ice skates that it was really fucking stressful."

"Ugh. Sounds like my U16 coach."

"Yeah?"

"Yep. One of my buddies said that guy would probably go home and watch the boot camp scenes in *Full Metal Jacket* and beat off."

The full-throated laugh that burst out of Avery made

my hotel room tilt. Christ, I was so stupid for him, especially when he smiled.

"Oh my God," he said, still laughing. "I bet Robs did the same thing." He mimicked jerking off, and he scrunched up his face as he said, "Yeeaah, do the bit about steers and queers again. Fuck yeah."

I laughed so hard I was cackling, and he did too.

It felt good, even if it was commiserating over (and making fun of) some awful past coaches.

As we settled again, I asked, "So you stayed because they brought in Coach Tabakov?"

Avery nodded. "I like his style and his systems. And I really wanted to stay because of—" His teeth snapped shut, and all the lingering amusement vanished from his expression. I wasn't at all surprised when he whispered, "Because I liked playing with Leif."

"I believe that," I said as gently as I could. "When you're that close to a teammate, you'll put up with a lot."

"Exactly." He met my gaze through the screen. "Did you have anyone you were close to like that?"

"I was pretty tight with Conrad Waverly. He was my roommate when I was a rookie, and we got to be really good friends." The memory made my chest tight. "Fucking sucked when they traded him."

"That's the worst, isn't it?" He winced at his own words, and once again, I didn't need to be a mind reader—no, someone being traded definitely *wasn't* the worst way two teammates could be separated.

"It sucks," I acknowledged. "We're still friends, and we always grab dinner when we're in the same city."

"That's good," he said, seeming to brighten a little. "I've got some old teammates—both from the Whiskey Rebels and major juniors—who I see when we're on the road." He paused, then laughed. "I swear, when we all retire, we should just form our own team of old crotchety-ass players who can't be traded because fuck trades."

I laughed, too, relieved at the break in tension. "Love it. Like the only way someone can be traded is if he and the other player are in total agreement and want to be traded."

"Exactly! We can all if the North American Because-Fuck-You-That's-Why League."

"Hmm, might have to workshop that one a little. Bit of a mouthful."

He huffed and rolled his eyes. "It's a great idea, damn it."

"It is! But, you know, maybe tweak it so it rolls off the tongue better?"

The answer to that was a middle finger, and I laughed.

Right then, I glanced at the clock on the nightstand, and my heart sank. "Fuck. It's late. I should get some sleep."

Was that disappointment on his face, too?

"Yeah, I should probably sleep myself." He ran a hand through his hair. "It's almost two and I've got therapy first thing in the morning."

"They make you show up in the morning?" I stuck out my tongue. "That's just *mean*."

I would seriously do or say anything to make this man laugh like that.

"It's my choice, honestly," he said, still smiling. "Get it all out of the way, and then I have the rest of the day to do whatever."

"Okay, that's fair." I sighed. "Well, I might not have time to chat tomorrow night; we're flying out right after the game, and then I have to try to sleep."

"Ooh, that's right—you guys have a back-to-back, don't you?"

"Ugh. Yes." I rolled my eyes. "Fucking hate back-to-backs on the road, but it's not like they consult me about the schedule."

"Those bastards."

"I know, right?"

He chuckled. "Okay, I'll let you go." Turning a little bit serious, but still smiling, he said, "Thanks for chatting. It's, um... It's been really good."

"It has for me, too. So... thanks for that."

We locked eyes.

The moment threatened to get unbearably awkward, so we quickly wrapped it up and ended the call.

And just like I had the other times we'd talked on this trip, I lay there and stared at the ceiling for a few minutes, trying to figure out what all I was feeling after talking to him.

I was no closer to making any sense of it than I'd been before. If anything, I was even more homesick than I was the first time we'd FaceTimed.

We still had two games to play on this trip. Three nights to sleep in hotels while I drove myself insane wanting to be back in Pittsburgh.

Wanting to be back in the same space as Avery.

Seriously. Is it time to go home yet?

CHAPTER 31
AVERY

Just landed. Care for company?

I responded so fast, I was surprised I didn't type a hole in my screen.

Definitely. We can order food or something.

The reply was a thumbs-up, and I'm not ashamed to admit that the relief was almost overwhelming. The damn road trip had gone on for-fucking-ever. I'd spent time with Rachel and the kids, and I'd skated with Marts, since he was trying to stay conditioned while he rehabbed his shoulder, but it just wasn't enough. I'd been missing Peyton so bad I was losing my damned mind.

And not a moment too soon, he pulled in my driveway.

As soon as I heard the engine outside, I whispered, "Oh, thank fuck," into the stillness of my empty house. The impulse to fling open the door and greet him like a boyfriend caught me off guard. Fortunately, I managed to tamp it down before I opened the door, and by the time I was face to face with Peyton, I was no longer in danger of grabbing him and kissing him.

That wasn't who we were. I wished it was, but it wasn't, and it never would be. I'd already fucked that up—including with a badly timed drunken kiss that I was still mortified about—so I didn't need to make it worse.

That wasn't to say it was *easy* to keep my hands to myself. It never was, but today he was wearing that gray-blue suit he must've worn on the plane. He always looked amazing in suits, and seeing him in one now was like seeing a glass of ice water in the middle of the desert. *Want.*

Somehow clinging to my dignity and self-control, I said, "Coffee?"

His smile—fuuuck. "Yeah. Sounds good."

After he'd left his shoes by the door, I led him into the kitchen.

While I got the coffee going, he said, "You're in a good mood."

Of course I am, I damn near said. *You're here.*

"I am," I answered instead. "Getting a little stir crazy and missing hockey, but... I'm doing pretty good."

"That's great." He leaned against the counter. "I take it therapy and all that has been going good?"

We hadn't talked much about that while he was gone. Too depressing. Too many other things to focus on that were so much more pleasant. "Yeah. Yeah, it's..." I exhaled, rolling my shoulders. "I swear this is the closest I've felt to myself since..." I hesitated, then quietly finished, "Since Leif died."

The words still hurt. On some level, I knew they always would. But it felt more like putting weight on an old, cranky injury than trying to walk on a broken ankle.

Peyton's smile made the whole world brighter. "That's great! I'm glad to hear it's been helping. You look..." He swallowed. "You *look* more like yourself, too. Not that I knew you before, but..." He actually blushed, which was too damn adorable. "You know what I mean."

I laughed softly. "Yeah, I follow. I'm just glad I wasn't too far gone when I got help. I can't imagine digging myself out of a deeper hole than this." I held his gaze. "So... thanks for that."

"You've done the work," he whispered. "Not me."

"No, but you gave me the swift kick in the ass that I needed." I swallowed. "To be honest, I think you saved my life. You definitely saved my sanity."

He swallowed hard, but then he smiled. "Glad I could help. I know it was rough there in the beginning, but... I'm glad it's helping."

"It is. I just..." I bit my lip. No, there was no way to say that without sounding like I was fishing for sympathy or something.

Peyton tilted his head. "What?"

"I..." I dropped my gaze. Then I laughed because, eh, what the hell? I doubted I could do much to look *more* pathetic to this man. "I can't lie—I'm still kicking myself for fucking things up with you."

"For fuck—what? You didn't fuck anything up with me."

I met his eyes with a skeptical look of my own. "Come on. Let's not kid ourselves. I'm grateful and I always will be, but nothing I've said or done over the past few months has been, shall we say, attractive?" Shaking my head, I turned away to get our coffee cups. "I don't blame you at all. I'm just fucking pissed at myself for—"

His hand materialized on the back of my neck, the

touch gentle but firm, and before I knew what was happening, he'd rotated me to face him.

And then his mouth was against mine.

For a second, I froze, but as he snaked his other arm around me and dragged his lower lip across mine, my brain and body caught up. I wrapped my arms around his neck, pulling him closer, and that little hum against my lips almost dropped my knees out from under me.

Peyton nudged me back a step so I was leaning against the counter, and he carded his fingers through my hair as he kissed the breath out of me.

When he finally came up for air, he was trembling almost as much as I was. Looking right in my eyes, he panted, "I've been... wanting to do that forever."

I stared at him, my heart thundering as my knees shook beneath us.

He licked his lips. "The last few months have been a lot of things," he said, still breathless. "Enough to make me stop being attracted to you?" He shook his head, and as he drew me back in, he growled, "Not a fucking chance."

Then he had my mouth again, and my spine turned to liquid.

Oh my God. This man's touch. His kiss.

There wasn't a damn thing I could do except hold on and just melt in his embrace. No one had ever kissed me like this. No one. Absolutely no one. If I didn't believe his words, I believed the unmistakable desire in the way he parted my lips with his tongue and explored my mouth. In the way he held me so damn tight—not so that I couldn't pull away, but rather like he was silently *begging* me not to.

I was the one to break the kiss this time, breathing hard and fast into the space between our lips. "You still... Even after..." I didn't even know why I was asking. He'd made it absolutely clear he wanted me.

Maybe I just couldn't quite get my head around *why*. *How*. After everything I'd said and done. After everything he'd seen. How in the world was he—

"I wanted you long before I ever came to Pittsburgh," he murmured. "Now that I know you?" He finished that thought with an even hotter kiss, sliding his fingers up into my hair and grinding his rock-hard cock against mine through our clothes.

I just whimpered and kissed him right back. It didn't make sense, him still being into me after all this, but his kiss didn't lie. The way he held on to me, fingers twitching against my scalp as soft moans vibrated against my lips— none of that lied either.

Holy fuck. Peyton Hall wants me.

And what could I do besides grab on and give as good as I got?

"God, I want you so bad," I mumbled against his lips.

That soft moan almost had me coming in my damn pants.

"Good thing we've got all day, huh?" he whispered.

Oh, hell. We did, didn't we? Nowhere to go except the bedroom.

"Think we'd be moving too fast if we jumped into bed?" I asked.

"Depends. Are we getting naked?"

"No clothes allowed in my bed."

He groaned softly. "Definitely not too fast."

"Didn't think so. C'mon." I nudged him back a step and took his hand. "Upstairs."

Peyton didn't object.

As soon as we'd stepped into my bedroom, he pressed

me up against the door and claimed my mouth again. Fuck, I could not get enough of the way he kissed—I'd heard of needing someone like air, but I'd never imagined what it would feel like to be on the receiving end of that need. To have someone kissing me so greedily. So hungrily.

And oh, hell, I hadn't realized until this moment how touch-starved I'd been recently, and now my whole body—every damn cell and nerve ending—tingled with the need for more.

"I'm game for anything," he murmured. "Just so we're clear. I'll fuck you if that's what you want. You can fuck me. We can sixty-nine all damn day. I just..." He paused to nip my lower lip. "I just want you."

"Ungh, me too."

He swept his tongue across his lips. "Why do we still have all these clothes on?"

I glanced down, honestly surprised our clothes hadn't just gone up in flames. Meeting his gaze again, I shook my head. "No idea. Let's get them out of the way."

The grin that lit up his face also lit up parts of me that I didn't know existed. I'd had plenty of sex in my life, including with a handful of boyfriends, but I couldn't remember anyone ever gazing at me like he wanted to devour me whole. Oh my God.

We separated and made short work of our clothes. It didn't take much for me—all I'd had on was a pair of jeans and a T-shirt.

Peyton still had on his suit, so he had a few more steps. Fine by me—that just gave me a chance to lie back in the bed and touch myself while I watched him strip down.

I'd seen him naked plenty of times, but ever since my earliest years as the queer kid in the locker room, I'd been in the habit of pointedly not observing my teammates. Especially what they were packing.

So color me seriously—and pleasantly—surprised to find that Peyton was *hung*. Not so big he'd be painful to take, but definitely thick enough to give my jaw a run for its money, not to mention my ass. I'd fantasized plenty of times about sex with him, and now I was on fire with need to feel everything he could do with that impressive dick.

Once he was finally, gloriously naked, he joined me in bed. I reached for him, ready to drag him own into a kiss, but he—

"Oh, fuck!" I cried when he ran the tip of his tongue up the length of my dick. "Holy..."

He glanced up at me, grinning. "I've been wanting to do this forever."

Before I could tell him to be my guest, he had his lips around the head and his hand around the shaft, and... oh, God. He didn't hold back at all—licking, stroking, moaning as if he were the one getting his brains sucked out his cock.

"Holy fuck," I murmured, arching off the bed. I had a split second to panic when I realized I'd pushed into his mouth, but his response was to take me even farther. I'd always loved when the guy I was with enjoyed sucking cock, and Peyton definitely enjoyed it. He blew me like this was his favorite thing in the world—the absolute main attraction.

And if he kept at it, I was going to come down his throat, which he'd probably love. I would too... except I wasn't ready for that. Not yet.

"Don't make me come yet," I whined. "That's so good, but... not yet. Please?"

He ran his tongue around the head once more, then came up to me, and I hauled him down into a deep, messy kiss. His hips settled between my parted thighs, and when he started rocking them, that thick cock slid alongside mine. I couldn't remember the last time a man had made the room spin like this; fuck, I was turned on.

"For the record," he purred, "I love giving head. So any time you're in the mood for a long, drawn-out blowjob..." He kissed me again, that talented mouth making me delirious.

Between kisses, I managed to ask, "Blowjob like that sounds *amazing*. What else do you like?"

"Being naked on top of you is pretty high on my list."

"Uh-huh. Do you like topping?"

Peyton growled against my lips, then murmured, "Baby, say the word and I will plow you like a driveway in Calgary."

I snorted, breaking the kiss, and we both burst out laughing. Still holding on to him, still laughing, I said, "A driveway in Calgary, eh?"

He offered a playfully innocent look and shrugged. "I'll fuck you so good, your neighbors will need a cigarette?"

Again, I collapsed into laughter. "Oh my God."

"What?" He dipped his head to kiss my neck. "I've got plenty more of those."

Between laughing and those soft little kisses he was planting on my throat, I could barely breathe.

He chuckled, then nipped my neck before he whispered in my ear, "Anything you want, baby. Anything."

I shivered, my humor evaporating in the heat of all this arousal. "Fuck me?"

He growled low again, shivering on top of me, and he purred, "Please tell me you're serious."

"Why? You want to—"

"*Yes*," he gritted out. "I've thought about that with my

dick in my hand so many damn times." He pressed his feverish forehead to mine. "Please tell me you really want it."

"Yes. I do. *Badly.*"

A low groan came from his throat, and then he was kissing me again, deep and hard and needy in that way that said he was this close to losing his mind. *Fuck*, yes.

It occurred to me then that he'd mentioned wanting me to fuck him. As he started down my jaw and onto my throat, now that my mouth was no longer occupied, I asked, "I'm a bottom. Like, exclusively. Is that—is that enough?"

Peyton's lips curled against my skin. "Baby, just making out in front of the TV would be more than enough." He slid a hand down and stroked himself between us. "And I can definitely top you to hell and back."

The helpless sound that escaped my lips didn't even sound like me.

But then reality nudged its way in, and I stiffened.

Peyton caught on even before I did. "What? You okay?" He pushed himself up, poised to get off me if I asked him to.

"I'm good. I'm good." I trailed my palm across his chest. "I, uh... I don't have any condoms, though."

"Oh." He chewed his lip.

"We can still do plenty." I grinned despite my own disappointment. "Save something for next time?"

"We could, yeah," he said with a nod. "But, um... I've got a test, actually." He gestured over his shoulder. "Recent one with the results on my phone. All clear."

I blinked. "Yeah?"

"Mmhmm. I was planning to be a lot smoother about all this if we got to—I'd bring it up *before* we were... well..."

"I don't know." I trailed my fingers down his back.

"Mentioning you want to fuck me bareback when you've already got me naked in bed—that's pretty smooth."

He laughed softly and kissed beneath my chin. Then he pushed himself up again and met my gaze. "I meant... I wasn't going to just..."

"Kiss me in the kitchen and then fuck me senseless?"

"Something like that."

I slid a hand up into his hair. "Well, I like this new plan of yours, so... feel free to keep improvising."

He was grinning again when our lips met. "So does that meant you want me to top you right now? Without a condom?"

"Something, something, driveway in Calgary."

Peyton laughed and buried his face against my neck. "Well." He bit my collarbone. "You do have lube, yes?"

"Plenty."

He let me up so I could get the lube out of the nightstand. As soon as I reached for it, though, he was against me, his arm around my midsection and his lips on the back of my neck. His hard-on pressed my thigh, and I let my head fall as I moaned with a mix of frustration and need.

"I can't get to the drawer," I protested. "I can't... oh, fuck..." His fingers had slipped between my thighs, teasing my taint and balls, and my brain went blank. "Peyton..."

He laughed softly. "What's wrong?"

"I want..." I flailed my hand toward the drawer. "I can't reach the lube."

Another laugh. "But I can reach you." He took full advantage, too, kissing my neck while he played with my balls.

I closed my eyes and exhaled. "You are such an asshole."

"Actually, since you're bottoming, I think that makes you the—"

We both burst out laughing.

I loved this so much. Even the frustration. Even the—

I realized he'd loosened his grip on my midsection, and I lunged forward to open the drawer. I snatched the bottle and held it up. "Got it!"

"Perfect." Peyton slid his hand up my arm until he reached my hand, and then he gently plucked the lube from my fingers. "Now to get you ready for me."

I twisted around and narrowed my eyes. "You're an evil tease in that department too, aren't you?"

He batted his eyelashes and shrugged.

I just laughed and rolled my eyes.

Peyton kissed my neck, then gently tugged my shoulder so I rolled on my back. Settling over me, he found my mouth, and we made out like we had all the time in the world. We did have all the time in the world, but goddammit, I wanted his cock... but his mouth was amazing... but I wanted...

"Fuck me, dammit," I demanded breathlessly.

His eyebrows jumped, but then he grinned. "Turn over." He opened the lube bottle. "Gotta get you ready."

For all he hadn't been able to resist grabbing me and kissing me in the kitchen, and for all he'd gone straight to going down on me once we'd made it into bed, Peyton took his sweet time now. And I didn't think it was just because he had a big cock and *needed* to make sure I was well-prepped, or even because he was a relentless tease—no, he was clearly enjoying himself, too. Especially when he molded himself to my back and started fingering me while he kissed up and down my neck.

"Touch yourself," he murmured in my ear as he finger-fucked me slowly.

I squirmed in his arms. "I'm afraid I'll come."

He nibbled my earlobe. "If you come, then I'll just have to turn you on all over again."

I was imagining this, wasn't I? I was lost in a fantasy, lying alone in my bed with my hand on my dick and my head full of the most deliciously pornographic thoughts of Peyton and—

"Ooh, yeah," I moaned as he crooked a finger just right inside me. I clawed at the edge of the mattress. "Fucking hell. I haven't... I haven't done anything for you, though."

"Oh, baby." He kissed my neck, his beard scuffing against my shoulder. "You're naked in bed and begging for my dick." He started moving his fingers a little faster. "Trust me—you've done plenty."

I bit my lip and shivered. "Won't... Won't say no to blowing you, though."

He groaned softly. "I'm definitely looking forward to fucking that beautiful face."

Jesus Christ. His dirty mouth was just... *fuuuck.*

"Right now, though," he went on, his voice husky with need, "I want your ass."

I rocked back against him, urging him on. "Good thing I love bottoming then, eh?"

"Mmhmm. Very good thing." He bit my shoulder—not hard enough to hurt, but enough to make me gasp. "We'll have to be more careful once you're skating with the team again," he whispered. "So you're not sore."

I bit my lip and arched against him.

"For right now, though?" The grin in his voice made my dick even harder. "I can rail you until neither of us can move."

"Fuck..." The word tumbled off my lips. "You have... the dirtiest mouth."

"Is that a problem?"

"Uh-uh. Keep... Keep up the good work."

He huffed a warm laugh across the side of my neck. Then he added a second finger inside me as he started kissing beneath my hairline.

I had to stop stroking myself. I desperately wanted the friction, but any more of that and I was going to come. "Damn it, Peyton..."

He laughed again. "What's wrong?"

"Nothing. But would you just fuck me already?"

I was sure he'd tease me for another hour or three just to drive me insane. To my surprise, though, he kissed my shoulder as he slipped his fingers free. "I would love to."

"Oh God," I moaned.

He dropped another kiss on my shoulder, then whispered, "I want you to ride me."

Any teasing I might've had about his cheesy lines died away because I was too turned on to think of anything except doing exactly what he said. Especially since this meant I could finally do something for him. Somehow, I managed, "Then get on your back."

He kissed my shoulder again, then pulled away. My back and shoulders were suddenly cool with the absence of his skin against me, and I almost whined in protest except I knew he was positioning himself so I could take him.

I was unsteady all over, so turned on I was shaking, but I managed to get up and straddle his powerful hips.

He gazed down at us, eyes full of lust and hunger. "Oh, fuck..." His eyes flicked up to meet mine, and I had to literally bite back a whimper. He'd been sexy before—naked, hard, and turned on within an inch of his life? *Perfect.*

I lifted myself up a little, and he steadied his cock as he guided me down. He felt even thicker than he looked, and I had to ease down slowly in order to take him comfortably.

Peyton didn't rush me at all. He just stared at me, and at us, heavy-lidded eyes on fire with desire and wonder. When I'd taken enough of him, he let go of his dick and started stroking mine, quickly bringing me back to full attention.

"Fuck," I whimpered. "Oh, fuck..."

"You are so hot," he breathed. "And so..." He closed his eyes and arched under me. "So *tight*."

Somewhere in my brain was a comment about how with a cock like his, tight was probably the default. The words didn't make it to my tongue, though, because that cock moving inside me had absolutely erased my ability to speak.

Slowly, I relaxed enough to take him easily, and then I was riding him, falling into a perfect steady rhythm. He matched my strokes, too, pushing up when I came down, and the absolute bliss was beyond intoxicating.

"Avery," he whispered. "Look... Look at me."

I hadn't even realized I'd closed my eyes until I opened them, and when I gazed down at him, all my own desire and arousal looked right back up at me. My God, he was so gorgeous.

He curved his hand behind my neck just like the first time he'd kissed me, and he pushed himself up on one elbow as he drew me down to him. We made out, and we rocked together, and my touch-starved senses *sang* as Peyton held me close and moved inside me. I wanted him thrusting—pounding into me so hard I couldn't catch my breath—but this was sexy and hot and amazing. His firm grip on my neck. Our fluid, easy motions. The way his cock stretched me. His *kiss*.

Was this even real? I'd been so convinced I didn't have a chance with him—that any chance I'd ever had was dead and gone—but here he was. Here we were.

"Let me get behind you," he mumbled against my lips. "I want to fuck you *hard*."

I damn near came, shuddering on top of him as I tried to find my breath. "Yes. *Please*."

We shifted positions, and I gripped handfuls of the sheets as Peyton guided himself to me. He had a hand on the small of my back, and he swore as his dick slid back in.

"This view is incredible," he slurred. "My God, you have the most gorgeous ass..."

I bit my lip, rocking back against him. I couldn't speak. I felt too damn good. Too damn turned on. Too ready to just lose my mind and come.

Somehow, I did find my voice: "Thought... Thought you wanted to fuck me hard."

"Mmhmm, I do." He curved his hands over my hips. "Just making sure I don't hurt you."

"You're not gonna—oh my *God!*"

He wasn't kidding about harder. He slammed into me, driving himself as deep as I could take him and knocking me forward with every thrust. My elbows gave, and I dropped onto my forearms. Fine—that freed up one hand to pump myself, and everything turned white. I distantly heard myself pleading for more, more, more. I didn't even know if I wanted it faster, harder, deeper, just that I wanted... *more*.

"Peyton..." I whined. "God, please..."

"You're gonna make me come so hard," he ground out. "Holy fuck, I'm—oh, yeah." His fingers bit into my hips, probably bruising, and he pulled me back against himself every time he thrust in. "Jesus Christ, Avery, I'm—" Then he shuddered, forcing his cock as deep as he could, and he held my ass against him while he trembled and roared.

With a shuddering sigh, he slumped over me, relaxing his grip as he panted hard against my sweaty back.

I closed my eyes, drunk on his pleasure as much as my own. He'd fucked me as close to oblivion as I could get without coming, and I was trembling as if I *had* come.

"Oh my God," he murmured. "I knew sex with you would be good, but..." He trailed off into a happy sigh.

Before I could speak, Peyton carefully pulled out, making me whimper in protest.

Then he had me on my back, flipping me over so fast I didn't even realize what had happened until I was, for the second time, fucking his eager mouth. His fingers pushed into my well-fucked ass, and he didn't hold back at all. He fingered and blew me for all I was worth, and I was already so close that it took under a minute for him to send me careening over the edge, shaking and shouting as I came in his eager mouth.

Sinking back to the bed, I was a dizzy, trembling mess. Had sex ever been this good? Not that I remembered. And I didn't care, because sex was this good now.

Sex with Peyton.

Holy fuck. Did I really just have sex with Peyton?

Right then, he settled on top of me again, straddling my hips, and his kiss was soft and languid now. Lazy, gentle, and tasting like me.

I wrapped my shaking arms around him.

And I didn't think I'd ever felt better than I did in that moment.

CHAPTER 32
PEYTON

Holding Avery while he came back down to earth had to be one of the sexiest things I'd ever experienced. I loved watching and hearing and feeling and *tasting* him lose control, and holding him against me while he trembled and caught his breath between kisses was seriously hot.

My God, this had been like every fantasy I'd ever had about him come to life. That kiss in his kitchen had felt like something that had been years in the making. One touch of his lips, all I'd been able to think was, *"yes, finally."* As if everything—the last few weeks, hell, my whole damn life—had been leading up to that moment, and it had finally happened.

In that instant, I hadn't thought any further ahead. It was both a complete surprise and made perfect sense that we'd gone from kissing against the counter to getting each other off in bed. When our lips had met, I hadn't imagined I was minutes away from being inside him and a few more away from him coming on my tongue. *How did that happen?* clashed with *Of course it happened* in my jumbled thoughts, but mostly, I was overwhelmed with... satisfaction didn't even seem to be the right word. Relief? Perfection? I didn't know.

I just knew I felt amazing right now, and I absolutely loved the way his man's beautiful naked body fit against mine while our mouths lazily moved together.

After God only knew how long, we came up for air. Avery gazed up at me with blissed-out eyes, then glanced down at our sweaty bodies and asked, "Join me for a shower?"

I grinned. "Is this a shower where we get clean?" I eased onto my side and slid a hand down over his perfect ass. "Or where we rinse off some cum and lube, and then just get started again?"

The hunger burning in his eyes almost had us getting started right then and there. "It's the kind of shower where we take a lube bottle with us just in case the bed is too far away."

"Ooh, I love the way you think." I pulled him back in for a kiss. "Because I'm pretty sure I'm going to end up fucking you over something."

Avery whimpered into my kiss. "Promise?"

Fucking hell, I'd hit the jackpot, hadn't I?

"Guess we'll find out." I stole another light kiss. "Let's go."

He grabbed the lube bottle, and we got up. It was a genuine miracle my legs stayed under me as we got out of Avery's bed. Judging by the way he leaned on me, he wasn't any better off.

But it gave us an excuse to lean on each other, so I didn't object. Especially once we were in the shower, attention divided between getting clean and getting close. Avery had the most gorgeous body, and I loved the way he felt pressed up against me, arms around my neck as we kissed and water cascaded around and between us.

"Shame we can't get away with this in the locker room," I murmured.

Avery's drunken laugh was musical. "I mean, we could try, but I feel like there might be a few objections."

"Just a few," I said, and claimed his mouth again. The shower swallowed most of his soft moan, but I caught the thrum of it against my lips, and I wanted more. One roll in the hay, one shower, and I was already hooked on everything about him, from the helpless sounds he made to the magic he worked with his mouth.

I'd had a crush or two in the past who'd been letdowns in bed, but Avery Caldwell was not one of them. He was everything I'd imagined and then some, from an artful kisser to a vocal, responsive bottom. I couldn't get enough of running my hands all over his body, tracing every muscle and plane and angle, memorizing contours as if I'd never touched another human in my life.

And predictably, holding him close and making out with him like this had everything below my waist stirring before too much longer. As my dick hardened between us, Avery rubbed against me, his own cock starting to come back to life too. The lazy kissing in between getting clean turned to hungrily devouring each other's mouths as we rutted and groped and wound each other up all over again.

"I swear to God, my sex drive has been MIA for ages," he panted. "But now that you're here..."

Then we were kissing again, and oh yeah, his sex drive was definitely alive and well. So was mine.

"We should get out of the shower," I growled. "I want to fuck you someplace we won't slip and fall."

The answer to that was the sudden silence of the water

shutting off. Avery met my gaze with smoldering eyes, and neither of us had to say a word.

We got out of the shower and started toweling off, but damn if I could concentrate on anything but him. His skin was flushed from the shower, his hair wet and falling over his shoulders, his cock completely hard—why the fuck weren't my hands on him?

I put my towel aside, grabbed him, and pulled him to me, letting his towel fall to the floor at our feet. The sound he made when I kissed him was all need and surrender; and his nails dug into my shoulders as he held me to him. We were still wet from the shower—too wet to get into bed—but I couldn't wait another minute.

I turned him and leaned him up against the bathroom counter. "I want to fuck you again," I moaned, rubbing my dick against him. "Jesus, Avery..."

His little whimper was the sexiest thing I'd ever heard. "Please do."

"Where's the lube?"

He snatched it off the counter since apparently one of us had been smart enough to get it on the way out of the shower. "Hurry up." He shoved the bottle into my had. "I don't want to wait."

"Greedy," I purred, and turned him around. "I love it."

He leaned over his forearms on the counter, offering up his ass like a perfect gift. I worked fast and put a generous amount of lube on both of us. Then I pushed his knees apart, and he gasped as if his brain had just caught up and realized this was really happening. Or like he was just aroused out of his mind.

When I guided my cock to his hole, he spread his legs even wider and leaned back against me. I went slow—he'd already come once, so he might be too sensitive to really rail him—and we both gasped as I breached him.

And just like that, I was in him again, holding onto his hips as our groans echoed off the bathroom walls while I slid in and out. Oh, God, he was beautiful. And tight. And *loud*. Those choked little moans were going to be my undoing, and I thrust just a bit harder to drive more of them out of him.

"Jesus, Peyton..." He took one arm off the counter, and when he started stroking himself, his hole tightened around me. I grunted and tried for all I was worth to match his rhythm, but hell if I could think about anything except this delicious friction and this stunning man in front of me.

The steam on the mirror was starting to clear. Vague shapes resolved into a clearer image of him and me fucking over the counter, and oh, hell, that was the sexiest thing I'd ever seen.

"Open your eyes," I ordered. "Look at us."

His eyelids fluttered, then opened, and when his eyes focused, a shiver went through him. "Oh, God..."

I ran a hand up the middle of his back and into his hair, which I gripped just tight enough to make him gasp. "You look so hot like this. Can't decide... Can't decide if I want to watch your face or my dick."

He just moaned and leaned back against me.

"Like that?" I asked.

"Uh-huh. Just..." he panted. "Fuck. Put on some more lube. I want... I want it *hard*."

Before he'd even finished speaking, I'd pulled out and grabbed the lube off the counter. A few strokes, and I was good and slick, and Avery whined as I thrust back into him.

"That better?" I growled in his ear, and thrust again.

He moaned, clawing at the marble wall. "Fuuuck, yeah."

"Not too sensit—"

"More."

"Oh, God..." I had to grab his hips just to keep myself upright.

Avery pumped himself furiously, his curses and groans echoing off the marble all around us. So damn hot. So damn...

I wanted to see more.

I stopped and pulled out, and before he could protest, I manhandled him around and started toward the bedroom. "Got a better idea," I whispered, and he went without arguing, stumbling a little on his way to the bed.

"Here." I stopped him beside the bed and stole a long kiss. Then I told him to lie back with his ass right up to the edge. From his grin, he knew where this was going.

With his legs around my waist, I pushed back inside, and Avery was already stroking himself as he arched off the bed and begged, "Hard. Do it hard."

"Exactly what I had in mind," I said through my teeth, and I gave it to him *hard*. The bed shrieked and shook, and Avery cried out all kinds of pleas for more in between curses and wordless, needy sounds as his hand blurred on his own dick. Totally worth stopping to change position, because this was an even hotter view. I loved the way he looked, laid out in front of me like that, jerking himself off for all he was worth while I pounded his tight ass. Every muscle in his body stood out, including that mouthwatering six-pack, and every stroke one of us took registered on his face as pure bliss.

"God, yeah," he breathed. "Make... Make me come, baby."

Oh, hell, that almost made *me* come.

"Yeah," I panted. "Come for me."

He bit his lip and squeezed his eyes shut, arching off the mattress again as he kept pumping himself. Fuck, he was so hot. I wasn't usually one to come at the same time as my partner, but I was sure that if he came, I was going to come with him. I was so damn turned on, so close, and watching him start to come unraveled was more than I could take.

I was a breath away from begging him to take us both there when he gasped and tensed. Cum dotted those six-pack abs, and I was right there with him, thrusting as deep as he could take me and coming until I couldn't possibly have anything left.

Then I exhaled and slumped over him.

Avery sighed, wrapping his arms around me, and I let my forehead rest on his collarbone.

"We're gonna..." I paused to catch my breath. "We're gonna need another shower."

He laughed and carded his fingers through my hair. "Probably won't need the lube this time."

"No, definitely not." I pushed myself up on shaking arms and met his beautiful hazel eyes. "Pretty sure that's all I've got for a while."

His smile was so sweet and adorable. "You and me both. But we can clean up and chill in bed."

That sounded like a great idea, and it was exactly what we did. There was some kissing and touching in the shower of course, but neither of us did anything to get the other spun up. We even managed to get dried off this time, and then into some gym shorts before we stumbled downstairs to the kitchen.

"I'm not as good a cook as you are," he said. "But I can probably put something edible together."

"Edible is fine. Do you need any help?"

"Nah." He flashed me that cute smile. "I've got it."

Fair enough. I took a seat at one of the barstools by the kitchen island while he rifled around in the fridge and cabinets.

He laid out the makings for what I suspected was a simple pasta dish, and my stomach growled audibly. He must've heard it, because he glanced at me and chuckled, but he didn't comment.

He put on a pot of water to boil, then started cutting up some tomatoes. "So, I guess the question is—what next?"

I cocked my head. "What do you mean?"

"I mean, are we..." He paused, gnawing his lip. "Like are we fuck buddies, or...?"

Oh. Okay, we were diving into that topic. "Well, I don't want to put any pressure on either of us. We're good at being friends. We're good in bed." I half-shrugged. "Maybe play the rest by ear? See how it evolves on its own?"

Avery studied me across the island before shifting his attention back to the knife and tomatoes. "That works. Though... if we're going to keep nixing condoms..."

I sat up a little and nodded. "Right. Right. Well." I cleared my throat. "I'm good with us being exclusive. We just don't have to start signing leases or looking for rings, you know?"

His sudden laugh was a relief. "No, no. Definitely not that. But yes to being exclusive." He looked at me through his lashes, his expression kind of shy. "I don't, um... I don't have any objection to being more than fuck buddies, though. Just so we're clear. We don't have to be, but if you want to be..."

I absently thumbed the edge of the granite countertop. "I... don't have any objection either. It, um... What we're doing so far feels right. I'm open to more—I just don't want us slapping names on things and putting too much pressure on. We can see where it goes?"

With a soft smile, he nodded. "I like that idea."

"Me too." I liked it a lot, if the thumping of my heart was anything to go by. Sex with Avery was all my fantasies and then some. Dating him? Possibly turning into something more?

Oh, hell. I could definitely get used to this.

CHAPTER 33
AVERY

After months on end of vacillating between feeling like shit and feeling worse than shit, I couldn't get enough of this new reality. There were still plenty of moments where I felt awful. Plenty of times when the grief, the guilt, and the shame caught up with me and beat me down until I could barely move.

But my therapists were helping me see that those were never forever. There was a light at the end of the tunnel, even if it still seemed far away, and the closer I got to it, the brighter everything seemed. As painfully slow as the process was turning out to be, it was forward motion. It was hope. It was more moments of almost feeling like myself again.

And it was also tumbling into bed with the sweetest, most amazing man I'd ever met. He could make me forget about everything except for him, and when we were together—whether we were fooling around or just watching a game on the couch—I felt *good*. That, more than anything, gave me hope for the future that was waiting for me at the end of this long, dark tunnel.

Today, Peyton had practiced with the team, then did some light two-on-two with me, Eminem, and Baddy. Afterward, we'd come back to my place where he'd drilled me into the mattress twice. That was followed by a long shower that involved a lot of making out, after which we'd returned to the rumpled bed, which was where we were now. He had his head on my chest, his scruff brushing my skin as we just lay there, basking in this comfortable closeness. I was still drowsy from two orgasms and a shower, but I wasn't falling asleep—I was just completely chill and happy. My body ached from both skating and sex, and that, too, felt good.

I absently carded my fingers through Peyton's hair, which was still damp and spiky from the shower. "I think I like this post-practice two-on-two."

"Yeah?" He lifted his head to meet my gaze. "Why's that?"

I smirked. "Mostly because the three of you are tired and I have an advantage."

He snorted and rolled his eyes, bumping me playfully with his knee. "Yeah, well, enjoy it while it lasts. When you come back to practice, we're going to bring you down a peg."

"Ha. You think."

"Uh-huh." He lifted his chin to kiss me softly, then shifted so he was partway on top of me. "Behave, or I'll tell them you've been talking shit."

"Oh. Yeah. *That'll* be a revelation." I draped my arms around his neck. "They'll just ask you what the fuck else is new."

Peyton laughed, then came down for a longer kiss. Not enough to get either of us spun up, just something gentle and languid. It had been so long since I'd dated or even hooked up, I'd forgotten how much I loved kissing lazily like this. And lucky me—I'd met a man who apparently loved it as much as I did.

After a little while, he broke the kiss and settled onto the pillow beside me. He was on his side, so I mirrored him, and that was when I noticed the slight furrow in his brow. An unspoken thought, if I had to guess.

I trailed my fingertips down his arm. "What's on your mind?"

"Well..." He held my gaze as he rested his hand on my waist. "There's something I want to ask you about, but... if you don't want to talk about, I'll understand."

Okay, now I was definitely curious. I found his other hand between us and laced our fingers together. "Sure. What's on your mind?"

He studied me, then swiped his tongue across his lips. "I'm curious about Leif."

My stomach somersaulted, but I tried not to let it show. "What about him?"

Peyton half-shrugged. "Anything, really. I know about him as a hockey player. Everyone does. But I never knew him, you know? As a person?"

"Oh." I chewed my lip.

"If you don't want to talk about him—right now or ever —that's fine. I'm just curious."

"No, no, it's okay." I breathed a soft laugh. "Just... trying to figure out where to start."

Peyton swallowed. "You guys met in major juniors, right?"

I nodded. "Yeah. He was a year ahead of me, and our billet families were across the street from each other. They traded off driving us to practices and stuff, so we spent a lot of time together right off the bat." I exhaled. "It was great, having someone there who knew the ropes. Like, I knew hockey, but major juniors, living away from home, a new city—it was a lot."

"I remember. It was overwhelming."

"Seriously. And we clicked pretty quickly anyway, on and off the ice."

"Were you guys linemates back then?"

"Not at first." I watched my thumb running along the back of his. "But five or six games into the season, his winger went down with the flu, so they bumped me up to the top line. The coaches liked the way we played together, so even after the winger came back, they kept me with Leif."

Peyton grimaced. "How did his winger feel about that?"

I half-shrugged. "Honestly, we kind of had a 1A and 1B situation instead of a first and second line, so it wasn't much of a demotion, you know?"

"Gotcha," he said with a slow nod. "So your team had two hot centers, then. Lucky."

I grinned. "We were, definitely. The second line center?" I whistled. "He was crazy good on faceoffs. Probably could've been a top ten overall draft pick if he hadn't gotten hurt."

"If he—" Peyton furrowed his brow. "Wait, was that Bryan O'Connor?"

"Yep. Shame what happened to him." I shuddered. "I will never forget that sound as long as I live."

Peyton shivered too. "I've heard a bone break one time. That was more than enough, thank you very much."

"I'm pretty sure I heard it when I broke my jaw, but I was in too much pain to notice."

He made a face and squirmed. "Ugh. No. No, thank you. Fuuuck that noise."

"My thoughts exactly, believe me." I shifted a little on the mattress. "Anyway, having him and Leif centering the top lines—we were gold, you know? So Gardener didn't mind getting bumped down. Honestly I think he clicked better with O'Connor anyway."

"Sometimes that happens."

"Right? So yeah, Leif and I were linemates for the rest of the season, and we were pretty much inseparable on road trips and stuff." I chuckled. "Some of the guys started wondering if we were dating. I'd been out since U14, so they just figured any guy I was close to must've been my boyfriend."

"That didn't bother Leif?"

"Oh, God, no." I laughed and shook my head. "He leaned into it, actually."

"Did he?"

"Yep. A couple of the guys were razzing him about it at practice one day. It wasn't mean-spirited—they were cool with me being out, they were just being guys, you know? So when we go to the bench between drills, he just comes over and parks his ass in my lap and says, 'Baby, they're being jerks!'"

Peyton barked a laugh. "Did he really?"

I nodded, laughing myself. "He did, and we played it up like crazy for the rest of practice, and we just sort of did the whole 'oh, look at us dorky boyfriends' thing for half the season."

"Half? What stopped you?"

"He started dating Rachel."

"Ah. Damn those women, getting in between two guys in love."

"Right? What the fuck?" I scoffed. "So inconsiderate." I paused. "The guys chirped us for *that*, too. They would threaten to tell Rachel that she was Leif's side piece. And then we're at a party with a bunch of teammates, and she's there. One of the guys comes right out and says, 'I can't believe you broke up Early and Calds.' She doesn't even miss a beat, either. Looks him dead in the eye, puts her arm around my waist, and says, 'What makes you think I broke them up?'"

"Oh my God," Peyton laughed. "There was no trolling any of you, was there?"

"It took work, let me tell you." I sighed. "My second year of major juniors was kind of boring, to be honest. A lot of hockey and traveling, but without Leif there..." I made a face.

"I can imagine. I was tight with our starting goalie during my first season. Not having him there the second year was tough."

I cocked a brow. "Tight with him, eh? So you were—"

"He's married with like five kids." Peyton rolled his eyes. "And no, he's not bi. We were just really good friends, and we roomed together on road trips."

"Ah." I flashed a toothy grin. "So you were *roommates*."

That got me an exasperated groan, and I laughed.

"You're a dick," he muttered.

"Yeah. Kinda." I laughed softly. "Anyway, yeah, it was a little quiet after Leif moved on."

"And you got drafted to the same team. That's some incredible luck."

"Oh. I don't know how much luck was actually involved."

"What do you mean?"

"Basically that I found out after the fact that he'd practically been running a political campaign for the team to draft me."

Peyton's eyebrows shot up. "Wow, really?"

I nodded, still chuckling. "I mean, here he was, this

eighteen-year-old rookie, bending the GM's ear like, 'dude, you've gotta draft this kid.' I guess it got to the point the GM would just sort of groan whenever he saw him."

"But he listened to him."

"I think he listened to the scouts more than anything," I said with a laugh. "But... yeah, he did tell us that Leif really put me on their radar." I rolled my eyes. "Leif said that entitled him to half my salary for the first season."

"I mean, that seems reasonable to me," Peyton said, eyes sparkling with mischief.

"Pfft. Whatever."

He just chuckled.

"There was another funny incident when he got married." I couldn't help smiling at the memory. "I was his best man, and I kept threatening to make my speech *really* embarrassing and inappropriate."

"Of course you did."

"Right? But then I actually wrote one, and it was bad—like, *all* the inside jokes from major juniors and the Whiskey Rebels, every embarrassing story I knew, plus at least half a dozen I'd made up. I printed it out on blue paper and showed it to him, and he just sort of rolled his eyes, crumpled it up, and tossed it back at me." I laughed. "Then at the reception, I pull out this wrinkled piece of blue paper."

Peyton snorted. "Did he recognize it?"

"*Ooh*, yeah. The look of horror on his face was absolutely priceless. Like, he was pretty pale to begin with, and he was suddenly whiter than Rachel's dress."

"Oh, shit. Did you actually read that speech?"

"Not the evil one, no. But I'd printed my real speech on the same type of blue paper, then wrinkled it up just to mess with his head."

"That's fucked up," he said with a laugh.

"I know, right? It was funny as hell, though."

"Did his wife think so?"

"Once she found out why he panicked?" I snickered. "Oh, yeah. She thought it was *hilarious*."

Peyton laughed. "She sounds like a spitfire from what I've heard."

"Oh my God, she so is." Another story came back to me, and I couldn't help grinning. "So, I was dating a guy my—second year with Pittsburgh? Third?" I shook my head. "I don't remember. Anyway, I'd been with him for a couple of months. Everything seemed fine, right? And like always, Leif and I would drive in to practices and games and stuff together. This one night, we're on our way home from a game, and he just pulls over—right there on the side of I-79 in a not-very-inconspicuous car—and tells me he needs to talk to me about my boyfriend."

Peyton's eyebrows were nearly in his hair. "Yeah? What was it about?"

"Well, it turns out there was a player on the farm team who'd been called up recently. Leif didn't tell me who it was, but I could put two and two together, since there were only three guys who'd come up recently. Anyway, the kid had come to dinner with a bunch of us one night, and my boyfriend was with me. The next day, the kid pulled Leif aside and said he was afraid to tell me, but he'd hooked up with my boyfriend a few nights earlier."

"No shit?" Peyton's jaw went slack.

"No shit." I rolled my eyes. "Leif told him he'd pass it on to me—that way I'd know. The kid was just terrified to tell me because he was afraid I'd be angry with him. I think he was also staying really tightlipped about his sexuality; Leif said he'd obviously been struggling hard to tell him, so he didn't want anyone else to know."

"Wow. He really looked out for the young guys, didn't he?"

"Oh, absolutely. And he also came prepared that night in case I didn't believe him."

"Yeah? How so?"

"He made a Tinder account specifically to find my boyfriend. The cheating doucheweasel was at least smart enough to hide his face, but there was a pretty distinctive tattoo that Leif recognized. He catfished him enough to get a face pic, then screencapped it all and showed it to me."

Peyton whistled. "Wow. That is some commitment." He grimaced. "I hope his wife didn't find out about the Tinder account."

"Pfft. He told her exactly what he was doing, and she even helped him set up his profile to lure the guy in."

"Seriously?"

"Mmhmm. I'm pretty sure she took the photos he used, too."

"He didn't use fake ones?"

I shook my head and laughed. "He was going to, but apparently Rachel said it would be a crime not to show off his abs and thighs." I made a face. "He also delighted in telling me what they did *after* they took those photos, because he's a dick like that."

Peyton laughed. "Oh my God. That's amazing."

"Oh, it gets better."

"Does it?"

"Yep. While Leif was trying to find my boyfriend, he thought Rachel was just scrolling on her phone next to him. Like, they're literally sitting on the couch while their kids watch a movie, both scrolling on their phones, and he's getting matched like crazy. He's ignoring it, but one of them starts messaging him."

Peyton cocked his head. "Don't you have to match with them too before they can message you?"

"Yep. Apparently while he was getting the kids refills on their snacks, she snuck onto his phone, found the fake profile she'd made, and matched with them."

"Oh shit, it was her?"

"Uh-huh." I laughed, rolling my eyes. "He figured it out pretty quickly because she'd send him these insanely raunchy messages, but every time he'd get one, she'd start giggling."

Peyton chuckled. "Seriously?"

"Uh-huh. He said it killed some time while he was waiting for my ex to connect with him. I guess they spent like an entire evening messaging back and forth with the cheesiest, raunchiest pickup lines they could come up with."

"That's amazing." Peyton stroked my arm, still grinning. "At least some good came out of your ex cheating on you."

"I know, right?" I tsked. "My friends got a whole evening's worth of entertainment."

"Eh, he was doing the Lord's work. Might as well get some entertainment value out of it."

"No kidding." Humor fading, I sighed. "Anyway, it didn't take him long to connect with the guy, and once he got those face pics and had some screencapped chats, he told me." I snorted. "And then he showed me like eight different guys who'd matched with his catfish account in case I wanted a rebound hookup or something."

"Oh, wow! Talk about being a bro!" There was a wicked glint in Peyton's eyes. "Did you take him up on it?"

I quirked my lips and shrugged.

Peyton rolled his eyes and nudged me. "Oh, come on. Indulge me."

Some heat was rushing into my face anyway, so it wasn't like I could deny it. "I... may have met up with one or two."

"One or two?" An eyebrow arched. "Like two at the same time?"

I shrugged again.

Peyton laughed and leaned in to kiss me lightly. "Sounds like the perfect way to get over a cheating dickhole."

"Exactly."

"I hope you bought that man a lot of beers as a thank-you for being your wingman. And anti-wingman, in one case."

"Beers, steaks, rounds of golf—oh, yeah. He was covered."

"Good." Peyton nodded sharply. "As it should be."

I just chuckled again, and the conversation drifted into a natural lull. I curled a little closer to him, enjoying his warmth and his touch.

It was then that I realized I'd been going on about Leif for... hell, for a while now. Just lying here, talking about my best friend and some of the shenanigans we'd had during the ten or so years I'd known him.

But my voice didn't feel like it was about to break, and neither did I. For the first time since I'd lost him, talking about him had felt good instead of like I was putting all my weight on a broken bone. The whole time I'd been grieving, I'd been focused on the loss, but I hadn't spent any time thinking about the good memories. About *Leif*. About all the things I missed rather than how much it hurt that he was gone.

I found Peyton's hand between us, laced our fingers

together, and pressed my lips to his knuckles. "Thank you," I whispered.

"For what?"

I swiped at my eyes, though they weren't tearing up as bad as I expected. "I haven't spent enough time thinking about the good things lately. I thought it would hurt, you know? Like rubbing salt in my own wounds? But I think I needed it."

Peyton drew me in closer and kissed the top of my head. He didn't say a word. Neither did I. There really wasn't anything that needed to be said, and I just closed my eyes and enjoyed this warmth and this closeness as something like peace settled over me. It would still be a long, long time before Leif's absence healed from an open wound to a scar. More and more, though, I had hope that that was even possible.

The hardest thing I'd ever done was try to move on without Leif.

And today I was grateful beyond words that I didn't have to do it without Peyton.

CHAPTER 34
PEYTON

Even as days turned into weeks, I still couldn't believe I'd landed in this relationship with Avery. That animosity between us at the start of the season was as distant a memory as the way I'd clashed with that one defenseman on my U16 team, but it was still surreal to be on this ground with him.

At the same time, it felt right, and whenever possible, we were inseparable. If I wasn't on the ice and he wasn't at therapy, we were together. At his place. At mine. Chilling on a couch. Eating in front of a movie. Tearing up the sheets in bed. Taking far longer showers than we probably should have. When I had to go out on the road, we were texting constantly, and as soon as I was in my room, we'd FaceTime. Sometimes those calls were just chats, catching up and enjoying each other's company even when we couldn't be together. Other times... well, it was a good thing I didn't have a roommate, let's put it that way.

I was utterly in heaven, and not just because I was having more sex than I'd had in ages—I loved this connection with him. I loved seeing him happy. I loved *making* him happy. He was still struggling and would be for a long time—I'd have been worried if he wasn't—but he smiled more. Though I hadn't known him before Leif's death, I was pretty sure he was more like himself than he'd been months ago—quick to laugh, smart as hell, seriously sweet.

I couldn't wait for the off season to start because then we could step back from hockey and focus on us for a few months. Still condition, still skate, but without the pressure of the regular or postseason, not to mention the pressure on Avery to come back from the player assistance program. Just a long summer of being together.

That was still a little ways off, though. We were in the homestretch toward the playoffs, and more and more, it looked like we had a shot of making it. Avery was due to start his conditioning loan with the farm team soon, and he'd be back at most two weeks after that. Then we'd have fewer than a dozen games left to make a drive at the postseason.

Tonight was a home game against a division rival. It was critical to win this one, ideally in regulation. We needed the points, and we also needed to prevent Jersey from getting any; we were neck-in-neck in the standings, and a regulation win tonight would give as an edge we desperately needed.

It was going to be a challenge, and not just because of the pressure.

"Any updates on Rachel?" Baddy asked after warmups.

I checked my phone. "Nothing yet. Avery said they're settled in at the hospital, but it could be a while."

"Don't count on it," Eminem said. "She went into labor with the last one right before a game, and Early almost didn't make it to the hospital in time."

"If she's anything like my wife," Willie chimed in, "this one will be even faster."

Some of the dads in the room nodded. Some of the others looked dubious.

"I don't know," Laramie said. "My son took like six hours, start to finish. My daughter?" He grimaced. "Almost thirty."

"Holy shit." Eminem shook his head. "My wife would've *personally* given me a vasectomy with her bare hands by hour twenty-four."

Laramie nodded solemnly. "Erin threatened to a few times, believe me."

"As well she should have," Falon chimed in. "You better believe my husband buys me something very nice on each of our kids' birthdays." She poked a finger at him. "I hope you do the same."

"Uh. Notice how I'm still alive?" Laramie gestured at himself. "I'm singlehandedly keeping an entire jewelry chain in business."

"Good." Falon nodded sharply. "Keep up the good work."

She and Laramie both laughed, and I chuckled to myself as I kept putting on my gear. I'd played with a couple of other guys who also showered their wives with lavish gifts every time their kids' birthdays came around.

"That woman went through hell with each of our five kids," Grayson had said after showing us the Rolex he'd just bought her. *"This is the absolute* least *I can do."*

There'd been exactly one guy who'd tried to blow off what his wife had been through in delivering their baby, and every dad in the room had eyed him like he'd lost his mind. He'd insisted that *"it wasn't that bad"* and *"she was made for that,"* and we'd all just shaken our heads and changed the subject. I couldn't begin to imagine why they were divorced now.

Tonight, we all dawdled in the locker room for as long as we could, hoping for an update from Avery, but none came. The show had to go on, so after making Coach, Falon, and Evan promise to let us know the instant they heard anything, we trooped out to the ice for the anthems and the start of the game.

By the time the puck dropped, I was almost entirely focused on hockey. A few synapses still wound themselves around the need for an update, but for the most part, I zeroed in on the game. My teammates did as well.

Jersey put up a hell of a fight, too, which forced us to concentrate even more than we already were. Their forecheck was well-known throughout the League, and they were dangerous as hell once they had possession.

So... we just didn't let them get possession. Our forwards and defensemen alike battled hard to keep the puck away from them when we were in their zone. Jersey managed a couple of breakaways, but they didn't get far. Trews made a highlight-reel steal in the neutral zone, poke-checking the puck right off their star center's stick, claiming possession, and firing it to Davis, who was just outside the crease. Davis tapped it in, and we were up 1-0.

Another intense battle later, I shot one over the netminder's shoulder. The celly after that one felt amazing—we were on fire, and I was on the board after two games without a point. Fuck yeah.

We were still up 2-0 when the horn sounded the end of the period, and we all clomped back into the locker room to recharge and rehydrate.

"Anyone heard from Calds or Rachel?" Laramie asked.

"Not yet." Falon peered at her phone. "Still waiting."

Coach and Evan also shook their heads.

After I'd stripped off my jersey, I took out my phone to text Avery and check in, both to see how Rachel and the baby were doing and to see how he was holding up.

But there was already a message on my screen. I read it, then held up my phone. "Oh, hey! It's a boy!"

The team broke into cheers.

"Told you it would be fast!" Eminem said with a laugh.

Baddy craned his neck toward my phone. "Are she and the kid doing good?" That quieted everyone down.

I read Avery's message aloud to the team: "'Tell the team it's a boy, born at 7:19, 7lbs 6oz. Mom and baby are fine.'"

More cheers, and suddenly everyone had their phones in hand, tapping furiously on the screens. I sent a text of my own.

> She's about to get bombarded with texts lol. Tell her I said congrats. How are you doing?

AVERY

> Yep, her phone just started blowing up lmao. I'm good. Holy shit newborns are TINY!

> lol bet Rachel doesn't think so.

> I'm not asking her. (lips zipped emoji)

> (laughing emoji) Good call.

> yeah yeah. Get back to work.

> (saluting emoji)

Chuckling, I tucked my phone away and went looking for a bottle of Gatorade.

Apparently I'd been more distracted than I'd realized, because when I hit the ice for the next period, I was *completely* focused. More than I had been earlier. The news gave everyone a jolt of energy, too, as if we weren't just playing hockey, we were playing to celebrate the addition to the Whiskey Rebels family. For a solid five minutes, no one from Jersey could even make it past the neutral zone into our defensive zone, and we hammered their goalie with shots—one of which went in. They were getting frustrated, too, which made them chippy; that wasn't good (for them) when we were this dialed in, because they were too easy to distract with checks and chirps, not to mention every time we stole the puck from them.

They did manage to squeak one into the net past Ziggy, but Davis answered with a second goal less than a minute later. Now he was on hatty watch, and at the end of the second, we had a 3-1 lead. Everyone knew that was the most dangerous lead, though; at 3-1, the winning team often let their foot off the gas at the same time the losing team got desperate. It wasn't unusual at all for a team to be winning 3-1 only to ultimately lose 3-4.

Not happening tonight. No fucking way.

During a commercial break in the third period, the announcer said, "The Pittsburgh Whiskey Rebels would like to extend our congratulations to Rachel Erlandsson, widow of our beloved captain, Leif Erlandsson. Their son Adrian arrived tonight at 7:19 pm. Mom and baby are both doing fine."

As the crowd went wild, an image appeared on the screen of Rachel holding the swaddled newborn with her older kids on either side of her.

The announcer's voice barely carried over the cheers: "Welcome to Pittsburgh, Adrian Avery Erlandsson."

Wow. They'd given the kid Avery's name as a middle name? Though... I wasn't surprised now that I thought about it. It was a sweet gesture, and Leif probably would've loved it. Hell, maybe it had been his idea.

What I did know was that the announcement gave the crowd a surge of energy, and that in turn gave us a surge.

I smacked Davis's shoulder. "Think you've got a hat trick in you tonight?"

He scoffed and smacked me right back. "Fuck yeah, I do. Let's go!"

I turned to Eminem, who was my right winger while Avery was out. "Let's get Davis a hatty, yeah?"

He flashed me a big grin and bumped my fist. "The fans will bring down the house if we do!"

"Perfect! Let's do it!"

A minute later, the third line was peeling away for a line change, and Coach sent us out. Jersey still had their fourth line on the ice, and they were both gassed *and* hemmed into their own end.

Eminem was first over the boards as our tired forwards came back. My skates had barely touched the ice before he was slamming a winger into the glass and relieving him of the puck. He came around the back of the goal, scanning the players. I slapped my blade on the ice and he passed without hesitating.

A defenseman tried to intercept it, but I bodied him out of the way. Two others were barreling down on me, but I spun away from one and took the other's hip check without flinching... or losing the puck.

A stick smacked on the ice, and I turned to see Eminem wide open. I sent the puck to him. It had barely hit his tape before he shot it toward the goal.

And there was Davis, waiting at the edge of the crease.

He tapped it in under the goalie's pads, and he was right —the fans brought down the house.

We all piled on Davis, hugging him and smacking him as hats fell all around us. When we skated to the bench for fist bumps, all the guys were roaring and effusive. The energy in this arena had already been off the charts, and now it was in the stratosphere.

In the end, the score was 6-1.

"Hey. Check it out." Davis gestured at the scoreboard, and he sounded a little choked up. "It's Early's number."

I looked at the score, then at the jersey hanging in the rafters.

Sixty-one.

Absolutely perfect.

Avery looked like death warmed over when I went to pick him up for our informal practice the next day.

"Come on in." He stood aside. "I still need to finish my coffee and hunt down some sneakers."

"No rush." I stepped into the house, and as he shut the door behind me, I added, "If we beat the guys there, they can wait."

He offered a tired laugh as he wrapped his arms around me. "Damn right they can." We shared a long, lazy kiss that almost made me reconsider going to practice at all. I'd already skated with the team this morning. Couldn't we just spend the afternoon doing... other cardio?

I wanted to help him be as close to game condition as possible when he came back, though; his conditioning loan to the minors was coming up fast, and the more he did now, the less ground he'd need to make up.

When Avery broke the kiss and gazed at me with heavy-lidded eyes, my resolve wavered again. Just a quickie before we left? That wouldn't hurt anything, would it?

Except for as much as he looked like he wanted to drag me into bed, he also looked like he was close to collapsing under the weight of his fatigue. Forget sex or hockey—he probably just needed some sleep.

"You sure you're up for this?" I ran my hands down his back. "There's no shame in taking a day to recover after last night."

"I'm good. Just need to wake up a bit." He let me go but gestured for me to follow him, and he led me into his kitchen. As he picked up his coffee off the island, he muttered, "Fair warning, though—I might stop in the middle of practice and take a nap on the bench."

"How would that be any different from usual?"

He choked on his coffee and flipped me the bird.

I snickered. "I'm just saying."

"You're a dick," he sputtered.

"I am what I eat."

Avery laughed again and rolled his eyes. "Oh my God. I am way too tired for this."

"Mmhmm. I know." I stepped behind him and slid my hands over his hips. Nuzzling his neck, I murmured, "That's the best time to do it—when you're too tired to form witty comebacks."

"Jackass." But he leaned against me and sighed as I wrapped my arms around him.

"You sure you're okay to skate today?"

"I'm fine." He put his coffee cup down and turned around in my arms. "It was a long night, and I'm tired as fuck, but I can skate."

I smoothed his hair. "How late did you stay at the hospital?"

He exhaled. "'Til almost three."

"No shit?"

He nodded. "Her mom took the older kids, and she didn't want to be alone."

"I don't blame her." I took his hand. "And I'm glad you stayed with her."

"Me too. And it was, um... It was quite the experience."

"Yeah?"

Another nod, this time with a tired smile. "I didn't think she'd want me in the delivery room with her, but things happened hella fast and her mom wasn't there yet, so..."

"Oh, so you were actually there when he was born?"

"Yeah." He whistled, shaking his head. "That was, uh... That was *intense*."

"I bet."

He laughed. "It's probably a good thing I haven't been reactivated yet." He held up his left hand and flexed his fingers gingerly. "I'd be day-to-day with an upper body injury."

I snorted. "She had a hell of a grip, then?"

"Oh my God, yeah." He lowered his hand. "I don't blame her at all, and I won't ever complain about it within earshot of her after what she went through—but holy shit, yeah, she's got a *strong* grip."

"I bet she does." I slid my hands up his sides. "We really can skip today, you know. No one's going to hold it against you if you need to rest."

Avery was already shaking his head. "No. I didn't skate yesterday, and I get twitchy if I go more than a day or two."

I frowned. "But you're—"

"I'm fine." He lifted his chin and brushed his lips across

mine. "I wouldn't trust me to play a *game* right now—not one that counted—but I can hold my own during practice."

"You sure you're going to be able to play, though? With your hand out of commission?"

"Eh, it's not that bad." He flexed his fingers again, grimacing as he did. "I won't be winning any stick-handling competitions, but I'll manage."

I smirked. "Oh yeah?"

He met my eyes, then rolled his. "Oh my God. I walked right into that one, didn't I?"

Chuckling, I patted his arm. "We'll blame it on the lack of sleep."

He grunted and shrugged.

"Look, in all seriousness," I said, "last night had to be really intense for you. Not just the lack of sleep, but... everything. It's okay to cut yourself some slack."

Avery lowered his gaze, and his shoulders drooped just enough to give away some more of the fatigue he was trying to hide.

"I mean it," I said. "One day of taking it easy won't hurt your conditioning. We can make up for it, you know?"

"I know, but I'm good," he whispered. "I'm tired as all hell, and I don't think I could handle practicing with the team. But a light practice with you and some of the guys? I can handle that. I think I need it, you know? To shake off the... Whatever is going on in my head after last night."

Something about that last part gave me pause.

Furrowing my brow, I asked, "What *is* going on in your head after last night?"

Avery dropped his gaze and rubbed the back of his neck. "It was just... It was a lot. Being in the room and all, but also... I mean, Leif should've been there."

My heart dropped. "That must've been hard. For both of you."

"It was. And I know he would've wanted everyone to be happy, but it's hard not to be aware that he's gone, you know? His kid was just born, and he's..." Avery swallowed hard as he shook his head.

I touched his arm. "I'm glad you could be there for Rachel, though. That she had that support."

"Me too. And I was thinking about it this morning—part of me is devastated that Leif couldn't be there." He exhaled. "But circumstances being what they are, I'm *really* glad I had my shit together enough that I *was* there. I don't know if I ever could've forgiven myself if I realized later that she needed me and I was too fucked up to be there."

I wasn't sure what to say, so I just gathered him in my arms, and he sighed as he leaned into my embrace.

"I think that's what's been hitting me the hardest," he said, holding me to him. "Realizing how close I came to not being the support my best friend's widow needed."

I stroked his hair and kissed his forehead. "But you were there. You picked yourself up and got yourself together. Don't tie yourself in knots over what could've been."

"That's easier said than done, isn't it?"

"Aren't most things?"

The response was a laugh that was dry as dust. "Isn't that the truth."

I pressed another kiss to his forehead. "I'm glad you were there, too. For her, and for yourself."

He loosened his embrace and looked up at me. "I wouldn't have been there if it hadn't been for you." He must've seen the protest coming, because he put up his hand. "Yeah, I might've gotten it together eventually. But there's no way I would've had my head together by last night. Not enough to be what she needed. So... thank you again for that."

"Of course." I carded my fingers through his hair. "I'd do it all over again in a heartbeat."

He gave me a tired smile, then raised his chin.

I met his lips, expecting a brief kiss, but neither of us pulled back. What started out lazy and languid turned hotter. Deeper. As my tongue slid over his, Avery's hands started roaming my body over my clothes, and I moaned. We were both wearing workout pants, so there was almost nothing between us as our dicks hardened, and I couldn't resist rutting against him. Avery's fingers twitched on my shoulders, a soft whimper escaping as he pushed right back against my hips.

Jesus. He was tired and we had someplace else to be, but... I just couldn't...

God, I wanted him so bad.

Abruptly, Avery broke the kiss and twisted around. "Fuck it." He snatched his phone up off the counter. "We're bailing on practice."

Anticipation crackled up the length of my spine. "Are we?"

"Uh-huh." He typed out a message, sent it, and tossed his phone on the island behind him. Then his arms were around my neck again, and that kiss said he fucking meant it. Forget putting on our hockey gear—we needed to take off all these clothes.

My phone vibrated in my back pocket. His vibrated on the counter.

Group chat, probably.

Avery tugged my phone from my pocket and let it clatter onto the granite beside his. "Bedroom?"

"Bedroom."

CHAPTER 35
AVERY

I was absolutely exhausted. If I'd tried to skate, I probably would've faceplanted and just gone to sleep right there on the ice.

Oh, but I found myself a second wind in Peyton's arms. As I dragged him down on top of me in bed after we'd left a trail of clothing from the kitchen, I was wide awake and rock-fucking-hard. Oh my God, I loved the way this man's body felt against mine. On top of mine. Wrapped around mine. I loved running my hands all over his hot skin and powerful, sculpted muscles.

He was just... so damn hot. And fuck, the way he kissed me when he was this turned on was *mind-blowing*. It was all consuming. I didn't know what it was he did differently, only that when his mouth was on mine, nothing else in the world existed. Just him exploring my mouth and stealing my breath and making himself the focal point of my entire universe.

Then he broke the kiss, and his lips were on my neck, and my whole spine turned to electricity. I arched under him, dragging my fingernails across his shoulders.

"So much more fun than practicing," he mumbled beneath my jaw.

Practicing? Practicing what?

Oh. Right. Hockey. The practice we'd blown off.

"Yeah, it is," I slurred. "Baby, that is so..." I trailed off into a moan as he bit my collarbone. "Fuuuck."

He laughed and continued kissing up and down the sides of my throat, along my jaw, and even my earlobes. Every time he moved, my dick rubbed against him and his rubbed against mine, and... Goddammit, I was so turned on I couldn't think. I didn't even know what I wanted us to do —fuck, sixty-nine, jack each other off—and I didn't care. As long as Peyton was driving me wild like this, I was in heaven.

He came up to kiss me, and after he'd finished making my head spin all over again, he growled, "I fucking love your mouth."

"Yeah?" I panted. "You love other things I do with it, don't you?"

Desire sparked in his eyes. "You know I do."

I grinned. "Well, then. Sit up." I reached back and knocked my knuckle against the headboard.

He gave me another kiss—another deep, hard incredible kiss—and then got up and did as I'd asked.

As soon as he was situated, I shifted around to go down on that amazing dick.

"Ooh, fuck," he breathed as I took him between my lips. "God, yeah..."

I moaned around him. I got off on giving head as much as he did, and he was so, so responsive. I loved the way he combed his fingers through my hair while I sucked his dick. There was just something so needy about his touch. About the way his fingers twitched now and then. About how he'd grab on just enough to tug at my scalp, but he wouldn't pull too hard or force my head down.

I teased him all over, from the head of his cock down to his balls and taint, reveling in the blissed-out sounds he made and how his whole body trembled when I touched him just right. He strained my jaw a little, and I couldn't deep-throat him quite as much as he could me, but I didn't hear anything close to complaints from him, so I wasn't worried. Like me, he loved when most of the attention was on the head anyway, and I could do that all day long.

And I probably would have, except he half-begged, half-ordered, "Get up here."

As soon as I sat up, Peyton pulled me onto his lap so I was straddling his powerful thighs, and he claimed my mouth again as he started stroking me between our bodies. I had to fumble a little—that kiss was as distracting as his hand—but I got my fingers around him, too, and my first stroke was rewarded with a low, rumbling groan.

He broke the kiss with a gasp, tilting his head back against the headboard. "Fuck..."

I took advantage and started on his neck, and holy shit, the thrum of his voice against my lips had no business being that sexy.

"God, Avery," he slurred. "You are so..." He moaned again, and his grip tightened around my dick, driving a hiss from my lips. "Get the lube," he ordered. "I want to make you come like this."

He almost made me come *exactly* like that. I shivered hard, biting my lip as I tried not to lose control and shoot my load all over him.

Peyton's laugh was low and wicked. "Mmm, somebody's turned on by that idea." He stroked me a little harder. "You close?"

I gasped, thrusting into his hand. "I've been close since we were in the kitchen."

"Exactly how I like you," he purred. Then he loosened his grasp. "Get the lube."

I got the lube. We both put some on, and a moment later, oh hell, now I was close to losing my mind. His slick strokes. His incredible kiss. I had to fight *hard* not to come, and I did fight it because I wasn't ready for this to be over.

We kissed hungrily as we pumped each other furiously. I couldn't help thrusting into his tight fist, fucking relentlessly against him as I chased my orgasm and worked like hell to get him there too. His cock was rock-hard in my hand, pre-cum joining the lube, and when I added a twist at the head, his throaty little moan was the sexiest thing I'd ever heard.

Peyton broke the kiss first, and he was deliciously breathless. "Come, baby. Oh, God. Come. Please."

I thrust harder into his hand. "You getting there?"

"Uh-huh." He leaned his head back against the headboard again, his kiss-swollen lips parted and his eyes on fire. "I am so..." He squeezed his eyes shut. "Fuck, baby..."

Then he cried out as he thrust up into my grip, and hot cum erupted over my hand and onto my stomach, and in seconds, my entire world exploded into bliss. We kept pumping each other until we both shuddered and relaxed.

As the dust settled, I trembled on top of him. He had an arm slung around me—when he'd done that, I couldn't say, but I loved the way it felt.

"Oh my God," he murmured. "This... This is definitely more fun than practicing."

I laughed, sounding about as drunk as I felt. "Think Coach will let us chalk it up as an off-ice workout?"

Peyton snorted. "Let's ask. See what he says."

"Yeah, let's not and say we did."

He chuckled and drew me down into a kiss. This was the lazy, gentle kiss I'd intended when we'd been leaning against the kitchen island. The hotter, sexier kiss downstairs had worked out pretty damn well, though.

After a moment, we reluctantly separated to get some tissues and clean up the cum and lube.

Peyton wrapped his arms around me, and we sank onto the mattress, all gentle kissing and soft touches now.

"Think the guys will be mad?" he murmured, grinning against my lips. "That we bailed on them?"

"Eh, I'll buy them dinner next time we're on the road." I slid my hands up his back. "Pretty sure they'll get over it."

He chuckled. "Should probably check our phones. Make sure they got the messages."

"Mmhmm. Probably." I pulled him in close, and we were off and kissing again.

He was right, though, and after a minute or two, I pried myself away from him and got up. I threw on a pair of gym shorts and went downstairs to grab his pants and our phones.

On my way up the stairs, I looked at my phone, and I let out a bark of laughter. As I walked into the bedroom, Peyton craned his neck. "What?"

I had to be bright red as I crossed the room. "Uh, well?" I handed him his phone as I sheepishly said, "They got the message about practice, buuut I think we're busted."

"Oh, fuck. Really?" He took the phone and looked at the screen, which showed the same incredibly busy group chat that was on mine.

AVERY

Hey guys, change of plans. Practice tomorrow?

BADDY

Is Halls bailing too?

EMINEM

I'm still skating even if Calds isn't there.

MIX

Halls, are you coming or not?

LARAMIE

LOL I bet he's coming. (devil emoji)

TREWS

Wait what does that mean?

BADDY

It means Laramie's full of shit (eyeroll emoji)

LARAMIE

I am not.

LARAMIE

Halls, you there?

EMINEM

Calds? What about you?

BADDY

FFS Calds was with Early's wife last night. Probably asleep you losers.

MIX

Yeah I'd be asleep too

ASTALA

yeah but where TF is Halls?

BADDY

IDK he wasn't on earlier

EMINEM

Laramie do you know something we don't?

LARAMIE

Just that I fucking told you they were banging.

MIX

WTF? You don't know they're banging.

BADDY

yeah dude you're full of shit

LARAMIE

Am I? When was the last time you saw Calds WITHOUT Halls?

EMINEM

wait really?

BADDY

huh. I mean... nah, that doesn't mean they're screwing though.

TREWS

Just cuz they're the only gay dudes on the team doesn't mean they're doing each other

ASTALA

IDK man, Laramie's kinda got a point

HALVES

Still haven't seen anything from either of them.

EMINEM

Whoa.

LARAMIE

Right? Calds bails, and now he AND Halls aren't answering texts? They're banging.

BADDY

100% banging.

MIX

You think?

LARAMIE

Absolutely banging.

EMINEM

Yeah, I'm convinced.

HALVES

ok a lot of things make a lot of sense now

TREWS

Damn I'm glad I didn't take you up on that bet, Laramie

LARAMIE

Chickenshit.

TREWS

(middle finger emoji)

Peyton lowered his phone, laughing and shaking his head. "Oh my God. And it just keeps going, doesn't it?"

"Yep. It does." I put my phone on the nightstand. "So much for keeping it on the DL."

"I know, right?" He paused, then gave me a wicked grin. "Since they've already figured it out, I've got an idea."

I straightened. "Oh, yeah?"

A few minutes later, he sent a photo to the group chat. It was a selfie of me and Peyton, very obviously in bed together and both flipping off the camera. He captioned it, *Stop fantasizing about us you weirdos.*

I was shaking with laughter as he sent the message. "I only wish we could see the looks on their faces when they get it."

"I know, right?" he snickered.

In seconds, both our phones started blowing up again.

LARAMIE

SEE I FUCKING TOLD YOU

EMINEM

That doesn't mean shit. Baddy and Mix do
that all the time.

MIX

Hey! Fuck you!

BADDY

Yeah WTF. I'd have way better taste in
dudes.

MIX

Baddy I swear to God (knife emoji)

EMINEM

Hey now. No lovers quarrels. Save it for
the ice.

BADDY

(middle finger emoji)

MIX

(middle finger emoji)

Peyton shook his head as he tossed his phone onto the nightstand. "God, I love this team."

"Seriously."

He gently plucked my phone from my hand and put it down next to mine. Then I was in his arms again. "Well, as long as we don't have to worry about them being mad about practice, I guess we can just chill, can't we?"

"Chill, eh?" I draped my arms around his neck. "Like, Netflix and chill?"

"Mmhmm. Minus the Netflix."

We were both laughing as our lips met. Then we weren't laughing anymore, but this was just as good. Better, actually.

Our phones were still buzzing and pinging, vibrating against the top of the nightstand, but we ignored them. The guys were cool with us, and I could catch up on all their chirps later.

There'd been a time when I would've been worried about something like that getting out—someone leaking the photo or otherwise outing us—but this was a good group. We could gossip among ourselves and give each other no end of shit, but private lives stayed private.

The team knew. Maybe down the line, we could come out publicly.

That was something to think about later.

In this moment, all I wanted to think about was this beautiful man whose dick was getting hard right alongside mine.

Everything else could wait.

The rest of that day was spent being absolute sloths. We ordered pizza, which we ate in the living room in our shorts while watching New York play St. Louis. A few of our teammates texted us throughout the afternoon and into the evening, mostly razzing us for bailing on practice to bang each other.

We wrapped up the night in the best place in the world—beneath the covers with Peyton's naked body against mine. No fooling around this time; we'd both stuffed our faces (what could I say, that pizza was amazing) *and* we were tired. Plus we were aching all over, and Peyton couldn't bail on tomorrow's morning skate.

So, we just curled up in my bed and kissed for a little while. That was almost better than the sex—as much as I loved getting hot and heavy with him, it had been way too long since I'd indulged in a long, languid session of making out without any expectations of more.

God, this was perfect. After months of hell, I was in heaven now, with the brightest glimmer of hope I'd had yet that I might actually heal from everything that had happened.

I drew back a little to gaze at him. How had I landed someone so good in so many ways? Despite me all but handing him a list of reasons to want nothing to do with me, he was looking at me like that—his eyes soft and his lips a little swollen.

And he was, more than anyone else, the reason I was closing in on my return to hockey. How much darker would my world have been if he hadn't stepped in and dragged me back to the light?

Holy hell, I was the luckiest man alive, in bed with the most amazing human being alive. I'd known that on some level, but something about lying here with him now, gazing into those eyes while I was in his gentle arms, drove it home so hard, every emotion imaginable wanted to come screaming out of me. I'd been sure just a few weeks ago that the best I'd ever feel again was a step above wishing I'd go to sleep and never wake up. Now...

Now *this*. Affection. Warmth. Opening my eyes every morning with something to look forward to. Actual excitement and—despite being sure it would never happen again—*happiness*.

A subtle furrow appeared between Peyton's eyebrows. "Hey." He slid his palm up my chest. "You good?"

"Yeah. Yeah, I'm..." I had to laugh, because *"good"* was the understatement of the century. "I'm definitely good."

A tiny smile tried to come to life, but concern lingered in his eyes.

"I'm good," I repeated. "Listen, I know I've said this before..." I trailed my fingertips down his cheek. "But thanks. For everything. You're the reason I didn't have to hit rock bottom before I started pulling myself together." I swallowed. "I don't know how bad things would've gotten, but I'm seriously grateful for what you did so I didn't have to find out."

Something unreadable flickered across Peyton's face, but it was gone too fast for me to make sense of it. He covered my hand with his and pressed a kiss to my palm. "I'm glad you asked for help when you did."

"I just asked for a lift home from the club," I whispered. "You could've taken me home, dropped me off, and left, and no one would—"

He kissed me just hard enough to shut me up. Then he touched his forehead to mine. "There was no way I was ditching you after that. You were obviously in a bad place." He drew back enough to meet my gaze. "You'd have done the same for anyone else on the team."

"Maybe. But... I'm glad it was you." I carded my fingers through his hair. "And that you stuck by me." I managed a cautious grin, and my heart went wild as I said, "Especially since I had a chance to fall in love with you."

Peyton's eyebrows flicked up. "Really?"

"Yeah." I caressed his cheek again. "If you're not there yet, that's—it's fine. I know people sometimes—things happen differently for everyone, you know?" I swallowed. "I just wanted you to know where I stand."

He studied me, a mix of disbelief and maybe a little bit of alarm in his eyes. Slowly, though, his expression softened. He leaned in, and when our lips met, my whole body tingled with desire for him. Maybe not for sex—my body had probably had enough—but for *him*.

No, he hadn't said it back. That was okay, though. I meant what I'd said—everyone came to things like that in their own time. I'd fallen fast for him—really fucking fast. I'd just wanted him to know that this was more than sex and catharsis for me.

So I just pulled him in close and got lost in this long, lazy kiss.

And we didn't talk anymore for the rest of the night.

CHAPTER 36
PEYTON

I loved the way Avery's body felt against mine, especially when he was asleep with his head on my chest. I loved having my arm wrapped around his shoulder and his hair tickling my chin. I loved the sound of him breathing, slow and relaxed like he didn't have a care in the world.

What I *didn't* love was when I was feeling and hearing those things because I couldn't fall asleep.

Sleep usually came easy for me. Hockey took a lot out of me, and even on off days—hell, even during the off season—I slept like the dead most nights.

Not tonight.

Because tonight, Avery had told me loved me.

Closing my eyes, I exhaled into the stillness of his bedroom. I trailed my fingers up and down his arm, searching for that peaceful feeling that always came when I was holding him.

It wasn't coming tonight and I knew it.

Our conversation before lights out pecked at me. Kept me awake. Kept me from relaxing into his warmth.

We'd agreed to just let things happen the way they

wanted to happen. Not taking it slow per se, but not rushing. And now... *this?*

I believed him when he said he loved me. And the words *"I love you, too"* had been itching to jump off my tongue as soon as he'd said it.

But I'd held back.

It wasn't that I didn't love him. I did. I was stupidly in love with this man. For the first time in my life, I had thoughts of going public with someone. Of being together in the long term—past retirement and into whatever came after hockey. Despite our rocky start, things with Avery were easy. They were... *right.*

That was it—being with him felt right. Like once that piece had clicked into place—once we'd finally crossed that line from friends to more—everything in the world had made perfect sense. They'd moved faster than we'd anticipated, but even that had felt right.

Lying here now, our earlier conversation echoing in my head, I realized how utterly naïve that had been. Without even realizing it, Avery had told me what this really was.

"There was no way I was ditching you after that," I'd said. *"You were obviously in a bad place. You'd have done the same for anyone else on the team."*

"Maybe. But... I'm glad it was you. And that you stuck by me. Especially since I had a chance to fall in love with you."

I pushed out a long breath through my nose.

I wanted to believe this was love. I wanted it *so damn bad.*

But.

I sighed and pressed a kiss to the top of his head. He stirred against me, then stilled, breathing slowly and softly in sleep.

Do you have any idea how much I want this to be real?

It was possible. The question was where this began and where everything *else* ended. How much of *"I had a chance to fall in love with you"* was, at its core, *"you stuck by me."*

It wasn't that I thought Avery was insincere or that he was lying. It was that he'd been through absolute hell over the last few months, and in his shoes, I'd be grabbing on to anything good, too. What relationship *wouldn't* feel like the love of my life if it was the first thing that didn't suck after my best friend's death and a new addiction?

If things had happened differently a few months ago—if a doctor had happened upon that aneurysm in Leif's brain and dealt with it before it had ruptured—then Avery's world wouldn't have been turned on its ass. I'd have come to Pittsburgh and taken my place on the second line. Leif would've continued to be the star center. Avery and I might've still danced around each other, letting that mutual crush lead us to something. We might've still ended up right here in his bed after some of the most amazing sex I'd ever had.

But Avery never would've crashed and burned. I never would've helped him out of the bar in that hotel, and he never would've called me from a nightclub where he was too fucked up to hook up with anyone *or* get himself home.

We might've landed here eventually... but not like this.

I closed my eyes and exhaled as I ran my fingers up and down Avery's arm.

I did love him. I was *painfully* in love with him. And I wanted to believe he loved me the same way.

But I couldn't shake this fear that the way Avery loved me wasn't the way one boyfriend loved another.

He'd told me he loved me in the same breath he'd told me how grateful he was that I'd kept him from hitting rock bottom.

What if he'd fallen for me because he saw me as someone who'd saved him? Or worse, because being with me was better than being alone with his grief? Where did that leave us once he'd grieved enough to stand on his own two feet?

Where did it leave us when he didn't *need* me anymore?

My dad had worried for a while that my mom had only stayed with him because she was grateful he'd saved her from herself. Their marriage had been in tatters before she'd finally started getting up from rock bottom, and then it had suddenly been like the honeymoon phase all over again. She'd fallen all over herself to be the wife she hadn't been while she'd been drowning in a bottle.

One night I'd overheard him saying he wanted to go to counseling.

"*Counseling?*" She'd sounded gobsmacked, and even a little affronted. "*But everything's going great with us!*"

"*That's what I'm afraid of,*" he'd admitted. "*How great will it be when you're done with rehab, and I'm just your husband again instead of the man who saved you?*"

The memory brought a lump to my throat and a sting to my eyes. Their marriage had very nearly collapsed again, this time under the weight of Dad's fears and Mom's anger that he didn't believe she loved him. Counseling had helped them get back on the rails, but that year had been almost as rough on all of us as the last year of Mom's drinking.

I didn't imagine Avery and I would be that volatile; we'd only been seeing each other a short while, and he was well into therapy and rehab. It was something we could talk about. We could work it out calmly like rational adults. We didn't have years and years of addiction and resentment to move past, so we'd be fine.

Right?

But I still couldn't shake the memory of my parents walking on eggshells that year because they couldn't figure out where they stood with each other.

Or sneaking up the walk after curfew one night and hearing Dad crying softly on the porch.

Or overhearing Mom on the phone telling a friend that if it weren't for us kids, Dad probably would've left ages ago, and how she wished he would leave because now she was afraid to lean on him.

I swallowed past that lump in my throat and held Avery closer. I wanted to believe that once we talked this through, we'd be fine. Hell, we could talk to his therapist or get a counselor of our own. It didn't have to turn into a shitshow.

I was just so scared that it would if I brought this up.

The alternative was to... not bring it up.

But then I'd just have to keep gaslighting myself that everything was fine until fear or resentment corroded me from the inside out or Avery finally realized he didn't need me anymore.

I didn't mind being my partner's rock. I loved being someone a partner felt safe enough to lean on when the need arose.

But where was the line between a rock and a crutch?

And if I was his crutch...

Then what happened when he realized he didn't need to lean? Or when I needed to lean on him?

I sighed into the darkness and kissed the top of his head again.

This isn't going to end well, is it?

CHAPTER 37
AVERY

Peyton wasn't in bed when I opened my eyes the next morning. For a second, I was worried, but the sound of the shower running calmed me back down. He did have to go to the morning skate, after all, and that wasn't a practice he could get away with bailing on. I was just amazed I'd slept through his alarm; he used the same alarm tone I did, so it should've woken me up too.

Huh. Weird.

Then again, I'd slept pretty damn hard. I hadn't noticed Peyton getting up, either, so... whatever. I couldn't complain after a night like that.

But a minute or so after the shower stopped, the alarm *did* go off.

My head snapped toward the beeping phone. What the hell? Maybe he'd forgotten to turn off his second and third alarms?

I grabbed the phone to shut it off. On the screen:
Morning skate Alarm 1

I couldn't unlock his phone to see if his second alarms

were set, but I could at least shut off this one. If the others went off, well, I'd deal with those.

After I'd put his silenced phone on the nightstand again, I sat up and peered at the closed bathroom door. While I couldn't quite explain the knot of worry forming in my gut, I couldn't ignore it either. Peyton always needed two or three alarms before he got up.

Yesterday had been perfect. Why was I so sure today was about to be very, very different?

I was pulling on some sweats when he came out of the bathroom. He, too, had on sweats and a T-shirt, which didn't help me unwind that knot of worry. At most, he'd wear a towel around his waist on the way out of the bathroom, and that was only when he hadn't completely dried off. Otherwise, he strolled around naked just like I did.

Something was up.

It could wait until we had some coffee, though.

Coward.

Yeah, probably.

But I did need the caffeine to clear my head, so whatever. In silence, we went downstairs, and I made some coffee while Peyton pulled out a couple of slices of leftover pizza.

"Breakfast of champions?" I asked, testing the water.

He laughed, but it sounded forced.

"Come on." I tipped my head toward the living room. "Let's sit. My hip is still annoyed about yesterday."

The nod to yesterday's marathon sexcapade should've prompted a chuckle with some actual feeling. Or at least a little grin.

Nothing.

But he did join me in the living room, and silence hung between us as we drank our coffee and he ate his pizza. I kind of wanted to get him talking now, but he did have to skate, which meant he needed to eat. This could wait a few minutes, if only so he didn't faceplant on the ice later.

When he'd finished, he took his dishes into the kitchen. He put his plate in the dishwasher, then topped off his coffee. I was relieved that he returned to the living room, but unsettled by the ongoing silence, not to mention how he struggled to even look in my direction.

Finally, I couldn't take it anymore. And he had to leave soon, so we either did this now, or it had to wait until after tonight's game.

"Hey," I said tentatively. "You're kind of on another planet. What's going on?"

He chewed his lip and stared into his coffee.

"Did I do something wrong?"

His head snapped toward me and he seemed poised to tell me I hadn't, but that second of hesitation didn't leave much to the imagination.

My stomach wound around itself. "What did I do?"

Peyton exhaled and dropped his gaze. "It's not that... I mean, you didn't..." He closed his eyes. After a moment, he admitted, "I keep thinking about what you said last night."

"What I said—" My teeth snapped shut and my spine straightened. "Oh. Did I... Fuck, did I jump the gun and say it too soon?"

Peyton shook his head slowly. "No."

I watched him, completely confused and this close to panicking. "Then?"

His shoulders fell, and he put his coffee cup on a coaster. Raking his hand through his hair, he finally spoke, and he sounded defeated. "I'm... worried you're not really in love with *me*."

My heart dropped into the pit of my stomach. "What? Of course I am! What does that even mean?"

He met my gaze. "It means you told me you loved me right after you said you were grateful I'd helped you into rehab."

"Yeah? And? I *am* grateful for that. Shouldn't I be?"

"It's not that. It's—" Peyton scratched the back of his neck and sighed as he met my gaze with tired, bloodshot eyes. "Would you love me like this if things had played out differently?"

"Differently? What things?"

Peyton took a breath. "If we... hadn't ended up line-mates this season." His expression begged me to put two and two together.

At first, I couldn't make the connection.

But then I did, and my heart sank deeper than I'd thought possible. We were linemates because there'd been a vacant spot for a first line center. Because our first line center had been very suddenly gone.

I struggled to find my voice, and somehow managed to croak, "You think this"—I gestured at the two of us—"is just because Leif is gone? And, what? Because I fell apart over that and you helped me get back on my feet?"

"I..." He chewed his lip, staring down at his hands. "Look, we were both attracted to each other before I came here. So maybe something would've happened, you know? But everything that *did* happen, it was because of..." He paused, and his shoulders dropped. "Fuck. There's no way to say it without sounding like I'm accusing you of anything or like I don't trust you. I *do* trust you. I..." He pushed out a breath as he met my gaze. "I'm worried you're not really in love with me. You're in love with something that feels better than everything you've been going through."

My lips parted. "That's... That's really what you think this is? I don't have feelings for you—I'm just grabbing on to the first good thing that came along?"

Peyton winced and avoided my eyes again. "I'm saying I don't know. And I'm not sure you do either. I want this. I..." He was quiet for a painfully long moment before he whispered, "I want this to be real. I'm just scared that neither of us knows if it is or not."

The emotions crashing over the top of each other in my chest were almost physically painful. Anger wanted me to jump to my feet and demand to know who the fuck he thought he was, questioning if I was sincere. Did he really think I couldn't tell the difference between love and *"well, this doesn't suck as much as everything else"*? That anger was bolstered by bone-deep hurt that he actually thought my grief for my best friend defined everything I did or felt.

And that grief wanted to drag me down to the floor and wrench some more tears out of me, because fuck me, maybe he was right. Everything in my world had been colored by Leif's death. Everything. How could I say it hadn't touched our relationship too?

"I'm sorry, Avery," he said. "I want this. I really do. But I need to know where the lines are between us and..." He pressed his lips together.

"Between us and everything that put me in rehab," I growled.

He flinched, still refusing to meet my gaze. "Considering I was part of putting you in rehab..."

All the air rushed out of me. "So, what? You regret that now?"

"No." The word was almost soundless—little more than a soft exhalation—and he finally looked at me through his lashes. "I'd do it again in a heartbeat. No doubt about it.

But... what happens when you're on your feet again? Done with rehab and therapy, and you're feeling more like yourself?" He swallowed like it took some serious effort. "Where does that leave us?"

All those emotions surged again, but none of them crystallized into an answer. Not one that could actually pull us back together.

Because we were...

Holy shit, was this *ending?*

"So you're..." I swallowed hard. "Are you calling this off, then?"

I didn't like how long he avoided my gaze and gnawed his lip.

"If you are," I said, my voice hollow, "then just say so. Rip the bandage off, okay? Because I don't want—"

"I'm not calling it off. I'm..." He stared down at his wringing hands for a long moment, his brow furrowed with unspoken thoughts. I held my breath, not sure what he was going to say next and without a clue what I wanted him to say.

That wasn't true. Of course I knew what I *wanted* him to say. I wanted him to tell me he loved me and everything was fine. But... I also wanted him to tell me the truth, and the truth in the way his eyebrows knitted together and his jaw worked—that wasn't "*I love you and there's nothing wrong.*"

After a fucking eternity, Peyton looked in my eyes. "I'm not saying it's over. I'm not. I just... I need to step back and think about what we're doing. And I think you do too."

It took a lot of work to swallow past both my dry mouth and the sudden lump in my throat. "For how long?" I croaked. "How does that even work?"

Peyton shook his head and dropped his gaze again. "I

don't know. I've—I've never done this before, so... I don't know."

"So this *might* be over." Anger crept into my voice, and I let it because that was a lot easier to deal with than all the other emotions trying to shove past it.

"Maybe?" He met me with a helpless look. "I mean it—I don't know. I don't want to walk away from this. From you." He spread his hands. "But I also don't want to get this invested when I don't know if you're here for who I am or what I did."

I blinked. "But... I do love you for you who are. It's not because—" I studied him. "Do you *really* think that's all this is?"

"That's the problem," he whispered. "I don't know. And I mean, I have no regrets. Helping you get into rehab—I'd do that again in a heartbeat. Being with you—that's been amazing. Like I said, I'm not saying we're done. I just need to make sure I know where one thing ends and the other starts. That's all."

I flinched away from his gaze.

"I'm sorry, Avery. I really don't want to end this over—"

"Yeah, I heard you," I snapped, locking eyes with him again. "But you're still stepping back and..." I flailed a hand. "If you need to take some time and go think, then fucking go instead of sitting here trying to convince me I should be happy about it."

He stared at me, lips apart. "I'm not trying to tell you you should be happy about it. *I'm* not happy about it! I just want—"

"Then maybe it's the wrong damn move!" I got up, suddenly restless and desperate to get away from him. "Fuck's sake. What do you even want me to say? That I've completely compartmentalized everything, and having feelings for you has absolutely nothing to do with anything?" I threw up my hands. "What am I supposed to say? That I'm sorry I fell in love with you because I fucking did it wrong?"

"Avery." He rose too. "You didn't do anything wrong. I'm not asking you to apologize for anything. You're not—"

"Then what do you *want*, Peyton?" I growled. "I can't change how things happened, and I can't change the way I feel." I set my jaw if only to keep myself from breaking down. "Tell me what you want from me."

Again he stared at me, but this time, his expression shifted from hurt and pleading to something harder. Something more closed off. Straightening a little, he said, "Maybe what we both need right now is some space."

I threw up my hands again and said nothing. I didn't say a word and neither did he as he went upstairs, collected his things, and left.

When the door clicked shut behind him, the tiny sound echoing through this huge, empty house, I sank onto the couch and pushed out a breath. My anger had already flamed out. I wasn't even really angry anyway—I was hurt. I was *crushed*.

I *wanted* to be angry. I wanted to light him up and tell him this was bullshit. I wanted to tell him he was reading too much into something. Seeing something that wasn't there.

But could I tell him—completely honestly—that everything between us *wasn't* what he thought it was? That it *wasn't* me falling for him because he'd pulled me from the mire? That I'd still have fallen for him like this if we'd just hooked up and started a relationship like normal people?

I groaned aloud. Fuck. Fuck! What if he was *right*?

Yeah, I'd had a thing for him long before I crashed and burned, but this? These feelings that tumbled through me every time I thought about him? The way my heart went absolutely wild every time I looked at him?

That was new.

And it had all happened since Peyton had brought me home from that club.

I wanted to believe all those feelings happened on their own, but I couldn't separate them from everything else.

I leaned forward and pushed my hands through my hair.

Fuck. What if he was right?

What if the best thing I'd ever had really *was* just me clinging to the man who'd saved me from myself?

CHAPTER 38
PEYTON

I was mostly numb after I left Avery's house. All the way to the arena, I was on autopilot, replaying everything we'd said and wondering if I could have—and should have—done something different.

But I'd had to say *something*. Maybe I'd timed it wrong or said the wrong thing or—I didn't know. But it wasn't something I could just pretend not to notice. I couldn't just sit back and wait for him to realize this wasn't love.

Not for him, anyway. It *was* love for me. I'd already known I was in love with him, and nothing had driven that home more than realizing he was slipping away from me. All I'd wanted to do was pump the brakes and make sure we both knew what we were doing, but all I'd succeeded in doing was losing him.

"Christ," I whispered. "What the fuck did I just do?"

And what could I have done differently? It wasn't like I'd told him I needed to end things. I'd told him the exact opposite! *He'd* ended everything.

I had no idea what could have or should have changed, only that this was all wrong. We could salvage this, couldn't we? Cool off, talk it through, take it slow, figure out what we both really felt? This didn't have to be the end.

I might've been able to believe that if the hurt in Avery's expression wasn't seared into my memory like an awful replay no one would stop showing.

I fucked this up.

I fucked it all up.

And I have no idea how to fix it.

Worse, I couldn't just stay home and wallow or go back to Avery's place and beg him to talk this through with me. No, I had to be at the morning skate, and I had a game tonight.

As I got off the freeway to get to the arena, my stomach wound itself into even tighter knots. That cold pizza and coffee from earlier threatened to lurch up my throat.

We'd come out to the team. They knew.

They'd had yesterday and last night to dream up all kinds of chirps about it, and there'd be no avoiding any of that once I walked into the locker room. What was I supposed to do? Tell them, *"Never mind, we actually broke up this morning?"* It was the truth, but it would mean questions and concerned looks and...

Was it too late to tell Coach I was too sick for practice or for tonight's game?

Yeah, it was, and I couldn't do that anyway. The team was counting on me. We were already down one top six forward. Plus there would be no end of heckling from the guys if I was suddenly scratched the day after quite obviously spending half the day in bed with Avery.

"Fuck my life," I muttered to the steering wheel.

There was no avoiding it. Any of it. Nothing to do but nut up and face the guys, and hope I didn't break down sobbing or lose my temper or God only knew what else.

When I pulled into the parking lot, I still had about fifteen minutes before I needed to be in the locker room. I hemmed and hawed a little, then swallowed my pride and did the only thing I could think of.

> Can we talk about this? I'm sorry. I don't want this to be over.

The word "Read" appeared beneath the message, so at least he hadn't blocked me.

He didn't respond, though.

Sighing, I closed my eyes and pressed back against the driver seat. We *could* come back from this. Right? It wasn't like one of us had committed some unforgivable sin.

You mean besides telling him he doesn't know what he's feeling and he's not really in love with you?

God, I fucked up so bad...

And somehow I was going to face my team and play hockey? When all I wanted to do was break every traffic law imaginable getting back to Sewickley to plead with Avery to talk this through?

Not like I had much choice. Avery wasn't interested in talking to me, and I had a job to do. Swearing under my breath, I got out of the car and headed inside, keeping my gaze down.

From halfway up the hall, I could hear the locker room's predictable noise, which was mostly voices talking over the rustles and squeaks of gear.

I thought I caught a glimpse of some guys in the hallway between me and the locker room, but they disappeared inside before I really paid much attention.

What I did pay attention to was how the noise suddenly ticked down a few notches. Gear still moved and people still spoke, but the relaxed vibe and loud heckling was conspicuously gone.

When I walked into the locker room, I glanced around, and almost everyone was looking my way. Everyone else was very interested in whatever gear they were putting on or adjusting. Even the equipment managers were suddenly very focused on their clipboards or, in one case, a helmet visor being tightened.

I pretended not to notice as I continued toward my stall.

As I started changing, people started chattering again, but the vibe was still subdued. Even those who chirped each other were quiet and half-hearted.

Awesome. I managed to kill my relationship and make the locker room unbearably awkward. I'm on a fucking roll today.

The guys who'd seen me in the hallway must've clocked that something was off and passed it on to the rest of the team, because they all gave me a wide berth. No comments about Avery and me hooking up. No comments about us bailing on our informal practice at the last second. Not a word.

I could only imagine what I looked like if all of them—even those who didn't always pick up on social cues—intuited that they should leave the subject alone.

Great. Nothing said *I'm a goddamned mess* like a whole room full of hockey players who were in possession of some juicy gossip but were conspicuously holding back their snark.

As we geared up, I noticed some of them sending texts and having hushed conversations as they showed each other screens.

If I had to guess, they were texting Avery to make sure he was okay. God, the guilt over that burrowed deep into my chest; he was struggling enough lately. I just *had* to pile this on him, too, didn't I?

This day just kept getting better and better.

I managed to get through practice much the same way I'd made it from Sewickley to downtown Pittsburgh without dying—rote memory and autopilot. I held my own during our various drills, and though it wasn't my best performance, I didn't fuck up while the special teams practiced.

The guys didn't keep their distance per se, but they were clearly nervous around me. Conversations were focused on hockey and nothing else.

It was Coach Tabakov who finally pulled me aside and faced the elephant in the locker room head-on. In the hallway, arms crossed over his jacket, he eyed me. "You're not here today, Halls. What's going on?"

I struggled to hold his gaze, and I finally gave up and stared at the concrete between our skates. "Just some... personal stuff."

"Anything I should be aware of?"

Oh, he probably needed to know this one. Especially with Avery getting so close to being reactivated, the prudent thing to do would be to let Coach know that his top line center and right winger had broken up. And that they'd been together in the first place.

That maybe his top line center was bringing more problems to this team than anything, and maybe the no-move clause in that center's contract needed to be revisited.

But I was anything but prudent right now. I was brittle and I was a coward, and I just shook my head. "No, Coach. It's—I'll have my head in the game tonight."

I sensed the skepticism coming off him. When I looked up, though, I wasn't ready for the concern that was also in his expression.

"Tell me honestly, Halls," he said softly. "Are you going to be okay tonight?"

I have to be. *If I* don't have my shit together tonight, *then...*

Then I don't know what'll happen.

I swallowed the lump trying to rise in my throat. "I'll be fine tonight."

His expression hardened, but only slightly. "I need to know if I can count on you." He gestured toward the locker room. "If *they* can count on you."

I nodded despite the roiling in my stomach. "By the time we suit up tonight, I'll be fine."

I wasn't sure if I was promising him, myself, or both.

But one way or another, it *had* to be true.

I should've been settling in for my pregame nap, but I already knew that wasn't going to happen. Instead, I wandered my apartment, trying to figure out what to do besides talking to Avery, since that was obviously not an option.

Finally, I realized I needed some outside guidance, so I sent out an SOS to the only person I could think of to ask for advice. Thank God I had someone I could talk to about things like this, too. I'd teased him that he owed me after I'd *finally* talked him out of getting back together with that douchewaffle he'd been on-again off-again with all last year. The reality, though, was that he was a good friend. He knew me well, and I trusted his intuition about a lot of things, even if he was—with one exception—terrible at picking men to date.

When Dan's face appeared on my screen, I breathed an actual sigh of relief.

"Thanks for talking with me," I said. "I really need a sounding board right now."

"Yeah?" He was in a hotel room, judging by the dull landscape painting above the plain headboard. "What's going on?"

"The short version?" I let my head fall back against the couch cushion. "Avery and I fixed our bullshit and we got together, and now I'm pretty sure I fucked it up."

Dan blinked. "Oh. Uh. How did you fuck it up?"

I gave him the rundown of how Avery and I had ended up together in the first place.

"So you guys got together after you helped him into rehab," he said.

I nodded.

"Wow." Dan pushed out a breath. "That's heavy."

"I know. And now I think I fucked it all up, but... I have no idea how to fix it." I almost choked on the words as I added, "Especially since he won't talk to me."

"It's only been, what, a few hours, though, right?"

"Yeah."

"Maybe he needs a little time to cool off." He laughed softly. "You know, like we both did after that one really awful fight we had?"

I breathed a laugh, too. "God, that was a shitshow."

"It was. But we got through it. And we were long-distance—we could've ghosted each other and been done with it." He offered a slight shrug. "You and Avery will have to be in the same room sooner or later."

I winced at the memory of the painfully awkward

locker room vibe this morning. "I'd kind of rather fix this before we're stuck together around the team."

"Yeah, I don't blame you."

"Any thoughts?" I asked. "Because I have no idea how to fix this."

"Well..." He was quiet for a moment, gaze unfocused. I didn't press; sometimes he did that when he was trying to gather his thoughts. Finally, he looked at me through the camera again. "The reason you're worried about him not really loving you? I think that has less to do with him and more to do with you. Specifically, your past."

I straightened. "What?"

"Listen, don't take this the wrong way..." He inclined his head a little. "But it sounds like your man isn't the only one with some baggage. Dude, I knew even before you told me about your mom that you and alcohol had a weird history."

"You did?"

"Well, yeah. You're not as subtle about it as you think." He must've seen the questions in my expression, because he continued, "You're fine for a beer or two, but you get twitchy when people start drinking heavily. I don't think other people notice, but I do—it's like you're just kind of uncomfortable, you know? Especially around people who get really fucked up. And when someone gets smashed enough they need a responsible adult to keep them out of trouble, that responsible adult is *always* you."

Heat rose in my face. I wanted to snap back that he didn't know what he was talking about, but... he kind of had a point. Hanging out with hockey players meant a certain amount of drinking, and I was okay with that. Once someone crossed into shitfaced territory, though—once they needed a babysitter—I exited party mode and became the guy who scraped people up, got them water, got them home.

I shifted on the couch. "You don't think I should do that?"

"I didn't say that," he said softly. "You're just the first to jump up and babysit the really drunk guys. The more people around you drink, the less you do. It's not a flaw, Peyton. None of it is. But the more I saw you in action, the more it became pretty obvious you're not real comfortable with all of it. Because as soon as that shit starts happening, you stop having a good time."

I definitely couldn't argue with that.

"I'm not saying there's something wrong with you," he went on. "But the shit with your mom—that's trauma, man."

I jumped. "It is?"

"Of course it is. And maybe that's something you need to deal with. Like... with some help."

"You think I need a therapist."

Dan gave me that arched eyebrow and half-shrug that always meant, *am I wrong?*

And... no. He really wasn't wrong.

"I'm not saying this to blame you," he said. "But I think it might be something you should explain to Avery. So he understands where you're coming from."

I chewed my lip. "What if it's too late, though? What if I've fucked this thing up with him?" I hated how pitiful and scared I sounded. "Like he won't want anything to do with me, and things will get awkward when he comes back from rehab, and—"

"Hey, slow down," Dan said gently. "It sounds to me like he's a good dude, same as you, and that if you two sit down and talk about this—like really talk and not try to act like you're too manly to discuss your feelings—you can figure it out."

"Hey! I've never been too manly to discuss my feelings!"

He rolled his eyes. "No, but I remember some of the conversations we had when we were trying to work things out. It was trying to get blood from a stone from both of us."

"Okay, that's fair."

"See? So go talk to him and see what you guys can work out."

I raised my eyebrows. "*Go* talk to him? Like..."

"Like stand outside his window with a boombox like this is the 1980s or something—I don't know. But if he's not responding to your texts or returning your calls, you might have to let him know you mean it. Show up and see if he'll talk to you." He paused. "I mean, obviously if he wants you to leave, then leave. But... you know what I mean."

"I do, yeah." I almost shuddered at the idea, if only because I was scared Avery would slam the door in my face. How angry *was* he over everything I'd said?

"Breathe, Peyton," Dan said. "It's probably worse in your head than it actually is."

"One can hope," I said with a humorless laugh. "Anyway, you're right. I'll see if he'll talk to me, and either way, I'm going to look into getting a therapist."

"Okay." He smiled. "Let me know how it goes, yeah?"

"I will. Thanks for helping me sort it out."

"Any time. You know that. And hit me up this summer and we'll do something." He paused, then laughed with a hint of sadness. "Something tells me we won't be doing another Tour de Debauchery together."

I chuckled. "Don't take this the wrong way, but... I hope not."

"Same." He smiled. "Good luck with him. He must be a great guy if he's got you tied up in knots like this."

"You mean like Will was such a great guy when he had you—"

"All right, all right. That's enough out of you."

I laughed, and I actually felt it this time.

We ended the call a moment later, and I sat back on the couch and stared up at my living room ceiling. I felt better after talking to my ex, but I also felt a lot worse. Panicked, almost. Like I needed to see Avery right this minute and talk this through, as if every second I waited was one more second he had to slip away from me forever.

I wanted to see him face to face like Dan had suggested, but I was still a coward. I also had to head back to the arena soon, but also... coward.

I needed to at least try something, though, so with my heart in my throat, I wrote out a text.

> I know I fucked up, and I'm sorry. Can we talk?

I got no answer.

CHAPTER 39
AVERY

There weren't words to describe how grateful I was that Shannon shoehorned me into her schedule this morning.

All day yesterday, I'd been a wreck over Peyton. I hadn't even been able to sit through the game because every time the camera landed on him, I wanted to fall apart. Both because I was hurting and because...

I mean, every time his face appeared on the screen, unless he was focused on a hockey play happening in that moment, the cracks showed. He was always so upbeat and lively, but this time it was like when someone was playing through a bad cold or a nagging injury—he just looked exhausted and...

Broken.

Fuck me, he looked broken.

I turned off the TV before the first period was over. The one bright spot of the night was that I resisted the temptation to drink. It was the first time since I'd gone into rehab that I'd wanted to get absolutely shitfaced, but I'd talked myself out of it. I was proud of that, even if I wasn't proud of all the reasons I'd been a mess to begin with.

Today, I needed to talk to someone who wasn't a complete disaster, and fortunately, Shannon was able to squeeze me in.

"Thanks for seeing me," I said as I sat down in her office.

"You're welcome." She studied me, worry pulling her eyebrows together. "So, tell me what's going on."

I did. I'm not too proud to say there were some tears or that my voice broke a few times, but I got through it. I laid it all out on the table, all the way through yesterday and last night and this morning, and then I met my therapist's gaze and whispered, "Where the hell do I go from here?"

"Well." She seemed to think for a moment. "Let's start with what Peyton was concerned about—that your love for him is rooted in gratitude and dependence more than affection."

I winced, staring down at my hands. "I *do* love him."

"Of course you do. I don't think anyone questions that, including him."

"But he doesn't think it's..." I chewed my lip, not sure how to proceed.

"He's concerned that you're not in love with him the way a partner should be."

I nodded.

"Do you agree with that?"

"No," I said quickly, but almost as fast, I sagged back against the couch cushion. "I... I don't think so? But what if he's right?"

"What makes you think he is?"

I pressed my lips together as I tried to pull my thoughts into order. "I mean, everything has been filtered through grief since Leif died. What if... What if that's all this is? That I'm jumping on being with him because it feels better than grieving over Leif?" I exhaled hard. "God, that makes me sound like such a dick. I'll be sad for him until I start getting laid? Ugh."

"I don't think that's what's happening here, though."

"You don't?"

She shook her head. "Grief and new love are not mutually exclusive. The fact that you're grieving as hard as you are for Leif just shows how much love you're capable of." She offered a gentle smile. "You can love Peyton while you're still mourning the friend you lost."

"But how do I know if I'm really in love with him, or if this is just gratitude for him saving me from myself."

"There's no reason it can't be both."

I stared at her. "But if it's just gratitude, then it isn't..." I chewed my lip, not sure how to finish.

"Well, let me ask you this, then." She folded her hands on top of her notepad. "When you're with him, or when you think about him, do you get butterflies?"

"Of course I do," I whispered.

"Okay." She tilted her head a little. "What about him makes you feel that way?"

I had to work to swallow. Staring down at my own hands, I said, "Everything, honestly. He's funny. I've thought he was hot for a long time, but when we're just hanging out together, I completely forget he was ever someone I had a crush on from a distance, you know? It's like he's... I don't know. Like he's been here all along. We just kind of... click, I guess? And he's, um..." Heat rushed into my face, and I felt like a shy schoolkid as I added, "He's an amazing kisser, too."

"So you enjoy the time you spend together."

"God, yeah," I whispered. "It sucks when he's on the road. It sucks being away from the whole team, but especially him. It isn't even..." I shifted a little, some more warmth rising in my cheeks. "It isn't just the sex, you know? That part's great and all, but..." I paused, trying to pull my thoughts into order. "I'm just happier when he's there than when he's gone."

"How much of that is rooted in what he did to help you get into rehab?"

I froze. "What?"

"You're worried your affection for him stems from him helping you," she explained. "But everything you've just described—none of it sounds related to that, does it?"

I stared at the floor between us.

"It's okay to be happy while you're grieving, Avery," she said softly. "It's okay to fall in love even while you're still sad."

I swallowed hard. "Peyton doesn't think it is, though."

"Didn't you say he's texted a few times about it?"

"Yeah. He, um... He said he's sorry and he thinks he fucked up."

"Did you respond?"

I shook my head.

"Do you *want* to respond?"

I had to think about that for a moment. "I want to fix things with him. I'm just afraid he'll tell me that what I feel for him isn't..." I trailed off when my voice threatened to crack.

"Well. Maybe what needs to happen first is you need to talk to him. And by that I mean you need to speak while he listens."

"What do I tell him?"

"Everything we talked about. That you are still grieving for your friend, and you are grateful that Peyton helped you when things were dark, but neither of those things precludes loving him." She paused. "Honestly, if it wasn't possible to love someone sincerely and genuinely while going through some other emotional turmoil, then no one would ever love at all."

I blinked.

"We're not always in the midst of a life-altering trauma," she clarified. "But everyone is going through something all the time, whether it's work stress or just worrying about the state of the world. No one is ever in the perfect place in their life or frame of mind to fall in love."

I sat back again, rolling her words around in my mind. "I, um... I hadn't thought about that."

"It's quite likely he hasn't either."

I nodded slowly as I let it all sink in.

Finally, I looked at her again. "Okay. I guess I need to talk to Peyton."

I was distracted all the way home. Not so much that I couldn't drive—I still had my situational awareness—but enough that nothing registered beyond traffic signals and what other cars were doing. I could've passed a presidential motorcade and a blazing housefire and not even noticed.

But I sure snapped into the moment when I turned up my driveway.

Peyton is here?

Oh, shit. I needed to talk to him, but I wasn't ready for—

I wasn't ready to see him, and I definitely wasn't ready for the spike of fury when I saw him. After my conversation with Shannon, I was ready to sit down and talk about this, but apparently I still needed to process things a bit, because just the sight of his car had me grinding my teeth.

"Emotions don't always seem to make sense," she'd told me during another session. *"But they are definitely real."*

Wasn't that the truth.

Peyton got out of his car as I was pulling into the garage. For a split second, I was tempted to hit the button and let the door come down in his face, but... I really did want to talk to him. I was angry and hurt, yes, but mostly I wanted to tell him everything I'd gleaned from my appointment with Shannon. See if we could salvage this after all.

What a weird contradiction of emotions as I faced him in the driveway—wanting to both tell him off and beg him to stay.

Was it too much to ask for a few minutes to process all this shit and get my head together before we talked? Apparently so.

"Hey." His voice sounded hollow. "Can we talk?"

I chewed the inside of my cheek. The words, *"No, get the fuck out of here,"* were dangerously close to tumbling out, but so were, *"I'm so sorry I made you feel like your only option was leaving."*

Instead, I nodded and gestured for him to follow me inside. I desperately needed some water, and he accepted an offered glass as well. Drinks in hand, we sat on the couch, and I tried not to think about how the conversation had gone last time we'd been here. Or that this was the place he'd slept that night he'd picked me up at the club, which had not been my finest hour.

After a sip of water, Peyton took a deep breath like he was about to speak.

"Wait." I put up both my hands. "Let me talk."

He stared at me, mouth still open like he wanted to protest. Slowly, though he relaxed, and he nodded. "Okay. Go ahead."

Oh. Fuck. I wasn't ready for this. But I was committed, so no turning back now.

"I get why you're worried that I don't really feel this way about you," I began. "And... yeah. I'm still broken over Leif. I probably will be for a long time." I had to swallow against the renewed rush of emotions. "But when I say I'm in love with you, I mean it. I can love you while I'm still grieving him."

"I know you—"

"Let me finish," I pleaded.

He closed his mouth again.

I rolled my shoulders. "You're not just the first good thing that's come along after I lost my best friend. And you're not just someone who scraped me up off the pavement. The truth is I've wanted you since long before you came to this team. And the more I've seen who you are, the more I've fallen for you. Not because you saved me from my own stupid self, but because you're the kind of man who would do that. Even for a teammate who was a jerk to him and gave him every reason not to."

Peyton lowered his gaze.

"Yeah, I'm still a mess after what happened to Leif," I whispered. "It's... That's going to be a long road. There's no way around it. But the way I feel about you? That has nothing to do with grief, and everything to do with you and *only* you."

He looked at me then, eyebrows up as if he hadn't heard me right.

"Like I said, I'm so fucking broken right now," I went on. "And I will be for a while. The fact that I still had the capacity to fall for you while I'm like this—you're just that amazing of a person."

His lips parted.

I hesitated, then steeled myself and moved a little closer to him on the couch. When he didn't back away, I said, "I know it also seems like it happened so fast. Like we jumped into bed and had some fun for a while, and now... this." I tentatively took his hand. "But I think I was falling for you long before we ever landed in bed."

"Me too," Peyton murmured. He hesitated as if he wasn't sure if I was done. Then he softly said, "I think that's why I was so surprised you thought I wasn't into you anymore. Because by then..." He trailed off, shaking his head. "I was so far gone for you and didn't even realize it yet."

My heart flipped, and for a goddamned change, it was a good feeling. "You are?"

He nodded, not looking at me, and he swiped at his eyes. "I'm so ridiculously in love with you, and I have been for a while. But after we talked, I think..." He wrung his hands and swallowed hard. "When I backed away, I don't think it was about us as much as it was about me."

"What do you mean?"

"I told you what I went through with my family. With my mom and her drinking." He pushed out a ragged breath. "I think that's affected me more than I thought it did." He laced our fingers together and gripped my hand so tight it was almost painful. "I think I need to get some help, too. To work through everything from my family."

The words caught me by surprise, and it took a second before I could speak again. "You... You do?"

Peyton nodded. "Yeah. Because I think I've got a lot of crap in there"—he gestured at his own head—"that wants to get in the way of what we're doing. And I need to do something about that."

I chewed my lip, fear keeping me silent for a moment.

The question on the tip of my tongue was an important one, but damn if I wasn't terrified of the answer.

This wasn't the time for easy subjects, though, so I took a deep breath and made myself ask, "Does that mean you're not in a good place for a relationship?"

"Probably." He met my gaze, a sweet and vulnerable smile coming to life. "But when you think about it, is anyone ever in the right place for one? We've all got shit we're trying to deal with and sort out. If we waited until it was all fixed, then we'd all just be single for the rest of our lives."

The hope swelling in my chest almost brought me to tears. My therapist had said as much, but Peyton was on the same page too? Did that mean... "So, you do want to?"

"Yes," he whispered, the smile finally breaking through for real. "Just, you know, be patient with me. I still need to find a therapist and figure out—"

"Peyton." I laughed and brought his hand up to kiss it. "I would be a hell of a hypocrite if I wasn't patient with you getting therapy and sorting things out. And even if I hadn't had to go through all this shit myself, I'd still be patient because I want you to be happy. And I want you to be with me."

Disbelief sketched across his face, which sent the same reaction through me. Did he honestly think I'd shove him away for needing help when he'd had to drag my ass in to get therapy? Not in this lifetime.

Then he relaxed, and he slid closer to me. "Any objections to seeing someone together?"

"Like a counselor?"

He nodded.

"No objections at all." I released his hand and reached for his face. "I'm game for anything that helps us both be happy and helps us be together."

He slid a little closer, and my God, that smile really was the best thing in the world.

No. Scratch that.

This *kiss* was the best thing in the world.

Being wrapped up in his strong, familiar arms, his scruff grazing my chin as his lips moved with mine, was like coming home after being gone for way, way too long.

Then he broke the kiss and buried his face in my neck, and he just held me, and that—*that* was coming home. I closed my eyes and held him close, just reveling in not being miles apart anymore. I'd expected to have to fight with him or beg him to understand where I was coming from or... something.

But no. I'd told him everything Shannon had suggested I tell him. He'd listened to me. He'd also shown some cards I hadn't expected. Suddenly it all made sense.

And still it seemed like a hard-fought miracle, holding him while the remnants of his kiss tingled on my lips.

"I love you," I whispered.

Peyton loosened his embrace. I had a split second to be afraid he was letting go, but when our eyes met, his smile soothed all that panic.

He cupped my face in both hands, and as he leaned in he whispered, "I love you, too."

God, my whole world felt perfect in that moment.

I knew it wasn't. I knew there were broken pieces, some of which would never completely mend, but this? A tender kiss after he'd said those words? This *was* perfect.

I pressed my forehead to his and sighed. "I'm sorry. I shouldn't have shoved you away."

Peyton gathered me into his arms and kissed the top of my head. "No. I should've known there was something else going on here. With me, not you. And... I don't know.

Explained it better?" He exhaled and stroked my hair. "I guess we can be a mess together, you know?"

I laughed, which felt amazing. "Yeah, we can."

"We can." He nodded. "And having a counselor together—I like that idea a lot. Maybe it'll make it easier for us to navigate everything, you know? We each have our own therapists, but then someone who can talk us through the rest."

A knot I hadn't even noticed before unwound in my chest, and renewed affection for him fluttered in my stomach. "You really want to do that?"

"Yes." He caressed my cheek and looked right in my eyes. "I love you, Avery. Whatever it takes to be what you need and what makes you happy—I'll do the work. No question."

It was suddenly hard to swallow and even harder to talk. I covered his hand on my face, and I teared up a little as I said, "And you thought it was possible for me to *not* really be in love with you?"

He laughed quietly as some color rose in his cheeks. "I *did* say I fucked up."

"No, you didn't." I cut off his protests with a soft kiss. "We just have a lot to work through. Each of us, and together. And I'm willing to do the work, too."

God, I was never going to get tired of that gorgeous smile. He curved a hand behind my head and drew me in, and just before our lips met, he whispered, "Deal."

That kiss was relief and love and everything in between. So much tension I hadn't even noticed before—in me and between us—melted away, and there was nothing left but this. Us. Two guys who had a ton of life's bullshit piled on our plates, but still found our way to each other.

When we parted this time, we were both out of breath.

Meeting his gaze, I wasn't at all surprised to see an entirely new set of feelings burning in his.

"Now that we've talked all that through..." He grinned and tipped his head toward the stairs, then raised his eyebrows.

I returned the grin as I took his hand and rose.

And oh, yes, we were definitely on the same page.

CHAPTER 40
PEYTON

I'd had makeup sex a handful of times in my life, and there was always a certain amount of both relief and release. It always meant that whatever had driven us apart or put us out of step was dealt with. Maybe not completely gone or resolved, but enough that we knew we could move past it. Whatever lingering emotions we had from the fight, we channeled into the sex until neither of us could move and nothing felt insurmountable anymore.

When Avery pulled me down onto his mattress this time, it was all that and so much more. This wasn't just landing in bed because we were back on the same page—it was coming home. I was absolutely turned on, hungry for his touch and aching to be inside him, but what we were doing now was a release in its own right. As if I'd already come once and now we were just getting each other spun up again.

Except I hadn't come yet. I hadn't come since the last time we'd touched. That hadn't been all that long, really—not even forty-eight hours—but it felt like too damn long. And yet, just holding him like this, making out while our hands rememorized each other's bodies, was as much a relief as the most powerful orgasm I'd ever had.

How stupid was I to think this was a crutch? Or that he was half-assing any of this?

I moaned into his kiss and held him even tighter against me as I rolled us over onto my back. He sighed into my kiss as he settled on top of me, and I was dizzy with need and relief. Never again was I second-guessing him, and no way was I backing away from this because of past-driven fear. All the therapy and God knew what else it would take to keep me from being scared of ghosts—well, I'd deal with that later.

Right now, all I wanted was Avery.

He broke the kiss, and I chased his mouth until our lips met again. From the soft whimper, he didn't mind at all, and we were lost in another long kiss that was somehow both languid and demanding. A kiss for its own sake, but also a means of driving each other wild until we were both shaking with need.

He *was* shaking when he broke away this time, and he touched his forehead to mine as he breathlessly whispered, "Would it be too much to ask for you to fuck me until I scream?"

All the air rushed out of me as I arched under him, nearly coming just from his plea.

"Not... Not too much to ask at all." I slid my hands up his back. "This might be quick if I do, though."

His grin was beyond sexy. "Then you'll just have to fuck me again, eh?"

Whatever smartass retort I might've had faded away as he rubbed his dick against mine. "God, Avery..."

"Is that a yes?"

"It's an 'anything you fucking want but get the damn lube already.'"

His laugh was wicked and when I looked up at him, so were his eyes.

Oh my God, I was so in love with him.

And I wanted him so, so bad.

"Get the lube," I whispered, the words coming out as more of an order this time.

Avery got the lube.

That wasn't to say we made much progress toward me sliding into him, though. Too much making out. Too much getting lost in each other. Even when we finally got the bottle open, we only got as far as slicking up my dick, and then his just for the hell of it, and suddenly we were pumping each other in between breathless kisses.

"We're both gonna come this way," I murmured against his lips. "We're gonna—I want to fuck you, baby."

He made a sound that was both hunger and protest, as if he couldn't decide if he wanted to keep going like this or if he wanted what he'd originally asked for. Finally, though, he stopped, and when he lifted himself off me, it was my turn for a mix of *"God, yes"* and *"wait, no."*

Then I was on my side next to him, his legs spread wide, and I indulged in more of his amazing kisses while I teased him open with slick fingers. Long after he was taking my fingers easily, long after he was squirming and moaning and trying to fuck himself on my hand, I kept going. Kept kissing him. Kept fingering him. Kept driving him higher and higher just because I could.

"Peyton." He grabbed my arm and met my gaze with fire in his eyes. "Fuck me. *Now.*"

I bit back a groan. "How do you want it?"

He shook his head. "Don't care. Just want your dick."

I kissed him lightly. "Get on top."

"Ooh. You like being ridden, don't you?"

"You better believe it." I lifted myself off him and got on my back. As he straddled me, I whispered, "What can I say? I love this view."

Avery grinned. "So what you're saying is—give you a show?"

I laughed, running my hands up his powerful thighs. "You already are, baby."

He just chuckled.

I put on some more lube, and then I steadied myself as I guided him down onto my cock. I liked this position a lot, but it also meant he could decide how fast and how deep he took me; I was well aware that my dick was on the bigger end, and that wasn't so much a flex as it was a reason to be careful. As much as I wanted to fuck him into oblivion, I didn't want to hurt him.

Avery eased himself down a little at a time, and it was just as well we were in this position. Not only could he control how deep and hard we went, I wasn't expected to do anything except lie here and stare up at him, watching his pleasure play out across his face. The flutters of his eyelids. The way his lips parted with soundless cries and curses. His hair tumbling over his face when he let his head fall forward.

And all the while, being overwhelmed myself from moving inside him. From his slow, slick strokes. From how hot and tight he was. Oh my God, I couldn't have kept up a rhythm or anything in that moment because I was just so mesmerized by him.

I was so, so glad I could really, truly feel him, too, even if that threatened to overwhelm me. I'd have happily worn a condom if that was what he wanted, but as I slid home, I was so damn glad we were going raw. The heat, the slick tightness—it just wouldn't be the same with that layer between us. I wanted to feel him, and oh, yeah, I did. Every stroke. Every moan. When he rocked his hips and changed the angle, we both gasped, and all I could do was push up into him and try not to lose my mind.

"Oh my God," he whispered, letting his head fall back. He sounded on the edge of tears as he ground out, "I fucking love your dick."

I just moaned, trying not to go insane as I matched his rhythm.

Like a lot of guys did when they bottomed, he'd gone soft, but he was getting hard again. I grabbed the lube, poured some on my hand, and I reveled in that strangled moan as I started stroking him back to full attention. He changed his movements again, fucking into my fist as he impaled himself on my cock.

"You are so hot like this, baby," I slurred. "Jesus..."

Avery bit his lip and moved faster. I matched him as best I could, and together we picked up more and more speed. He was rock-hard in my hand now, too.

"Do you want to come like this?" I panted.

He squeezed his eyes shut and whimpered before he gazed down at me. "You want me to?"

I nodded. "Yeah. I'm..." I arched under us as a shiver ran through me. "Oh, God. Yeah. I won't be far behind you if you do."

That drew a deliciously helpless moan out of him, and he was the one to shiver this time, tightening around my dick as his rhythm faltered for a couple of strokes. He recovered, though, moving even faster than before—oh, yeah, we were on a mission now. Round two could be long and indulgent; I needed us both to get off this time before I went absolutely out of my mind. I needed him to clench hard around me, come all over me, and drive me over that edge to my own desperately needed climax.

"Oh, God," he rasped. "Don't... Don't stop. Don't..." He leaned forward enough to grab the headboard, and he used that leverage to ride me so damn hard, so damn fast—

"Fuck, baby, I'm gonna come," I slurred. "Oh, fuck... Fuck, I'm—"

Avery's whole body jerked, and he cried out as his hole clenched impossibly tightly around me, and then hot cum landed on my stomach. I didn't even know what I was saying—just mumbling and babbling as his orgasm sent me crashing into my own. I let go of his cock, grabbed his hips, and pulled him down on me, and I shouted God only knew what as I came inside him.

With one last shudder, I stilled.

Above me, Avery was trembling and out of breath, and I wrapped my arms around him and tugged him down. I didn't worry about the cum or the sweat. We'd take a shower in a minute.

First, though, I wanted to just hold him while we both came back to earth.

All my earlier emotions came back to the surface as I held my shaking, panting boyfriend against me. When I closed my eyes, I wasn't at all surprised to squeeze a couple of hot tears free.

Stroking his hair, I sighed into the quiet.

We were here. We were back.

I was home.

It took a shower, a marathon fuck in almost every position I knew, and another shower before we finally collapsed into a satisfied heap in his rumpled bed. He had his arm around my shoulders, and I rested my head on his chest, and for the longest time, we just lay in comfortable silence. I think I even dozed off for a little while. I know he did.

What eventually drove us out of bed was our growling stomachs. We were hockey players, after all, and there was only so long we could go without eating, especially after engaging in some, shall we say, intense cardio.

We ended up ordering delivery from that awesome Thai place again. While we waited, we settled in Avery's living room, curled together on the couch instead of sitting too far apart.

"I feel so much better," he said on a happy sigh.

I chuckled. "Most people would after a couple of orgasms."

"Well. Yeah." He drew away enough that he could look at me. "But I meant... about everything else. Being back here again."

Sobering, I nodded, and I ran my fingers through his hair as I said, "Me too. It feels like we were apart a lot longer than two days."

"Yeah. It does." He clasped my hand in his and brought it up to kiss my palm. "I'm just lucky you're this stubborn."

"And I'm lucky you were willing to listen, so I think we're even."

He cuddled a little closer to me. "Eh. I'm not keeping score."

"Neither am I." I stroked his hair again. "And... I'm sorry. For freaking out on you."

Avery was already shaking his head. "No." He sat up again, opening up more space between us but not letting go of my hand. "You had a lot going on that I didn't know about. Sounds like stuff even you didn't know about." He ran his thumb along the back of mine. "I think we can just chalk this up to both of us realizing we need some help, but we can still make this work."

I nodded as he spoke. "Yeah. It's been... eye-opening, that's for sure."

"It has." He searched my eyes. "And you really think seeing a counselor would be good for us? Together, I mean?"

"Absolutely. We're both coming into this with a lot of baggage that we don't need to trip over, you know?" I trailed my fingers down his cheek. "So let's talk to someone while we're still good instead of waiting for problems to crop up."

Avery blinked. "Oh. Hell. I never thought of that. People usually go to counseling when they're already in trouble. I didn't even realize it was an option when..." He gestured at himself, then me. "When things are okay, you know?"

"I never thought about it before, but this whole thing—it spooked me. I'd rather we nip things in the bud than let it get as ugly as my parents' marriage did."

His forehead creased. "They're still together, aren't they?"

"They are. And they're happy now. But..." I whistled, shaking my head. "It was pretty bad there for a while."

"I bet." He kissed my palm again. "I agree—let's not do that."

I smiled and reeled him in for a kiss. "So... off season? We'll find someone for us?"

Avery nodded. "Good idea. Things are going to get pretty crazy soon. Playoffs and all that."

"Yep. And you'll be back to playing again soon, too."

"Yeah. I will." He smiled faintly, but he dropped his gaze as some worry crept into his expression.

I tipped up his chin. "What?"

"Just..." He pressed his lips together, then took a breath. "My conditioning loan starts next week. So I'll be in Wheeling until I'm reactivated."

My heart sank a little. We'd just put ourselves back on the rails after that brief but awful bump in the road. I wasn't ready to be away from him. "It's only a couple of weeks, though."

"Yeah. It's... It won't be bad." He swallowed hard. "I'm not worried about that part. Being away from you, yeah, but..." He trailed off as his eyes lost focus.

"So... what's bothering you?"

"Getting reactivated." He flicked his gaze back to mine again. "I've been gone for—God, almost two months. What if I've lost a step? What if I can't get back to how I was playing before?"

"You've been on LTIR before, haven't you? For even longer?"

He nodded.

"This won't be any different, will it?"

"Except it will." His shoulders dipped a little. "When I'm out with a broken jaw or a concussion, everyone gets it. It's an injury—they happen. But being out for..." His face colored and he dropped his gaze.

"I know a lot of people can be shitty about addiction," I whispered. "But you know the guys can't wait to have you back. The fans, too—they've been asking about you for a while. They *want* you back."

"Yeah?"

"Of course." I leaned in and pressed a kiss to his temple. "You'll see. Everyone's been rooting for you. Everyone." I carded my fingers through his hair. "Anyone who thinks less of you for grieving and for needing help—their opinion isn't worth a damn. The people who care about you—including the fans—want you to be healthy, and they want you back playing hockey as soon as you're ready." I smiled. "I think you'll be pleasantly surprised when you come back."

He held my gaze, uneasiness still etched all over his expression. After a moment, he relaxed, though some of the uncertainty lingered. "I guess we'll find out after I get back from Wheeling, won't we?"

"Yeah. We will."

I understood why he was nervous. In his skates, I'd probably feel the same way.

But I knew our team. I knew the fans.

And I knew all the way to my core that Avery had nothing to worry about.

CHAPTER 41
AVERY

My conditioning loan to the minors turned out to be a lot more fun than I anticipated. It sucked being away from Peyton for two very long weeks, but it was great to get back out onto the ice. Playing and practicing alongside the younger players was a blast, too; our GM had been working some serious magic in building up our farm team, which meant we'd have some excellent young talent coming up in the next couple of years.

I played five games with them, and I didn't care what level this was—scoring four goals and six assists was still satisfying as hell. The fans seemed thrilled, too, and I signed quite a few autographs before and after the games.

Tonight, though—tonight I was nervous.

Because this would be my first time playing in a Whiskey Rebels sweater since I'd entered the program.

I'd kept up my conditioning, and I'd had the time in the minors to help in that department too, but I wouldn't be a hundred percent tonight. There was no avoiding that. Every point was critical right now, and the last thing we needed was a player who was still getting his timing back.

I even suggested that Coach drop me down to the bottom six for a game or two just to help me find my stride, but he refused.

"I've got faith in you, Calds." He put a hand on my padded shoulder. "You haven't been out that long, and I know you've been practicing with the guys. You'll be fine."

Well, we'd find out, wouldn't we?

I'd had teammates before who'd returned from the player assistance program, and they'd always been met with enthusiastic cheers from the crowd. None of them had ever been booed—everyone was always as thrilled to see someone return from the program as from an injury or an illness.

That didn't stop me from expecting them to boo me.

"We always expect the best reactions for everyone but ourselves," Shannon had told me this morning. *"But most people are kind and supportive, and I think you'll be pleasantly surprised."*

She'd also mentioned she and her wife had bought tickets for tonight's game. That meant that as I stepped out for warmups, somewhere in this arena, my therapist was probably smiling to herself because she and I both knew she'd been right.

The second I came out of the tunnel, the crowd went nuts. I could tell whenever the camera was on me because they'd go wild all over again. There were signs. There were people banging on the glass. People were chanting my name.

When I skated behind the goal, I saw a teenage boy holding a sign that read, *We knew you could do it—welcome back #72.*

Holy shit. I almost lost my damn edge. I almost choked up right there on the ice.

Instead, I focused on finding a puck, and when I had one, I sent it up over the glass for the kid. It caught in the net a couple of times, but it finally went over. He looked like I'd made his entire year as he held up his puck and his sign.

Smiling, I tapped my glove in front of the sign, then put it against the glass. He grinned and fist-bumped me.

Then I skated away to continue my warmups, wondering if I could make it through this game without losing it.

And if I did fall apart... well, would anyone really judge me? Everyone in this arena knew what I'd been up against for the last several months. They all knew I'd lost my best friend in the world. Just being here on this ice at all felt like a small miracle; quite frankly, if I shed some tears and someone decided I was too soft or too weak, they could get fucked.

It was getting harder to imagine them actually doing that, though. As Shannon, Rachel, and Peyton had all pointed out to me more than once, the fans had grieved Leif too. From the signs and the cheers, they were as happy to have me back as I was to be back.

Our warmup routine didn't vary much from game to game, and sliding back into that felt amazing. It felt *normal*, and there weren't words to describe how damn good *normal* felt these days.

When it ended, we left the ice in our usual order, retreating to the locker room to hydrate and get ready for the first period. All normal. All the same as I was used to.

Right up until Baddy walked up and hugged me tight. "It's good to have you back, man."

The words and the hug both caught me by surprise, as did the rush of emotions they ignited, but I returned my friend's embrace. "It's good to be back." Nothing had ever felt more like an understatement than those words. Being back here was second only to being back in Peyton's arms. It was like my world was finally back on its axis for the first time in too long.

As he let me go, he clapped my shoulder. Then his eyes flicked to my jersey—to the C on my chest, I thought—and something like regret slipped into his expression. Meeting my gaze again, he said, "We shouldn't have made you captain, dude."

My heart hit the floor. "Oh. Uh..." How the fuck was I supposed to respond to that? "I shouldn't have let you guys down."

"Let us—what?" Baddy yelped. "No! Man, no. That's not what I meant. You're captain material. A hundred percent." He squeezed my arm. "But we shouldn't have put that on your shoulders. Not when you were having such a tough time after we lost Early."

Damn, now I really didn't know what to say.

Coach appeared beside us, and his hand landed on my other shoulder. "He's right. We all knew you were struggling harder than the rest of us. Because you were closer to Early than anyone." He gave my shoulder pad a light smack. "It wasn't right for us to pile the captaincy on you too."

My throat tightened, and I had to take off my glove to wipe my eyes. "Someone had to do it."

"No." Coach shook his head as he withdrew his hand. "We could have had three alternates instead of two As and a C. I'm sorry we did that to you."

Several of the other guys chimed in, murmuring their agreement and nodding.

I closed my eyes and released a long breath as some weight slid off my shoulders. I hadn't even realized how much pressure I'd been feeling from the captaincy, and knowing the guys understood why I'd buckled under it was more of a relief than I'd anticipated.

Another hand appeared on the small of my back, and I didn't have to look to know who it was. I did look, though, and gazing into those sweet, concerned blue eyes gave me a whole different kind of rush.

"You going to be okay tonight?" Peyton asked softly.

I smiled, wrapping my arm around his shoulders and leaning into him. "Yeah. I'll be fine." I laughed. "If I go another night without playing hockey, I'm going to lose my damn mind."

That broke some of the tension in the room, and there were more nods, coupled with chuckles of "I'd go crazy without hockey, too" and "there's no therapy like hockey."

I laughed with some more feeling as I rested my head against Peyton's shoulder. The real therapy had done more for me than I could ever put into words, but there was some truth to what the guys were saying, too—hockey was cathartic and energizing in ways I desperately needed right now. The sport itself, and also being out there with these men. With this team that was like a family in so many ways.

My best friend was gone, and there was nothing I could do to change that.

But tonight, for the first time since that awful night at the hospital, my world didn't feel so damn empty and bleak.

I patted Peyton's chest, then straightened and looked around the room. "What do you guys say we go out there and knock two points out of Charlotte?"

The cheer that went up was more exhilarating than the roar of the hometown crowd after an overtime goal.

Peyton ran his hand up my back, and his smile sent a rush of heat through me.

Good God, I loved this man.

I lifted my chin for a soft kiss. "Let's do this."

He grinned. "Yes, captain."

I snorted and rolled my eyes.

"See?" Eminem said, and there was a loud smack. "I told you they were back together!"

"Pfft. You were guessing as much as the rest of us." Baddy rubbed his arm, which Eminem had apparently whacked with a glove. When he caught my eye, he smirked at me and Peyton. "You boys know you're never hearing the end of this, right? Like ever?"

Peyton chuckled. "Eh, it's a small price to pay for—"

"La la la!" Eminem covered his ears. "I don't want to know!"

"Get wrecked, Em." I flipped him off. "Your jealousy is so transparent."

"Wait, who's he jealous of?" Trews asked. "Calds or Halls?"

"Both," Peyton said.

Baddy nodded. "Definitely both."

Eminem gave him a shove. "Act like you're not!"

"So you admit it?" Peyton asked. "You're jealous of—"

"Gentlemen," Coach said, his voice stern but laced with humor. "Can we perhaps focus on tonight's game and not who's jealous of Calds and Peyton hooking up?"

My jaw went slack. Peyton's spine straightened.

As our teammates chuckled around us, Coach looked at me and shrugged. "What? Did you think I didn't know?"

"I..." I paused, then shook my head and started for my locker stall. "Should've known. Can't get anything past Coach."

He smacked my shoulder as I walked by him. "And yet you still try."

The chirping continued, of course, but we did dutifully

hydrate and get ready for the game. Moments later, we were filing out to the ice again. Some of the guys went straight to the bench. Some of us skated a few circles to stay loose while the announcer read the names of our starting lineup.

I didn't usually pay much attention to the lineup announcement or the fans' reactions to our names.

Tonight, though, not gonna lie—I got one hell of a rush when the crowd almost drowned out, "At right wing, number seventy-two—welcome back your captain, Avery Caldwell!"

I smiled to myself as I took my place on the blue line for the anthem. The sound of the crowd was a balm to my soul; for all I'd convinced myself I'd let my team and Pittsburgh down, both the players and the city were welcoming me back as if they'd never lost one iota of faith me.

I glanced at Peyton. Then I looked up.

The spotlight illuminated the American flag, but it also lit up the row of jerseys a few rafters back.

My gaze locked on the one sporting number sixty-one.

I had to swallow hard, but I didn't feel as brittle as I had during our home opener or during the ceremony when they'd retired Leif's number. If anything, determination swelled in me. Leif would've understood the need to grieve, but he also would've worried himself sick if someone couldn't get back on their feet. If they were struggling so hard that they couldn't move forward.

In fact...

Standing there on the ice with Leif's jersey high above me, it occurred to me that Rachel had been right. Had the roles been reversed and I'd been the one with my jersey raised long before my time, Leif might well have collapsed the same way I had. He was tough as nails, but he had the biggest heart of anyone I'd ever known. How had I thought for even a moment that he would've disapproved of or been disappointed by my collapse, when I knew—I fucking *knew*—he'd have struggled just as hard in my skates?

Maybe he wouldn't have crashed and burned the same way I had, but I was a damn fool to think he wouldn't have been an absolute mess after losing a friend. Or even a teammate he didn't know well.

Until this moment, I hadn't realized how much I'd been afraid I was letting my best friend down by coming unraveled the way I had. And somehow, gazing up at his number right now, I understood that Leif would've tried to hold up the team the same way I had. He'd have piled everyone's grief and shock onto himself and tried to carry us all, hiding his own pain and soothing everyone else's until he—being as human as anyone else—would've crumbled.

I closed my eyes, surprised I didn't squeeze a tear free. As the anthem wrapped up, I took and released a deep breath, feeling lighter as yet another anchor chain fell away.

I'm not weak. I'm not a fuckup.

I'm as human as the man I'm still grieving.

And tonight, I'm going to do his memory proud.

Just before we broke away to set up for the faceoff, Peyton bumped my glove with his. When I turned, he was smiling, and I smiled right back.

My first game with these men in way too long, and then I'll spend the rest of the night sleeping next to you.

Hell yeah.

A minute later, the puck dropped, and we were off and running. The Pittsburgh Whiskey Rebels were bound and determined to wring two points out of this team, but Charlotte was going to make us work for it. Though we won the first faceoff, they stole the puck and broke away, speeding into our zone, three-on-two against our defensemen while we forwards were hot on their heels.

Eminem got to the puck carrier first with a hard hip-check that almost sent the guy sprawling. Somehow, the guy didn't lose possession, and even a viper-fast poke check from Trews didn't relieve him of the puck. They were almost on top of the crease now, the puck carrier dancing through the defensemen as he tried to either pass or shoot.

I'm pretty sure he didn't see Peyton coming, though.

Just as the puck carrier deftly avoided another check from Eminem, Peyton swiped the puck right off his stick. He spun away from another of Charlotte's players, and I—hovering near the blue line—slapped my stick on the ice.

There was too much traffic for Peyton to pass it to me, so he did the next best thing—he whipped around behind the goal and saucer-passed over everyone's heads. I was wide open, and I tracked the puck, mentally calculating if I should chase it or—

Nope, it was low enough.

I jumped up, snatched it out of the air, dropped it to the ice, and tore across the red line, then the blue one. I had no idea what was going on behind me because the crowd was going absolutely insane, drowning out every sound and even my own thoughts.

I skated for all I was worth toward the goal, focusing on the goalie, tracking his movements, watching him watch me. Fake it? Backhand? Top shelf? Five-hole?

I wound back to rip a shot over his shoulder, and when he rose to anticipate it, I snapped it under his pad.

The roar that came out of me was swallowed up by the crowd. Elation surged through me, and I banged myself off the glass in the same instant the red light came on.

My first game after rehab. My first shift. My first *shot*.

I was fucking *back*.

My teammates crushed me in hugs, smacking my helmet and shoulders.

"Welcome back, Calds!" Eminem shouted over the noise.

"Fuck yeah, Captain!" Trews said.

Peyton didn't say a word, but he didn't need to. The pride and love in his eyes said it all.

The impulse to knock our helmets off and kiss him was almost overwhelming. If not for the deafening roar around us, not to mention the hands pounding on the glass behind me, I might have forgotten we were in front of thousands of fans, not to mention all the cameras. I might have locked lips with him right then and there.

And goddammit, I wanted to do exactly that.

Fortunately, I kept my head together. He and I exchanged a gloved fist bump, and then I was leading the guys to the bench for more fist bumps.

Our shift was over, so we took our places on the bench. As Peyton dropped beside me, his shoulder touched mine, and I had to fight hard not to put an arm around him or rest a hand on his thigh. Physical affection was just so easy between us. So habitual. And damn it, I'd had to spend two weeks away from him while I was on my conditioning loan, and Peyton had been on the road with the team until yesterday morning, so we'd only had one night together lately. I needed to be able to touch him.

Not now, though. Hockey now. Hands all over Peyton later. I could wait.

Or, well, I thought I could.

I kept it all under the surface until early in the third period. We were up 4-2, and we had Charlotte on their heels. The fourth line kept them hemmed into their end the way they were so good at doing—keeping them busy and unable to do even a partial line change despite their players being absolutely gassed. Then our guys started to peel away one after the other, and my line along with Eminem and Trews hit the ice to push hard against the exhausted Charlotte players.

Davis was the last to join us, and his timing was perfect —a Charlotte defenseman had made a desperation play, flinging the puck toward the penalty boxes to get it out of the zone without icing it. Two of them had seized the opportunity to drag their tired asses toward the bench, probably thinking the puck was about to leave the zone, so we'd also have to leave, regain possession, and re-enter the zone to keep it onside.

What they didn't expect was Davis intercepting the puck just before it would've crossed the blue line.

Now it was still onside, they had two players way out of position, and the remaining three were ready to collapse.

Davis passed to Eminem, who shouldered his way past a breathless defenseman, and fired the puck toward the goal.

Peyton was waiting at the edge of the crease, and he tipped it in easily.

The horn sounded. The red light came on. The crowd lost it.

And fuck me, but the absolute joy radiating off Peyton almost dropped my knees out from under me.

How had I landed such an absolutely stunning man?

And how the hell was I supposed to keep my hands off him for another—I glanced at the clock—seventeen and a half minutes?

Fuck it.

Just before we were going to skate to the bench for fist

bumps, I couldn't resist, and I asked, "You care if the fans know about us?"

Surprise took over his expression, but only for a second. Then his grin lit up the whole arena, and he pulled off his helmet. "Absolutely the fuck not."

My heart went wild, and I took off my own helmet, glided a little closer, and kissed him.

I thought the crowd had gone nuts when my name was announced or when I'd scored, but I was utterly unprepared for the way they responded to the two of us kissing. If anyone didn't like it, their distaste was completely lost in the deafening, stadium-shaking roar that went up.

We broke the kiss and looked up, and sure enough, we were on the Jumbotron. We laughed and waved, which only egged the crowd on.

No one needed a delay of game penalty, though, so we kept it short, and we went to the bench so Baddy's line could go out.

I had my nose buried in the iPad a moment later, watching the replay of our last shift, when the crowd started going nuts yet again. I snapped my head up to see what was happening.

But... there was nothing really happening on the ice. There'd been an icing call, and everyone was getting ready for another faceoff.

Then Peyton elbowed me and pointed up.

As soon as I saw the Jumbotron, my jaw went slack.

The camera was on *us*.

And there was a pink heart around us with the words KISS CAM blinking below us.

Suddenly all our teammates were banging their sticks on the boards and telling us, "Give the fans what they want!"

"Oh my God," I said.

"You heard 'em." Peyton touched my face and turned me toward him, and...

And oh, wow, we gave the fans what they wanted.

Brief. Chaste. Nothing that would cause a scandal beyond *"OMG two men kissing."* But I could guarantee that *no one* in this building or watching at home had *any* question about if Peyton and I were together.

Yeah, we'd probably hear about it from PR.

Quite frankly?

I really didn't care.

CHAPTER 42
PEYTON

I had no idea if we were going to make it into the playoffs. If we did, it would be by the skin of our teeth. Losing Leif and, for a little while, losing Avery had been hard for the team, and there was only so much we could play through that.

With our record, we'd probably be comfortably in third place or *maybe* have the first wild card spot in a less competitive division. The Metropolitan division was, however, the most competitive in the League. Our third-place team had more points than did the first-place Pacific team, and Central's third-place team was tied with our second wild card. This was *not* an easy division.

There was still time, though. Unless one of the teams ahead of us fell apart—and it did happen sometimes—we'd have to play balls-to-the-wall for the remaining weeks of the regular season to secure a wild card spot.

As I watched Avery stripping off his gear and smiling and chirping with the guys after tonight's game, though, I didn't care if we made it into the postseason. The Whiskey Rebels' season had been nothing short of miraculous given what we'd been up against all year. The team had lost their captain, and then we'd watched as our new captain had crashed and burned, but we'd kept going. Kept playing. Kept holding our own out there even when we brought all the wrong emotions on to the ice.

And Avery...

The man I'd met at training camp had been broken and lost.

The man who'd skated out to the roar of the crowd tonight had been the hockey player I'd admired, the captain this team had believed in, and the man I'd fallen in love with.

Definitely not what I'd expected when I'd signed that contract with Pittsburgh less than a year ago.

As we finished up showering and getting dressed, the wives and kids came down from their box. Several wanted to congratulate Avery on his return, so I hung back, assuring him we didn't have to leave until he was good and ready.

The locker room was getting a little crowded, though, so I told him I'd wait for him in the hallway, and to take his time.

Out here... much better. Quieter. Not so many moving bodies. I leaned against the painted cinderblock wall and released a long breath. Tonight had been incredible. Whatever fears Avery had about losing a step, I was pretty sure they were gone.

I knew from experience with my mom that addiction was a lifelong battle. And I knew Avery's grief wasn't going anywhere any time soon. But tonight, I had even more hope than I'd had before that he could and would move forward. He was strong as hell, and he was willing to both put in the work to get better *and* to make peace with the pain that would likely follow him for the rest of his life. I couldn't help but admire how strong and committed he was.

Falling in love with him? That felt like it had been inevitable all along despite our rocky start.

Footsteps coming out of the locker room pulled my focus back into the present, and I looked up to see Rachel with her new baby in a sling. She was coming right toward me, too.

"Oh. Hey." I smiled at her.

She smiled back, and when she stopped in front of me, she shyly asked, "Can I hug you, Peyton?"

I blinked. "Um. I... Yeah. Yeah, sure."

It was a little challenging with her son between us, but she wrapped her arms around my neck and I carefully returned the embrace.

"Thank you," she murmured in my ear. "For everything you did for Calds."

I drew back and looked at her.

She smiled, a hint of tears in her eyes. "I don't know if we would've lost him like we lost—" She swallowed, then swiped at her eyes. "What I do know is that with the way things were going, we would've lost him one way or another." Her smile returned. "You saved him, and you brought him back to us."

I had to fight back the lump in my throat. "He did all the work."

She was already shaking her head. "He did the therapy and all of that. But he told me how it all happened. There's no telling how far down he would've gone if you hadn't stepped in."

That lump got a lot thicker, but I managed, "I saw someone go that far down once before. Twice, actually. I couldn't..." I shook my head as I cleared my throat. "I couldn't watch him go there too."

"I'm glad someone was looking out for him." Her smile

grew. "And the way everything *else* worked out between you, well..."

That chased away the threat of tears, and I laughed, knowing damn well I was blushing. "I can't complain about that. Don't know if it sounds like a great love story, but..." I half-shrugged.

She snickered. "Eh, by the time you need to tell your kids how you met, you'll have figured out how to tell the story."

"Our kids?" I scoffed even as a warm feeling rushed through me. "Let's not get ahead of ourselves. We just started dating."

Rachel just grinned.

Honestly, I hoped it went from her lips to God's ears. I didn't know what kind of future lay ahead of Avery and me, and we were still in that shiny honeymoon phase, but I hoped—really, really hoped—that this was only the beginning.

A future? Kids? Forever?

Why the hell not?

After a moment, Rachel broke the silence. "By the way, I think you and Leif would've gotten along." She laughed softly. "Between the two of you, you'd have kept Avery in line."

"Hey!" Avery appeared beside her. "Peyton would've been trouble, too."

"*Nobody* is as much trouble as you and Leif were." She glanced at me, an eyebrow arched. "Though, I don't know. Maybe you could give them a run for their money."

I flashed them both a grin. "I could sure try."

"Oh my God." She rolled her eyes. "Two peas in a pod, right here."

"You have no idea," I said.

"I think I can guess." She glanced down and bounced her baby just a little. "I should get out of here." She looked at us with an apologetic expression. "It's late, and I need to find my other three."

"Locker room." Avery nodded in that direction. "They were playing with Eminem's kids."

"I figured. Well, they need to get to bed, and quite frankly, so do I." She smiled at him. "It was great to see you out there again tonight."

He returned the smile. "It was great to be there. And I'm glad you and the kids came, too."

They shared a quick, careful hug over the baby, and then she hugged me again too before heading into the locker room.

Avery watched her go, a sweet, serene expression on his face. It was almost impossible to imagine what a wreck he'd been not very long ago. At the same time, it wasn't—a man with a heart as big as Avery's was bound to be hit hard when he lost someone, and when someone dear to him had lost her husband.

After Rachel had disappeared through the door, he turned to me. "Ready to go?"

I made an *after you* gesture and we walked down the hall toward the player parking garage. In the car, I started the engine but didn't put it in gear. Instead, I rested a hand on his leg. "Do you want to go out with the guys? Or head home?"

He quirked his lips. "What do you think?"

"It's up to you." I drew him in a little and pressed a kiss to his temple. "Tonight's your night."

He held my gaze. Then he smiled and lifted his chin for a kiss. "Well, if it's my night, I think I'd rather spend it with you."

I grinned. "Yeah?"

"Mmhmm." He curved his hand behind my neck and claimed that kiss, and I let it linger for a moment, reveling in this gentle touch and this closeness. Touching his forehead to mine, he whispered, "It's so good to be back with the team. And with you."

"It's good to have you back. That conditioning loan felt like forever."

"Seriously" He drew back a little and met my gaze. "You know, Rachel was right."

I blinked. "What about? That Leif and I would've gotten along?"

"Well, that, yes. But also, I heard what she said outside the locker room."

"Oh. You did?"

"Yeah." He studied me over the console, the streetlights casting harsh shadows over his beautiful face. "She's right, you know. I don't know how bad things would've been without you." He took my hand and squeezed it gently. "I'm just really grateful I didn't have to find out."

I leaned over and kissed him. "I'm glad you were receptive to it. Not everybody is."

He blinked.

I caressed his cheek. "The morning after I picked you up at the club, I was fully expecting you to tell me to pound sand and kick me out of your house."

Avery's lips parted. "But... you did it anyway?"

"Yeah. I couldn't just sit back and let you self-destruct. I had to at least try." I exhaled. "I can't tell you how relieved I was that you didn't fight it. And I mean it—that takes a *lot* of guts. Admitting you need help, and getting that help. Especially for someone who's in the public eye like you are."

"I... never thought about that."

"I watched two people in my life crash and burn," I whispered. "One had to hit absolute rock bottom and *almost* lose everything before she finally admitted she needed help. The other..." I shook my head. "So I've seen for myself how hard it is. It took a lot to accept help the way you did. I'm proud of you for it."

Avery smiled as a blush rose in his face. Clasping my hand, he said, "Well, it definitely helped to have someone step up and stop me from destroying myself. All of this?" He held up our joined hands. "I'm still amazed you can see past everything I did and said and still want me."

I drew him in again and brushed my lips across his. "You'd have to try a lot harder than that to make me lose interest."

His lips curved against mine. "I think I'd rather try to keep you interested."

I grinned, too. "Oh, yeah?" Sliding my fingers up into his hair, I asked, "Any thoughts on how you're going to do that?"

The hand on my thigh made me gasp a second before Avery had my mouth.

When he broke that kiss, his hand was nearly at my groin and we were both out of breath.

"Am I on the right track?" he asked in a sultry voice.

"Mmm, I think so." I nipped his lower lip. "But how about we go back to one of our places so security doesn't bust us?"

Avery laughed, making me warm all over. "Good idea." He gave my thigh a squeeze before pulling his hand away. "Let's get out of here."

We did.

And Avery had no trouble keeping my interest for the rest of the night.

EPILOGUE
AVERY

August

The last time I'd been to this place, I'd been an impossible mix of numbness and excruciating pain. Absolutely torn apart from the inside out, but also detached and certain I was never going to feel anything again, least of all anything good.

That had been the second worst day of my life, just ten days after the absolute worst.

Today...

Today was bittersweet.

Walking across a gentle slope of sun-dappled grass beneath sheltering trees, I was happy despite the lump firmly lodged in my throat.

I carried a small bouquet of flowers in one hand. In my other, I laced my fingers between Peyton's, grateful for the company and the affection.

Am I ready for this?

I'm ready for this.

I took a deep breath of the warm air.

I think I'm ready for this.

"You okay?" Peyton asked.

I nodded. "Yeah. It's just hard. Coming back to..." I gestured around us.

He gave my hand a reassuring squeeze. "We can do it another day if you want to."

"No." I kept walking. "It's going to be hard no matter what, but... I want to do this."

He didn't argue or protest. He just stayed with me as we followed the path.

Peyton and I had flown into Örebro, Sweden, a week ago with Rachel and the kids, and we were staying at a hotel in town while they stayed with her in-laws. Since coming here, we'd divided our time between helping her with the little ones, spending time with Leif's family, and playing tourists.

The whole time, today had been in the back of my mind. I'd needed to do it. I'd wanted to. I'd just been afraid I couldn't handle it.

It had taken me until today to work up the courage to come here. No one had pushed. Not Peyton. Not Rachel. Not Leif's family.

This morning, I'd finally been as ready as I would ever be, and now here we were.

When we stopped, my skin prickled with goose bumps and my eyes stung, but I didn't cry. Mostly, I just took in my surroundings, letting reality settle onto my shoulders.

There'd been people crowded around last year. A casket. A hole in the ground.

Now it was just us and a headstone:

Leif Adrian Erlandsson.

There was more inscribed, most of it in Swedish, but I was too fixated on his name to try to parse any of it.

I pushed out a ragged breath as I knelt. I tucked a crisp hundred-dollar bill into the bouquet—I had lost the bet, after all—and carefully put the flowers along the base of the headstone. Then, with my heart in my throat, I traced my fingertips over his name. Seeing it carved in stone like that was just so... *final.*

I can't believe you're not here anymore.

My therapist had assured me that moments like this were normal. Moments when it took my breath away to realize Leif was gone, and I had to recalibrate to this new normal. These moments, she assured me, would be fewer and farther between over time, but if one hit me a year from now or twenty years from now, it didn't mean anything was wrong with me. It was just how grief worked.

"They're hard," she'd said. *"They're painful, though they will probably hurt less over time. But it's okay to sit with those moments. Pause and let yourself think about him and how much you miss him. Part of keeping his memory alive means keeping a certain amount of grief alive, and that's okay."*

I'd understood at the time what she'd meant, but it was times like this—when I was running my fingertips over my best friend's name carved in stone—that I felt it to my core.

Yeah, it still hurt. Sometimes it even hurt physically, from my aching chest to that uncomfortable lump in my throat to the sting in my eyes. But that was the price of having someone as amazing as Leif in my world. I couldn't love someone that hard without grieving them this hard. Especially now with some time, distance, and therapy, I wouldn't trade the friendship we'd had for anything. Not even if it meant never feeling grief like this again.

I traced a letter in his name one more time, then rose, my knee cracking because I'd been crouched for so long. I exhaled and rolled my shoulders.

Peyton's hand landed gently on the small of my back. "You all right?"

"Yeah." I turned to him, and his concerned expression ignited a completely different ache in my chest. Leif would've been insufferable, watching me fall for Peyton like I had. He'd have gotten back at me for all the playful teasing I'd done when he'd been stupid for Rachel, because God knew I was that stupid for Peyton now.

I wished Leif could've been here for this. To see how ridiculous I was over this man. To give me all the heckling and chirping I richly deserved. And to, at some point when we were alone, look at me and say in all seriousness, *"I'm glad to see you this happy with someone, Avery."*

That moment had never come, but I could see it and hear it and feel it as clearly as a memory. I could feel its absence, simultaneously hating how it had been taken away and being grateful that I'd had time—however short it had turned out it be—with the man who I was sure would've eventually said those words.

Peyton must've seen something in my eyes, because without a word, he reeled me in close. Arms wrapped around me, he stroked my hair as I leaned on him. I didn't cry. I'd been sure all the way here that I would, but now, I just relaxed into Peyton's embrace and let the peace settle over me.

"I'm glad to see you this happy with someone, Avery."
Yeah. Me too.

Carding his fingers through my hair, Peyton softly asked, "You sure you're okay?"

I exhaled, then drew back to meet his gaze. "I'm good.

It's hard, you know?" I nodded toward the headstone. "I think it always will be. But I'm not a mess like I was before."

Peyton gently cradled my face in both hands. "You were never a mess. You were going through hell." He pressed the softest kiss to my forehead, then another to my lips. "If I'd lost someone like him, I wouldn't have been in any better shape."

The lump in my throat grew, and I leaned into him again, resting my head against his shoulder and closing my eyes as he wrapped his arms around me. If I'd learned anything going through the last year, it was how fortunate I was to have so many good people in my life. That whole time I'd been trying desperately to be stronger than I was, I'd been oblivious to just how many people cared about me. They didn't want me to be strong—they wanted me to be okay.

And more and more as time went on, I believed I would be. I believed I *was*.

Though I'd long since finished the player assistance program, I still saw Shannon twice a month, and she'd been a godsend. When she'd told me I'd have moments where the grief would stop me in my tracks, she'd also gone on to explain that contrary to popular belief, grief didn't just go away. There didn't come a point where it was wrapped up in a neat little bow and stored on a shelf. Closure was more like turning a page than closing a book—it was forward motion, it was distance, but wasn't the end. For many people, that grief never completely went away.

At first, I'd been devastated by the idea of feeling like this forever, but she'd gone on to tell me that understanding that if I still grieved, I wasn't broken or overreacting. The more she'd explained it, the more I'd realized what she was getting at: that once I let go of the idea that it would be gone

forever, the more I could make peace with it being a dimin-
ishing constant. The more I could be gentle with myself and
let myself experience those periods of grief when they came,
rather than worry I was backsliding or wallowing.

"*Twenty years from now,*" Shannon had told me one
day, "*you might have gone for quite a while without thinking
about it. Or you've thought about him, but it's happy memories now, and you're at peace. But then one day, you see or
hear something that reminds you of Leif, and it makes you
sad. That doesn't mean you need to rush into a therapist's
office or worry that you're not healing as much as you should.
It just means you still remember how much you loved him
and how much you wish he was still there. You can sit with
that feeling for a little while, let yourself be sad and feel that
grief, and then the next day you'll be thinking about happy
memories again. It's okay.*"

These days, I understood what she'd meant. In the year
since Leif had died, I'd been able to remember the happy
times more and more. I could talk about Leif without
choking up, though sometimes that still happened. I'd made
peace with the fact that there were bad days as well as good
days, and slowly, the good days had begun to outnumber
the bad.

And credit where it was due—the man holding me right
now had been a godsend. There'd been a few times where
I'd been having an awful day—when everything had caught
up with me and I'd been overwhelmed with grief—and
Peyton would sit me down and ask me to talk about the
good times. He never seemed patronizing, either. He
genuinely seemed to want to know all about the friend I'd
lost just before we'd met, and he listened intently while I
reminisced. I'd usually struggle through the first couple of
stories, but as I went on, I'd feel better, and by the time I'd

finished, I was still raw, but less brittle. Less focused on the void Leif had left behind and instead reminded of all the reasons he'd been so hard to lose.

Though my relationship with Peyton had been heavily intertwined with the aftermath of losing Leif, that grief and heartache didn't define us. As the season had gone on—and especially during the off season—we'd been able to focus on each other. We'd roomed together on road trips, and nothing in the world left me more refreshed and ready to play than waking up from a pregame nap in Peyton's arms.

It helped, too, that I wasn't the only one getting therapy. Peyton hadn't been able to lock anyone down until the season was over, especially since he had no time during the playoffs. Barely three days after we were eliminated, though, he was in his new therapist's office. They were slowly working through the trauma he hadn't even realized he had from his mom's alcoholism and the effect it had on the family, and it had been tough for him. There were some days he came back from therapy and just wanted to curl up on the couch and watch stupid movies. Other times, he wanted to go shoot pucks for a while until he could finally let a few tears fall and talk to me about his session.

About a month into the off season, his therapist had dug into the feelings Peyton had about Jeff Richards, his former teammate who'd lost his marriage and career to his addiction. Turned out Peyton had been harboring a lot more guilt about it than even he'd realized, and it was eating him up that he hadn't helped him. He'd wondered all this time if Richards was even alive, and his conscience had been a wreck because he blamed himself for not stepping up.

After that session, Peyton had reached out to some other players from Detroit. They, too, were carrying a lot of shame and guilt. With some help from the League, Richards's family, and—from what I'd gathered—law enforcement, they'd managed to locate their former teammate. Richards was still in a bad spot, still struggling hard with his addiction and he'd been living in his car for the past two years. He was alive, though, and—to Peyton's immense relief— receptive to help.

In between giving him that help, Richards's former teammates were now working to start an organization. Their plan was to not only help athletes struggling with addiction, but to offer help and resources to the friends, family, and teammates of those addicts. I'd joined them, and the Pittsburgh and Detroit clubs were both eager to pitch in. Hopefully in the coming season, the organization would launch, and people like Peyton, Richards, and me would no longer feel quite so alone.

The week before we'd left for Sweden, Richards was settling into an inpatient rehab facility in New Mexico. Peyton spoke to him on the phone, and he'd cried after they'd ended the call. I'd cautiously asked if everything was okay, and he'd smiled as he'd wiped his eyes and told me, *"He wants us to visit when we get back."*

We would, too. They kept in constant communication via text and the occasional FaceTime, and they were both looking forward to our visit. So was I.

For that alone, I decided Peyton's therapist was worth his weight in gold.

Our couples counselor was a godsend, too. Right now, he was mostly helping us navigate each other's therapy— how to talk about things, what to ask, how to be what the other needed. Between him and our individual therapists, we were on much more solid ground than I'd thought possible.

We'd initially agreed to take our relationship slower

than we had at the start, but at least one step ended up being unexpectedly accelerated. It was a combination of a downstairs neighbor driving Peyton insane with too-loud bass-heavy music at all hours of the day and night, and us spending almost every night together anyway. Then at the trade deadline, the team had acquired a player from the western conference, and Peyton suddenly had an opportunity to jump ship from his lease so the other player could take his apartment. The team didn't have to fuss with finding a place to put up the new guy, the new guy wore earplugs to sleep and headphones the rest of the time—it worked out for everyone.

So... now we were living together at my place. We had the odd squabbles that came with cohabitating—I wasn't great about keeping up on the dishes, he was the worst about leaving beard trimmings in the sink, and neither of us could ever remember when trash day was—but I wouldn't trade it for anything. It was like we'd butted heads and struck sparks off each other in the beginning, sorted all that shit out, and now everything was smooth and easy.

Sighing, I drew back again. "We should probably get out of here. Don't want to keep the family waiting."

Peyton didn't move. "Are you ready to go?"

I stared down at Leif's headstone for a long moment. I couldn't say I felt particularly *good*, standing beside my best friend's grave and rubbing up against the raw spots of my grief, but there was a sense of peace that I was pretty sure I'd been chasing all this time. That settled feeling that even though it sure felt like it sometimes, I was not going to crumble beneath this weight.

Taking a deep breath and rolling my shoulders, I met my boyfriend's gaze again. "I think I'm ready, yeah." I swallowed. "Do you, um... Do you have any objection to coming back here before we fly home?"

"Not at all," he whispered. "We'll spend as much time here as you need."

I smiled, lifted my chin, and kissed him softly. "Thank you."

He smiled back, and we shared another kiss. Longer this time, but still chaste—still appropriate for where we were.

And yet, in the back of my mind, I could hear that scoff followed by the Swedish-accented, *"Jesus Christ, you two. Get a room."*

The thought drove a laugh out of me, which broke the kiss.

Peyton eyed me. "What?"

I shook my head and took his hand. "Just imagining Leif heckling us." As we started back down the path, I added, "Because he absolutely would."

He chuckled as he fell into step beside me. "From what you've told me about him? I believe you."

We exchanged glances, both laughing softly, and we headed back toward the rental car.

Coming here hadn't been nearly as bad as I'd anticipated. Definitely not as bad as the last time; the funeral had been hell on earth. Now I was leaving with Peyton, and I promised myself we'd be back at least one more time before we left Sweden.

Then we'd be back to Pittsburgh. Back to training with our team, ready for the next hockey season.

Last season, for all I'd wished at one point that it would be over sooner than later, had ended earlier than we would've hoped. The Whiskey Rebels made it to the second round of the playoffs before being knocked out by Long Island. That was tough, but we were proud to have made it as far as we did. When Coach told us in the locker room afterward that Leif would've been proud, I wasn't the only one who cried.

Next season, we'd all vowed, we were going all the way to the finals.

But that was next season. For now, we had this time to let injuries heal, spend time with our friends and family, and relax. Peyton and I were religious about working out, and we had ice time scheduled with several other players from the League who were summering in Sweden. Leif's nephew would be joining us, too. I was looking forward to that.

In between, we played tourist, especially since Peyton had never been here before. We had side trips planned to Norway, Finland, and a couple of other places.

We were also here to help Rachel and the kids, which had had a side benefit that I hadn't anticipated. I'd never been particularly sentimental about watching a man interact with kids, but the first time I saw Peyton playing with Kalle and Linnea... oh Lord. He was just so damn cute with them. And the first time I saw him holding baby Adrian? Whoa. That was the first time I'd ever thought that I didn't just want kids of my own—I wanted kids of my own *with him.*

Not yet, though.

As much as losing Leif had given me a sense of urgency for everything—the intense fear that everything needed to be accelerated so we didn't run out of time—I made myself be patient when it came to this relationship. I hadn't want it to be based in my grief, and I didn't want it to be rushed because of it either.

We'd get there.

For now, we were here, enjoying our time in Sweden

even with the reminders of Leif's absence at every turn. For the first time, I was beginning to understand what Shannon had meant when she'd said to me once that I'd eventually be able to celebrate Leif's life more than I grieved his death. Mentioning him or being reminded of him always stung, but more and more, the happy memories could stand on their own.

More and more, I believed that when I came to Sweden again in the future, I could smile without getting that lump in my throat.

I would always miss my best friend, but the dark felt like it was behind me now. There was joy in my life again. I still saw his wife and children all the time, and I'd vowed to her that I would help her keep his memory alive in them as they got older.

As the days grew brighter and the weight of grief on my shoulders lightened into something I could carry, I knew there was love and happiness ahead of me.

Especially because there was already love and happiness with me right now.

At the car, I turned to face Peyton. "Thank you. For coming with me."

"Of course." He released my hand and wrapped his arms around my waist. "We can come back as many times as you need to."

I smiled, draping my arms over his shoulders. "Maybe. But... I think I got what I needed."

"Okay. If you need more, though..."

The words *"I have exactly what I need right here"* were on the tip of my tongue, but that sounded just a little too corny. Instead, I drew him in for a soft kiss.

When I broke that kiss, though, some words did come.

"A year ago," I whispered, "I never imagined thinking

this ever again, but... I think I might be the luckiest man alive."

Surprise registered on his expression, but then he smiled. "I don't know. I think I hit the jackpot."

I laughed quietly and shrugged. "Maybe. But I met someone who saw me at my absolute worst, pulled me out of the fray, and still managed to love me like this. Pretty sure it doesn't get any better than that."

Peyton was already shaking his head. "Nothing that happened was any reason to love you less." He caressed my cheek. "You're amazing, and you're a lot stronger than you think." The corner of his mouth twitched. "And those six-pack abs don't hurt anything, so—"

I burst out laughing, which felt absolutely incredible. Here in this place where I'd wondered if I'd ever feel anything but sadness and loss ever again, Peyton had me laughing and rolling my eyes and... feeling *good*.

As I sobered, I trailed my fingertips along the edge of his beard. "Thank you again. I mean it. For... everything."

He just smiled and drew me in, and I let his kiss make me as dizzy as the laughter had.

The man I'd been a year ago couldn't have imagined where I'd be now.

The man I was now couldn't imagine things turning out any other way.

And I couldn't wait to see the beautiful future I was going to have with Peyton.

For more books by L.A. Witt,

or to subscribe to my newsletter, please visit

http://www.gallagherwitt.com

Newsletter perks:

- Exclusive discounts & giveaways
- Access to ARCs
- All the latest news about pre-orders, collaborations, and more!

Romance * Suspense

Contemporary * Historical * Sports * Military

HOCKEY ROMANCES BY L.A. WITT

The Gentlemen of the Emerald City Series

The Pucks & Rainbows Trilogy

Rookie Mistake (written with Anna Zabo)

Scoreless Game (written with Anna Zabo)

Injured Reserve

Name From a Hat Trick

Brick Walls

Interference

Aftermath

Red Line

Own Goal

Burner Account

Conditioning Loan

Man Advantage

Punchline (co-written with Cari Z)

Writing as Ann Gallagher

Even Strength (co-written with Cari Z)

Writing as Lauren Gallagher

Playmaker

Romances by L.A. Witt

The Anchor Point Series

The Husband Gambit

Name From a Hat Trick

After December

Leave

Romantic Suspense by L.A. Witt

The Hitman vs. Hitman Series (written with Cari Z)

The Bad Behavior Series (written with Cari Z)

The Venetian and the Rum Runner

If The Seas Catch Fire

The Truth in My Lies

...and many, *many* more!

ABOUT THE AUTHOR

L.A. Witt is a romance and suspense author who has at last given up the exciting nomadic lifestyle of the military spouse (read: her husband finally retired). She now resides in Pittsburgh, where the potholes are determined to eat her car and her cats are endlessly taunted by a disrespectful squirrel named Moose. In her spare time, she can be found painting in her art room or destroying her voice at a Pittsburgh Penguins game.

Website: www.gallagherwitt.com
    Email: gallagherwitt@gmail.com
    Twitter, Instagram, & Threads: @GallagherWitt